CAUGHT

By Janet Periat

Caught

This is a work of fiction. Names, characters, places and incidents are either the product of the author's imagination or are used fictitiously. Any resemblance to actual persons, living or dead, events, or locales is entirely coincidental.

Published 2011 by Madison Avenue Press

www.janetperiat.com

First Edition: 2011

ISBN 978-1-937813-03-1

Book Design: Frank Higgins

Edited by: Ann Fischer

For Frank

ACKNOWLEDGMENTS

Countless people helped me write this book. I've tried to remember them all here. Unfortunately, my brain has limited capacity and I'm sure I've forgotten someone. If so, I owe you a beer.

First of all, I'd like to thank my husband, Frank, for supporting, helping and encouraging me for the past twenty years in my writing career. He believed in me when no one else did. And he is a rock. Love you, big guy.

Next, huge mega giant thanks to my beloved critique group, the Armadillos: Ann Fischer, Anne Maragoni, Linda Baxter, Teri Bradburn and Linda Hill. Without their help, I would not have finished this book. Nor would it be any good. Nor would I be as good. You girls are treasures.

I'd also like to thank the Silicon Valley chapter of the Romance Writers of America. I was lost without them. I've learned more about writing in the last five years than I had in the previous fifteen. They hooked me up with the Armadillos and were instrumental in helping me find an agent. You guys ROCK!

I'd like to give a big shout out to Laurie McLean, my agent, for her amazing guidance, help and advice. She believed in me when few others did.

Super big thanks to Randy Cleveland for his amazing cover art. And for being a great friend to me.

I'd like to thank therapist Delores DeAlba for providing psychological background advice on my characters. But mostly I'd like to thank her for being a beacon of light during some of my darkest times.

I'd also like to thank Linda Sullivan for her heroic caretaking of my sister (and me) and for the inspiration for the character of Sam.

I want to thank Diane Castle, Linda Castle, Carla Roberts and Cathy Norris, for being there and always believing in me.

Thanks to Tet Dychioco for inspiring the character of Mary. I don't know what I would have done without her help during the roughest part of my life.

Thanks to Bill Tidwell and Jeff Banke for teaching me about guns and Jeeps.

Thanks to Google and countless websites for providing me with information. Yachtforum.com for Burke's boat, Sfnewdevelopments.com for Burke's penthouse, and Rob from cockeyed.com for the size of one million dollars in hundreds.

And last, but not least, I'd like to thank my sister, Judy, whose bravery and courage after suffering a debilitating stroke continues to inspire me. If it weren't for you, my dear, this book would not have been possible. I love you.

PREFACE

The beginnings of this book were created during the most painful time of my life.

In late May of 2008, my sister Judy came to my house and announced, "I've been having seizures and just found out that I have a brain tumor. It's so big, I may not survive the operation."

What ensued was three months of pure hell for the both of us. I have included scenes in *Caught* that came directly from that experience. Emma's emotions in the beginning of the story are mine. Nearly all the scenes with Lizzie are born of truth.

The following is an account of the events that led up to writing the first chapter of *Caught*. It makes the Preface hideously, unusually long. After a long argument with myself, I've decided to go ahead and include it. While reading this will give you a deeper understand of Emma's mindset, the story carries itself. Feel free to skip to the first chapter.

After Judy informed us of her condition and we all had a good cry, we made plans to handle the crisis. Since Judy is single and has no children, I became her primary caregiver. Because she lives an hour away from services and could no longer drive, she moved in that day. After two crazy, lawyer-and-doctor-appointment-filled weeks—and after Judy said good-bye to everyone she loved—the operation went perfectly. We were ecstatic.

The following morning, I got a call from the hospital. Judy had "an event". Which turned out to be a severe left hemisphere stroke that had paralyzed her right side. We were informed by her neurosurgeon that she would more than likely live in a permanent vegetative state for the rest of her days.

My beloved, funny, amazing sister was now a vegetable.

I've never felt that kind of pain in my life. My heart and stomach have never hurt that badly.

Thankfully, the doctor turned out to be wrong. Quite quickly, Judy began communicating with us. A yes. A no. A gesture. Soon, it became clear that she was all there, just locked inside her mind. Slowly, she began to heal. But one of us (my brother Dan was an amazing hospital advocate) had to be at the hospital at all times to ensure she got the care she required. Catheters were left in, she wasn't turned, she was in pain and ignored.

After ten days in the hospital and two weeks in a nursing home, Kaiser Health Foundation released her, stating that they didn't cover the costs of the care Judy required. They believed she wouldn't get much better and needed to be "housed". I saw my sister's improvements and argued, but had no recourse.

Besides, Judy kept signaling that she was ready to come home.

As it turned out, my sister is an amazing actress. When I visited, she was perky and showed me how she could get to the toilet. She led me to believe she could walk. I don't blame her for her con job. The nursing home was frightening and depressing.

Judy moved in with us on Friday, July 4th. Two minutes after I got her home, it became clear that she was in no shape to be out of the hospital. She couldn't walk, talk or care for herself. She required 24-hour-a-day nursing care.

That weekend, I learned firsthand how badly our health care system is broken. How could any hospital release someone in her condition without telling me her requirements, without showing me how to lift her and get her in the car? Try to get a hold of anyone on a holiday weekend. I had one nurse—an old high school friend and a total star—but she quickly became overwhelmed. (Later, the Kaiser home health care nurse admitted they'd made a huge mistake in the way they released Judy to my care. *Thanks.*) I rushed to the pharmacy for supplies, wondering where the hell I would get another nurse.

What happened next made me a true believer in God.

As I walked into CVS, I "just happened" to run into my late aunt's nurse, Tet Dychioco, a wonderful human being who took amazing care of my aunt and grandmother and attended many family functions, including my wedding. I'd fallen out of touch with her since my aunt's funeral. Tet was unemployed and looking for work. She'd prayed that morning for God to send her a job. We cried and hugged. She came on board that day.

Thankfully, Judy had saved enough money to pay for a full-time nursing staff for a short period of time. I don't know what I would have done without the nurses. Her care was far beyond my capabilities. Tet was amazing. She brought in more help and saved me. More importantly, she and the other nurses saved Judy.

At the same time, my husband Frank and I were on the verge of losing our home. Frank had been out of work for several months and our finances were grim. The day my sister told us about her brain tumor, my husband had finally acquired a short contract with a new client. Unfortunately, his office was at home. I have no idea how he got anything done.

From July to September, our three-bedroom rancher turned into a hospital with round-the-clock nursing care along with visits from occupational nurses, speech therapists, home health care nurses and physical therapists. These trained professionals gave my sister therapy, inspected my house to make sure it posed no hazards to her, and ensured we were taking good care of her. (It would have been nice if they had displayed this type of compassion and diligence when my sister was in the hospital.)

In addition to the hoards of medical staff, we had a ceaseless parade of visitors and relatives coming through the house. Most of them needed refreshments and a full report. Many needed emotional support. All the while, I took Judy to doctor appointments, paid her bills, shopped, coordinated her nursing care and tried to handle the affairs of her business as best I could. While also trying to protect Frank's time and privacy so he could work, run my own household, and meet the deadlines for my column. I gave up doing anything for myself, including writing novels and short stories.

While I had some help, I'm still shocked by how many people went out of their way to torture me during the ordeal. Questioned me. Called me up to tell me my decisions were horrible and I was horrible. Huge health events bring out the best and the worst in people. I experienced far too much of the worst. But thankfully, a lot of the best, too. Like Judy's nursing staff. There were also angels in the small community where Judy lived. They cared for her cats, her home and helped her transition back into her old life. I will never forget their kindness. (Sam, Lary, Bev and Cuz, you are *stars*.)

While Frank and I complained about the constant intrusions and complete lack of privacy, we still felt lucky. We weren't facing death. We didn't have a brain operation. We hadn't had a stroke. We remembered how to brush our teeth and wash our hair. We weren't totally dependent on others for survival. We didn't have a store we couldn't run, pets we couldn't hold, a garden we couldn't tend. We didn't wake up in a horror movie of a nursing home, totally dependent on an uninterested staff and unable to fully communicate our needs.

We were fine.

But we all have limits. At a month and half into the ordeal, despite all my attempts to keep it together, I was on the verge of a mental breakdown.

Six months before, I'd booked a trip to San Francisco (a whole half hour away) to attend the Romance Writers of America conference, which was coming up fast. But I couldn't see how I could go. Judy still needed care, Frank needed me, I had to supervise Judy's appointments and coordinate the visiting therapeutic care nurses. I knew I should probably cancel, but held out hope I could go. I'd scored appointments with a great editor and a top New York agent. But Judy came first.

As I got closer to the date, Judy's condition improved greatly. And my mental state deteriorated even further. Judy wanted me to attend the conference—probably because she could tell I was about to spontaneously combust—but also because she's the biggest champion of my writing career. So I finally decided to attend.

I'll never forget the day I left for the conference. Horrendous.

That morning, my sister and I had a long, drawn out argument about where she would go next. I wanted her to try an apartment nearby to practice her occupational therapy and gain some independence while still being close to doctors. She wanted to return to her home in the country. An hour away from civilization. Out in the middle of NOWHERE. While she had limited speech, my sister could still argue as well as she ever could. We fought for an hour until we both ended in tears. I finally gave up and packed for the conference.

About fifteen minutes after I started assembling my stuff, my elderly parents, niece and sister-in-law arrived to visit my sister. While they were eating lunch in my kitchen, I tried to pack and give last minute instructions to Tet while my relatives asked me questions. The doorbell rang. It was the occupational therapist from the hospital and her supervisor. Inspection time. Time to answer a battery of questions and prove I was taking great care of my sister. While I appreciated their diligence, that day, all I wanted to do was slam the door in their faces.

Still, I held it together and was super polite because I liked the occupational therapist. A real cute gal. But that day, because she had her boss with her, she pulled the authoritarian card. Her normal sweetness had been replaced with the demeanor of a policewoman.

When I told her that Judy had decided to return home in a month, she said, "We'll see. I'll need to inspect the house. We may not allow her to return home."

I told the woman that there was no way to make my sister do anything. That I'd tried to get through to her with no luck. That she didn't understand my sister's stubbornness. That I had no power over her or her decisions.

The therapist held her ground.

It was at this point that I informed her that I was on the verge of having a complete mental breakdown.

She sent me a pitying stare and talked to me like I was a mentally ill three-year- old. "We understand this is difficult for you, but we have our rules. But clearly you're distressed today. We'll discuss this at a later date," she said with an imperious expression.

My vision shifted and I let loose on the woman and her supervisor, screaming at the top of my lungs.

I don't know how it happened, but somehow I ended up in the car and Frank was driving me to San Francisco. All I remember was images coming at me. The cars ahead of us on the freeway. Frank, calm beside me. Driving by Candlestick Park. The tall buildings of the City. But only impressions. I was so crazy, I wasn't even there. I'd completely left my body.

Frank dropped me off at the hotel. I kissed him good-bye, stumbled inside and somehow managed to check in and find my room.

I headed right for the mini-bar and chugged a nine-dollar Heineken. About a half an hour later, I remember arriving back in my body and being surprised I was in a hotel room in San Francisco. I couldn't believe it was real. I couldn't believe I was alone.

It was so quiet.

The room was still. No one was asking me for anything. My actions weren't under a microscope. I didn't need permission to do anything.

The craziness had been replaced by calm.

Then I realized I had to pitch my books to a top New York editor and agent the next morning. And I got to work.

One of the Saturday workshops was on the plot elements of romantic suspense. That night, with these ideas rambling around in the back of my head, I looked out my hotel window and thought about San Francisco's exciting stores and restaurants, but didn't want to walk around the City alone at night. I imagined what I would do if a bad guy jumped out at me and demanded my wallet.

At that moment in time, the answer was clear. I would lose my mind. I was barely sane. I'd go all nuclear on the robber's ass and get myself killed.

Then I wondered how the criminal would react if their victim started screaming at them like a madwoman. Would they back off? Would they kill her?

At that moment, I saw the opening scene with Emma Holsten, Burke Cherlenko and Rollin Hanson you are about to read. I quickly grabbed a notebook, sat on my hotel bed and wrote the first twenty pages of *Caught* in longhand.

At the time of this writing, my sister is doing great. She's living on her own, loving and caring for her cats and running her store, even though she still has speech issues. She continues to improve every day and is an inspiration to everyone who knows her. I feel so blessed to have her in my life.

-Janet Periat, May 2011

ONE

"Dead people don't shop," Emma argued into her cell phone, trying to sound reasonable when all she wanted to do was scream at the Franklin Mint service rep. She pulled into the narrow alley behind her antique store and drove slowly by the overflowing dumpster and three sleeping homeless guys.

"I'm sorry, ma'am, but our records show that the order for the *Faberge Star Wars Jedi Knight Victory Egg* was placed on July 26th by a Mrs. Dolly Holsten."

Emma gritted her teeth and forced her rabid emotions to quiet. "And I'm telling you my mother was dead on the 26th. And she was dead for seven months before that. I know, I buried her." She slammed on the brakes and her Prius jerked to a stop in her tiny parking spot, jammed between a dingy brick wall and a delivery truck covered in graffiti.

"I'm very sorry for your loss. But in order to cancel this charge, I'll need proof she is deceased."

Her mind went red with rage and tears blurred her vision. "Well, how about if I dig her up and ship her body to your office?" Emma snapped and hung up the phone with sharp flick of her wrist. Throwing her cell into her purse, she took a deep breath. "Good one, Emma, take out all your frustrations on a sales rep…Christ, I'm losing it." Guilt tweaked her gut. "I should call back and apologize."

Her cell phone wolf whistled at her. She grabbed it and checked the number. Her sister's nurse. Her back and stomach tensed so hard, they hurt. Her entire body geared for action. "Mary? What's going on? How's Lizzie?"

"I'm in a store with her and can't get her to leave."

Emma clutched the phone harder, her mind reeling. "What?"

Mary made an exasperated noise. "We were driving back from the doctor, she made me stop at Safeway and help her into the store and now she won't leave. She keeps going up and down the aisles and pulling stuff off the shelves. I don't know what to do."

Emma's tenuous hold on reality almost snapped. Somehow, she dug down deep and found some reserves. "Christ. Here, let me talk to her," she said, rubbing her forehead and steeling herself.

"Lizzie! Lizzie!" Mary said urgently, her voice further away from the phone. "It's your sister, Emma, here."

Muffled sounds of the cell being handled came over the receiver, then Lizzie's breathing. "I…um. Um. Face! Need face!"

Emma's mind went dark and her interior burned with frustration. All she wanted to do was take care of her sister and keep her calm, but Lizzie made her job nearly impossible. Her left-brain stroke had wiped out her speech center so thoroughly, she couldn't even mime what she wanted. But that didn't stop her constant and adamant demands. It was like taking care of a giant, sick baby. "Calm down, Lizzie. Look, go home."

"No! Face! Um…face!"

"Here, give me that," Mary said. "I'm sorry. I'll get her out of here. I thought maybe you were close by and could stop and help me."

"No, I wanted to get to San Francisco early today, I just parked behind the store." Emma rolled her shoulders to loosen them.

"Oh. I'm sorry. Don't worry. I'll get her home. Oh, and happy birthday."

Emma grunted.

"Your birthday's September twelfth, isn't it?"

"Yeah. Thanks, Mary."

"What do you want for your birthday?"

"All I want is Lizzie to get better. I'll talk to you later." Emma closed the phone and held her head. Grief tore at her belly. The Lizzie she'd known was gone. She missed her more than she thought possible. Not only had she lost her only family, it ripped her apart to see her amazing, accomplished sister so damaged. Horrifying.

Emma wished she were stronger. She'd never been this close to the edge. If one more bad thing happened, she'd wind up in an asylum.

She got out of the car and locked it behind her. Taking a furtive glance at the sleeping homeless guys, she hustled to her back door, unlocked the five deadbolts and slipped inside her tiny antique shop. She relocked the deadbolts before turning to disable the alarm.

Somehow, just stepping inside her store centered her. This was a realm she could handle. Thank God there was one place where she had control.

On her way to the front of the store, a musky smell met her when she stepped by the 18th century German curio cabinet. She stopped and sniffed the air. Masculine. Cologne? No. Not quite. Hints of patchouli. She did a quick check around the store. No sign of Jerry. Nothing unusual. She'd unpacked a pair of old Scottish candlesticks the day before with stubs of stinky candles left inside. Probably that.

A half an hour later, the store open, Emma stood behind the glass U-shaped display unit that served as her counter, ready for the day to start.

"It's my birthday, so it's going to be a good day," she announced to her empty store and the Universe. "I see people coming in here, buying expensive stuff. Hopefully that stupid Polar bear—no self-recriminations, Emma. We're being positive now. So let's ask for what we want. A hot rich guy to come in here, buy everything, fall in love with me and help me take care of my sister." She chuckled. At least she still had her sense of humor.

The bell on the back of the front door announced there were customers. She looked up to greet them.

Four men oozed into her shop like an oily malevolent fog. Their faces shadowed by the hazy morning sunlight coming through the window behind them, they fanned out, each one dominating an area, crowding her tiny store. One by one, the fluorescents illuminated their hard, fortyish faces. Three dark-haired guys and a bald one. Dressed in black, they surveyed Emma and her wares like they owned the lot.

Her skin prickled, her body went cold and adrenaline jacked her system. Definitely not customers and not the sort of men she'd ordered. Her heart thumped hard against her ribs and she took a step toward her baseball bat.

Careful not to show any fear, she smiled at the group. "Good morning, gentlemen, how can I help you today?" Damn it, she should have kept the gun. Where the hell was Jerry? While useless, at least he would be another body in the shop. She took another step toward her bat.

Baldy smiled, eying her in a proprietary way. All the hair on the back of her neck and arms stood up. Sweat broke out on her forehead. About six foot, he had dark, even features—technically pretty hot—but his mahogany gaze was ice cold.

She fought a shiver.

He walked straight up to the counter. "You're in my store."

She took a step back. "Excuse me?"

A half-smile played on his full sensual lips. "I suppose I should start with some pleasantries, but I'm really not in the mood. So I'll be blunt. Your scumbag partner Jerry owes me five hundred thousand dollars. Last night, after I had him beaten, I discovered he doesn't *have* five hundred thousand dollars. Outside of 2,476 dollars and 97 cents at the San Francisco Credit Union, the only other thing he owns is this store."

Emma blinked. "He owns half. And only because my dead ex-husband lost it to him in a poker game."

"Now I own the whole thing. Unless you think it's a good idea to fight me." He withdrew some papers from an inner pocket of his jacket, unfolded them and slapped them onto the counter. With a menacing darkness in his eyes, he pushed them over to her. "Sign these."

She stared at the man, unable to make the leap to comprehension. As they locked gazes, his words penetrated her brain. A high-pitched whine filled her head and he suddenly seemed far away. This wasn't real. She must be hallucinating. She was so stressed out she was having waking nightmares.

Baldy's henchmen took up defensive positions behind their boss.

Baldy was a conqueror. Clearly. The power in his dark brown gaze, the way he held his broad shoulders, the simple way he told her he'd had her partner beaten, all of it, the man was a king. An underworld king.

After a long pause where Baldy's intense gaze never left hers, he said, "Sign them and you may leave." He turned to his men. "Gather whatever you can to give to Banana and get the paperwork into file boxes. We'll burn the place and collect the insurance." He turned back to her. "Before you go? I'll need your passwords for the computer. I'll send a man around to collect whatever else pertains to the store at your home. Checkbooks, petty cash, all of it."

This was real. This was really happening. Her dead ex-husband's criminal world had finally claimed hers in its entirety.

Wild images flew at her. Lizzie lying in that horror movie of a nursing home in her own filth. The house for sale. Her car repossessed.

A thermonuclear bomb of fury exploded inside her. A deafening pounding pulsed in her ears as fuzzy images of the men whirled in front of her. A voice erupted from the depths of her gut like she'd summoned a demon from the fires of hell. "No! You will not do this to me!"

She blasted Baldy back three feet and made his men reach for their weapons.

"The bullshit stops here and now!" she roared, pounding her fist on the glass-topped display case, making the rare English teapots inside rattle. "You will not take away my only way to care for my stroke-victim sister, you will not leave me destitute and penniless, you will not cause me to lose what little I have left of my mind! You will get the hell out of here or I'll jump over this counter and kill you all with my bare hands!"

Baldy didn't react. He merely stood there, his arms crossed over his broad chest, watching her as if she were a fascinating TV show. Taking his cue, his bodyguards relaxed and put away their guns.

She glowered at him, her entire body shaking. "No way am I going to let some evil overlord of the underworld *bastard* come in here and take my store from me!" She pointed at the door. "You turn your ass around and you get out! I'm done taking shit from abusive men! Done! Burnt, spent, crispy. Get out!"

Baldy continued to stare at her with that detached, yet interested gaze.

It finally hit her. She had no power here. She'd lost. Totally utterly lost. She collapsed on her tall stool. "Right. I'll just kill you all with my bare hands," she said in small and removed voice. "This is so bad." Suddenly, she started laughing. "I mean, it couldn't get any worse, could it? Look at you, you're a bloody criminal overlord."

Belly laughs ripped through her and tears streamed down her face. Gasping for breath, she laughed until her sides hurt. "Oh, I'm dead. So dead."

Something clicked. Death. Here was her way out. These guys would shoot her and her life insurance would take care of Lizzie. Her sister would never have to go back to that state institution. A weird, peaceful calm came over her. "Dead. Wow. Does that sound good," she heard herself whisper. "Did I just say that aloud?" She laughed again. "How dumb am I? How about I grab a gun and shoot myself with it? Christ." She held her head and groaned.

Baldy studied her as if she were an interesting bug in a laboratory. Without taking his eyes from hers, he said, "You're cute. And insane. Just my type. Boys, we're leaving." He picked up the papers from the counter and slipped them back into his pocket. A smile twitched at the corners of his mouth and his gaze shifted. He took time to appraise her body, his eyes resting on her breasts for a good long moment.

She suppressed a shudder.

His dark gaze snapped back to hers, the coldness returned. He pointed a finger at her. "You owe me."

And with that, he turned and walked out the door, his men on his heels.

Emma didn't move. Did that just happen?

She waited for him to return. A couple minutes passed. She stared at the door. Nothing. No one.

A loud squeaking came from behind her, terrifying her. She yelped and swung around.

A man was extricating himself from the broom closet in the corner of the store next to the twelve-foot-tall stuffed Polar bear.

Anger ignited her insides like a match lighting a tank of gasoline. Had the world suddenly gone crazy? Was there a sign outside her shop that read: Woman Seeking Attackers, Apply Within?

She grabbed the baseball bat and got a good hold on it. She wished she could call the police but the last time she did that, the stupid cops tried to pin her ex-husband's murder on her.

Mystery Man fought the closet door, pushing hard to get it over the old warped floorboards.

She got more and more infuriated. This was it. She was going to kill this guy.

He finally opened it wide enough, stepped out and gave a satisfied sigh. He had neck length dark hair graying at the temples, and a very tanned, distinctive face. Hooked nose, strong chin, carved cheekbones and a penetrating dark, almost black gaze. Maybe six feet tall with a wiry build, he wore a black leather jacket and dark jeans.

He sent her a radiant smile revealing perfect white teeth. "Happy birthday," he said cordially.

"Get the fuck out of my store now or I will beat you to death," she growled.

He eyed the bat, but didn't seem afraid of her. "Emma, don't worry. I'm here to help you, not hurt you."

She snorted. “Oh, right. That’s how I met all my friends, they broke into my house and then we partied.” She seared him with a glare. “Get out or I’ll call the police.”

He stood his ground and chuckled. “Right. And Detective McCoy would rush right over here to help you, wouldn’t he?”

A chill came over her. She took a step back. How did he know the name of the detective who’d been persecuting her? “Who the hell are you?”

He sauntered over a bit closer, but stayed out of bat range. “An ally.” He shot her another grin. “I’m here to save you, believe it or not. Because you, my dear, are in more trouble than you can possibly imagine. I can help you. And maybe you can help me. He likes you. That’s good. And very, very bad. But useful. Let me buy you a birthday brunch.”

That masculine smell! As the man neared her, it was clear the scent belonged to him.

She studied him. This guy had a different energy than Baldy. Not a conqueror, but definitely a soldier or detective or something. For some reason, he didn’t frighten her. He didn’t have the same coldness behind his eyes. Still, he was playing with Baldy and therefore dangerous.

She held up her bat. “Get out.” Her eyelid twitched. She tucked the bat under her arm and held the lid closed to make it stop, her stomach tight with frustration. “Quick before I go all nuclear on your ass.”

He leaned on the counter. He was very comfortable in his own skin and about ten years older than she. Kinda hot on second look. Almost familiar in a way.

“Saved your hide, that temper of yours,” he drawled, flashing her a winning smile.

“Save it, Mr. Charming, I’m immune.” Even though there was something she instantly liked about the guy. Which made her instantly dislike him, too.

He didn’t even react. “Sorry to hear about your sister. Tough break. She looks better though, since you got her out of that nursing home.”

Her body went rigid and her jaw set. Gripping the bat more tightly, she held it high, walked around her counter and stopped within a few feet of him. "You stay away from my sister. Leave now or I bash you to death," she bit out. "I swear I will."

His smile faded, revealing a glimpse of a very different person underneath. Not cold like Baldy, but still a calculating player. She had something he wanted. And he wanted it badly.

His gaze darting between the bat and her, he held himself more defensively, hands at the ready in case she went for him. "I wouldn't dream of hurting Lizzie, Emma. I'm here for you and believe me, you need me."

Good move. Open, direct hook. "Doubtful."

"I didn't have to reveal myself, you know. I could have gotten out of here without you knowing it. The reason I'm talking to you right now is because your safety depends on it. If you haven't already figured it out, you're in danger. From that guy and a bunch of others. You have information certain people want. Which is why he didn't kill you."

The news almost sent her over the edge, but she held on. She'd learned long ago not to trust strangers. Especially strangers associated with her ex. "What information?"

"Information your husband died trying to protect."

"Adam? He wasn't my husband, I'd prefer if you didn't refer to him as such."

"He wasn't?"

"He died two days before the divorce was final. And he was an idiot. You must have got your story wrong. The only person he'd ever die trying to protect was himself. But I do have one question. Which one of you jerks tried to pin his murder on me?"

He held her gaze steady. Strength radiated from the depths of his dark brown eyes. And confidence. "It wasn't me. And I don't recommend trying to find out. That information will get you killed. Well, faster than they're gonna kill you, anyway."

Talk about overplaying his hand. "Stop trying to manipulate me and get out."

"I'm not lying."

"Bullshit. Get out."

"All I ask is ten more minutes of your time."

"I said, get out!" She advanced on him and took a swing.

He jumped back out of the way, his eyes dilated. "Okay, okay. I'm going." His expression went neutral and he studied her. Ran his tongue along the inside of his cheek. "You *are* cute. And insane. Just my type, too." He rolled his eyes. "Hanson," he said to himself, "we need to have a talk." He reached into his jacket pocket, withdrew a card and put it on the floor in front of him, all the while keeping an eye on her bat. "Day or night." He backed up to the door and opened it. "After ten in the morning is better. Before eight at night. Need my beauty sleep."

He took a step through the door, then stopped and swung back to her. "Oh, yeah. Just because I came out of the closet in San Francisco," he said, pointing to the broom closet, "doesn't mean I'm gay." He laughed heartily and stepped through the door. "Heh, closet, good one." Holding the door open, he paused. "Don't wait too long to call me, Emma," he called out over his shoulder. "I hate to see nice people get hurt." He left, walked past the front window and gave her one last glance. With a smile and a wave, he disappeared.

Emma dropped the bat, raced to the door and locked it. She caught herself and snorted at the futility of the action. Locks worked great with Closet Man, hadn't they? Baldy wouldn't have a problem with them, either. Even with all those locks and her alarm, the place was as porous as Swiss cheese and as easy to break into as a kid's piggy bank. Great.

But what did they want? What information? What the hell was Adam killed for?

She hadn't seen Adam for the last six months of his life. Not ever since he moved in with the toddler/stripper.

The longhaired guy seemed sincere. Which meant he was just a really good liar. A thug like Baldy.

She grabbed the card and read it. "Rollin Hanson and a number. Nothing. No occupation, just a name and a number. So informative!" She threw the card down onto the counter and paced over to an English suit of armor. "Adam's dead, damn it!" she railed at the five-foot-tall antique. "When will that asshole stop affecting me? How much more crap am I supposed to take?"

She stomped over to her cash register to close it out. Universe had sent her a clear message: *Close the shop. Go drink alcohol.*

She opened the drawer. Jerry's key fob sat near the change.

Emma pictured him unconscious and bleeding. Shouldn't she be more upset by the thought? She felt strangely numb. On some level, perhaps even gleeful. Drunk jerk. If he wasn't trying to bully her into walking away from the store, he was driving away the customers. Another one of Adam's gifts that kept on giving.

Of course, the last time she'd seen Jerry, he'd pushed her too far. Emma smiled at the memory. He'd learned a very important lesson that day about her limits.

The only bad part of Jerry's karma was Baldy. Clearly a creep of the worst kind.

You owe me. She did a full-body shudder.

Rollin walked down Valencia Street, scanning for Cherlenko's bald head. A bracing foggy wind bit through his open jacket and chilled his sweaty body. Closet had been like a sauna. He shivered and zipped up his leather coat, continuing his search.

He thought of Emma swinging that bat at him and smiled. Hoo boy, what a woman.

Artsy white yuppies sat together at an outdoor café; a lone Mexican lady pushed a grocery cart down the sidewalk; a group of gay men chatted in front of a clothing store. No Cherlenko. He checked the parked cars, looking for Cherlenko's silver Mercedes SUV.

Over his Bluetooth, Bobby said, "He's gone, just drove away."

Rollin stopped at the street corner and waited for the red light. "Damn it, no more cheap batteries for the transmitters. And next time, you change them out, you would have fit better in that dumb closet."

"I told you not to buy those," Bobby said through a mouthful of food. Sounds of chewing came over the com. The man never stopped eating and was skinny as a supermodel. Rollin figured by the time he hit twenty-five he'd fatten up, but Bobby was just as thin as he'd been at twelve years old when Rollin found him in that dingy Bangkok alleyway. Amazing metabolism. "So did you hear that? Isn't Jerry in Vegas?"

"Maybe he got back without us knowing it."

Two men flanked Rollin. His heart stilled and his body went hard. He had twenty ways to take them down if they attacked. Casually, he glanced at them. A tall skinny Goth twenty-something in guyliner and a gay bodybuilder whose waxed chest was on display through his open collared shirt. Rollin's defensive posture broke and he relaxed.

The light turned green. Crossing the street, he said, "Check on Jerry. I think Cherlenko lied about him. Makes no sense that Jerry would be taken out of the picture this soon. Not until Cherlenko knows for sure that he can't help him find the money. I think Jerry got Cherlenko to bully Emma out of the store in exchange for information. And I think Cherlenko just figured out what we did, that Emma's the key to the money that Adam stole, not Jerry."

"Cherlenko's timing worked out perfect for us," Bobby said, slurping his drink. "We couldn't have planned that better."

Rollin rubbed his forehead. "Yeah, poor woman. I don't feel too good about this one."

"Now don't go soft on me."

"For her?" Rollin said with a chuckle. "Uh…I'm goin' the opposite."

Bobby broke into a mild version of his distinctive donkey laugh. "Why do you always go for the crazy ones?"

"No idea. With this one, aside from the fact that she's hella cute, it's probably the sister thing. I'm a sucker for family loyalty. And she's not really crazy. She had her shit together before she married that idiot Adam Ramsay."

"I hope she can lead us to that money. What a sweet paycheck."

Rollin walked past a trio of twenty-something white kids in pork pie hats. He stopped to check the street for traffic so he could cross. Super heavy. He kept moving. "She knew more about Adam than anyone else I've found. All his family's gone. And even though I tore her house apart, I still think the money could be there. Or maybe a clue to where he put it."

"I don't know. You combed that place pretty good and so did Cherlenko."

"Yeah, but I'll bet Emma's got some idea of where Adam might have hidden the cash."

Sounds of chewing, then a large swallow. "What about Adam's new girlfriend, Jennifer? I know you checked her out, but didn't Adam say 'Jenn's goofy song' was where the money was hidden? Weren't those Adam's last words?"

Rollin's mind clouded with darkness and guilt tweaked his gut. He should have never handed Adam over to Cherlenko. If Adam hadn't been such an asshole that day, he might not have. "Yeah, but Adam would have said anything at that point. Let's see what I can get out of Emma. All I gotta do is pull out some of the ol' Hanson Magic."

Bobby snorted. "Here we go."

Emma's sweet face came to mind. Her large green eyes, short dark hair, amazing jaw line, cute pert nose and those full sensuous lips. Followed by her astonishingly hot body. Smokin'.

Finally, a break in the traffic. "Hey, I can dream, can't I?" Rollin ran out behind a Porsche and crossed the street. "Besides, she may not live long enough to date." He walked up behind a large Comcast van.

"Wait," Bobby said.

A group of people came out of a nearby Italian restaurant and clustered near him on the sidewalk. Rollin turned toward the street so his conversation wouldn't be overheard. "But damn, Cherlenko's gotten even creepier and more delusional since I saw him last. I don't like the way he looked at her. I know that look. And no good has ever come from it."

"Last thing Emma wants is a man. She's said that about a million times to her friends this week alone."

Rollin blew some air through his lips. "Cherlenko's got some weird power over women. He even got that CIA ice queen to flop on her back."

"You're clear."

Rollin gave a quick check around. The crowd had dispersed. "Still, I think I'd better try for this one, just to protect her from Cherlenko." He opened the back door of the Comcast van. The stench of salami assaulted his nostrils. "Jeez, what the hell are you eating in here?" he asked, climbing inside their mobile command center. He shut the door behind him and clicked off his earpiece.

Sitting in front of a bank of surveillance equipment wearing headphones, Bobby laughed, his dark eyes crinkling with amusement. He held up the rest of a sub. "Anchovy and peanut butter surprise," he joked. He always threatened to eat the most disgusting combinations of food while they did surveillance together in the van.

"You're sick."

As Rollin squeezed by him on the way to the front, Bobby turned and breathed at him with an impish grin, engulfing him in a toxic cloud of salami, onions and mustard.

Wincing, Rollin waved his hand in front of his face. "Jesus, that's terrible."

He opened the small door to the front cab and started to go through it. At the last second, he punched Bobby in the shoulder and dove into the cab. A light touch grazed his back from Bobby's return jab, but no solid contact. Rollin turned and sent him a triumphant grin.

"Getting slow, old man," Bobby said with a smirk. "I almost got you."

"Respect your elders, kid."

"Ha, you're the only elder I had who didn't beat me."

Rollin snapped his fingers. "I knew I forgot somethin'. Should have beaten you when you were young. Blew it."

"Sure did." Bobby flashed him a huge, food-filled grin.

Rollin started up the engine. Damn it, the more he watched Emma and listened to her, the more he liked her. Unexpected.

He sighed. He hated using people. Especially nice people.

"Oh, well, all's fair in love and when money is involved," he mumbled under his breath. "Especially five hundred million dollars."

* * * * *

Burke Cherlenko sat back in his Mercedes-Benz SUV and smiled. What a spitfire. The sparks from Emma's flashing green eyes had sent an electric shock straight to his cock. He loved the way her red lips curled lusciously with anger and the way she bared her straight white teeth at him. Delicious creature.

Withdrawing his cell from his jacket pocket, he punched in a number. "Dubois? I need everything on an Emma Holsten Ramsay. Everything she's done since she was born. I want to know her spending habits, eating habits, education, friends, every boyfriend and husband, things no one else knows about her. All of it. As soon as possible. A bonus if I get it tonight. Thanks." He hung up and set the phone on the seat.

Emma would look so good naked and underneath him.

He took a sip of his espresso. "David? Let's stop by Burberry on the way home. Their fall line came in."

"You got it, boss." His driver signaled for a right.

Emma had surprised him from the onset. Number one, from the pictures on the walls of her home and by the way Jerry described her, Cherlenko expected a dowdy middle-aged woman with grey hair and a permanent scowl. He must have mistaken Emma's mother for her. The only thing he'd been right about was the scowl, but he'd never seen a lovelier one. Creased in nearly flawless white skin, even her frown made her beautiful.

His biggest judgment in error was associating her with Adam. He figured anyone who married that parasitic imbecile had to be one too. As soon as she opened her mouth, he'd realized his mistake. Emma was sharp as a razor. And gutsy.

Sunlight broke through the fog and streamed in through his window. He pulled out his Gucci sunglasses and slipped them on.

Surprisingly, she had taste, too. She dressed simply, but very chic.

Such a contrast to that horrid décor of her house. He couldn't decide whether it was the bathroom covered in Pez dispensers or the collection of Disneyana that sealed his opinion. Or her newly started collection of tin Japanese space toys.

While she also displayed English antiques on her shelves and Egyptian artwork, the woman was clearly a bit of a nut.

Still, she had a power about her. A deep, rock solid power.

Titillating. Arousing. And an enticing challenge.

His cell phone rang. Jerry. Right on time.

"Well? How'd she take it? Did she cry?" Jerry sounded like he was practically salivating.

Rage itched at Cherlenko's spine and quickly took over his gut.

Interesting reaction. Protective of her already.

"No, she laughed," Cherlenko replied. "Fascinating woman, actually."

"Laughed? So is she out? When you gonna burn the place? Oh, yeah, I got an idea I'm following up about Adam. Could be the big payoff, my man."

Disgust and revulsion washed through him. While he deplored killing, he'd make an exception in Jerry's case. Once he got what he wanted out of him. More than likely Jerry was lying about his "idea". His time was almost up.

"Great," Cherlenko said with little enthusiasm.

"I'm on your team, man. So what about my store?"

Emma was a much more promising lead. Not to mention much more fun to court. She might even know the location of the weapon.

"Yes, about the antique store, that didn't work out as planned," Cherlenko said. "I've decided you're going to walk away from it."

"What do you mean, *you decided*? That's my store!"

"Now your share is mine. Don't worry, I'll compensate you." *Right before I kill you.*

"What if I don't want to be bought out? I want her to suffer! That bitch hit me with my own gun, then kicked me in the balls in front of a bunch of people! Hey, we were partners in this and you may think you're all high and mighty, but I'm gonna tell you a thing or two, man…"

While Jerry ranted, Cherlenko took out his Blackberry and typed in a one-word command.

"…yeah, so you'd better—hey," Jerry exclaimed. "What the hell are you doing, man, breaking into my pad? Cherlenko, what the fuck is Banana doing here? Don't! Put that down! That's an antique! Emma paid a lot for that!"

A crashing sound came over the receiver followed closely by Jerry's scream of pain.

Cherlenko laughed and clicked off the Blackberry. Idiot.

He pictured Emma beating up Jerry and a charge went through his dick. What a wild girl. She was going to be so much fun. Fun to play with, fun to tease, fun to seduce. He'd bet she'd be outrageous in bed. All teeth and nails. He couldn't wait. That beautiful mouth twisted in tortured sexual agony. Her white ripe breasts in his hands. Diving between her delicious thighs. His cock got even harder.

Everything was coming together perfectly. The biggest deal of his life plus a bonus playmate.

He smiled.

I'm King of the World, ma.

With the weapon, the girl and the money, he would be.

TWO

Lizzie wouldn't let the nurse in the bathroom. "I quit! I quit!" she screamed from inside.

Mary, the Filipino nurse/saint, pounded on the door. "Lizzie, you're gonna make me mad! Now open this door! I have to help you take a shower! You didn't rinse your hair yesterday! Remember? It all stuck together, now let me in!"

Her stomach in knots, Emma knocked on the door, hard. "Lizzie! I swear, I'll take the goddamned door off the hinges if you don't let Mary inside! I'm sick of this shit! You have to listen to us!"

"I quit! I quit!"

Lizzie's new favorite words for the day.

Her blood boiling, Emma frowned, shook her head and turned to the nurse. "Mary, just wait for her to come out. She has to sometime. Then deal with it."

Mary pursed her lips and crossed her small arms over her chest. "I know, she just makes me so mad. Like a big two-year-old."

"I'm glad you knew her before," Emma said with a smile.

Mary pouted. "Doesn't make it any easier."

Was Lizzie ever healthy? Not crazy and sick?

As Emma walked to the front door to see if the mail was there, she passed a picture of Lizzie taken in March, just six months before. Happy and smiling, in front of her garden store. A wealth of sadness weighed on her, making her feel twice her one hundred and thirty pounds. Sorrow ate at her gut. Was it really only six months? Seemed like a century.

As she opened the front door, Emma shook off the emotion. She couldn't allow herself to reflect yet. She had to stay strong. Put all that grieving on the back shelf. Getting Lizzie back on her feet, that was the only priority.

Thank God, the doctors' first prognosis of a permanent vegetative state had been wrong. Lizzie would get better. Was getting better. She couldn't walk just the month before and now she was showering alone. Well, that was a little messed up, all her life skills had somehow vanished with the stroke. While she was improving, no one could predict how far she'd recover. She may never be able to live on her own again.

Emma walked down the bricked pathway to the mailbox. Light glinted off something across the street. Several parked cars in front of the condo complex. Nothing shiny of note. She grabbed her mail and shut the box. Another flash of light. It came from inside a dark sedan. The window was partially rolled down.

The engine started, the car pulled away and headed toward her. As it passed, the driver, a bald man in sunglasses, gave her a slight nod.

She dropped her mail. Her heart leapt into her throat and she broke out in a full body sweat.

Baldy.

Fuck.

"This is good. And very, very bad," came a deep voice from the other side of her hedges.

She yipped, jumped and spun toward the voice. The longhaired man with the crooked nose appeared. Rollin Hanson.

Shaking, she held up her hand in a firm gesture. "I can't handle you right now." She sighed and looked at Baldy's car, now halfway up the block. "He's not gonna leave me alone, is he?"

"Nope."

She turned back to the handsome irritant. “Look, I didn’t speak to Adam for the last six months of his life except to get him to sign the divorce papers.”

“I and the other guy think you still might know something.”

“Great. So Baldy wants information. And a quick piece of ass. Great news.”

Rollin laughed. “Wouldn’t be quick with him. He normally holds onto women for a couple years. Then he…lets them go.”

“Kills them.”

“No. Not always. Sometimes. If they piss him off.”

A breeze kicked up sending Rollin’s scent over to her. Hints of patchouli, pine and musk. Really nice, actually.

She thumbed behind her. “Who is he?”

“Burke Cherlenko, like you said, an underworld overlord. Actually, he’d love to be one, but he isn’t that high level. Enough to do major damage to anyone who gets in his way. Enough to stay out of jail. Even out of the courts. But he’s not that big on the scale of things. But as far as you’re concerned, he’s got the power of Satan. He owns your ass, lady. And if you want to come through this okay, you’d better make friends with me.”

Her muscles tensed, she narrowed her gaze and pointed at him. “Look, don’t tell me—”

Without blinking an eye, he talked over her. “Your partner, Jerry, is about to show up dead. And I think your new friend there might set you up for his murder.”

Her head rang like someone clanged it with a couple of garbage can lids.

“If you don’t let me help you soon, it might get beyond the place where I can repair it and save you.”

Way too much information at once. Incomprehensible. Jerry’s murdered, she’s to blame? What? Shields on full, she crossed her arms across her chest and hardened her face. “What is it that he wants that I supposedly have? And just a stretch here, I would assume it’s the same thing you’re after. Yet you’re painting yourself as the good guy in this little game. How do I know the two of you aren't working together to get whatever this thing is you think I have?"

His gaze sharpened. "Cherlenko and I are not on the same team."

She sent him a half smile. "Bull. Main evidence being the fact that my house was torn apart. Two bloody times. By the way, do you like my new bedspread?"

His head jerked back ever so slightly.

She grinned. "Asshole. You could have cleaned up after yourself. What the hell do I supposedly have?"

He blinked, then studied her. She'd clearly surprised him. "I think you might know."

She rolled her eyes. "Oh, for crying out loud. Let me guess. This is the part where you torture me to death for information I don't have. And I thought my life was going so well. I just have to say something here, Mr. Nice Guy, if you were really nice, you'd stay the hell away from me so I can focus on getting my sister well."

A flame lit his dark gaze and his stubbly jaw tightened. "I'm trying to protect you. You're already involved and there's no way out. Now that he's targeted you."

She shot him a cold glare. "You want what he wants and you're trying to get it first using the nice guy routine. I'm done and you can go."

"It's not a routine. I am a nice guy."

She burst out laughing. "Nice guys don't spy on people."

"They do if they're trying to protect the person."

"Why would you want to help a complete stranger?"

"Because I was in your position once and someone helped me."

This stopped her. He was either the best actor in the universe or he was telling the truth. Knowing her husband and his world, she decided the former. "You're good."

His gaze darted over her shoulder. "He's here. I'll see you later."

She followed his line of sight. The dark sedan was back. Adrenaline swamped her, her heart pounded, her body screamed at her to run. She turned back and Rollin had vanished, seemingly into thin air.

Cherlenko pulled up into her driveway and rolled down his window. “I want to talk to you about your partner.”

He and the other guy were working her. Timing was just too good. Too smooth.

She feigned indifference and sighed. “Don’t tell me.”

“I know you’re suffering right now, but this is important. I want you to come with me.”

A wave of fear made her head swim. She steeled herself and stood taller. “Is that an offer I can’t refuse?”

His symmetrical face hardened. “I wouldn’t recommend it.”

Her gut roiled and a wave of nausea made her salivate. She swallowed hard. “I am about to snap.”

“I’d appreciate it if you didn’t.”

She felt like a fly caught in a web. Using some strength she didn’t know she had, she forced her exterior to appear calm. She had to take care of Lizzie. That was her priority. And to do that, she needed more information on her enemy. No matter how she looked at it, she had to go with him. “I need to drop the mail off and tell my nurse that I’ll be gone for…?”

“Less than an hour.”

All the voices in her head screamed at her to stop. The dude was a murderer. Getting in his car was suicide. “Look, I’m so not in the mood to be maimed or killed. I have to take care of my sister. Why don’t you find someone else to menace?”

“No harm will come to you. You’ve become valuable. Which is lucky. Don’t make me chase you down. I hurt people when they anger me. I don’t want to hurt you. But I will.”

Blood rushing in her ears, her throat constricted. “You terrify me,” she said without a shred of irony.

He gestured to his passenger seat. “Tell your sister and her nurse you’ll be right back. I promise you’ll arrive back here unharmed.”

Somehow she got her feet to move. She went inside, grabbed her coat, cell phone and her pocketknife. The only weapon in the house. Pathetic, but it made her feel about one percent safer and at this point, she'd take anything that helped.

Mary tuned into her and studied her face. She jerked her head toward Cherlenko. "Who's that man?"

"A friend of Adam's," Emma said, averting her gaze. "I'll be back in an hour or so. I'll have my cell, anything happens, you call me."

"We'll be fine." Her attention went to Emma's trembling hands. "Don't know about you."

Emma ran out and opened Cherlenko's car door while a cacophony of voices in her head bellowed at her to stop. Some part of her wondered if this was the last car door she'd ever open.

Emma sat next to him and she swore she could feel his black energy radiating out at her. Like she was in the company of the Beast himself. The look in his eye was so controlled, so focused, so dark, the smile on his lips seemed a complete contrast to his interior.

His cologne, however, smelled good. Really good. Dressed nice. Expensive tailored black shirt, black dress pants, black boots. Really clean. Kind of guy who shaved twice a day. Nice teeth, nice lips. If he weren't so bloody scary, he'd be super hot. The shaved head suited him.

He shot her a grin. His gaze warmed and sparkled. Unexpectedly charming.

Her heart beat a bit faster.

The mask fell away and coldness returned to his depths.

She wanted out of that car.

He took the freeway and headed north toward San Francisco.

The way he turned the steering wheel, the way he checked the traffic, signaled, checked his mirrors—his movements were precisely controlled. And fluid. Like he was a fantastically tuned machine. She got the feeling he had such mastery of his body he could control each hair on his arm.

He glanced at her a few times, an expression of amused superiority on his sculpted face. Obviously, a mind reader. Unsettling. Of course, at this point, duplicity was far beyond her reach. This whole Sister With A Stroke/Murdered Husband thing had zorched her brain cells. Her autopilot feature only had one mode: transparent.

He only drove a mile or so, took the 3rd Avenue exit and headed toward the Bay. He drove to Seal Point Park and parked up on top of a deserted hill.

Ducks, geese and sea birds hung around the shoreline and floated out amongst a few old dilapidated piers. Just north of the park, airplanes landed at San Francisco Airport.

She loved this place and visited often. And now Cherlenko was ruining it.

He shut off the engine and turned to her. His dark gaze pierced hers.

Her shoulders tensed into rigidity. Sweat pooled behind her knees. She held her hands in her lap so he couldn't see them shake.

"I need your help."

Not what she expected him to say. She found herself relax a bit. "With what? I thought you were taking my business."

"No. That's yours to keep. But I would like a favor in return."

"Which is?"

"Your partner…well, he didn't quite make it," he said with a creepy smile.

The willies hit her hard, but she forced her body to remain still. While she didn't feel any grief about Jerry, she could have easily been the one Cherlenko killed. "Why doesn't that surprise me?" she tossed off.

"You don't seem too upset over it."

"One less abusive asshole male on the planet."

His gaze hardened and a muscle in his jaw twitched.

A slap of fear smacked her across the face and her stomach hollowed. Shit. Where were her filters? She decided not to apologize and draw any extra attention to her flub. "You do realize you aren't getting my normal reactions. If you told me this six months ago, while I hate the guy, I'd probably be having a little fitty."

His expression lightened and a hint of a smile crossed his full lips. "Fitty. I like that."

"Okay, enough chitchat, just tell me straight out, don't sugarcoat it, don't smear lube on it, I want it straight. What do you want from me?"

"Lube." He let out a chuckle. "I like you." After a pause, the planes of his handsome face went hard and he straightened his muscular shoulders. "A man contacted you. Don't bother denying it. He was there, in the closet when we first met. I found that out later. I know you were surprised. And don't trust him anymore than you trust me and rightfully so. He probably warned you that I am an evil man. Since I've killed your partner and almost took your business from you, you probably believe it. I am not evil. I'm a very fair man who does not like to be cheated or made a fool of. Not for ego, but for the principle of it. I hold myself to very high standards and I hold those in my employ to the same standards. Your partner worked for me."

"And cheated you out of money for his gambling debts."

"Yes. You lost, what? Thirty thousand, seventy-seven hundred and some odd change?"

"I won't ask how you know all that."

"He was rather forthcoming with information toward the end. Do you want to know what he stole from 7-11 when he was nine?"

"No thanks. And please never tell me what you did to him." She gave a small shudder and blocked the vivid, gruesome images flashing through her mind.

A slight nod. "So, this man who visited you, Rollin Hanson, doesn't have very long to live, I'm afraid."

"Not surprising."

"If you help me, you'll never have to worry about your sister again. She'll get the best care money can buy. I know you only have one more month's worth of money to pay that nurse and Elizabeth will need care far beyond that."

"Go on."

"I need you to help me pin your partner's murder on Mr. Hanson."

A burst of anger burned through her, and her stomach and fists tightened. Right, on top of taking care of her sister and trying to keep the store afloat, she'd just pin a murder on a stranger. Her hatred for the man deepened. "And if I don't?"

"Then I'll pin it on you."

It felt like he kicked her square in the chest with steel-toed boots. Her chest constricted and all the air left her lungs. Her head buzzed with a loud roar. This was real. If she didn't do what he said, she'd be in jail for the rest of her life and her sister would go to back to that horrible place. For good. Like a butterfly stapled to a wall, she had no way out.

She held her chest and tried to get her breath back. "Pardon me while I hate you here for a minute."

He laughed. "I like you. I think you like me."

Snorting, she gaped at him. "No, I don't. I don't like people who blackmail emotionally wrung out people into helping them frame other people for murder."

A slight smile. "How soon we forget."

"What are you talking about?"

"Planting murder evidence on your stepfather's partner?"

A gut punch slammed her and her mind went gray. It took her a second to breathe again. "How did you find…never mind." Her body at battle stations, she rubbed her forehead, then hugged herself. Totally scary what this man knew about her. No one knew that. She hadn't told anyone what she'd done. "That was different. I-I w-was nineteen and…"

He sent her a sympathetic look. "You were protecting your mother."

"Yeah."

"And you were very surprised when Mother didn't turn out to be the murderer. Strange twist of fate that the partner actually turned out to be the culprit, wasn't it?"

"So what's my blood type and what grade did I get in History in fifth grade?"

"AB positive and I think it was a B," he said with a slight twinkle in his eye.

She laughed, shocking the hell out of herself. What was wrong with her?

He seemed delighted. When he smiled, he looked so normal. "I knew you'd like me."

"Dude, how could I like you? You're terrifying. You're this overlord—"

"—of the underworld," he finished with a huge smile. "Love that. I want that on a little plaque on my desk," he said, miming a square object. He pointed to the imaginary words. "Burke Cherlenko, Overlord of the Underworld."

"Look, I know myself. I can't pin some murder on—"

He gave a short laugh. "You can't be this dense."

"What?"

"I wouldn't have to pin this murder on you."

"What?"

"You'll be the police's prime suspect. Have your forgotten your very public fight with Jerry in middle of the street the other day?"

Tink! A nail went into the lid of her coffin. Wait, that wasn't enough of a motive.

"And the fact that he stole thirty-three grand from you?" Cherlenko added.

Tink! A second nail drummed into her coffin. She fought the blackness that threatened her mind.

"You haven't even been cleared in your husband's death. Detective McCoy will be all over you."

Her jaw dropped into her lap, her mind went blank and her stomach twisted so hard, bile crept up her throat. "Holy God." The car spun and she gripped the door handle to steady herself.

"I'm not a monster," he continued smoothly. "You're lucky I came along and liked your spunk. Other men in my position would have killed your spunk along with you. Or done worse to you," he said with a glance at her breasts. "I've kept many people away. I've protected you."

Breathing hard, sweat trickled down her neck. "Sounds familiar. Am I supposed to thank you at this point?"

"Yes. But I won't be offended if you don't. At least right now. Before you know me."

Before you know me. A whole body shiver.

"The police will be paying you a call. If you follow my instructions to the letter, they'll move on and leave you alone."

Visions of being carted off to prison while her sister howled jolted her brain. Tears stung her eyes. She wiped them away. No way was she crying in front of this asshole. "How? Like you said, I'm screwed."

"No, you're not. I can help you. Throwing the suspicion on Rollin won't be that difficult. I'll provide you with an airtight alibi and all you have to do is tell a story about how Rollin came into the shop and threatened Jerry. You have Rollin's card, don't you?"

"Yeah..."

"This will be simple for you," he said with confidence. "I know you want your focus on your sister's well being. Not only will I take some of the monetary burden off you, I can arrange for better care."

"I want Mary."

He gave a slight nod. "She took good care of your mother."

Unnerving, the way he kept throwing out tidbits of information about her.

"All you need to do is fabricate a story about Rollin coming into the store to harass Jerry," he said with a small, simple gesture. "Write it out. Memorize it. They'll ask you a million times."

Detective McCoy's sharp, Terrier-like face popped into mind. That awful sneer. His horrible accusations. Toxic, dark emotions polluted her mind like clouds of radioactive fallout. "I know. Been through it recently," she grumbled.

When would she stop being at the mercy of assholes? When would it end?

"You do this for me, I'll greatly appreciate it. I'll make sure that shop becomes entirely yours."

"Because you're a generous man," she added tartly.

A hidden smile grew on his handsome face. "Because I'm a generous man."

She blew out a long breath of air. "I should have shot Adam the moment he approached me in the museum. I'm gonna end up in jail someday because of that bastard."

"No, you won't," Cherlenko said with that same air of supreme confidence.

He started up the car and drove her back home. She didn't remember anything of the ride there, suddenly he pulled up in the driveway.

He put the car in park and turned to her, his face hardening. "When I call you and tell you to be somewhere for that alibi, you do what I say," he clipped out like he was the king and she was his servant.

She wanted to punch him. Hard.

"Okay," she said for lack of any other response. She hadn't made any decisions yet. No way was this dickhead going to bully her.

His gaze sharpened. "Do I need to mention what will happen if you don't help me?"

"No."

He smiled warmly like she'd just told him how much she enjoyed his company. "Good. You'll be hearing from me."

"I can't wait," she snapped coldly.

His smile widened. "Someday, that line will hold no sarcasm." He winked at her.

She suppressed a shudder and scrambled out of his car.

Without looking back, she walked into her house. Mary's dark eyes wide, she rushed up to her.

"Where's Lizzie?" Emma asked.

Mary waved a hand. "Oh, she's fine. Sulking in her room, watching TV. I'll try to feed her later. So what happened? You don't look good. Who was that man?"

"I don't know, Mary." The sympathy on the nurse's face nailed her. Tears filled her eyes.

Mary reached out and hugged her. "If Adam wasn't already in Hell, I'd pray to God to send him there."

Emma fought her emotions. She pushed away from Mary and forced a smile. "I'll be fine. I just have to think. Keep Lizzie busy for me. I'm gonna go into the backyard with a beer and think."

Mary's brow furrowed and she twisted her mouth to one side. "My cousins might be able to help you. They're mean, too."

"No. Let me see what I can do. I don't want to drag you into this. Those guys are very dangerous, very sophisticated criminals. They have resources you and I couldn't even dream about."

"You sure?"

"You being here for Lizzie is all I want. Thanks."

"You need me, you let me know. We're family."

Her heart lightened and she hugged Mary hard.

An hour and three beers into her backyard brood, the answer came to her. Totally crazy, her worst fear, her worst nightmare, but she'd be in charge. And Lizzie would be protected. It was all that mattered.

Two hours later, her heart hammering, her knees shaking, Emma walked through the door of the San Mateo Police Department and up to the reception desk.

A young police officer with bright blue eyes, a buzz cut and a bad case of acne nodded at her. "How can I help you, ma'am?"

Emma cleared her throat. "I'm here to confess to a murder."

THREE

Rollin stood with his mouth open, holding his phone and staring out the living room window of his Pacifica beach house. The waves crashed on the rocks below, but he barely registered the ocean scenery, he was too blown away. "She *what*? Say that again, you have to be kidding me."

"No, I'm not," Bobby replied. "Emma confessed to Jerry's murder. I'm sending you the report. Check your email."

Sweat breaking out all over his body, his heart went into double-time. "Is that where Emma's been? How did she get there without us knowing it? Don't we have full surveillance on her? And when did Jerry's body surface? I haven't heard anything."

"Here's the deal, Jerry isn't dead. The cops found him by accident, hiding out in Vegas. They did an undercover sting operation on some gun smugglers and Jerry was in the wrong place at the wrong time. He's in jail in Vegas right now."

"*What?* But Jerry was in that hole in Brisbane—in the old shoe manufacturing plant—being beaten to death. Shit." Rollin smacked himself on the forehead and paced across the hardwood floor. "I'm so blind. David Mangrove is a double-agent. Thank God, we got two guys inside Cherlenko's organization, because David just screwed us. Man, am I gonna fry his ass. Shit, I needed him."

"At least Banana is still there and hasn't turned on us."

"I can't believe David," Rollin said in disgust. "After all Cherlenko did to him, he's still loyal. Unbelievable. Shit. Cherlenko used me to get to Emma. And I made it so easy on him. Of course, it made no sense to kill Jerry. I thought maybe Jerry did something to Cherlenko that he didn't want people knowing about. Still, I smelled something wrong with David, I should have known better."

"He was good, don't blame yourself."

"Who else can I blame?" Rollin demanded.

"Okay, your fault," Bobby replied cheerfully. A bag rattled then crunching sounds came over the receiver. Sounded like potato chips.

"So Banana's still on our team? How come he didn't tell us about Jerry?"

"Banana's been on a different job for Cherlenko," Bobby said through a mouthful of chips. He chewed and swallowed. "He just called me to tell me what's going on at Cherlenko's headquarters. Banana swears he didn't know about the Jerry thing."

Rollin's shoulders relaxed and he took a deep breath. "Thank God. Still, let's keep an eye on him. We have to have someone on the inside. So what did Banana say? Emma confessed, cops found Jerry, is this what Cherlenko wanted? What was he up to?" He collapsed into his overstuffed leather loveseat.

"No, he didn't want her to do that. He's freaking out. Big time."

"So she went against him? He didn't force her into that?"

A flock of pelicans in the shape of a V flew by his living room window.

Slurping and a swallow. "No, Cherlenko forced her into it, but not the way you think. Emma told Mary she confessed because she didn't want to give into either of you."

Rollin's gut tightened, a wash of guilt went through him. He hated adding to her stress. Hated. It.

Bobby continued. "Cherlenko said if Emma didn't pin Jerry's murder on you that he'd pin it on her."

Leaping off the couch, Rollin felt walloped. His heart wrenched at the thought of Emma in such an untenable situation. How much more could she take? "Holy shit. What an asshole. Not only trying to get to me, but probably testing her out to see what kind of power he could get over her." He walked over to the window and gazed out; three seals basked on a sunny rock below unbothered by the waves that lapped at their tails.

"And he wants you all tied up with the local cops and out of the picture."

Rollin burst out laughing. "Well, she sure showed him. God, I love that girl. What a firecracker. Okay, we have to get her out of there."

"She'll be out of the hospital in a couple hours."

"Hospital?" Rollin exclaimed.

Bobby gave one hee-haw. "She went ape-shit when they told her Jerry was still alive. Started laughing hysterically and confessing to all sorts of other crimes. Said she was the Unabomber. McCoy wanted her ass, too. Kept her up all night questioning her. My guy in the police station said that his boss was pissed at McCoy for wasting the department's time on her and not recognizing her as being mentally unstable."

"So they sent her to the emergency room for a psyche evaluation?"

"Yeah. Last I heard, she was still waiting to be seen." A bag rattled. Crunching.

"Shit. Wonder how she thought she'd take care of her sister from jail."

"Emma—" Bobby choked and coughed. Slurping. Coughing. More slurping.

"Told you huffing potato chips was dangerous," Rollin cracked.

Bobby grunted. Finally, he cleared his throat. "Emma signed her house and business over to the nurse in exchange for taking care of Lizzie until she gets better."

Rollin walked into his kitchen to press out another cup of Kona coffee. "Damn, that woman has heart. She's whacked, crazy, desperate, but she's got heart." He reached for the French press and stopped. "Shit. Cherlenko's gonna fall hard for her. She has no idea how she just screwed herself. Once he gets over being pissed, he'll be all over her. He's never had a woman he couldn't completely control." He laughed and grabbed the press. "She's good. Poor lady," he said, withdrawing the lid.

"Gives us a great opportunity."

"Doesn't it, though? Time to play the White Knight." He tapped some ground coffee into the press and turned on the electric teakettle.

"Wait…just got a text. Emma's out. Mary picked her up."

"I'll let her sleep for a day, then I'll go pay her a visit. Burke's probably already there."

"No. Not yet."

"He will be," Rollin said with a sharp nod.

* * * * *

Emma glared at her bushes, spraying a geranium so hard with the hose, flowers flew off and sailed over the fence. Ever since she got home, she'd been alternately sleeping and brooding. Minutes before, Mary had caught her in her room, staring at the darkened TV and muttering threats about what she wanted to do to Cherlenko. Mary'd pulled her up off the recliner and pushed her outside for some fresh air. Poor woman. Taking care of two crazy people.

Emma took a deep breath and eased the water pressure, careful not to damage the flowers any further.

After a bit, she began to relax. She had to get over this. So she'd been manipulated into confessing to a murder of a person who turned out to be alive. At least she wasn't facing a long prison term. Nor did the cops think she killed Adam any longer. In fact, now McCoy's superiors thought she was a total whack job. She'd overheard his boss order him to let her go and leave her alone. To concentrate on other suspects in her husband's murder. Jerry being one of them.

Cops didn't seem to know about Rollin or Cherlenko. Not that she'd mentioned either. She wasn't stupid. Criminals like that could get you killed in prison. Or anywhere else for that matter.

Still, she'd wanted to get out from underneath Cherlenko and Rollin and since she hadn't seen either, she figured mission accomplished.

Even if they showed up, she'd get rid of them. Whatever game those two were playing had nothing to do with her. She didn't have any hidden information about Adam.

She watered her way up the long driveway. As she absently stared at some iceplant, a dark car pulled up and parked in front of her house. The home health care nurse from Kaiser in charge of Lizzie's case was due any moment.

She checked the driver.

A bald man wearing sunglasses.

Her heart thumped hard, her blood turned frosty and she squeezed the hose nozzle in a death grip.

Cherlenko.

His face stony, he got out of his car and slammed the door in a big display of anger.

Rage erupted from within her like a bucket of C-4 exploding. She pointed at him. "Get back in your car and get the fuck off my property or I swear I'll hose you!" she yelled so loudly, her voice echoed all down the block.

He stopped and put his hands on his hips, his mouth hard. "I'm not pleased with you."

"Oh, yeah? Well, I don't care, you asshole! Get into your car or I swear, I will hose you down! I mean it! If you don't want your precious expensive Italian clothes destroyed, get in the car, drive off and never come back here again!"

Cherlenko fingered his lapels. "Louis Vuitton. French, not Italian," he drawled in a snotty tone.

Snap! Screaming, she charged him, nailing him full on with the spray.

Sputtering and yelling, he tried to protect himself, but she kept his head and entire front in her target zone. Soaking wet, his face beet red, he ripped open his car door and dove inside. She continued toward him, hosing his car and bellowing at him to leave.

Gunning his engine, he peeled out. As he passed her, he pointed at her, his mouth open in a yell. She followed him, dousing his car until he was out of range.

"Asshole!" She flipped him off.

She turned away with a huge huff, moved back to where she'd been and continued watering.

Mary came rushing out of the house, laughing. "You got him! You got him!"

The joy on Mary's face broke her fury. Emma smiled. "Guess I did, didn't I?"

Mary slapped her thighs. "Oh, that was so great, that idiot deserved it. That was so funny. He was so mad!"

Emma finally chuckled. "Ruined his perfect French clothes. Probably just cost him some heavy-duty dry cleaning bills. Jerk."

"You think he'll come back?"

"Probably," Emma replied. "I think I'd better install a bigger hose. Maybe I'll tap into the fire hydrant next time."

"You might need it now, look," Mary said, pointing across the street.

Rollin stood leaning on a tricked-out dark green Jeep Wrangler with a huge smile on his face.

Fire blasted through her veins. She advanced on him, waving the spray nozzle. "I'll hose you, too, buddy. Get lost!"

"Yeah, you go away and leave her alone!" Mary yelled.

Emma turned back to her. "I don't want you involved, Mary."

Mary stuck out her chin. "I'm already involved."

"I know. Let me handle him."

The pint-sized Filipino beauty glared at Rollin. "I want to help you beat him up."

Emma laughed at the fierceness on Mary's sweet face. "Go check on Lizzie. I'll get rid of him."

Mary's dark gaze blazing, she pointed at him. "You're a very bad man!" With a toss of her head, she turned and walked into the house.

Emma returned to her roses and watered them, ignoring the big jerk across the street. He watched her.

After a good five minutes, Emma couldn't stand it. "Will you please go away?"

"I want to talk without getting a shower. I'm staying out of spray range."

"I don't want to talk to you."

"Got that. But I'm not leaving."

"Fine. Suit yourself."

She turned her back to him and finished watering. Rollin stayed put.

Without another glance his way, she rolled up the hose, went into the house and sat down at the kitchen table where Lizzie was eating. Or attempting to eat. Her left-brain stroke had partially paralyzed the right side of her body. Her right hand was so weak, she had to use both hands to get the spoon to her mouth. But she was getting most of the food in her mouth, a huge leap forward from the week before.

"You're doing great, honey," Emma said.

Lizzie gave her a bright smile and nodded, pureed peaches clinging to the sides of her mouth.

Despite the food on her face, Lizzie did look better. Her gaze was clearer and her long, white hair looked cleaner. Even with the stroke, she didn't look forty-five. Her face was so youthful, her premature white hair had never fit. Emma'd been trying to get her to dye it for years, but Lizzie was the Earth mother/hippie type. Natural was more important to her.

Emma got up, gave her sister a pat, then went into her bedroom to check her email. She answered a couple inquiries into her sister's health from friends, not mentioning her other issues. Soon, she got sleepy and crashed on her bed.

Two hours later, she got up and shuffled into the kitchen.

Mary sat at the table, drinking tea and reading a magazine. "Lizzie's taking a nap and he's still out there."

Emma stared at her. "You're kidding me."

"No."

Shoulders slumping, Emma rubbed her brow. "Christ. All right, I'll get rid of him."

"You want my help, I can get my cousin to get rid of him for you."

"No, honey. I'll take care of it. But thanks. Means the world to have you in my corner."

Mary gave her a bright smile.

Emma combed her hair, had a half a cup of tea to wake fully, then went out to confront the jerk. He sat in his Jeep, reading the paper.

As she approached, he set aside the newspaper. "Hi," he said, with a large smile on his rugged face.

Her heart beat a bit faster. An inadvertent thrill went through her. Where the hell did *that* come from?

Ignoring her response to him, she sighed. "What will it take to get rid of you?"

"Come get a burger with me."

Not what she expected him to say. She stared at him blankly. "A burger."

"Yeah, I'm jonesing for *In and Out*. Millbrae. I'll bring you right back here. And I won't make you pin a murder on anyone, I swear."

She snorted. "You want me to just get in your car with you."

"That's the general idea. Burger? You probably haven't eaten since this morning, huh?"

Her stomach growled, as if on cue. A burger did sound good. And she loved *In and Out*. "It would be stupid of me to get in that car with you."

He sent her a half-smile. "If I'd wanted to kidnap you, I would have done that by now. And I wouldn't have sat out here for the past three hours. I do have another life."

"So why don't you go live it?"

"Because you've made sure that Cherlenko won't leave you alone."

She rolled her eyes. "And how did I do that?"

"You outsmarted him. Good one, by the way. The confession. Good job. I heard he lost his mind. He didn't expect that. Neither did I, for that matter."

She shook her head and placed her hands on her hips. She examined his face carefully. "You won't leave me alone, will you?"

He didn't skip a beat. "Not likely."

Blowing out a breath of air through her lips, she ran her hands through her hair. "Shit. You're lucky I just took a nap."

"Or I'd be dripping wet?"

She cracked a smile. "Yes."

"Go get your purse or whatever you want to bring with you," he said, nodding toward her house. "Stun gun. Machete, whatever."

She couldn't help but chuckle at the guy. "Okay. I'll let you buy me a burger."

Slack-jawed, he seemed astonished. "I didn't say anything about buying you a burger. Make sure you bring some money, I'm almost out."

She gaped at him.

His serious expression broke, he flashed a giant smile and pointed at her. "Ha! Gotcha." He jerked his head toward her house. "Go get your stuff."

Who was this guy? A joker one minute, a high-level criminal the next. She couldn't keep up. Muttering to herself, she went inside and got her purse.

Mary came out of the kitchen, saw Emma's purse and her eyes went wide. "You aren't going with him?"

Emma ran her hand down the nurse's slim shoulder. "If I don't return, the house is yours. Just take care of Lizzie for me. These creeps clearly aren't going to leave me alone. Maybe if I go along with this guy—he seems to be the least horrible of the two—maybe I can figure out how to make them both go away."

Mary's mouth went hard. "I don't like this."

"I don't either."

"I'm going to call you every fifteen minutes."

"Okay."

Mary gave her a quick hug. "Good luck."

Emma crossed the street and climbed into Rollin's jacked-up Jeep. His distinctive interesting scent hit her upon sitting. Musky, with hints of jasmine and earth. Peculiar, yet…sumptuous.

He sent her a grin and her heart skipped a beat. She had to give it to him, with his long dark hair and his black leather jacket, he was hot. Got hotter the more she saw him. With his intelligent dark gaze, crooked nose, that strong chin and goatee, guy made a striking package. Not your typical good looks, but very tasty.

Mental note to self: Resist the sexual interest, please.

"This is probably stupid on my part," she said, clicking the seatbelt into place.

"Nah. You can tell I won't hurt you. And I won't. Unless you call feeding you greasy carbs hurting you. Calorie Police might consider this an assault."

She snorted, reluctantly breaking into a smile. Bastard was very charming. Luckily, her brain was burnt. No worries on getting too caught up in him. She simply wasn't capable.

He turned the car around and soon they were on the freeway headed north.

Rollin was such a contrast to Cherlenko. Rollin's floormats were filthy, the Jeep hadn't been washed in months and there were pens and coins and candy wrappers on his dashboard. Between the seats held more of the same. While he personally was clean—and so were his clothes and leather jacket—they showed lots of wear. This was a guy who got his money's worth out of his belongings. Didn't go in for the big show. Clearly didn't care much about how he looked or appeared to others.

He was also much more relaxed about his driving than Cherlenko. He checked his mirrors and all, she wasn't afraid, but he drove sort of casually. Elbow up on the door, slumped a bit in his seat. Seemed very comfortable with himself. Which made her more comfortable with him.

"Did you see me hose Baldy?"

He burst out laughing. Had a really nice laugh. Deep, natural. "Yeah. I'd just pulled up. Probably pissed about his clothes. He's a clothes whore. You ruined his Gucci."

"Louis Vuitton. At least that's what he said right before I turned the hose on him."

He sent her an admiring grin. "You rock. Women don't say no to that guy. He's got some weird power over 'em."

"Not me."

With a raise of his eyebrows, he nodded. "Heard that before. Watch yourself, he's tricky and smooth."

"Will he try to kill me?"

"No. Well, hopefully not."

"Wow. That was super reassuring."

He chuckled and waved his hand. "Sorry. No, he won't kill you. I won't let him. But I don't know what's going on with him. He's changed over the past couple years."

"So you know him."

"Oh, yeah."

"How?"

"Served in the military together."

Like a slap across the head, this shocked her. She couldn't picture the two of them in the same room, let alone in the same platoon. Nor could she picture either of them in the service. "*You were in the military with him?*"

"Yeah. Known him a long time, actually. He wasn't like this. He changed. He used to be cool. A good friend, actually. Best friend, if you can believe it."

"You have to be kidding me."

"Yeah, I know. He's changed that much." His dark gaze clouded. "I don't know who is he is anymore. Got all deluded and high on himself. Freaked out. It sucks, to tell you the truth."

Rollin clearly still loved the guy. And was hurt they were no longer friends.

She couldn't get her bearings.

"Now he's…scary, actually. At first I thought his new badass act was just an act, like he was under deep cover or something. But now, I really think he believes he's a criminal. What he did to you the other morning? If I hadn't seen it with my own eyes, I wouldn't have believed it. I watched this guy put his life on the line to save two Iraqi kids from a building the Marines were about to blow."

"Cherlenko? Really?"

"Yeah. But something happened to him after this last mission we did. He changed personalities and went nuts."

"Was he, like, some war hero or something?"

"Yeah. But don't let that influence you. He's not that man anymore. And the thought of guy with his knowledge and skills turning to crime is…bad. I can't think of anyone more dangerous. Not to scare you."

"I'm beyond fear at this point. Which is why I hosed him."

"That was awesome," he said, breaking into hearty laughter. "Hosing Cherlenko. Too funny. Sorry, I know you don't find any of this amusing. But I'm loving watching you outsmart him. But soon, my dear," he said, meeting her gaze, "you're gonna need more people on your team." He turned his attentions back to the road and exited the freeway.

"And you want to be on my team."

"Yeah. You are no match for Burke Cherlenko. I'm barely a match for him. But I got a ton of people who want to help me. All the guys he screwed over."

"So you'll help me in exchange for whatever the two of you are after."

"Might help you, too," he said, pulling up at the stoplight.

"What is this all about?"

The light turned green and he hung a left onto Millbrae Avenue. "Let me buy you a burger first. I think better on a full stomach."

"Okay."

They pulled up in the drive-through.

He turned to her. "I want to grab the burgers and park out by the airport and watch the planes land, and eat, okay?"

"Sure."

He ordered a Double-Double. She went for her usual. Two meat, one cheese, grilled onions, Protein Style.

Shooting her a grin, he said, "You really know your *In and Out* burgers."

"Yep. A connoisseur."

He drove out Anza Blvd and parked in the Embassy Suites parking lot overlooking the Bay.

They ate in silence, only breaking to comment on how good the food tasted.

After she downed her burger and wiped her chin, she turned to him and sent him a serious stare. "So will you please tell me what this is all about? Neither of you have told me anything so far."

"Adam stole five hundred million from a friend of mine. My friend wants it back," he said casually, crumpling up the paper that had held his burger. He put it in the bag.

Her heart nearly stopped and her chest squeezed together. She had to gasp in a breath. "Five hundred million dollars? Adam did? That idiot? Do you know how much dumb was packed into that tiny brain of his? More dumb than Paris Hilton. More dumb than it'd take to fill up Lake Michigan. Dude had nearly the entire supply of dumb on the planet stuffed into that pretty head of his."

Rollin cracked up. "You got that right. No, Adam just stumbled into it. For the first time in his life—well second, meeting you in the museum was awfully good luck—but for the second time, he was in the right place at the right time."

"Apparently. Damn, five hundred million dollars. Hell. That's crazy. Money. And here I thought it was some super-secret-spy-crazy-underworld-criminal-organization-Mission Impossible-guerilla-subversive-type crap."

He raised a brow at her. "That was a lot of words."

"That was nothing. So why am I alive, exactly? Five hundred million? I should be floating in the Bay now after having suffered the same fate as my ex-husband."

"Everyone knows you don't know. But after some investigation, I believe you might know. But you don't know it."

She couldn't help but smile. "I know but I don't know that I know."

He gave her a cute smile back. "Right."

"Sounds like you're grasping at straws." She dug through her burger bag and fished out a fry.

"Perhaps. But I got a gut feeling you'll lead me to it."

She snorted. "Same gut feeling Cherlenko has about me."

"Yes, even though with him and you? It's beyond that. You're a challenge now. He won't leave you alone until he conquers you."

Groaning, she rolled her eyes. "Lovely."

"Once he sets his sights on a woman, it's all over. But I'll help you get rid of him."

She noted a few scars on the back of his hands. "So this is your job? Money recovery?"

"Sometimes."

"Huh. So…do you work for the government?"

"Not officially."

"Do you work for the evil overlords of the underworld?"

"Not officially."

"What do you do officially?"

"As little as possible."

She pursed her lips at him. "You're just a punch-line factory, aren't you?"

"I try." He grinned.

Sighing, she stared out over the Bay. “So Cherlenko was trying to pin a fake murder on you to get you out of the way so he can get his hands on the money. I mean, me.”

“Yep. We’ve both been hired to recover the cash. But again, Burke also did that to you because he’s playing you. Loves his mind games. While he freaked out when he found out you’d gone to the police, he’s probably falling in love with you right about now.”

Her stomach twisted like it was in a taffy puller. “I almost retched up my burger.”

“You think that way now. He’s a charming fucker. I’ve seen him take down stronger women than you.”

A weird, eerie echo in her brain warned her that Rollin could be right. She attempted to wipe the thought away, but the fear remained. “My life is so much fun. It just gets better and better. This is all so completely enjoyable,” she muttered, gloomy. “Wait. How could I possibly be involved with that money? And why did you search my house? Adam only visited when my mom lived there. Not while I’ve been there.”

“Adam was at your place two days before he was killed, while you were at the store.”

Emma checked to see if he was lying. Didn’t seem to be. “Adam? At my house? Oh. Probably trying to steal something from me. But why? He had five hundred million.”

“Don’t know. Any ideas where he might have hid the cash?”

“No. If you guys couldn’t find it, how could I? You guys are professionals.”

“Do the words, ‘Jenn’s Goofy Song’ mean anything to you?”

Her ears went back and her jaw tightened. “Jenn? As in Adam’s new girlfriend, Jennifer?”

“I don’t know.”

“Jenn’s Goofy Song? Why would I know anything about his relationship with the adolescent-stripper-slash-meth-whore?” She wadded up her burger bag and tossed it to the floor.

“I’m just asking.”

"Wait, is this why all my Disneyana got ripped off? You guys took all my Goofy stuff."

"Sorry."

She glared at him. "You destroyed my collection. Talk about boundary crossing. My mom's body was barely cold. Same with Adam's. And then you guys destroyed my house. Twice."

He shrugged slightly, but there was no apology on his rugged face. "You married the wrong guy."

"I know. But damn it, that stuff cost me upwards of a few grand. I can't even get some of those pieces anymore."

"Sorry. Actually Cherlenko got to the Goofy stuff before I did. He didn't find anything in it."

The sight of her destroyed house flashed through her mind. Upended couches, all her clothes on the floor, the empty shelves that had held her Disneyana. "Damn him! And damn you, too. Christ what a mess."

He snorted. "I bought you a burger," he said like it made up for everything, clearly joking.

She couldn't help but laugh. This guy was so hard to stay mad at. "Okay, so we're even."

He flashed her a lop-sided grin. "See?" His attention went to his dashboard. "Is it really five o'clock?"

"Yeah."

He lit up. "Awesome! Hey, you want a beer?" He got his wallet out of his pocket and went through it, withdrawing an Embassy Suites room key. He held it up with a triumphant grin. "Killer, I still have it."

"You staying here?"

"No, but they have this great afternoon booze reception. You produce a key and voila! Free drinks. Come on, you want a cocktail?"

She stared at him, waiting for him to admit that he was joking. The bright anticipation on his face didn't fade. "You're not kidding."

"Hell no."

"You're insane."

He opened his door. "Come on, this location makes great popcorn, too."

"You just ate a whole wad of food," she said, indicating his burger bag.

"Popcorn takes up no space in the human stomach. It's been scientifically proven. Come on."

Emma couldn't figure out why she was going along with the madman, but she found herself following him into the lobby of the Embassy Suites. At the center of the hotel was a six-story-tall indoor garden atrium with a Koi pond. He led her through it and up to the "complimentary" bar.

Flashing his room key at the barkeep—a large overweight, bald sixty-something guy with glasses—he pointed at the beer taps. "I'll take a Sierra Nevada. And Emma? What would you like?"

"Uh…"

"Why don't you get your usual, honey?" he said with a wink.

She couldn't help but laugh at his audacity. "Okay, give me a Long Island Iced Tea."

Rollin looked at her with mock astonishment. "Goin' wild on me, woman." He turned to the barman and nodded toward her. "Gotta keep my eye on this one, even after twelve years of marriage, she still surprises me."

The bartender smiled. "Twelve years, good for you. You still look happy together, too. You know, you can really tell people who've been married a long time, can't you? People got a way with each other."

Emma coughed back laughter.

Rollin tipped the guy a few bucks, grabbed their drinks and led her to a table next to a little waterfall. "I'll be right back, *wifey*, I'm gonna grab us some popcorn."

She watched as the strange, yet very hot man walked over to the popcorn machine and filled up two small bowls. She had to admit, he had a really nice ass. Perfect size and tight.

He returned, sending her a huge grin. "Here, *honey*." He set the bowl in front of her and sat, chuckling. "That was funny. *Really can tell when people have been married a long time, can't you?*" he said, doing a spot-on impersonation of the bartender. "Man, that was good. Your face turned bright red. Good cover on the coughing there."

She burst out laughing. It was all so surreal. And he was so funny! The way he handled the barkeep, his smooth manner—so self-assured—and his flawless imitation. But carrying a room key to get free drinks? Who was this guy? She shook her head. "I don't think I've ever met anyone like you."

He winked at her. "Never met anyone like you, either, Emma. The way you hosed down Cherlenko, turning yourself into the cops, you're a firecracker, lady. Never knew any woman who could stand up to that bastard. I know you're not exactly yourself with the strain of dealing with your sister, but still, you're funny."

She took a sip of her Long Island. Really hit the spot. "So how did you get into this…thing you do? You were in the military?"

He leaned back in his chair and ate a handful of popcorn. Gesturing with his beer, he said, "Yep. Officer in the Navy. Went into special forces…" His gaze clouded, his mouth went tight and his attention shifted to his beer. "Saw some…ugly stuff. Changed me. Realized that there are no good guys or bad guys." He met her gaze. "Governments, rich people, the way the planet really works—very different than I thought. Really popped my cherry. So I quit. Became a surf bum for a year in San Diego. Got bored, had an offer from an old buddy, some mercenary stuff. Crazy, but it parlayed into more surveillance opportunities, information gathering, recovery of lost items. Now I'm freelance."

He took draw off his beer.

"So how long have you known Cherlenko?"

"Jeez. Like eighteen years. We got stationed in Germany together right out of the academy. He was a junior officer. I was his immediate superior. Then he got promoted to my level, like in about a minute. Brilliant guy. We became friends pretty fast. Bonded on computers, history and movies. Excellent company. But…" His expression fell, pain lines appeared on his lean face. "You saw him. He's lost his mind."

"So who killed Adam? The guy he stole the money from? Or Burke? Or you?" She studied him carefully.

His gaze darted to his drink, then back to her. "I told you, that information could get you killed."

For some reason, she wasn't afraid of him, nor put off by his statement. "Did you kill him?"

He held her gaze. "No." His expression didn't waver.

"Okay." Rollin clearly wasn't going to spill anything else about Adam's death. She sipped on her Long Island. "So what do you think I should do?"

"Help me find that money. Once it's out of your possession, you'll be safe."

"I thought you said Cherlenko wanted to prove something to me."

"If you keep hosing him down and there's no money at stake, he'll go away. Besides, he has so many women—after him, with him—eventually, he'll forget about you."

"Ladies' man."

He gave a knowing nod. "Oh yeah."

"Did he take one from you?"

"Try dozens."

"Yet you still hung out with him."

"He was like the brother I never had. Despite the woman problems, we were really close."

Rollin was such an interesting character. His face had seen some fighting. Along with his crooked nose, there was a small scar on his chin and one near his left eye. The sparkle in his eyes, his humor and his lightheartedness were such a contrast to his rugged features. So compelling.

Adam had been pretty, but not as manly.

A Koi fish swam up and stopped below them. Begging for food, probably. Rollin peered down at the fish, then turned to her. Mouth open, his eyes bugged out and his face transformed into the Koi. An absolute perfect likeness. Astonishing. And hilarious.

She cracked up.

He broke his pose and joined her, his eyes sparkling. "You got a great laugh, girl. Good audience, too. Sorry if I've added to your stress here. But I have to tie up the loose ends of yours and Adam's life or you'll never be free."

"He was my stupidest mistake, ever."

He sent her a searching look, then gazed at his drink. "So how'd you end up with him?"

Her face warming, she snorted sourly and her attention went to the Koi pond. "I'd just been dumped by my first husband, an older college professor with a legion of mistresses. Adam should have been a one-night-stand. But he needed the layout of the museum and the alarm codes, so he stuck with me until he got them. Even went so far as to marry me. Then the idiot left his plans for the break-in on the coffee table. I went to my boss immediately. She thanked me profusely—I was the big hero for about a minute—then she fired me and got me blackballed from the museum world."

"Sorry, Emma."

"Yeah. So I set up the antique shop—which actually turned out to be fun and a lot less ass-kissing—and Adam lost half of it to Jerry in a goddamned poker game. Finally, I'd had enough and kicked the jerk out. And all this happened because I couldn't say no to a pretty face. Life would be infinitely easier without hormones."

"Yeah, but a lot less fun." He sent her a cute smile.

Her heart beat harder.

She suddenly realized that she was enjoying herself. She was relaxed with Rollin. He seemed sincere, smart and relatively sane. If she'd met him under other circumstances, she'd have slipped him her phone number.

But aside from being a tasty little nugget, could he really help her? It was clear the situation wasn't going away on its own. She needed someone on her side. And she liked this guy. A lot more than Cherlenko.

She gestured toward him. "If I went along with you, how would we proceed?"

"I'd come over and we'd take a closer look at the house. And I want you to think long and hard about Adam's words: 'Jenn's Goofy Song'. Because that's supposedly what he said right before…" His attention went to his beer.

Emma made a face. "They tortured him to death. Or no, he had an inconvenient heart attack while they were torturing him."

Rollin kept his eyes on his drink. "Uh…yeah."

"I can't believe that stupid cop thought that I'd murdered Adam," she said with disgust.

"You were set up."

"Wasn't I though? Love to get my hands on the bastards who did that to me." She checked his face and swore she saw a flash of shame in his dark gaze.

Did he plant the murder evidence on her?

No. She couldn't picture Rollin doing that to anyone.

He nodded. "You were very lucky you got rid of that evidence."

She shuddered and held herself, rubbing her arms. "Shit, that was close. I'd been camping. I got home and was putting away my cooler in the garage and found this bloodied part of a baseball bat stuffed in a bag near my recycling. That's when I thought Adam had beaten someone to death and hidden his evidence at my house. I had no idea it was Adam's blood all over that thing."

"So what did you do with it?"

"Walked straight to McDonald's and dumped it. Then I came back home and was puttin' away my underwear and found Adam's credit cards in the drawer. Man, all the hair stood up on my arms and neck. I grabbed 'em and buried 'em in my yard. By this time, I was completely paranoid. I checked out my front window and noticed these scary guys staring at my house. So I called the cops for help." She took a draw off her Long Island.

"Uh, oh."

"Yeah. I couldn't believe it when they showed up with a search warrant and tore my place apart." She sighed heavily. "I didn't even know Adam was dead. Then they dragged me down to the police station and grilled me. Thankfully, I knew enough to keep my mouth shut. With Adam's body being dumped two blocks from my store, if they'd found those cards, I'd be in jail right now. McCoy's a pitbull."

She got the distinct impression Rollin knew more about her frame up than he was letting on. He had difficulty keeping eye contact and kept picking at a thread on his jeans. He knew who'd done it. It was all over his face.

Then, like a light switch, his expression changed. His gaze sharpened, he shifted in his seat and sat straighter, leaning into her. "So I know it bugs you, but what Adam said before he died could be the key here. Think about that 'Jenn's Goofy Song' thing, okay?"

Her jaw tightened and a flame of anger burned her insides. Even though she'd kicked Adam out, why did he have to hook up with a cute teenager? Such an operator. Amazing face and powerful Svengali-like charm.

Red Flag! So is this guy! Don't get all lulled here. Don't let your heart flutter at the thought of joining him on this money search thing.

Standing shoulder to shoulder with him, looking for the money up in her closet. He'd turn to her…

Dear God, she wanted to kiss the guy.

Abort! Abort! Run away!

She was on the Adam conveyor belt, headed straight back to heartbreak and destruction.

Damn her hormones! She couldn't wait for menopause. Maybe she'd get her senses back.

His dark brow furrowed. "Are you all right? You just went pale."

Damn it, too tired to mask her emotions. "Huh? No. Sorry, I'm tired and this alcohol is hitting me hard."

"Better get you home," he said, patting her arm. "You need rest. You got enough last night, right?"

He certainly seemed caring. And his attention made her feel good. “Some.”

“I know McCoy kept you up all night. What a jerk that guy is.”

Disconcerting. This guy had more information on her than she did. “What don’t you know about me?”

He smiled and his dark gaze twinkled. “What your favorite flavor of ice cream is.”

“That’s right, I haven’t been buying it lately. I’ll let that be a mystery to you. Gotta keep some secrets from you,” she said, sending him a flirty smile.

He lit up and returned the grin, only with a wicked gleam in his eye.

What is wrong with you?

Her muscles tight, her stomach jittery, she followed him back to the car. She hadn’t meant to flirt with him. It’d happened naturally. And far too easily. She had to avoid him.

But how was she supposed to handle this terrible situation without help?

She didn’t know. But she had to figure it out.

No matter how much she wanted to believe Rollin was on her side, she knew better. With five hundred million at stake, she’d be stupid to trust anyone.

And she was done being stupid.

FOUR

Next morning, coffee and a doughnut from the shop around the corner was the only answer. The only things Emma wanted to think about. Because thinking about Rollin and the five hundred million dollars was making her mental.

Adding to her stress, Lizzie had refused to eat breakfast. Suddenly, Lizzie didn't like eggs. She kept trying to say what she wanted, but all that came out was "non-negotiable damages." Really odd the phrases her wounded mind decided to keep. And Lizzie clearly thought she was saying something else. The fight had escalated into a full-on screaming battle. Far too much emotion, far too early in the morning.

Once at the doughnut shop, Emma had to sit on herself to stop from ordering more than one. After much ruminating, she chose a chocolate twisty and some Kona coffee. Yummy! She headed back home with her prizes. She'd sit in the sun on the back porch, read the paper, eat her precious doughnut and drink the coffee. A ten-minute break from all the craziness.

As she walked by the entrance to the bank parking lot next to her house, a black limousine pulled up beside her.

She continued walking and suddenly, she was flanked by two refrigerator-sized men. A behemoth with long blond hair and a bruiser with a red crew cut and goatee. Cherlenko's goons.

Adrenaline blasted through her limbs and she sprinted for her house.

Not two steps away, they grabbed her, dragged her backwards and shoved her in the back of the limo. The doors locked, they jumped in the front and the car sped away, slamming her back against the seat. Thank God, she had a lid on her coffee or she would have been scalded in the attack.

She looked over and no surprise, there sat Cherlenko. With a smug grin on his overly handsome face.

Her blood turned to molten lava. Her teeth clenched. She held up her cup of coffee. "I've got half a mind to throw this at you."

"You'd have to have half a mind to try," he countered, his dark eyes flashing.

She leveled her best glare at him. "You *bastard*." She put her coffee in her lap and backhanded him across his thick shoulder. "What's wrong with you? Kidnapping me? What are you thinking?"

The corners of his mouth twitched as he fought a smile. "I'm thinking you're probably the most adorable woman I've ever met."

She yelled at him in an unintelligible shout of exasperation. He winced from the noise, but broke into a wide grin. Wholly amused. She wanted to slap him, but she already knew the backhand across the shoulder was as far as she could go.

"Adorable. Absolutely adorable," he said.

Even though she was furious, couldn't stop from smiling back at him and chuckling at the absurdity of it all. All so ridiculous. And the bottom line, he probably wouldn't kill her. He liked her. She could work this to her advantage.

She sighed and relaxed back against the plush leather seats. "I know you want the five hundred million, okay? Rollin told me. But I don't know where it is. I've told both you this. But why the hell did you try to blackmail me into framing Rollin for Jerry's murder when he was still alive? You needed to control me? Prove that you could pull my strings?" She glowered at him and jabbed a finger his way. "Stop this shit. You're really starting to piss me off. Now will you please turn the car around and let me go enjoy my doughnut and coffee in peace?"

His amused expression didn't waver. "Afraid I can't do that."

Anger raged through her veins. Her jaw popped from being clenched too hard. "Please don't make me want to smash my doughnut in your face. It's a good doughnut."

"So eat it."

"I want out of your car. You are kidnapping me. I don't want to be kidnapped."

"Don't think of this as being kidnapped. Think of it as an apology."

Her thoughts exploded in a giant mushroom cloud of confusion. "*What?*"

He laughed. "An apology. You can eat that doughnut or have eggs Benedict and cracked crab and champagne at the Ritz-Carlton in San Francisco in about twenty minutes."

She stared at him, baffled. "You're taking me to the Ritz-Carlton?"

"Yes."

She blinked, carefully examining his symmetrical face. No duplicity whatsoever. "You're crazier than the other guy. What is up with you guys? Why are you feeding me?"

He snorted and rolled his eyes. "*In and Out Burger* is not food. This brunch we're going to is food," he said with a regal air.

"Why are you feeding me at all?"

"Like I said, as an apology. And a belated birthday gift. My timing was rather off the other day, wasn't it?"

What was his intent? "You can have the money if I find it," she offered.

"I know that. This apology is unrelated." Behind his dark gaze, the wheels of his mind clicked rapidly.

She narrowed her eyes. "You're trying to work me."

"Yes," he said with no hesitation.

She couldn't help but laugh. He joined her. At least he was upfront about his deviousness. But underneath his cordial exterior lay a dark and ugly beast.

He could easily kill her.

But right now, he liked her. And for some reason he liked it when she spoke her mind. That would fade quickly, but for the time being, she'd tell him what she thought. Well, not all of it.

"This hurts my brain. An overlord of the underworld wants to feed me. At the Ritz-Carlton." She ran her hand through her short hair, then rubbed her tense brow. "Life is too weird. So if we find that money, will you go away?"

A slight smile twitched on his sensual lips, he scanned her body quickly. "I'm not sure yet. I think I like you."

Breathing out loudly with frustration, she gestured at him. "Only because I've foiled your evil plans so far. Look, could you do me a favor and stop using me as a pawn? You have no idea how hard my life is right… now…"

The man didn't react. At all. Her words had zero effect.

She threw up her hands. "Oh, Christ, like you care. You want the five hundred million. And I may be the key to it. So, I'm stuck."

Cherlenko gave a slight nod. "I'm glad you have a clear understanding of the situation." His eyes and mouth went hard. "Mr. Hanson won't leave you alone, either."

Emma took a sip of her coffee and tried to figure a way out of this trap. She came up with nil.

She glanced over at the hot creepoid. Damn, the guy was masculine. Really, overly goddamned masculine. His aura, the way he held himself, his buff body. She hadn't met many men like him. So self assured. So self confident. He had no doubts about his abilities or his future. Rock solid.

Strangely, Rollin had the same manly inner confidence. But she wasn't afraid of Rollin.

She nodded at Cherlenko. "So what happened between you guys, anyway?"

"What did he tell you?"

"Well, you stole a couple girls from him and—"

His eyes wide, his mouth open, he coughed and sputtered and then nearly shouted, "I *what?*"

This was the first time she'd seen this level of emotion out of him. Underneath his smooth exterior, the man had some serious firepower. A volcano of passion. His calm exterior was clearly an act.

Which was why he seemed so controlled. She'd been right. He thought about every move before he made it. Expended tons of energy containing his emotions and projecting his carefully constructed image. She guessed there was an insecure boy hiding behind his badass armor. Didn't mean he wasn't a badass, either. It meant he was more unstable than she previously thought. And complex. Very complex.

She forced herself not to react. "Let me guess, your side of the story is different."

Burke shook his head, his dark gaze fiery. "I can't believe his audacity. I stole a girl from him—sorry, that is the most ludicrous lie I've ever heard. Not six months ago, he stole MY girlfriend in France. Damn him. Rollin's one of my biggest disappointments. We were friends, did he tell you that part?"

The man clearly felt betrayed in a big bad way. And hurt. She got the sense Cherlenko's hurt went beyond what happened with Rollin. He had some damage from childhood. The boy inside him wasn't just insecure, he was wounded.

"Yeah, he told me," she finally said.

He ground a tight fist into the palm of his other hand. "Let me guess, he said I stabbed him in the back."

"No. He…said you were different than he first thought."

His jaw set, even more fury raged in his gaze. "What an idiot. Bastard," he bit out. He noticed his fists, sent her a quick worried glance and relaxed. He clearly hadn't meant to show her his true feelings. A veil of coldness dropped over him. The emotion left his face. "No matter. That's all over. I just wish he'd stay out of my way," he tossed off like he suddenly didn't care.

"He said the money was stolen from someone you both worked for."

Fire heated Cherlenko's gaze once more and his mouth twisted into a sneer. "He's lying. That's my money," he said, jabbing a finger into his broad chest. "Adam stole that five hundred million from me. Not his boss. Rollin apparently isn't done with me. When that man turns, he turns all the way," he spat. "This is why I wanted him put away for Jerry's murder. I just want him out of my hair. Well, so to speak," he said running a hand over his smooth pate.

Emma let out a reluctant chuckle. "Very different stories."

"I'll bet." He snorted. "Rollin always comes off as so honest and forthright," he said with disgust. "He's good at that White Knight act. But it's all an act. He's more ruthless than I am. And that's saying something."

"Well, you two had a falling out, that's for sure."

"I trusted him and he betrayed me. More than anyone ever has. Not even my father could compare to his level of deceit."

And there it was. Daddy screwed him over, leaving him with trust issues for life.

Cherlenko continued, seeming unworried about revealing his true emotions. "I'll never let my guard down again like that," he vowed, anger lines deep on his handsome face. "I thought Rollin was like me. Had the same ethics. But as it turned out, he's a greedy bastard like the rest of the morons I deal with."

"Wow, that was almost verbatim what he said."

Another snort. "Of course. Don't be fooled. At least I'm honest about my greed. Honest about my lack of conventional morality." He said "conventional" like it was bad word. Something tawdry and cheap. "That man hides behind a shield of honor that masks a black heart and an even blacker soul. He's in total denial about who he really is. Lies to himself constantly. Runs away from himself. Probably trying to escape the memory of those kids he killed in Bangkok. Of course, that was an accident. Supposed to be a terrorist cell, turned out to be a school. Bad intel. Twisted his mind. Military will do that to you."

Could it be true? Was that the bad stuff Rollin talked about? Would account for that haunted look behind his eyes when he spoke of his past. Poor bastard.

Damn. Cherlenko made an impressive case for not trusting Rollin. If he turned on Cherlenko, he could turn on her. Especially with that sum of money at stake.

But Cherlenko was the one who kidnapped her. Rollin hadn't given her any reason not to trust him. Except for the fact he was involved with a dark world.

"I wish I could tell which one of you is telling the truth."

"You'll figure it out soon enough," he said, his emotions winding down. He took a deep breath, his face relaxed and turned cold again. "So you'll help me search for my money, right?"

"I guess."

"I know he wants you to do the same."

"Yeah."

"Fine." He leveled an intense stare at her. "I want to know if you find something. Like within thirty seconds of finding it. Not three days after he's acted on it. The same time you tell him. And if you remember something when you're alone, you call me directly. Before you do anything else. Before you call him. You pay me with your loyalty and I'll pay you with mine."

"And if I screw up?"

His eyes went icy and his mouth tightened. "I don't recommend that."

A chill went through her. Followed closely by a wave of profound fatigue. "I can't take much more stress right now. I will blow."

"I don't care if you have another emotional outburst, I want my money back."

"And I will do everything in my power to make that happen."

He studied her face carefully. After a moment, he smiled and warmed. "Good."

"Of course, the best idea would be for me to move out of that house and let you guys take it down to the foundation, then burn it so I can get the insurance and rebuild."

His shoulders relaxed even more, he settled back in his seat and his demeanor softened. "I'm not sure it's there. But I think you might know where it is." He reached over and tapped her temple.

All her nerves tingled and her heart skipped a beat.

"I think it's right there," he said in a husky voice.

Her body heated under his seductive gaze. Then her gut roiled with revulsion at her reaction. She gave her head a mental shake. Stockholm Syndrome and so soon?

She pretended her physical response to him hadn't happened. "Rollin believes the same thing. I'm the only one who doesn't. I have no idea what 'Jenn's Goofy Song' means." The empty shelf that once held her prized Goofy antiques flashed through her mind. She glared and pointed at him. "And you owe me some Goofy Disneyana. That shit cost me plenty," she said, her anger centering her once more.

He made a dismissive noise. "You were done with Disney three years ago," he scoffed. "Aliens and toy space ships are your new thing." His gaze penetrated hers, making her feel like he could peer inside her mind. A slightly wicked smile came over his full lips. "Why don't you let me buy you a set of Japanese vintage space toys? A 1960 Namura Space Moon Car, in box, perhaps?"

She gasped and her heart rate spiked. Little tin space ships danced in front of her eyes. The Holy Grail! Cost like nine grand, easy. Wow, that would be the crown jewel of her—

What the hell are you thinking, woman?

Repulsed by her toy greed, she wanted to slap herself for reacting to his bribe. She pretended not to be interested. "Uh, no thanks."

He laughed delightedly. "I saw your eyes light up, don't bother denying it. You want it and you want it badly. No need for self-recrimination, we all have our peculiarities."

"And I'm sure yours would scare the hell out of me," she cracked, angling a glance at him.

He laughed and for the first time since she got in the car, it seemed like he stopped playing his game. Now at ease, his gaze was open and playful. His anger gone, he regarded her like an old friend. Weird. She couldn't help but relax, too.

"I'm far more normal than you believe," he said.

"You're right. I don't believe you at all."

"Wait," he said, his gaze turning predatory, his smile hungry. "You will."

His sexual energy transformed into a large beast that leapt across the seat, bashed her over the head and dragged her back to his Cave of Sin. Her instinct was to flop on her back and pull him on top of her.

Like a swift kick in the head, that thought derailed her. Fear jolted her body. She froze to her seat, wishing she could jump out of the moving limo and run for her life.

Okay, this wasn't going away. This wasn't a momentary aberration. Her attraction to the man was growing by the second. She had to deal with it. Denying her feelings would only feed them.

Her fear of him was probably fueling her lust, some weird hard-wired survival response. An ancient Mate-with-the-Scary-Alpha-Male self-protection mechanism.

She concentrated on sipping her coffee, forcing herself to relax. Thank God for therapy. She'd learned she couldn't choose her feelings, but she could choose how to respond to them. Denial would be the quickest way to wake up in bed with him. Jesus, how scary. One minute he'd be kissing her, the next he'd have a gun to her head.

No wonder her love life was rife with failure. Attracted to the exact wrong type.

No worries. She'd stay aware of her feelings. As disgusting and perverse as they were, they were real. But that didn't mean she had to act on them. She had all the power in the situation. He could kidnap her and force her to be in his company, but she wasn't giving into her misplaced lust. Now that she knew what was going on, she could control herself.

He read her like a billboard and grinned knowingly.

She had to change the subject, fast. "Listen, Cherlenko—"

"Please, call me Burke."

"Burke, then. You know there's a ton of ways to apologize other than kidnapping me."

"Would you have come with me otherwise?"

"No."

A slight shrug. "I needed to make things right with you."

"By terrorizing me?"

He gave her a quick head-to-toe examination. "You don't look terrorized. Have I hurt you?"

"No."

He laughed easily.

Her protests were clearly futile. "For pity's sake." She sighed. "Can I borrow your cell to let Mary know I'll be back…when?"

"After brunch. Say two o'clock," he said, withdrawing his Blackberry from his jacket pocket and handing it to her.

She called Mary who was properly alarmed. Took Emma several minutes to calm her down. When she was done, she handed the phone to Cherlenko. He took it, his fingers brushing hers, softly, purposefully, it seemed. Still, he had nice hands. Long strong fingers, manicured nails, smooth skin.

He sent her a half smile. "Mary's very loyal to you. That's good. Rare."

"Tell me about it."

"Her cousins work for me occasionally."

Her attention sharpened. "So Mary wasn't kidding. Didn't think she was. She wanted to send them after you."

"Did she?" He seemed very amused by this idea.

"Or Rollin."

He flashed a bigger smile. "I might let them."

They rode in silence for a time. She sipped on her coffee and tried to figure out a way to get rid of him. She finally turned to him. "I have no idea how I'm going to help you get that money. I had nothing to do with Adam for the last six months of his life."

"Not true. You went to the bank together," Cherlenko replied.

"He owed me money, I drove him there to make sure he put into my account because he was a such a slimewad, if I wasn't there to make it happen, it wouldn't."

"Still, you had contact with him."

"Yeah, I guess so. I…"

"As you get rested, I want you to think about each instance you saw him since early March. Mostly you accompanied him to the bank. And once somewhere else. In May. I was wondering where?"

"I went with him somewhere other than the bank?"

"Apparently."

She couldn't remember what he was talking about. Her brow hurt from wrinkling so hard, she rubbed it. "Jeez, so much has happened since then. I blacked out everything with him that I could."

"Would help if you remembered each instance."

"I'll do my best."

"That's all I could ask," he replied with a smile.

They pulled up at the entrance to the magnificent San Francisco Ritz-Carlton. One of Cherlenko's goons opened the door for her. She had half a mind to run and create a ruckus, but playing along with Satan was probably the best approach at this point. Besides, he knew where she lived.

Cherlenko kept a gentle hand at the small of her back as he guided her into the hotel. The action was so natural, his manner was so self-assured, she didn't question it. Until she realized he had his hand on her back. And that it sent a public signal that she was his. She raced for a subtle way to disengage. Right as she was about to stop to "check her shoelaces" he let go.

Soon they were seated in a fancy-schmancy dining room surrounded by well-dressed rich people, mostly tourists.

Emma looked around at all the nicely pressed and starched women's clothing and then examined her own black Bermuda shorts and white tank top. She felt like Cherlenko's poor relation. She had a dark dot on her tank, probably one of her ever-present chocolate stains.

She picked at it and it came off. Fuzz, thankfully. Then she noticed a light discoloration around her nipples—holy crap. She could just get a hint of them through the thin material. She'd meant to wear a thicker bra, not this stupid sheer job. No wonder the guy at the doughnut shop had been staring at her tits.

"You look fine. Better than fine," Cherlenko drawled in soft tone.

She looked up and he had an approving, very sensual grin on his handsome face.

Her heart tripped and a little flicker of joy burned inside her.

Damn it and damn him. Being aware of her attraction apparently wasn't much protection. *What was wrong with her?* How could she be sexually aroused by the creep? He'd blackmailed her, forced her into that ordeal at the police station and was probably the one responsible for killing her ex-husband. She was sick. Totally sick. She had to get away from him.

His grin widened and got hungrier. "I knew you'd like me," he purred.

"Oh, please," she said with a dismissive gesture. "Don't go all egotistical on me. You have plenty of women. You don't need me."

He sent her a devilish smile. "Need is not the issue. Want is all I care about," he said, his voice a bit deeper, with a hint of sultriness.

The man could really deploy the Charm Bombs. She steeled herself. "You're one hell of a flirt, buddy."

One side of his mouth turned up. A slight waggle of his heavy dark brows. "You inspire me."

She laughed and his grin widened.

"I'm glad I amuse you," he said. "You certainly amuse me."

"You didn't look too amused wet," popped out of her mouth.

His smile faded some, but his dark eyes gleamed with challenge. "You were a very bad girl that day," he said in a low rasp. "Very bad."

A thrill went through her loins, her heart beat faster and the bottoms of her feet tingled. Immediately following, her stomach nearly turned in on itself.

This bastard knew how to work a woman. Must have got a PhD in Seduction from Evil Overlord University. Dickhead.

Cherlenko raised his eyebrows briefly. "And after I got angry, I did laugh. No one has dared to hose me since I was in training for the SEALs. Humbling experience. But in retrospect, understandable."

"Yeah, do you know what you put me through?"

"Ten hours of interrogation," he replied crisply. His gaze flared. "But that was your choice."

"I'm not playing your game. I'm not playing Rollin's game."

His expression relaxed into an almost smirk. "You're here with me."

She snorted. "You forced me into the limo."

"You could have run just now."

"Yeah, like I'd get very far. Like you don't know where I live. And…" She shrugged and sighed. "I wanted the food."

He burst out laughing and shook his head. "Adorable."

"You say that to all the girls."

"Yes, but I don't mean it with them."

Emma let out a reluctant chuckle. "You are a very bad man."

"And I can be very good, too," he said to her breasts. He met her gaze and sent her a sexy grin.

Her pulse raced and her sex gave a little throb.

She took out a mental fire extinguisher and doused her lust. Why couldn't she distance herself from the guy? Stupid misguided hormones.

As they shared the meal, she fought for mental clarity. But soon, she couldn't help but relax with Cherlenko. He directed all his attention to her, treating her like she was the only woman in the room. He knew a lot about French Impressionism, one of her favorite subjects. He knew a lot, period. History, geography, computers, whatever topic arose, he had something intelligent to say about it. Rollin was right. He was excellent company.

Cherlenko ate the way he drove, methodically and perfectly. Not one crumb on his lips, ever. The fluid movements with his hands—

cutting his tenderloin with the precision of a heart surgeon—the way he sipped his champagne, the guy was the epitome of controlled cool.

As she watched him, her thoughts drifted to those amazing hands of his. What would they feel like on her skin? His sensual mouth, what would he kiss like? How would he taste? As good as he smelled? How dominant would he be in bed?

He nodded at her and indicated her shoulder, breaking her out of her reverie.

Convinced he'd read her mind, her throat tightened. She stared at him, her heart beating fast.

Cherlenko sent her an easy grin, reached over and picked a salad leaf off the top of her tank, far too close to a breast. His fingers brushed her shoulder. His soft touch sent a buzzsaw of sexual electricity through her interior. A wave of hunger for him nearly paralyzed her.

Good, holy God.

So much for fighting her attraction. She'd never been more unwillingly aroused by a man in her life. Inconvenient and frightening.

After a superb meal, Emma and Cherlenko got into the limo and headed back to San Mateo.

They talked about the Bay and how the area had changed since they were kids. He grew up in the Sunset district of San Francisco, she in San Mateo. They remembered the Circle Star Theatre in Redwood City, when Mission Delores was a bad part of San Francisco, and before Half Moon Bay and the coast became popular and overcrowded.

She found herself warming to him, this time emotionally. Why did their local connection have an effect on her? Who cared? Ted Bundy grew up near lots of people, too. Didn't mean they had an affinity toward the guy.

Disturbing.

When they pulled up in front of her house, she opened her door, fast.

Before she could escape, Cherlenko gently took hold of her arm, his dark gaze sharpening. "Try to avoid him."

"Rollin."

"I'd appreciate it if you didn't encourage him."

"I'm not encouraging either of you, believe me."

His expression turned amused, playful. "I think you enjoyed our date."

"It wasn't a date. Your goons forced me into this limo."

"I took you out for a meal, that's a date."

Emma turned toward him and straightened her shoulders. Leveling a full force glare at him, she said, "Let me make this clear. I don't like you. And I don't like him. I want both of you to fuck off, is what I want. Okay? I'm being nice to you because I'm afraid of you. I'm being nice to him because I'm afraid of him, too. I'm not choosing to be with either of you. I will do what I think it takes to survive this situation and take care of my sister."

His expression varied as she spoke. He didn't like hearing that she didn't like him, he didn't like it when she said "fuck off", but he softened when she admitted to being afraid of him. Was his mask slipping? Was that on purpose? Or was he playing her? She'd bet the latter.

Cherlenko studied her.

She grinned at him. "I knew my honesty would start to grate on you."

He brightened, laughing. "Still charming. Blunt as a hammer, but very charming."

"Well, what do you expect? One brunch doesn't exactly make up for what you've done to me and are continuing to do to me. I don't like people who mess with me."

"Understandable, but misguided. I'm not messing with you. I'm trying to protect you. The sooner I get that money off your hands, the sooner you and your sister will be safe. I'm not the enemy here, Emma. I know I've done bad things to you and I couldn't be more sorry. But you have to let me help you now. Helping me is the only way to protect yourself. You align yourself with Mr. Hanson and you'll be dead and your sister will wind up in a state institution."

Cherlenko seemed damned sincere, but he was the one who launched the assault on her, not Rollin. "He hasn't kidnapped me or tried to blackmail me into pinning a murder on someone. By his actions, he's the more trustworthy of the two of you."

His gaze went cold. "Then let me put this another way. You hold the key to some very valuable information. While I like you, I have other ways to get this information. Hope I continue to like you."

Fury blew through her, firing up her limbs and fists. "Do you have to threaten me all the time?" she blasted at him. "You appear not to get your way for one second and you lower the boom on me. You got one hell of a bedside manner, Cherlenko. You could learn a thing or two about manipulating people."

His cold expression broke and his mahogany gaze warmed. Laughing, his body relaxed. "I really like you. Okay, let me try this one more time. Realize the position you're in, is all. Keep that in mind. Not only with me, but with my adversary. Don't believe his nice guy routine."

"I don't."

"You'll be hearing from me within 48 hours. Please answer my calls. And if I want to see you? Don't make me come after you. I want to keep protecting you. While I like you and your spunk, you're right, all this blunt honesty and aggression will start to grate on me. Make it easy for me to protect you. Don't keep running from me."

Her stomach, neck and back tightened. This guy was exhausting. Absolutely exhausting.

She practically leapt out of the car.

"Until we meet again," he said, flashing her a warm and charming smile.

"Yeah," she replied in a neutral tone.

"And call me Burke next time," he called out behind her.

Next time. She suppressed a shiver.

Emma walked up the driveway, kicking a rock out of her way. She didn't have the mind power to play these games. And with her new disgusting attraction to the demon, she had to do her best to stay away from him. But how was she supposed to do that with five hundred million dollars at stake? Shit.

She walked inside and his scent hit her just as she saw him.

Rollin. Sitting on her living room couch.

FIVE

Emma's heart thumped hard and anger burned through her. "What the hell are you doing here?"

Rollin leapt to his feet and came over to her, his handsome face full of concern. "Are you all right? Did that bastard hurt you?"

His caring attitude threw her off. "No. But look, you have to go. I need some time here."

"What did he want?"

She sent him an incredulous stare.

"Okay, stupid question."

"Cherlenko's right out there," she said, pointing dramatically out the front window. "What would have happened if he'd walked in here? Huh? What the hell are you thinking?"

He gave a slight shrug, but seemed completely unmoved by her attack. "I would have hidden."

"Did Mary let you in here? Where are they?"

"The park. Mary wanted to get Lizzie out of here for some fresh air. They just left ten minutes ago. I came in with the extra key you keep under the frog on the back porch."

She roared at him with fury.

His eyes went wide and he stepped back. Then he broke into a wide smile.

"They make doors to keep the unwelcome out," she bit out. "Just because we shared one burger does not give you the right—why are you smiling?"

"Sorry. You're really cute when you're mad."

Rage blew her mind apart. Screaming at him, she leapt forward and shoved him back. "Don't patronize me!"

He held his hands up in a defensive posture, but continued smiling.

"I am not to be laughed at, you jerk! Stop smiling at me!"

He pantomimed a big struggle to contain his laugh. Then he finally allowed his smile to burst through and breathed heavily with exhaustion from the effort.

She laughed. And then was so mad at herself, she screamed again. "I can't take this. You have to get out of here. That's it, I'm done. All I wanted was a doughnut!" She stormed off to the kitchen.

"Doughnut?" he asked quietly behind her.

She ignored the big fool and turned on the automatic tea kettle. Cup of oolong would calm her.

No sounds came from the living room. No doors shutting. Nothing.

After a few minutes, she walked back in. He sat on the couch, playing with a small wooden puzzle from her coffee table. He saw her and set it down.

"Would you please leave?"

"Look, all bullshit aside, I can't do that. You don't know what you're into here. I leave, you're toast. We have to recover that cash. It's the only way to protect you."

She glared at him. "Have you guys compared notes? You and Cherlenko have the same pitch. I know you're different, okay? But how different? That I can't tell. With five hundred million at stake, I'm not going to trust that your motives are simply about protecting some stranger. Me."

His expression softened. He stood and walked over to her. "Emma, you—"

"Look, I don't trust you any more than I trust him, okay? And I'll tell you the same thing I told him. I want you both to fuck off. I have no bloody idea where the money might be. None. Zero. Zip. And if I found it at this point, I'd burn it. I'm probably going to die, anyway. I can't see a way out with a good ending here. So if you'll excuse me, I'd like to enjoy what little life I have left without spending any time with either of you."

Finally, Mr. Joker wasn't happy. His gaze didn't go cold, however, it went fiery. His jaw set. His anger, unfortunately, made him even hotter looking.

"Fine. You're right. Initially I got into this for the money. I planned on using you, getting the cash and splitting. Then I got to know you."

She gave a harsh laugh and crossed her arms over her chest. "You don't know me at all. We've spent nearly nil time together. You're projecting some other woman onto me."

Putting his hands on his hips, he gave a short laugh. "Hardly. I couldn't make you up, lady. You're one-of-a-kind. From your Egyptian art jones to those weird Pez dispensers in your bathroom to your actually very good poetry to the chocolate you have hidden in your underwear drawer—why do you hide chocolate there, by the way?"

"Habit. Only way I got some in my last two relationships."

"Really? Anyway, you don't get it. I like you, woman. For you. What really showed me your character is what you've done for your sister. I had a sister once who took care of me when I was a kid, like yours did for you. And when she needed me, I was there for her."

He cracked her defensive shield. Maybe he was okay.

His gaze clouded and his pain lines grooved deep. "She didn't make it, but I gave her my all. So I understand you. This job has crossed over into the personal for me. I want to make sure this calms down around here so Lizzie can get better. And the only way to do that is to find the money. Once it's over, I'll take care of Burke for you. I'll make sure everyone leaves you alone. But you have to help me now."

He was working her. At first she went along with him, but nobody was this nice. The guy was an amazing mimic and actor. The pain lines? So persuasive. She chuckled and shook her head. "Nice speech. I can't tell who's better at this shit, you or Cherlenko."

His face turned crimson and his dark eyes went wild. Surprising her. "Not everyone in your life is trying to fuck with you," he blasted. "Half your problem is that you don't trust the people you should—like Tom Trafton and Randy Cleveland—and you trusted people like Adam Ramsay and Bob McCahon."

How the hell did he know about them?

"You gotta open your eyes, lady, or someone is gonna close them permanently." He pointed at her dramatically. "You need me. I know Burke's good. I know you don't trust either of us. But goddamn it, woman, you'd better put your faith in me. You want me to leave? Fine, I'll go. But you'd better call me. And very shortly. I can't stress this enough: Time. Is. Running. Out. It's not just me and Burke, there are others who want the money. When they find out that a lady with no team behind her is between them and five hundred million, I won't be able to protect you or your sister. You don't even need to put much trust in me. Just help me find that goddamned money. Call me."

And with that, he turned and stalked out the door, slamming it behind him.

She stared after him, numb. What the hell was that?

Remember his acting skills. Damn, he was good.

As she made herself a cup of tea, an idea occurred to her. What if Rollin was telling her the truth? What if he actually cared about her?

Five hundred million dollars.

Forget it. He and Cherlenko were two of a kind. Good cop, bad cop. They knew each other, wouldn't be a total shock to find out they were scheming together against her.

She took her tea and walked out onto the back porch to sit in the sun. A bit of a chill in the air this late September afternoon, but the sun was warm. She sat down on a cushy outdoor chair and surveyed her garden. Double Delight roses were still blooming. Nasturtiums had taken over the orchids. Apples were almost ready for picking.

She got up and walked down to the orchid bed and grabbed a handful of nasturtium vines. Thankfully, they came up easily. The spicy smell of nasturtiums filled her nostrils.

Damn, she loved this property. Even though it reminded her of some horrid scenes with her stepfather, it was home.

She'd love to make it a real home and find a nice husband. A real man.

A guy like Rollin without all the bad stuff.

Guy was a pest, but he sure was cute. From his sparkling dark gaze to his crooked nose and long dark hair to his sense of humor, man was a hot package. It wasn't fair. Adam was hot, too. Why the hell did the Universe keep tempting her with handsome jerks?

Damn it, she wished Rollin had been telling the truth.

She pulled a giant wad of nasturtiums off her biggest orchid and tossed them onto the lawn behind her.

Maybe there was something wrong with her DNA. Her mother had sure attracted some losers. Men with pretty exteriors and rotten interiors. Like mother, like daughter. Sheesh. She had to take control and end this trend. Lizzie'd been smart and given up men years before due to the same issue.

But what a rotten fate. Emma didn't want to be alone.

Of course, she wanted lots of things she'd never received. Perhaps this lifetime was about something else.

She swept the pile of nasturtiums into her arms and walked back to the garage and dumped them in the compost bin.

Maybe this time around she was supposed to learn to be there for herself. Maybe she was supposed to be alone. Learn how to be in her own corner.

If so, she was doing a crappy job so far. She needed to take control. While she'd tried to evade Rollin and Burke, she'd let them manipulate her plenty. She had to get rid of them and permanently. And to do that, she had to find that money.

Emma walked back across her lawn toward the orchid bed and stopped mid-stride. Wait a minute. If she found the money and didn't tell Rollin or Cherlenko, she'd hold all the power.

A rush of energy whirled in her belly and spread through out her body. Now this was a good idea. She returned to her chair on the back porch and drank some tea.

She thought about her rat bastard husband. She'd go over this one more time. Where would Adam have hidden five hundred million that she hadn't already checked? Where did he ever store stuff?

They'd cleaned out their safe deposit box, so it wouldn't be there. He'd taken everything of his with him. She had a storage unit, but it was in her mother's name and held only her mother's stuff. And Adam didn't know about it.

Wait a minute. He did know about it. He was over at her apartment when she was moving, scamming some money from her. She agreed to give him the money only if he'd helped her move the piano out of her mother's house. A couple guys were going to charge her four hundred bucks, she'd given Adam a hundred. One of their only exchanges that had come out in her favor.

Couldn't be that obvious. Besides, a storage unit would be the first place Rollin or Cherlenko would check.

But the storage unit wasn't in hers or Adam's name and she paid the rental yearly. She'd made the last payment the previous December from her mother's account, two weeks after Mom died. Maybe Rollin and Cherlenko didn't know about the unit.

She set down her tea, got up and went into the kitchen. She opened the junk drawer that held the keys.

The key to the storage unit was gone.

She gasped and her heart jump-started. "Holy shit!"

Key hadn't been marked, either. Only Adam and her mother knew what it looked like. Maybe that's what he was doing at her house two days before he died, collecting that key. But why didn't they find the key on him when he died?

They probably did. Great, the storage unit was probably destroyed. Another huge mess to clean up. Still, it would be worth a trip over there to check it out. She'd bring the bolt cutters and snap off the lock.

Wait. If the money was still there, she'd lead both Cherlenko and Rollin right to it. She had to be smart about this. She had to check it without them following her.

She thought about movies she'd seen where people had escaped surveillance. *The Pink Panther* was the first one that came to mind. In the opening scene, the female burglar ripped off an apartment, escaped and changed clothes in the elevator.

Emma could do the same thing, maybe not necessarily in an elevator.

A perfect plan came to her.

This sounded fun. Outsmarting the jerks. That would be a coup.

She left Mary a note: *Be back later, going shopping in the City. My cell is dead so I'm not bringing it. If I don't get home or call by nine tonight, call the cops and put out a Missing Persons Report on me.*

Emma's cell wasn't dead and she took it, but left it turned off. The cell was old, so it didn't have a GPS in it, but she was still concerned they could trace her if she used it. She'd rather have Mary think the phone wasn't working rather than worry her with details of her current drama.

Rummaging around in the back of her closet, she retrieved some old clothes and a new pair of shoes. If they'd put tracking devices in anything, it'd be in the stuff she wore daily. She was probably being paranoid, but couldn't be too sure. After putting the clothes and shoes in a backpack, she snagged a wig from her Halloween box along with big dark glasses and a baseball cap.

This better work.

She walked from the house to the Hayward Park train station, seven blocks away. On guard, her muscles tight, she looked around, but didn't see anyone. But they had to be watching her.

Emma took the northbound train to the end of the line, the downtown San Francisco station. Bustling and loud, the place teemed with people. She slipped into the bathroom and changed into her disguise as fast as she could.

Her heart pounding like Cherlenko or Rollin was about to show up any moment, she headed out into the throng, this time with a limp and different posture. She boarded the southbound train and headed to Redwood City.

Forty-five minutes later, she arrived. Clutching the straps of her backpack so hard, she had white knuckles, she stepped off the train. Her legs shaky, she carefully watched her feet so she didn't do a face plant into the sidewalk. She expected to be surrounded and attacked, but no one approached her.

As she cleared the train station, she began to relax. No one suspicious around and no one following her.

The storage facility was a couple miles from the station, but she saved time by taking a few shortcuts through old industrial yards. She checked around fairly constantly, but rarely saw anyone. Still, she felt like a tightly wound spring about to pop. Jittery and terrified, she kept expecting Rollin to walk up to her. Or Cherlenko to pull up in his limo.

After snapping off the old lock, she went inside the fifteen by fifteen foot storage unit.

All the boxes were stacked neatly. Everything was just as she'd left it. Didn't look like anyone had been inside.

To make sure, she began a methodical search through the boxes. Good idea, anyway. At some point she had to deal with getting rid of the stuff. After her mother died, she couldn't bear to part with Mom's belongings, so she'd packed them up. Once she got Lizzie back on her feet, she'd bring all the boxes home.

First stack: Christmas ornaments, books, her mother's sewing projects.

"Why did I keep Mom's half-finished sewing? Sheesh."

She stood back and stretched a moment before continuing. The old family piano stood in the corner. Needed to get it tuned and brought back to the house.

She did a double-take. "I covered that with an old quilt. I made sure all the surfaces were covered. Where the hell did it go?"

Her body tensed and her pulse quickened. Adam had been there! She moved more boxes and saw a peek of the quilt. Her heart rate jumped higher. She took all the boxes off the quilt, which covered a very long box about six feet long by three feet wide by three feet tall.

She gasped. "A dead body? A freakin' dead body in my storage unit!" She clamped her hands over her mouth.

Great! Tell it to the whole world why don't you?

Her heart ramped up to near heart attack mode and her limbs shook. "Adam, you idiot!" She dropped her voice. "A dead body in…"

Five hundred million dollars.

"Wait a minute. This should be the money. Why would he put a dead body in here? It doesn't stink and it would. Unless the person is embalmed."

Clammy with sweat, she lifted the quilt. Underneath were five vest-like things sitting on top of a long black plastic case with words in Russian printed on the outside. She moved the vests; they were heavy. She finally recognized them from the dentist's office. Lead vests they used on patients to protect them from x-rays.

"That's weird. Why would they cover this in x-ray protection? Oh, who knows? But Russian? Maybe it's five hundred million in Russian dollars. No one said anything about it being US money. What a weird twist of fate. Ain't gonna be dragging this to the money exchange office. Excuse me? I'd like to exchange *five hundred million dollars*." She laughed.

Hands shaking, she bent down to unlatch the case and found that the latches were already busted off. She lifted the top slowly, hoping all to hell to see a wad of greenbacks, not Russian dollars. When she caught sight of something white and metallic, she sighed and her shoulders drooped.

"Damn it. Of course, there couldn't be any money. Adam couldn't do anything right. No, as usual he stole some stupid huge and bulky thing that's totally worthless. Which is why he left it here. Rollin and Cherlenko are out of their minds. I suppose I should be relieved it's not an embalmed body."

In one sharp motion, she flipped open the lid the rest of the way.

A four-foot-long bomb sat inside a specially molded gray plastic interior.

She froze and stopped breathing. Her heart kicked into a speed metal rhythm.

A bomb? She blinked. Well, if it wasn't a bomb, it was doing a damned good imitation of one. The cylindrical object was about four feet long by ten inches in diameter and painted white. The front end was pointed and there were flanges or wing things on the back. Words in Russian were printed along one side. There was a hatch near the back end with big red letters on the cover that seemed like some kind of warning.

A bright yellow and black symbol was stamped next to the lettering.

Took her a full second to recognize it.

A radioactive symbol.

The floor shifted beneath her. She stumbled and fell backwards against the metal wall of the storage area, clanging her head. Pain seared her scalp. She held her head and stared in horror at the bomb.

Images of mushroom clouds flashed through her mind. Burned Hiroshima victims. Clips of black and white movies of nuclear bomb testing where houses were blown away. Scenes from *Terminator 2.* The bright flash and kids melting.

Her stomach imploded and bile rose in her throat. Her limbs trembled.

This was it. The enemy. Her biggest fear. Ever since she was a kid, she'd been waiting to die by nuclear blast. Her mother said it often: *The Russians are going to kill us all.* Emma never thought she'd see her tenth birthday. She'd been so relieved when the Cold War ended. Those were the first nights she felt safe going to bed. After all those years of fear.

And here it was. Her worst fear embodied in one metal case.

This one bomb could wipe out a city. Hundreds of thousands of people vaporized and so many more to die horrible deaths in the following weeks. Survivors scarred for life, both mentally and physically.

She always said she wanted to be at Ground Zero if there was ever a nuclear war. She didn't want to die in agony over a few weeks. She wanted to die unaware. Hear a noise, look up and by the time she asked the question "What is that thing?" she was gone.

"God? I didn't mean this," she whispered.

She should get up and run. Call the military. Do something before this…this *thing* got into the wrong hands.

Oh, God, the trouble she was in! They'd put her away for life and throw away the key! She'd be sealed up in a lockdown facility forever.

But she couldn't take the chance that Cherlenko would take the bomb and…

Would he use it? Was he masterminding some scheme to destabilize the country?

No. Cherlenko was not an extremist. He was a businessman.

He was selling it.

That was it. Clearly going for Badass of the Year. That fit. Cherlenko was exactly the type of man to want to sell a nuke. What a feather in his Louis Vuitton hat.

And Adam got in his way.

And now she was in his way.

He would kill her the moment he got his hands on the weapon. She knew too much.

Rollin must know about it, too. He and Cherlenko had to be in cahoots. No matter how sincere Rollin seemed, this changed everything.

She shuddered. She had to go to the cops. It was the right thing to do.

It was the only thing to do.

Gloom smothered her. She fought for breath. She couldn't go to jail. She knew that now.

She flashed back to that interrogation room. Facing McCoy all night. That horrible ordeal. As soon as she started confessing, she knew she'd blown it. She wished she'd waited and come up with a better way to rid herself of Rollin and Cherlenko. But she'd been too burnt. Too desperate.

Those ten hours convinced her that she couldn't handle the situation again. She couldn't imagine how much more exponentially horrible her interrogation would be if she were accused of treason or terrorism. They'd waterboard her. Send her to some other country and torture her. She couldn't go through it. She wasn't strong enough. Nuke or no, there had to be another solution.

She had to calm down and focus. There had to be a way to keep the bomb out of both Rollin and Cherlenko's hands and get it to authorities without involving her.

Emma pushed on the box with her foot. Very heavy. Couldn't move it alone.

Maybe it wasn't a real nuclear weapon. Maybe it was a fake bomb. A dummy bomb used for practice.

She snorted. "I'm lying to myself. I'll bet there's no money at all. I'll bet both of those assholes want this fucking bomb. Which accounts for those vests. Blocking the radioactive signal."

No wonder they killed Adam. The knucklehead heisted the stuff before he knew what he had. Adam wasn't a long thinker. He was more of the instant gratification type.

"Damn, I'm glad I sneaked here. Holy God, they'd better not have followed me. I'd be dead. Totally utterly dead. That is if I don't get killed by nuclear radiation poi… son…ing. Shit!" She leapt forward and closed the lid. Frantically, she covered it with the vests and quilt, then gingerly set all the boxes on top, hiding the bomb as best she could.

Her body screamed at her to flee the scene and moreover, to get away from the nuke. She wanted to run in all directions at once. Where should she go? What should she do?

"I gotta get out of here. And run far away until I figure this out. Oh, damn. Lizzie! I can't run away."

Tears stung her eyes. She leaned against the cold metal wall and it gave. Clank!

Her heart rate jumped at the sound and she quickly moved back.

She held her chest and concentrated on slowing her breathing. "Must calm down. Get a hold of myself. God? This is too much," she said to the ceiling. "Could you please stop this shit?"

Now it was more important than ever that no one found out about the storage locker. No way did she want to be responsible for bombing a city in America. Who knew who Cherlenko and Rollin wanted to sell it to? Al-Qaeda? The Mafia? She needed to run the other way and quick.

But why hadn't she been tortured to death for the information yet?

Maybe they didn't know Adam had it. Maybe they just suspected he did. They were probably using the excuse of the money as a reason to search for the bomb.

Whichever, the longer she stayed at the storage unit, the better chance of getting caught there.

Emma took out the new lock, put it on the storage unit door and headed home. But she wasn't anxious to get there. Lizzie needed to be in a healing environment, not in the orbit of the Nuclear Drama Queen.

Taking a long involved circuitous route home, Emma stopped at a bar eight blocks from her house and downed three beers.

The beer didn't dull her guilt, not one iota. She needed to be a better caretaker to her sister. With all this craziness, how was Lizzie supposed to get well? Emma should have sold the house and taken off after Adam got murdered. At the very least, she should have moved Lizzie somewhere safer after Cherlenko and Rollin appeared in her store.

Too late now. Her body hot with shame, she walked home.

When Emma put her hand on the doorknob to the front door, she heard loud voices coming from inside. Adrenaline pumped through her. She turned to run when she recognized one of the voices as Mary's. The other was the deep voice of a male.

She had to help Mary.

Shaking and terrified, she opened the front door.

SIX

Rollin stormed over to her and towered above her, eyes blazing. "Where the hell were you?"

She relaxed. At least it wasn't Cherlenko.

Mary grabbed him by the arm and yanked him away. "You don't talk to her like that." Then she turned to Emma. "Where the hell were you? Shopping in San Francisco with no phone?"

"I'm sorry," Emma said, backing up, her hands in a defensive posture.

Rollin wedged his body between them and grabbed Emma by the upper arm. "You're coming with me." He dragged her down the hallway toward her bedroom.

Mary gasped. "What are you doing? You leave her alone!" She followed, swatting at him.

Emma couldn't help but laugh. "Mary, it's okay. I'll talk to him."

"You bet your ass, you will," he growled.

Her vision shifted. White-hot rage flamed her insides. "Excuse me?" she demanded, ripping out of his grip.

He grabbed her again. "Shut up. We need to talk."

Pushing her in front of him, he hustled her down the hall and shoved her into the master suite. Slamming the door, he locked it behind him.

The sliding glass door was open, so she didn't feel trapped, just pissed that he was throwing his weight around.

She spun on him. "Now, look, you—"

"No, you look," he said, jabbing a forefinger into her face, his features hard, his gaze roasting her. "This isn't a game. Your life is on the line."

"You think I don't know that?"

"Where the hell were you?"

"Adam's grave, okay?" came flying out of her mouth. "I wanted some privacy. I hated him and I'm all conflicted about his death and I didn't want anyone following me there and tearing up his stupid grave. So I gave everyone the slip." She sounded much more convincing than she thought she would. *Good one, Holsten.*

His shoulders relaxed and some of the fire went out of him. "You had me half scared to death. If you tell me what you're doing, then I don't have to worry and get other people worried like Mary." He gave a nod toward the door. "She's scary, that little woman. She's got fangs," he said earnestly.

As what seemed like usual with this guy, she couldn't stay mad at him. Plus he actually seemed to care about her.

Duh. The bomb. No wonder he "liked" her. She was the key to a bloody nuclear weapon. Same with Cherlenko. He could care less about her, too.

Rollin sent her an easy smile. His attention drifted momentarily to her boobs.

Okay, so both guys wanted her, too. They wanted the bomb and to get in her pants.

Which was odd. She'd never exactly been a guy magnet. She liked her looks, but she wasn't technically that beautiful. Adam had been the best-looking man she'd been with and as it turned out, his looks had been compensation for an extremely limited interior. Nice coat of paint on a freakin' Yugo.

So what was up with all this weird sexual attraction? Did she have some odd hormonal power over Rollin and Cherlenko? Some weird pheromone release from turning thirty-two? Were her ovaries sending out a distress signal? *Mate with me before my eggs get old!*

She let out a long sigh. “Rollin, look. I actually think you have good intentions here, but you have to back off.”

The urgency returned to his carved face. “I can’t. People have found out about you. We have to go undercover. I was gonna to let you come to me, but there’s no time left to win your trust, Emma. They’ll hurt you.”

She studied him. “You seem so sincere.”

His eyes went wild and his nostrils flared. “I am sincere, damn it!” He stormed across the room, running his hand through his long hair. “You’re driving me nuts. Shit, Bobby took less time to trust me and he’d been living in a gutter in Bangkok, beaten by everyone who knew him.”

“Who’s Bobby?”

He flipped his hand dismissively, clearly impatient with the digression. “My technical guy. My son. Sort of. We’re family. Even though technically we’re not related.” He drew a bead on her.

Part of her wanted to wither, dart away and hide. The guy had an intimidating edge. He came off as laid-back, but he clearly wasn’t. An amazing power lay at his core. Formidable opponent.

She rubbed her forehead. The day’s events, the three beers and all that walking had taken its toll on her. All she wanted to do was escape his intense scrutiny. “Rollin, I can’t trust you. How could I? Put yourself in my situation.”

“It’s been a long time since I was that naïve,” he said, his mouth tight.

“I’m not…shit.” She rolled her eyes. “Okay, so I’m naïve.”

“My point exactly,” he said, walking up to her. He took her by the shoulders. “You have to trust me so I can protect you. Where did you really go today?”

No bloody way.

She took a step back, disengaging from him and broke eye contact. “I’m not ready to tell you.”

He stepped forward again, closing the distance. "Did you find the money?" His gaze pierced her.

She looked him right in the eye and told him the truth. "No."

He examined her carefully for a long few seconds. She held his gaze easily.

He finally nodded. "Okay, okay. But don't scare me. I'm…"

She made an exasperated noise. "Rollin, look. You're either a fantastic actor or you're overly emotionally involved here. I'm just one of your cases."

He sent her a sharp look. "No, you're not."

"What do you mean?"

He blinked rapidly, looked away and then turned back to her. His expression softened. "I like you. I mean, like… *like* you… like you." He gestured vaguely, then put his hands on his hips and frowned.

"What do you mean you like me?" The truth slammed her hard. "Wait. Like *like* me, like me?"

He pursed his lips. "I didn't plan on it. Believe me. I don't want to like you like this, but I do. The sister thing, your humor, the way you stood up to Burke. Shit, woman, you're fuckin' awesome. Why wouldn't I like you?"

Her mood soared, then she hit the brick wall of reality. He wanted her, that was all. A quick piece of tail. She shook her head. "You're confusing lust with like."

"No, I'm not," he said simply, yet with a resolution that rang of absolute sincerity.

Emma stared at him, her mouth slightly open, her mind unable to make the full leap to comprehension. But as he stood there, his face full of emotion, it hit her. He meant it. He liked her. Like really liked her.

Her heart skipped, then swelled so much, her chest felt tight. Little giddy bubbles of joy popped inside her. He was so hot! She looked at his mouth. She wanted to taste him. Feel those firm lips on hers. His hard body, pressed against her naked flesh, skin on skin, drinking in his heady scent—

Shit. *He got her.* Manipulating her again!

Blowing out a breath through her lips, she crossed her arms across her chest and sent him a weary grin. "You had me goin' there."

His gaze went nearly black with anger. His face reddened and veins popped out on his forehead. "Oh, yeah?" he sneered.

He lunged forward, latched onto her and kissed her.

Rollin's smell and taste bombarded her senses. His intense energy enveloped her. Her entire body buzzed. He tasted delicious. His heady scent transformed all her brain cells into little bombs of lust. His lips, hard, yet soft and smooth, hungrily possessed hers.

A rocket of desire blasted through her body, the explosion centering on her clit.

Her sex cried out for his cock.

What are you doing? He's trying to manipulate you, you idiot!

Damn him! She pushed on his hard chest and wiggled, trying to get out of his grasp. He clung to her, keeping his mouth firmly on hers. Wrapping his long arms around her, he deepened the kiss.

Time skipped and her train of thought vanished in a poof of hormones.

Spinning the tip of his tongue around hers, he greedily explored the depths of her mouth. She dug her fingers into his shoulders, her body tingling and on fire. Tightening his grip on her, he forced his tongue deeper and pressed his hard body against hers.

Her knees nearly gave out. She clung to him, her mind whirling with images of his naked chest above her, his hands pinning her wrists to the bed. The feel of his rock hard cock inside her. She pressed her hips against his and felt his steely need. A searing hot rush of sexual energy coursed through her.

He pulled away, his gaze dark and heavy lidded. "That's how I feel for you," he said in a soft, tortured rasp.

Reality came storming back. Fear gripped her.

What the hell was THAT?

She tried to step back, but he wouldn't let go.

"I know you feel what I do. Don't be afraid of me, Emma. I won't hurt you. I couldn't."

She pushed harder and he reluctantly let go.

"This can't happen. I…" she stammered.

"It is happening. Genie's out of the bottle, girl."

She fought for mental clarity. "This is completely inconvenient timing on your part. I probably don't have long to live."

His jaw went hard. "You'll live until you're a hundred if I have anything to do with it."

Her head cleared a bit. She shoved her desire for him aside. "I need time to think about this."

"We don't have it. If you found the money today, I have to know."

Was he manipulating her?

"I didn't."

"Okay. I won't ask again."

"Good."

He ran his hand down her arm and she instinctively leaned into his touch.

Hunger grew in his dark eyes. "Damn woman, I want you. Badly. But I like you too much to screw with your head right now. We have to concentrate on getting that money back. Now that I just blew your mind—and mine—could you think for two minutes about that song thing? Or any places Adam might have hidden a large stash of money?"

Walking away from him, she gave her head a shake, still reeling from the kiss. She thought Burke had sexual power over her. Didn't compare to Rollin. She liked him a lot, too. Too much.

She fought to concentrate on what he'd just asked her. "Yeah… hiding places. Wish I knew. Honestly. I want this to end. I want this all to stop. But I've come up with nil."

"I hope you're telling me the truth."

She turned back to him and glared. "And I hope you're telling me the truth. I don't like people who play with my emotions."

"I'm not," he replied forcefully.

"Okay, so how long do you think we have?"

"Not long. We need to get you out of here tonight. I heard some buzz about you. Scared me. Right now, Burke's able to keep people away. His reputation is pretty off-putting. But when I heard your name, I knew the timer had just gone off. We need to send your nurse and sister into hiding, too. Got a line on a nice apartment right near the hospital. Then you come with me and we'll try to find that money."

Pacing across the room, she rubbed the back of her neck. "Seems like a pretty iffy plan. Where do we search? My brain hasn't come up with anything."

He shrugged. "Well, at least it will buy us some time."

She let out a long sigh. "Can I think about it? Could you give me until tomorrow morning to think about it?"

He walked up to her and took her in his arms. Sending a thrill through her. She boxed her lust and packed it away. Unhelpful.

He sent her an intense stare. "No, I wish we could. I'd love to have the luxury of time, but I have to get you out of here tonight."

"Shit."

"I'm worried. And I'm not the kind of guy to worry unnecessarily. I know you don't know me. But you have to trust me."

"Cherlenko wants me to report directly to him. If I don't give him what he wants, he'll probably kill me."

"No, he won't. I'll protect you."

"He'd kill me, wouldn't he?"

"No, I don't think so. But you'd wish you were dead once he was through with you. He breaks women. Down to nothing."

"I'd never let him that close to me."

"I've seen him take down stronger women than you. First he lures them in with limo rides, fancy restaurants and gifts. Then he seduces them, then he owns them. I've never seen anything like the power that guy can get over a woman. These talented, smart ladies turned into zombies. It's unreal. He really gets off on controlling them."

"That fits."

"He's into some pretty kinky sex stuff, too. Gets off on whipping girls."

Her stomach felt like a flock of hummingbirds burst into flight inside her. She fought a shudder. Cherlenko, a Dom? Scariest. Thought. Ever.

Rollin didn't seem to notice her reaction. "Granted, girls who are into that sort of thing, but from his stories, I think he's gone too far a few times. He tried to seduce you, didn't he?" He examined her face carefully.

"No. He flirted, but I'm immune," she said, praying her face would stay neutral.

She pictured Cherlenko dressed in leather, a sadistic grin on his face with a long whip in his hand. Her body went cold and goosebumps covered her arms.

Rollin seemed to believe her. "Watch him. I'm telling you, he's good. Women I know who thought they were immune to him, fell for him. Suddenly, without knowing how they got there, they woke up in bed with him. The next thing you knew, they were enslaved."

Alarming news. "Like he used Roofies on 'em?"

A quick shake of his head. "No. He likes the conquest. Likes his women to be alert and awake and aware that he's conquering them."

Emma made a face and nodded. "Then once they're conquered, he gets bored. What does he do with his discard pile?"

Rollin's face fell and his gaze hollowed. "He doesn't know and he doesn't care. When he's done, he's done. He throws them out. If they bug him too much, he makes them disappear. The survivors I've seen are like shells of people. Enslaved, dependent, broken. Takes a few years of therapy to recover from what I've heard."

"What happens if he can't seduce them?"

He shrugged, a dark look on his face. "I don't think you want to find that out. Nor would you want to find out what he does to women who betray him. That's not pretty at all."

Looking away, she bit her lip.

No matter how she looked at this situation, she saw her own death. Either Cherlenko would kill her or these other people. More than likely Cherlenko. He already had a bizarre interest in her. He could misconstrue any of her actions as betrayal.

Especially if she ran off with Rollin.

Rollin took her chin and gently turned her face toward his. "But you don't have to worry about him, Emma. I'll protect you. Stick with me and you'll be fine." He hugged her. His arms felt wonderful around her.

She wanted to believe him so badly. He seemed so sincere.

His attention dropped to her mouth. Leaning in, he kissed her.

Spinning, her thoughts crazy, only one coherent thought came out of the swirling mess: *Get naked with him, NOW.*

But she still didn't trust him. She might end up in bed with him, but she wasn't going to trust him.

Not with that nuke at stake.

How could she?

SEVEN

"Lizzie, honey? We have to talk. Mary, please stay."

Emma sat down on Lizzie's bed and took her by the hand.

Concern etched Lizzie's beautiful youthful face. She reached out and wiped a tear from Emma's cheek with her good hand. Her right hand lay limply in Emma's. "You?"

Emma took a deep breath. "There's no way to say this so I'll just say it. The men who killed Adam are after me now. You're not safe here. And you're not safe around me. You and Mary have to get as far away from me as you can. And I have to hide." She burst into tears. "I'm so sorry. I just want to take care of you and all I've done is fuck everything up."

Lizzie took her in her arms and stroked her back. "Good, good. Love. No…worry. Okay."

Mary ran her hand down the back of Emma's head. "Don't worry. I'll take good care of Lizzie. I've got a cousin who said we can come anytime. I'll call her now."

"I'm so sorry." Emma's heart shredded like wild animals tore at it.

Lizzie pushed away and sent her an intense stare, clearly wanting to convince Emma she was fine. "No worry." She pointed at Mary. "Mary. Okay."

Emma could see her sister locked inside her mind, wanting to jump out and reassure her. From books she'd read, she'd learned that a person's intellect wasn't affected by strokes. And despite the trauma, Lizzie was still her rock. She couldn't yet physically take care of herself, but she still had the inner strength to take care of Emma.

Emma cried harder.

Lizzie hugged her and petted her head. "You not bad. You good. No… no…" She pushed Emma back and wiped her tears away again. "No. Me…fine."

Emma sent her a weak smile. "Yeah, Mary will take good care of you."

Emma helped pack up Lizzie's meds and her clothes, and loaded them into Mary's car. Then she and Mary helped Lizzie out to the car. Mary stayed on her weak right side and Emma had hold of her left arm. Lizzie moved her left leg, then dragged her right along slowly. Emma opened the car door and Mary helped Lizzie turn around and guided her into the seat. Lifting Lizzie's right leg, she put it inside.

It felt so wrong to be sending her sister away. So counterintuitive. Her entire being cried out for Lizzie, to care for her, to mother her.

Emma leaned on the door. "I'll have my cell with me always," she told Mary. "Don't tell me where you are on the phone. I don't want anyone else to know."

"Are you going to be okay?" Mary asked.

"Sure. I'll let you know the minute all this is over. I don't know where I'll be, but I have your cell number and I'll be in touch as often as I can."

"I want to call my cousins to help protect you."

"Your cousins work for Cherlenko."

Mary's eyes went wide. "Oh, that's bad."

"I know."

"Still, don't worry," Mary said with a dismissive gesture. "I'll take good care of her. Please call me at least once a day."

"Okay."

Emma turned to her sister and her gut wrenched. Pangs of guilt stabbed her insides.

But Lizzie just smiled. "Fine. Love…love…you."

"I love you, Lizzie. I'll see you as soon as I can."

"Bye-bye," Lizzie said. Her smile broke and tears appeared in her brown eyes. The normal pink glow of her cheeks faded. "Safe. Love... you. Safe."

Emma forced a confident expression on her face. "I will," she said with a final pat on her sister's arm.

They pulled out of the driveway. Emma watched the taillights of the car disappear into the night. Sorrow engulfed her, her body wracked with sobs and she dropped to her knees on her front lawn. Anger at Cherlenko and Rollin boiled inside. It was all their fault she was involved. And Adam. God, how she wanted to beat him. She punched the soft grass. Asshole. For the first time since he'd been gone, she was glad he was dead.

She got to her feet and kicked a rock across the yard.

Didn't matter if she'd just made out with Rollin, that look on Lizzie's face alone made her want to smack him. And Cherlenko.

Rollin was off making arrangements for a safe house, due back in a couple hours. She'd promised to be ready by midnight.

But fuck that. Fuck both guys. She was ditching. She'd done it once and she could do it again.

Emma quickly got her essentials packed up. She thought about grabbing her entire cash stash, but if she happened to get ripped off in the next couple days, she'd have nothing left. She could sneak back later and grab more if needed.

She put on black cargo pants and a black sweatshirt, grabbed her backpack and locked up the house. Stealing out the back, she wheeled her old, decrepit bike to the back fence and threw it over. After hopping the fence, she rode away on her ten-speed and headed for Belmont.

As the cool night air bit into the exposed skin on her face and hands, niggling doubts scratched at the back of her mind. Was she running away from the one man who could help her? Her heart said yes, but her head said no. She liked Rollin. A lot. She kept thinking about that kiss. His taste. His smell.

But she couldn't trust her hormones. With the lives of millions of people at stake, she couldn't take the chance.

Maybe after a good night's sleep, she'd feel differently. Maybe she'd call Rollin and let him help her. But on her terms, not his.

And while Rollin seemed okay, at the moment, she was comparing him to Satan. Next to Cherlenko, even Voldemort seemed like a cuddly teddy bear. In the scheme of things, she couldn't trust either man.

* * * * *

Next morning, Emma rolled out of her squeaky motel bed in Belmont and called Mary. Lizzie was doing fine and had settled in nicely at Mary's cousin's house in San Bruno. A slight wave of relief.

Then she checked her messages. Five from Rollin, demanding to know where she was. Acid scorched her innards at the sound of his frantic voice. She distanced herself from her reaction. She was in charge of her life, not him. She knew what was best for her. Even though he sounded so tortured on the phone. Could he really like her that much?

No, it was about the money and the nuke. She had to remember that. No matter how sincere he seemed, she had to keep things in perspective.

Which wasn't easy. Just hearing his voice made her want to rip off all her clothes and jump on him. She actually hoped he was lying to her at this point. What if he was telling her the truth? Her stomach twisted hard. She couldn't go there.

Rollin was shouting by the second message, so she erased the last three without listening to them. Maybe he did like her. She'd certainly elicited some strong emotions out of him.

Five hundred million dollars. Yeah, that kind of money elicited strong emotions out of anyone. And so would that nuke.

Speaking of a plan, she'd successfully escaped and hidden, but now what? What should she do? Where to go from here?

Pacing the tiny, stinky seedy room, she noticed her socks were getting dirty from the few steps she'd taken on the avocado-green-with-light-yellow-stain-spots carpeting. Ewwww. Her clever idea for staying somewhere no one would look for her didn't seem so brilliant after all. Maybe she'd move to an airport hotel.

A wallop of fear hit her. She wouldn't feel safe in a nice big hotel. Too many people around. Not to mention the cost.

Okay, back to a plan. First things first, she needed to get rid of the nuke. She didn't want to be stupid, she'd entertain thoughts of calling Rollin. She really could use someone in her corner. Especially someone so hot and sexy.

Hormone Alert! Forget it. No more making decisions from below her waist. Contacting Rollin was out.

Quick plan: stay in Motel Hell and write up plans to dispose of the nuke. Then get rid of the weapon.

Then what? She couldn't stay away from Lizzie for long. Somehow she had to protect and care for her sister—with dwindling resources—all the while protecting herself from Rollin and Cherlenko.

A tear rolled down her cheek, she wiped it away. No time for weakness.

She clearly didn't have all the answers yet. Maybe by the time she figured out what to do with the nuke, all the other answers would fall into place.

Emma sat on the bed—which made a weird *clank* sound—and listened to the last message on her phone. From Sam, her best friend. Just the sound of Sam's voice made her feel better. God, she missed her. And needed her. But she couldn't involve her in this horrible drama.

"Where the hell are you? Where's Lizzie? I just drove by the house and it's dark. Your ass better be around because tonight is your birthday party. We're picking you up at six, have your overnight bag packed. Remember, we're going to Escapade in the City. We got a table reserved in a corner. Diane, Carla, Peggy, Cathy, me and you, and watch out boys, the cougars are on the hunt!"

Emma burst out laughing.

"Put on your mini-skirt and fuck-me pumps, we're gonna rock that club like it's never been rocked before," Sam proclaimed. "We got a hotel suite for the night. We're gonna get blasted and take a cab back to the room. And boy, do we all need it. And take a nap, we'll be out late. Six o'clock. Be ready."

Emma had forgotten all about the party. Damn, that sounded so good. She wished she could go. The past few months had been horrific for all of them. Peggy had just lost her husband of fifteen years to a drunk driver; Diane's mother had Alzheimer's and had recently moved in; Sam had ended a five-year relationship; and Cathy and Carla were in the middle of divorces.

Intense longing wrenched her insides. She had to go. She had to see her friends. She felt so disoriented, so lonely. Stuck in this nasty little motel room away from everyone she loved and everything familiar.

Emma glanced at a chair in front of a chipped desk. The seat was covered in spots. Anything was better than staying there and playing Name That Stain.

She walked into the bathroom and turned on the overhead fluorescent, which flickered, casting an eerie green light over the peeling paint on the walls and the lidless toilet.

What if she met them at the club? She could sneak there, dance and drink with them, go to their hotel room and then steal back the next morning. Why wouldn't it work? Neither guy had found her so far. She could probably pull it off.

And if she was about to die—an excellent possibility—she wanted one last night with her girls.

A shiver raced through her and her eyes filled with tears. *A last night with her girls.* How had her life come to this?

Forcing herself to calm, she called Sam and spun a lie about how Lizzie was going to a rehab center for therapy. And that she'd been out shopping when Sam had stopped by. She'd meet the girls at the club that evening because she'd already be up there at her shop. Sam bought the whole story. Which made Emma feel like a skunk. But she had to protect her friend.

A glimmer of joy appeared on Emma's horizon. Doing something so normal sounded so fun. So healing. It'd clear her head and give her the juice she needed to handle her upcoming challenges. Perfect. A night out with her best friends always put things in perspective.

And it would get her out of Motel Hell for a few hours.

* * * * *

"We look so hot!" Emma crowed as the five took their places in the chic lounge area of a hot club in downtown San Francisco.

"Better than hot! We're on fire," Sam pronounced, doing a shimmy. With her wavy auburn hair and flashing hazel eyes, Sam looked particularly radiant this evening.

The girls hooted.

Diane pointed at Emma. "And you're lookin' damn good for thirty-two."

"Boo-yah!" Emma did a saucy little hip cock.

Sam pumped her fist. "Whoop-whoop!"

Three Cosmopolitans into the night and very buzzed, Emma hit the dance floor with the girls.

The music was great. She and her buddies made fun of the other dancers and laughed like hell. Emma lost herself in the dance beat and the booze, reveling in her temporary freedom.

A man grabbed her hands and danced with her. She gazed up at him to protest and felt gut-punched.

Burke Cherlenko. Dressed to the nines in a sophisticated black suit with a red silk shirt underneath and reeking of expensive cologne, he had a wicked grin on his handsome face.

A bomb of fury exploded in her gut, fueled by the Cosmos. She wanted to kill him. Frustration and exasperation threatened to blow her body apart. Not only had he found her, she'd put her friends in danger. This wasn't happening.

Glaring up at him, she pointed at the back of the club. "Now!" she shouted, storming off.

She reached a deserted corner of the club and spun on him.

He wore his normal superior and amused grin. It took all her effort not to pop him one.

"How dare you! What the hell do you think you're doing? You stay away from me and my friends! If you hurt one hair on any of my girls' heads, I will kill you. I mean, it, Cherlenko. Stay away from us."

His smile faded and his expression grew serious. "At three-thirty yesterday afternoon, two contract killers landed at SFO with you as their target. I neutralized them."

A loud whooshing in her ears made the club's music fade out. Freezing fingers of terror latched around her heart; she clutched her chest. The club tilted. She had to rest a hand on the back wall to steady herself. "Who wants to kill me?"

"People who don't want you divulging the information in your head. The same people who killed your husband."

"Holy shit."

"I'm here to protect you, Emma. Not to terrorize you. Not to upset you. Not to hurt your friends. I'm here to protect all of you. You're playing a very dangerous game. Running from me, coming out here in public with your friends. You're the one who's put yourself in danger, not me."

A chill came over her, tears blurred her vision and she wrapped her arms around herself. "I...I have to get out of here. I can't hurt them. I thought I could just have one last night with them before I took off. I can't—"

He came closer to her and put a hand on her shoulder. "Shhh. It's okay. I know the pressure you're under. I understand you're not thinking clearly. Saying good-bye to your sister must have been so hard for you. Let me protect you, Emma. Let me give you this night. I know you need it. I'll make sure no harm comes to you or your friends."

"I…"

"Rollin can't protect you the way I can. He had no idea about the hitmen. You were right to run from him. But you need to let me help you now."

Shaking, adrenaline flooded her. She wanted to bolt out into the night and keep running. She couldn't believe how selfish she'd been coming here. What an awful mistake it'd been. She wanted to shoot herself for putting her buddies in danger.

He took her by the hand. "Come and let's dance. I have men guarding all of us. Nothing bad will happen to you. I'll make sure of it."

She studied his face. Dude was a master game player and not to be trusted. Who knew if he was telling her the truth? He was probably manipulating her.

"How did you find me so quickly?" she said, pulling her hand away.

"I've followed your every move since we met."

"That creeps me out. I have no trust in you, Cherlenko. As far as I'm concerned, you're part of the problem here."

"Do you want me to leave? I'll leave if you'd like me to. But I can't guarantee your safety. If I found you this easily, others can, too. I'm worried about you, Emma. I know you don't trust me, but you should. This has gone beyond the money for me. I like you. I don't want to see you hurt. Let me help you. Come on, dance with me. You'll feel better."

Her mind swirled like someone tossed her brain in a blender. She took a deep breath and examined his deep brown eyes and expression carefully. On second look, she didn't see any duplicity. She actually saw caring and concern on his symmetrical face.

What if he was telling the truth? Even Rollin had said that Cherlenko was very powerful. He was offering her protection. And her girls.

Her other option was to tell the girls she had to leave and abandon them at the club, hoping that she'd take the danger with her. But all the creeps had to do was kidnap her friends and she'd have to hand them the nuke. Shortly thereafter, more than likely, all five of them would die.

The only logical decision was to accept Cherlenko's offer. Which meant exposing her friends to even more danger. In no way did she want the two worlds colliding, but she saw no other way out.

She met his gaze. "Please don't hurt my girls."

"I'd never do that to you, Emma. I'll take care of them the same way I'll take care of you. Completely. I promise."

She sighed and bit her lip. After a pause, she gave him a nod.

"One favor?" he asked.

She raised an eyebrow. Here it was, the payoff. So soon?

He smiled. "Call me Burke."

Her shoulders relaxed a bit and she gave him a small smile. "Okay, Burke."

He took her by the hand and led her to the dance floor.

It took a long while for the beat of the music to penetrate her overwhelmed mind. And she had to admit, Cherlenko looked hot. And he was watching out for her and her girls. Two very powerful persuaders to allow him to be there.

With his focus completely on her, that smoldering look in his eye, he began to have an effect on her. The way he moved his hips, the admiring looks he kept sending her, the boy was so bloody gorgeous. Playful, yet very cool. Lethal combination. And he could dance. A white guy who could dance? Unreal.

She finally relaxed and began to enjoy herself. She did a turn and the women sent her *what the fuck?* looks. She burst out laughing. She grabbed Cherlenko's hand, very naturally—and on some level a voice shouted a warning about all this ease—and brought him over to meet the girls.

Dude was so smooth. He shook their hands, danced with each one a bit and treated them like they were queens. Seamlessly, he returned to her. A slow song came on and she was in his arms.

His warmth, his scent and his attention sent shivers of joy racing through her body. He was so strong, so self-assured and so classy.

She always wondered what it would be like to be properly seduced and now she knew. This guy could write a book on it. He didn't try to cop feels, didn't talk to her breasts, he made her feel like the most important person he'd ever met. And more importantly, like the most beautiful woman in the room. He didn't glance at the young twenty-somethings that desperately tried to draw his attention away from her. All his focus was on her.

Cherlenko was a formidable weapon. And a great distraction.

Which was weird. While he was the one man she feared most, he also provided her with escape. Odd combination.

He escorted her off the dance floor and to their table. After ordering a round of drinks and a ton of expensive appetizers, he told the waitress that the entire night was on him and to give "his" girls anything they wanted.

Her four friends looked like they'd won the lottery.

Cherlenko made a simple gesture to his goons. The two hulking bodyguards joined the group and were soon dancing with Cathy and Diane.

Sam came over and plopped down on her other side, away from Cherlenko. "Okay, the scoop, now. Where'd you meet Burke and why were you two arguing? Looks like you already have history. How come I've never heard of this guy?"

Tricky. Sam was a mind reader. Emma had to make this good.

"Yes, we have a weird history and this is why you haven't heard about him. I met Cherlenko, uh, Burke, about a month ago in my store. He accused me of selling him a fake antique and I didn't take that too well. We had a huge argument, I proved where I'd bought it and he finally believed that I hadn't cheated him. But I wasn't very happy with his approach. He asked me out then and I said no, even though he's hot."

Sam raked Burke with her hazel gaze. "I'll say. He looks like he should be on the dessert menu."

Emma laughed. "And I hadn't seen him since then until just a few minutes ago. I needed to set things straight with him. But he's very persuasive."

Sam elbowed her. "And hot. And rich."

"Yes."

"Well, he sure as hell likes you."

"Apparently, but the jury's not out yet. I'll have to see how things go tonight."

Sam leaned forward, made a huge exaggerated point of looking at Cherlenko—who returned a quizzical stare—then she arched a brow at Emma. "I give you two hours before you're fucking." She burst out laughing and clinked her glass with Emma. "Whooooooo!"

Dear God, you'd better be wrong. Emma laughed to cover her terror.

Sam got up, still laughing, and moved back to her place next to Peggy.

Cherlenko leaned into her. "What did you tell her about me?"

Emma brought him up to speed. "And please remember the story. Sam is tenacious. If she catches wind that was a bunch of bullshit, I'll never hear the end of it and neither will you."

He smiled. "You did well."

The waiter brought a round of drinks. Cherlenko handed her another Cosmo. "How are you feeling?"

"Um, better with this Cosmo," she said, taking a long draw.

It was then she noticed he'd been rubbing her naked back. Very gently, sensually. A part of her told her to shy away, but his touch was so comforting, so delightful, she took another drink of her Cosmo instead. And another. She nearly drained the glass.

Rollin popped into her mind, followed shortly by a pang of guilt. She'd ditched him and now she was cozying up to Cherlenko. Hadn't it been just the night before that he'd kissed her? Seemed like ten years ago.

She liked Rollin a lot, too. But now? With contract killers descending on her? What was the right survival choice? Should she have stayed with Rollin? Could he protect her?

Who'd she rather be with? Well, easy: Rollin. She really liked the guy. And he didn't scare her. While she felt safe with Cherlenko, he terrified her. Iron fist in a nice soft glove. Rollin was squishier inside. Candid, and his charm was authentic, not practiced like Cherlenko's.

But Cherlenko had more power. And he'd found her fast. Rollin hadn't. And if Cherlenko was telling the truth, he'd saved her bloody life. From not one but two contract killers.

And she had to admit, he had a nice touch.

Oh, God. Did he think she was going to sleep with him? Hot as he was, how could she sleep with a man she feared so much?

But then again, if her life and the lives of her best friends were on the line… Should she sleep with Satan if it meant saving them all?

Well, duh. That was a no-brainer.

But that wasn't apparent yet. She'd try to find a way out. She wasn't going down on him without a fight.

Of course, if he kept drawing circles on her bare back with that light, delicious touch of his…

Rattled by that thought and the whole freaky evening, she took another sip of her Cosmo. The glass caught her attention. It was full. She was sure it had been nearly empty a minute before. Maybe she hadn't drunk as much as she thought.

Cherlenko slipped his arm around her and she instinctively leaned into him. His hard body felt so reassuring. So intoxicating. Alarm bells sounded in her head.

She wanted Rollin, not this guy. Even though Cherlenko seemed to have her body under some kind of black magic spell.

Sam and one of Cherlenko's bodyguards broke up laughing after having shared a private joke. All of her friends were having a great time with the thugs. Maybe she should just let go and enjoy herself.

Could be the last time she got the chance.

The waiter arrived with a plate of delicious-looking baked oysters, one of her favorite foods.

"Oysters, m'lady?" Cherlenko asked with an adorable smile. He stabbed a particularly nice looking oyster with a fork and fed it to her.

Her girls cheered.

Well, as long as she was selling her soul, she might as well enjoy it.

* * * * *

The Beast was in bed with her. Bright red skin, pointed ears, black mustache and evil laughter. His features were familiar. He reached for her.

Emma awoke, her heart pounding. A bomb of pain went off in her head. Way too much light in the room. Painful. Nuclear fallout hangover. She shut her eyes, willing herself back to sleep, but with a different dream.

Her bladder sent her an alert. No. Bed was so soft. Softer than normal.

The mattress moved, someone was with her. That's right, she was in a hotel room somewhere in the City with the girls. Normally they got a room with a couple beds and shared.

"Weirdest dream," she mumbled to her bedmate. She wrenched open her eyes and tried to focus on the person. "Dreamt I was in bed with Satan. And he looked just like…"

Her vision cleared and there was half-naked man grinning over at her.

Burke Cherlenko.

Satan in the flesh.

EIGHT

Emma screamed and leapt from the bed. Cold air chilled her, her stomach lurched and she almost barfed. She looked down at herself. Stark ass naked. She screamed again and dove back under the covers, pulling them up around her neck and gasped at Cherlenko in horror.

He burst out laughing. Propped up on an elbow, the covers went to his waist, revealing tight abs and gorgeous worked-out pecs with a perfect amount of dark chest hair.

The adrenaline dump made hammers pound her head. Her gut churned and her tongue felt like a big, dry mattress as she stared at him, terrified to the core of her soul.

Flashes of the night before popped into her mind. Running her hand over his hard thigh, massaging his amazing chest and kissing his superb lips.

"Oh, God, I kissed you." They'd been at the bar. She saw the swirling lights behind him as she leaned in and kissed him. *Oh, no.* "I initiated the kiss," she said in a hoarse, horrified whisper.

His amused grin grew wider. "Yes, you even asked permission first. You asked if I'd be offended if you kissed me. You were quite polite about it."

Holy shit! Did she fuck him? *Please, God, no!*

Sweat broke out all over her body. "Did we…"

"No. But you were fairly adamant that we should," he said, clearly holding back more laughter.

Her face flushed hot. More memories attacked her. Horrid, horny memories. She'd touched him, all right. She remembered what his butt felt like. Rock solid, wonderful. His ropy arms and his hard chest. She remembered what he tasted like. Unfortunately divine.

She clapped her hands over her face. "Oh, God. I remember. This is horrible. I'm sorry. I don't usually get like that."

"I know."

"I apologize."

"No need. I fully enjoyed it. I didn't exactly fight you."

"How far…I mean…"

"Nothing happened outside of some kissing and…" He sent her a wicked grin. "Some touching."

He relished telling her. Bastard.

"Damn it, the Cosmos!" Anger burned through her and she pointed at him. "That glass stayed full the whole night."

"Yes, it did," he replied with an almost proud edge.

What a player. While he'd protected her, he'd still snared her in a trap. This was why she couldn't trust him, he was always playing a game. Shit! "You wanted to see what happened to me."

"Yes. You can tell a lot about a person by the way they react to alcohol."

"What did you learn about me?"

His expression softened. "That when you're happy, you're the most beautiful woman I've ever met."

Thwack! He flattened her. No one had ever said anything like that to her in her life. Her heart cracked open a bit. This guy was good.

His smile grew and his gaze sparkled. "And you're sweeter than you let on, you're funnier than I thought, you've got a wild streak a mile wide—and you're not a bad singer." He sent her a teasing grin.

"Oh, God," she said, sliding back down into the bed. She hid her face in the covers. Even her ears felt hot.

She finally peered out at him. He watched her with an expression of delighted amusement and fondness. Weird.

"I also learned that you inspire amazing amounts of loyalty in your friends. Your friend, Sam…"

Emma sat up, instantly concerned. Sam was a wild woman. And she had no idea who this guy was. "What did she say?"

His gaze darted upwards. "Uh, I think her direct quote was: 'She's hurting right now and if you take advantage of her, I'll hunt you down and chop off your nuts.'" He smiled, clearly amused.

She chuckled and relaxed back into bed. "Sounds like Sam." Damn it! She should have never gone out last night. She should have known she'd been exposing her friends to danger.

A stab of pain knifed her skull. She groaned and rubbed it.

"I liked her," Cherlenko said. "I liked all of them. Very nice ladies—wild as hell—but very nice. And they love you. Fiercely loyal to you."

"Yes. We all are to each other. We've been through a lot together."

"You're lucky to have each other. Rare to find that kind of connection with people."

She wanted to use the bathroom, but there was no way she was getting out of that bed naked again. She searched the vast bedroom suite. "So…what happened to my clothes?"

"They're being cleaned."

"Cleaned," she repeated, confused.

"Yes, you didn't quite make it all the way around the fountain in that conga line that Peggy started."

Dark night sky, a brightly lit tiled fountain, a very narrow ledge around it. Cold water. Very cold water. Burke reaching in and fishing her out.

She fell back against her pillows. "Not the conga line. Damn. Normally, it isn't somewhere precarious, like around a fountain. Well, once it was around a pool. With the same results."

He laughed.

"Yeah, those girls are a bad influence on me."

"Seems like you're all a bad influence on each other. When we all got here, I gave you my robe and sent out your clothes."

The entire group sitting on cream-colored furniture. She was dancing. Cathy laughing so hard, she was on the floor, holding her sides.

Damn it. She'd actually brought her best friends in the universe to Satan's house. She'd never forgive herself.

"We all hung out here for a while, right?"

"Yes. Peggy greatly enjoyed a bottle of my Cristal. Rest of you girls couldn't get enough Cosmos. Then my boys took your friends to their hotel room. You insisted on staying here. I mean, truthfully, I wasn't going to let you go with them. I can't protect you from there."

The contract killers.

Two faceless thugs with guns walking through the airport popped into her mind. One held a piece of paper with her name on it and her picture. She shuddered.

Burke's lips quirked. "However, I was going to put you up in my guestroom, but you…"

Groaning, her face went hot again. "I probably shouldn't be embarrassed, but I really came onto you, didn't I?"

A barely hidden grin spread across his handsome face, speaking volumes. "Yes. Quite enthusiastic."

She wanted to turn in on herself and disappear. "Shit. I apologize. And thanks for not taking advantage of me."

His smile vanished. "I don't sleep with drunk women." His gaze went dark, predatory. "I like my women coherent. I like them aware of everything I'm doing to them. For them," he said in a husky tone. He winked at her.

Turned on, terrified and overwhelmed, she held back a long scream.

"And don't worry, I prefer women without hangovers. I only want women who want me. But I like to be the initiator."

Thank GOD!! She finally breathed. "Sorry."

"Please don't apologize. You were fun last night. I haven't laughed like that in years. You ladies, when you get going—I laughed until my sides hurt. I haven't seen my boys laugh like that, either. Sam and her jokes and the way she kept making herself crack up—"

"She's a riot, always has been."

His gaze shined with affection. Damn, he could be charming. "You two have many shared mannerisms. How long have you been friends?"

"Since we were nineteen. I met her at a party and I was too drunk to drive—the only other time in my life that I was wasted—and she drove me home. And stayed."

"Stayed?"

"Yeah, I passed out and she and my mom talked and hit it off. Sam mentioned that she'd been kicked out of her place because of a bad roommate and had nowhere to go and Mom offered her Lizzie's bedroom. Then we moved out together a year later and lived together for five years until I moved in with the professor. Sam's been more loyal to me than anyone. She's a tiger. Yeah, and her jokes. Most of them aren't funny, but what's funny is the way they crack her up."

Burke grinned, showing off straight white teeth. "She was a riot. And a beautiful girl. But I pity the man who falls for her. She has no filters on her mouth, does she?"

"No. At least you always know where you stand with her."

"I'll say. You tell a good joke, too. And your impressions of the other dancers at the club was highly amusing."

Her face went hot again. "God, I haven't been that drunk since that night Sam drove me home. I never get drunk. Tipsy occasionally, but never drunk."

"If you'd like to use the bathroom, there's one on your side of the room, through that door." He pointed to a closed door on her side of the vast bedroom suite. "Or there's one over here," he said, pointing to another closed door near him.

"Stereo bathrooms, how convenient."

The corners of his mouth twitched.

Now that her sight had cleared some, she gave a quick look around his room. So this was Satan's bedroom. Very classy, actually. Floor-to-ceiling cream-colored drapes covered two walls of windows. The room was about the size of half her house, nearly a thousand square feet with cream-colored carpet. The modern and chic warm wood furnishings were sparse, yet arranged perfectly. Airy, masculine, understated.

"Um, where are we?"

"One Rincon Hill Tower. The penthouse. 60th Floor. The whole floor," he added with a slightly smug edge.

"Holy shit. You are rich."

"Yes, I am."

"I can't wait to see the view, but…"

He pointed to the end of the bed. "My robe is right there."

The robe had blended in with the cream-colored blanket on his king-sized bed. She reached for it while desperately trying to cover her naked body at the same time.

He chuckled. "No reason to hide. There isn't any part of you I haven't seen."

Her face, ears and chest warmed.

"I love that particular shade on you. Goes great with your green eyes."

"Shut up."

He nodded at her. "Have a question for you. Where did you get that odd tattoo on your lower back? Looks like it's been there for ages. And what is it? Looks like a set of random numbers and letters and a name."

She rolled her eyes. "I've wondered the exact same thing since I was little."

"When did you get it? How old were you?"

"My mother says I was three and a half. I don't remember."

His gaze went wide and his brow furrowed. "They tattooed you when you were three—"

She sighed. "My dad lost a bet is all she'd say about it. *Your father lost a bet,"* she said, doing an imitation of her mother wearing her "prune face". "She wouldn't say anymore."

His expression turned thoughtful. "I've seen one like it before."

"You have?" He must be wrong. Maybe looked sort of like it, but couldn't be the same.

"Yes. I can't remember where. It'll come to me. Let me see it again."

She shot him a worried look.

Cherlenko laughed and made a spinning gesture with his forefinger. "Turn over."

She tried to move without him seeing too much of her. She wrapped the sheets as tightly around herself as she could.

He had to push the covers down to see the tattoo. He touched the tattoo, igniting her skin. A little tingly spark raced through her and her sex gave a throb. He had the most marvelous touch. Damn it.

"0-2-Charles-0-0," he read. "Very interesting. Wonder what it means." Your father was murdered, is that correct?" he asked, drawing light circles around the tattoo.

The delightful buzz in her body grew stronger, she fought the urge to grab his hand and put it where it would really do some good. "Yeah. Apparently. Sometime right after he lost the bet and I got tattooed. Mom said if someone hadn't murdered him, she would have. Penny ante crook, apparently."

"He was more than that. Part of a very large and very successful crew wiped out in a gangland slaying."

Through her horny and foggy haze, his words hit her like a spear between the eyes. She turned to him, reeling, her heart pumping harder. Her lust retreated. She'd never heard any of this. "What the hell? How do you know that? Tell me what you know."

"Just that. He was part of a successful crime cell, but they stepped on someone's toes and all got murdered on the same day. Eight of them."

Goosebumps raced over her. She couldn't get her head around the news. "Wow. This blows my mind, I had this idea of who he was. Where can I find this information?"

"Get a copy of the police report."

"Why didn't I think of that?"

"I saw the files on all your father's friends."

"Damn, you are blowing my mind. I thought he was a pipsqueak."

"Uh, no. Not a godfather, either. Somewhere in between. Successful. Sophisticated. You never tried to find out anything about him?"

"No. It's…my mom terrified me. Told me if I found out too much, I'd become a target. She told me to forget about him. I didn't even know he existed until my stepfather was murdered four years ago and my sister finally slipped it to me. I always thought my stepfather was my real father. When I confronted Mom, she nearly killed my sister and denied it forever. Then about six months before she died, Mom finally came clean. Blew. My. Mind. My mother said she never told me to protect me. That my real father was murdered and I shouldn't go poking around in his old life or let anyone know we were alive. I just found out his name recently when I went through Mom's stuff. She got rid of almost everything of Dad's. All I have is his ring and birth certificate, their marriage certificate, two wedding pictures and that's it. She even changed my birth certificate and my sister's. But I know nothing about him. This is wild."

"I'll send you the files I found."

"Cool."

Her bladder protested loudly. Cherlenko was going to get quite a show when she got up.

"Oh, screw it." She threw aside the bedcovers and stood up. The floor slid sideways and she gripped the bed. "Whoa. Too fast."

He grinned and feasted on her with his dark eyes. She grabbed the robe and headed to the bathroom.

Closing the door behind her, she used the toilet, then staggered to the mirror, horrified by her raccoonish make-up and gray pallor. She should have scared off Cherlenko with this ugliness.

Jesus, what a pickle. Flirting, fine, why did she have to kiss him? And enjoy it? Absolutely repulsive behavior. But what the hell happened? She couldn't have been that drunk.

A wallop of nausea and dizziness slammed her and she gripped the sink. Okay, so maybe she had been that wasted.

She tried to remember the events leading up to the decision to kiss him. In retrospect, aside from the hormones, there had been some fuzzy reasoning. A) He was protecting her. B) He terrified her. And C) He was deliciously hot. Basically, it came down to self-preservation and the protection of her friends. She couldn't blame herself for that. And her actions certainly made him like her more. Which she could use to her advantage. Maybe she hadn't totally blown it.

She washed her face and removed the Alice Cooper look. Her overnight bag sat on a chair in the corner of the large bathroom. She brushed her teeth quickly and slipped on a t-shirt and sleep pants.

Okay, so now what? She'd successfully made him like her. But in the blinding light of day, there was no way she was prepared for the follow-through. So how was she supposed to get out of this gracefully? Men like Cherlenko were used to getting what they wanted. And he wanted her. Shit.

Stupid alcohol. Stupid death threats. Stupid hot creepy asshole.

Rollin's voice popped into her mind. *Women find themselves in bed with him.*

Oh, God, Rollin! A twinge of guilt and shame burned through her. She'd kissed Rollin, then went out and freakin' made out heavily with Satan.

Well, she didn't want to kiss Cherlenko now, that was for sure. She wanted to run and never look back. There had to be some way out of The Cherlenko Trap. She only had to find it.

With as much dignity as she could muster, she tottered back into the bedroom. Cherlenko was gone. The door to the other bathroom was shut. She heard the water running inside. She sat on the bed and formed and discarded fifty plans for escape. She simply didn't have the money or the experience or the resources to play on the same field as Cherlenko and Rollin.

Cherlenko came out, looking horrendously cute. Blue silk pajama bottoms, nothing on top but tanned muscles. Lovely, buff muscles. He looked like a pin-up boy.

She sent him a weak smile and gravity sucked her back down on the bed. She groaned.

Laughing, he walked over and sat next to her on the bed. He reached up and brushed some hair out of her eyes. Thrilled by his touch, her body responded to him like a well-trained dog. A dog she'd like to drop off at the pound.

He picked up her hand and examined it, lightly stroking her fingers.

Prickly energy raced over her skin and set fire to her lust. Her body sent a rush order for sex. She told it to shut the fuck up.

Cherlenko read her well. His sharp gaze didn't miss one of her reactions. He seemed absolutely delighted with his sexual power over her. "What would you like for breakfast?"

"The last twelve hours of my life back."

He smiled. "Other than that."

"All I could probably get down is some toast and black tea."

He continued to lightly massage her hand. "You could use some protein and vitamins too. How about some eggs and fresh fruit with that?"

"You're kidding."

"No. Got everything in the kitchen."

"Seriously?"

"Seriously. If you can make your way out there."

She giggled. "I'll make a concerted effort."

"I'll get you some water to start, how's that?"

"That would be lovely."

He got up and left and returned with a cold bottle of water. With a wink and a grin, he said, "Food will be ready shortly. Come out when you can manage."

And then he left.

A weird feeling came over her when he shut the door. Disappointment. She liked his attention.

Her brain shattered a bit more.

Curious about the rest of his apartment, she somehow dragged herself out of his bed and went in search of him.

The place was like a gigantic glass labyrinth hovering in the sky. She felt more outclassed and outspent with each step. Crime sure paid for this guy. Each room afforded floor to ceiling windows with astounding views of San Francisco. Tall skyscrapers, the Bay Bridge, the bay and the Oakland hills beyond. Breathtaking. Live postcards everywhere she looked.

Cherlenko decorated his home in Criminal Overlord Modern. Boxy white leather couches in the living room sat around an Eames era, swoosh-shaped, clear glass coffee table. An ancient Japanese sword collection along with colorful abstract paintings hung on the interior walls.

One of the abstracts looked familiar. Expressionist. In reds, blacks and various whites with a dash of yellow. She checked the signature. She almost fainted. *Pollock.* A freakin' Jackson Pollack! Outrageous. She'd never been exposed to this kind of wealth before. Unreal.

This guy had far more money and power than she'd imagined. Seductive and terrifying.

His kitchen was immense and outfitted like a professional's. Cherlenko, still shirtless, stood before a huge twelve-burner Viking stove. Behind him, fancy stainless pans hung from the ceiling above a granite-topped kitchen island. Clear-glass-faced cupboards on the wall revealed perfectly ordered white china. A giant Sub-Zero stainless steel fridge stood near her at the doorway. Everything was spotless.

A dining table set up for two sat in front of a wall of windows.

He grinned when he saw her and beckoned her closer. “Have a seat, we’re almost ready to eat.” He gestured toward a pair of chrome and black leather bar stools that sat at the end of the kitchen island.

“’K.”

He worked the stove like a pro, again with those precisely controlled movements.

She couldn’t believe an overlord of the underworld was cooking breakfast for her.

Like magic, the guy had a fruit salad, fresh coffee, eggs and toast all set up on his dining table. Plus a steaming hot mug of black tea for her.

The scrambled eggs were done perfectly. The luscious fruit salad contained ripe kiwi, blackberries, orange slices and three kinds of melon. She couldn’t remember the last guy who cooked for her. First husband. Once. On their first anniversary. And that was it.

The view kept distracting her away from the food—not just of his magnificent chest—but of San Francisco. They were so high up and the window next to her was so clear, she kept getting the sensation that she was about to fall. Instead of scaring her, the view invigorated her. So exciting to see the bustling city from this vantage point.

She gestured at him with her fork. “Do you cook often?”

“When I feel like it. I prefer my own cooking. But mostly, I don’t have the time.”

“Huh.”

He smiled. “You’re not used to it.”

“Um, never seen many guys cook before except for chefs in restaurants.”

“Glad I’ve surprised you.”

“Oh, you’re full of surprises, all right.”

He sent her a wicked little smile. Her heart gave an extra thump. Damn it.

She wished she could remember more of the previous evening. Disjointed bits and pieces kept flashing through her mind, but nothing too coherent.

She saw herself in his living room, performing some song. Groan. "So was I singing a lot?"

"Oh, yeah."

"I have a vague memory of singing a song about my old cat."

He pressed his napkin to his lips and dotted them clean. "Adam's pet name for you was Gem. Gemma or Gem."

"Yeah, so?"

"Gem's goofy songs."

It took her a long second to catch up to what he meant. Adam's last words. The clue to the five hundred million. She was happy and disappointed all at the same time. Of course, he didn't like her that much. He got her drunk to pump her for information. "Holy shit. You got me to sing all of them."

A slight raise of his brows. "Quite a repertoire."

"Well? Anything?"

"I don't know," he said with a laugh. "There's a lot of material to sort through. I've got a man working on it now."

Her face blazed hot. "Did you record me?"

He grinned. "Yes. Would you like a copy?"

Emma put her head down on the table. "I'm going to die."

"Come on, you were cute. I especially liked the Sniffy Butt song. Sam made you sing that five times."

Keeping her head on the table made her dizzy. Plus she wanted to finish that delicious food. She carefully lifted her head up.

Cherlenko's dark brown eyes warm and playful, he leaned in a bit. "But it was the imitation of your cat sticking his nose in your other cat's butt that killed me."

The heat traveled to her neck and ears. "Please stop." She partially hid behind her hand, unable to keep eye contact.

He laughed. "I don't know what's more adorable, you last night or you right now. Both reactions, I think, are equally delightful."

She sighed heavily and rubbed her face. "So wrong. It's all so wrong."

"I don't know, feels right to me," he said with a smoldering look.

Her face burned even hotter. She suddenly pictured a guy in headphones, listening to her sing the Sniffy Butt song and writing down the lyrics. She burst out laughing and laughed until she almost puked. It took her a long few minutes to tell Cherlenko the picture in her head.

He cracked up, seemingly relishing her sense of humor. "So where did you go when you disappeared on Friday?"

"When?"

He smiled like *don't play with me,* and his attention on her intensified.

Bastard! Right when her guard was down, he went in for the kill. This guy had to be carefully watched at all times. She didn't allow herself a reaction. She waved a hand dismissively. "Oh, hell. I just wanted to see if I could get away from you guys. Freaked out Rollin, too. And then I did it again."

"Yes, but I had you followed Friday night. I'm speaking about Friday day."

"You had me followed Friday night? But…"

"Yes, I had a man follow you to the motel in Belmont. I've kept a close eye on you. All except for four and a half hours. Where did you go?"

"Baylands. I took a long walk. I wanted to be alone. Took myself out to dinner and then came home."

"You didn't go to Adam's grave like you told Rollin?"

This guy was a snake and she was too hung over to match wits with him. "Nope. Why would I go there?"

"He believed it."

"Good for him."

A half-smile. "I like that you lied to him."

"I'll bet you do."

His demeanor turned icy. "But don't lie to me. Ever."

Her stomach did a twist. "Okay."

"Now, really, where were you?" This in a matter-of-fact tone.

Forget it, she couldn't lie anymore. Some truth was in order. "Not ready to tell you. And no, I didn't find the money."

A muscle in his cheek twitched and he seared her with his gaze. "Playing a dangerous game, Emma." Then he forcibly softened his expression. She could tell he didn't want to either. The man was not used to having his authority questioned. "How can I protect you if you don't let me help you?"

She suddenly saw an aspect to the man that she'd missed. And it was so apparent. Cherlenko was playing her stepfather's game. Adam tried, but didn't have the balls. When Daddy wanted something, he wouldn't stop. Whatever it took to get his objective was okay. First would come flattery or a bribe. Then a direct order. Barely hidden threats soon followed. Then eventually, an open threat. If that didn't work, he followed through. A few slaps for her mother, a spanking for her.

So how soon before Cherlenko tried to physically intimidate her? Was he a spanker or a slapper? With his sexual proclivities, she'd guess both.

At this point, he wanted in her pants. This was a great bargaining chip. But soon, it wouldn't be enough. She wondered how much time she had. He would get the truth from her, eventually, and he'd do whatever it took to get it. And then he'd get his hands on that nuke.

And that thought terrified her.

His eyes darkened. "You need to trust me, Emma."

She played the same defense she used with her stepfather. No reaction. "Got that."

"I want you to tell me where you went."

"And I don't want to tell you."

He looked a bit pissed at that, then he recovered and his features softened. He shrugged. "I will find out."

"I'm sure you will. I'm surprised you didn't get it out of me last night."

"I am, too. Wasn't for lack of trying."

She laughed to cover her fear. "So what did I tell you?"

"Something about a bar and the train," he said, leveling a penetrating stare at her.

She looked at her tea. "Oh, yeah, I did go to a bar. Had a few beers."

"And you went somewhere else, too."

"Cherlenko, I'm not telling you. Stop asking."

"Call me Burke. And I'm only trying to protect you."

"I heard that one. Burke."

He sighed. "You'll trust me soon enough."

Not bloody likely. She concentrated on her food.

Cherlenko set down his fork and frowned. His gaze darting around the table, he appeared to be cogitating. He took a deep breath and focused in on her. "I meant to say this earlier, Emma…this isn't easy for me. I'm not known for my apologetic nature. Of course, I'm rarely wrong. But with you, I was. I misjudged you in the beginning and I apologize for that. You didn't deserve what I did to you. And I don't blame you for being angry with me. I just want you to examine your feelings now and make sure that anger isn't clouding your judgment. Those two contract killers won't be the only ones coming after you. There will be more."

"Could we have this conversation after I eat?"

He smiled. "I don't want to cause you any upset, but this is important. You must trust me. You must tell me where you went."

She studied his face. This was the crux. He wanted what she had badly. More than anything else in his life at the moment. She could feel his urgency from all the way across the table. Which meant she had to think carefully about how she proceeded.

His focus on her sharpened. "Whatever you found, it's important. Why else wouldn't you tell me?"

She said nothing. The less she opened her mouth, the better. She turned her attentions to her food.

"I respect the fact that you don't know who to trust, but if whatever you found disturbs you this greatly, it makes sense to share that responsibility with someone who has the power to handle it."

He knew about the nuke. What else could he be talking about?"

She snorted. "Who said I found anything? You're doing all the conjecture here. Maybe it's somewhere cool I can hide from both of you guys. If I divulge it, maybe I'm screwing myself."

He smiled. "You couldn't hide from me."

"I already did."

"But I'm watching you much more closely than I was. See, your problem, Emma, is that you don't understand the world which you've been drawn into. My world. There are no in and out privileges. There is no escape. Only when the money and whatever else you found is recovered, only then might it be over for you. Which gives you two choices: being on your own with all your current resources, or aligning yourself with someone more powerful who can provide you with protection."

Dude should be a used car salesman. He was good.

"At this point, you have a choice, me or Rollin," Cherlenko continued. "While Rollin can provide a certain level of protection, he doesn't have near the resources I do. He had no idea about those contract killers. If you'd stayed with him, you'd be dead right now. And so would he. He's a pawn. I'm a king."

"Were you on the debate team in college?"

He smiled despite himself, but his face reddened. The line between his eyes deepened and his expression darkened. And then it looked like he flipped a switch on his emotions and his face relaxed. The man had amazing control over himself. She knew he'd rather smack her at this point.

"I want you to stay here with me," he said in a neutral tone. "I can protect you here. And if you hang around me long enough, you'll learn to trust me. You'll see me for who I am. I don't think you'll be disappointed."

She studied him. "Rollin said you've made some of your women disappear. That you break them. That you enslave them, turn them into zombies and then kill them if they bug you too much."

His face turned to granite, his eyes to flames. "He'd say anything to drive a wedge between us."

"That's an evasion."

He frowned, seeming annoyed. "Of course I haven't killed any of my women," he said as if the thought was ludicrous. "Shit. Kill them. Enslave them. Hardly. I've let them bleed me dry, but I haven't killed any. I don't date women I would ever consider killing. Nor would I consider dating someone who was so weak they couldn't stand up to me. But…" He leveled a cold stare at her.

Her stomach clenched. "Uh, oh." Here it comes. The threat.

His freezing gaze didn't waver. "Yes. I have only two rules with those in my circle: don't lie to me and don't betray me."

"Or?"

A slight shrug and a raise of an eyebrow. "I wouldn't kill you…"

She let her anger show. "Is that a threat?"

He didn't blink. "Yes."

She laughed at his pure evilness. At least he admitted to his games. Stepdad never did that. "Cherlenko, this is—"

"Burke."

"Burke, this is not the way to seduce me."

He held his gaze steady. "I don't want any bullshit between us. I want you to know what I think. It's the only way you'll learn to trust me."

"Okay, do me a favor? Lie to me sometimes."

His serious expression broke and he laughed. "Damn, you are adorable." He got up, pulled her out of her chair and kissed her.

She wasn't sure she was ready for it, but she was too afraid to push him away.

Fully awake, kissing him freaked her out. Her stomach fluttery, her brain alerted all quadrants of her body to battle. She couldn't believe she was kissing the guy. Thinking about it and doing it were two different things.

He tasted like coffee and man. Really good man. Heady, thick, musky. He lightly ran his hands up her shoulders, traced her neck and cupped her face.

His intense focus uprooted her. His talented tongue slowly worked her own, sensually, patiently. Slowly, she became aroused.

Then, seemingly out of nowhere, a full-charge blast of lust rocked her body, so powerful it annihilated her doubts and torpedoed her barriers.

She wanted to devour him. Take him inside her. Feel him inside her. Fuck his whole being. Drink in his power.

He pulled away and her body cried out with hunger. A heavy hormonal fog made him appear as if he had some sort of sparkling light shining on him.

The smug smile on his handsome face cleared the fog away. Revulsion at her reaction boiled inside her. Her mind snapped back. Anger flared through her and she balled her fists. He didn't like her. He liked controlling her.

So different than Rollin. When Rollin kissed her, she could feel his heart. Rollin wanted to love her. Cherlenko wanted to own her.

But mostly, he wanted that nuke. And he was ruthless enough to sell it. She had to keep control over herself. She had to put him off. Somehow, she had to get away from him.

"So you'll stay?"

"I need time to think."

"You don't have the time. You leave here and you're bait. Rollin will get you killed. I won't."

She held his gaze. "I need time."

The ropy muscles in his neck twitched, his mouth went ugly and his dark gaze fired into her. "I won't make you stay."

"You'd like to."

"That stubborn streak of yours could get you killed."

"More than likely."

His stern expression broke; he smiled and sighed. "You are a troublesome woman."

"Where have I heard that before?"

"From every man fool enough to fall for you."

Did that mean he was in that group? She checked his expression, but it was guarded now. This guy was a total mindfucker.

Right at the end of their meal, the doorbell rang. The dry cleaners with her clothes. They took showers—separately—and she got ready to leave.

She grabbed her overnight bag and went to his front door to wait.

A while later, he appeared, his mouth and eyes grim. "You still insist on leaving?"

"Doesn't mean I won't come back."

"Rollin will find you. He knows you're here."

Gulk. Gut punch. A bit of shame burned in her cheeks.

"He won't be happy with you," Cherlenko added unnecessarily.

She sent him a cold look. "I don't care if he's unhappy. All that matters to me is if I'm happy. And I'm not talking to him, I need a few hours away from both of you. Look, I'll call you tonight."

"No, you won't. You're going to run. Know this, Emma: I won't let you get too far. I won't stand by and watch you get hurt. You've come to mean too much to me."

"And you really want to get your hands on that cash. Let's be real, Cherlenko."

"Burke."

"Burke. Whatever. Look, you care sooo much more about the money than me. And if you'd start being honest about that, I'd probably trust you more."

His gaze went fiery, his mouth, hard. "You really think that little of me, don't you? For your information, I have more money than I could spend in fifty lifetimes. My life is about challenges. What I want, I can't buy. And I want you. But I won't hold you hostage. If you want to go, I'll drive you wherever you want. But I'll say this one last time: I'm your only chance for survival. I'll give you today to think and then I'm taking control whether you like it or not. I won't see you killed because you've misjudged me."

"Great. I love being imprisoned."

"Fine!" he exploded, storming away from her. "Get yourself killed! What the hell can I do about it?"

"If you're being honest with me, I apologize. But I don't want to be with you because I'm afraid of you. I want to be here out of choice."

"Fine. I'll take you to the motel," he bit out.

When they pulled up in front of Motel Hell, Cherlenko angled a glance at her, grabbed her arm, pulled her to him and planted one on her. Anger blasted through her. A half second later, his off-the-scale sexual energy annihilated her. Her skin tingled like he'd attached little electrodes to it. She completely lost touch with where they were, all she could think about was diving inside this man to quench her overwhelming thirst for him. She didn't want to make love to him, she wanted to fuck him. Hard.

When he pulled away, his eyes were dilated and his mouth hungry. "We're going to be good together, Emma."

She put as much distance between them as she could. "If it happens. Yeah, enough fireworks to light up a continent. Still doesn't mean I'm going to sleep with you. I need to be clear about your intentions first." A total lie. She knew his intentions and her physical reaction said it all: *run and keep running and don't look back.*

She wanted to make love with Rollin. Cherlenko was pure playground. And at this point in her life, she'd slept with enough playgrounds. She wanted a home.

His mouth went tight. "I wish you trusted me. I don't like leaving you like this."

"Look, since you won't let me go far, this is a moot conversation. I'll call you, okay? Give me a few hours to clear my head."

His expression went hooded and a brief flash of anger flared behind his eyes. He liked her more than she'd thought. And more than he'd thought.

His taste on her lips, her mind scrambled, she stumbled out of the car and into her first floor seedy motel room.

Rollin's sweet, smiling face popped into her mind. Her heart tweaked, a sickening twist of guilt roiled her gut. She hoped she wouldn't run into him. She liked and believed him more than Cherlenko. But with that nuke in her storage facility, all bets were off. She'd disappear, get rid of the weapon, then see if Rollin still liked her.

She flicked the lights and nothing happened. Of course. Motel Hell strikes again. Kicking off her shoes, she ripped off her top and skirt, then walked over and flicked on the light by the bathroom and screamed.

Rollin sat in a chair in the corner of the room, glowering at her.

NINE

Rollin's expression broke briefly into a quick ogle when he saw she wore only her underwear. But he straightened up quickly and sent her a blazing glare. "Ran away from me to jump in bed with Burke. Nice. Damn, Emma, I expected more out of you."

Searing hot fury shocked her body. "Go to hell and get out of my room. I don't have to take this shit from you." She stalked over, opened her backpack and yanked out a t-shirt and jeans.

Her anger centered her. She was glad he was being an asshole. Made it much easier to distance herself from him. Talk about a great cure for her case of the guilts.

Donning her clothes quickly, she turned and he stood no more than three feet away, his face red.

He assaulted her with his angry gaze. "You're playing on the wrong side."

"I'm not playing on any side."

"You were all over him."

Did she suddenly have her own TV show? How did these guys find out everything about her?

She sliced him with a glare. "I drank five plus Cosmos. After that, I could have been kissing on Rush Limbaugh, thinkin' he's George Clooney. At least I kissed you when I was sober."

His hard expression broke and he looked away. A half second later, his gaze went volcanic and bore into her. "I was there, you know," he said, hands on his hips.

"Where?"

"The club."

Unwanted shame burned through her. *Shit.*

"Burke saw me. You didn't. You were too busy hanging all over him."

Her humiliation turned to anger. "Fuck you."

She went to brush by him, but he caught her by the arm. "You have no idea what you're into."

She tried to yank out of his fierce grip. "Oh, I have a really good idea."

He held her more tightly. "Once he sleeps with a woman, he owns her. Now he owns you."

"I didn't sleep with him."

He laughed and let go of her. "And you expect me to believe that?"

"Idiot. He doesn't sleep with drunk women. You know that. Remember you told me about him liking his women alert for the conquest? He did pump me, but only for information."

He'd forgotten about Cherlenko's sex rules. His face went from dark to light. Then he narrowed his gaze. "You wanted him. You initiated the contact."

She jabbed her forefinger into his hard chest. "Don't play these jealousy games with me. I went out last night for me. To let loose and be with my girls for my birthday—which you and he both ruined, by the way. I did not intend to end up with Satan. That was not what I wanted. I don't want him. The only reason I let him come onto me is because I'm afraid of him."

His mouth twisted and his gaze blackened. "So you'd fuck him to protect yourself, is that it? How noble."

She leveled a proud stare at him and brought herself up taller. "If it came down to it, yes. If my life was on the line or the lives of my friends, you bet I'd sleep with him. And if you judge me for it and think I'm a tramp, well, screw you, I don't care. We shared one kiss, Rollin. I don't owe you dick."

He waved three fingers at her. "Three. We kissed three times. And you ditched me. For him."

"No, I didn't. I ditched you for me. Because you make my head swim. Because I like you too much and I can't trust my hormones. I don't want him, okay? I want you, but I screwed that up, didn't I? So why the hell are we having this stupid pointless conversation?"

He seemed startled. He examined her closely. "You want me?"

"Yes, you idiot. It's not like me, what I did with Burke, but these are pretty goddamned extreme circumstances and I expect you to cut me some slack here. I'm moral, goddamn it. I mean, two contract killers came after me and he stopped them. How come you didn't know about them?"

"What contract killers?"

She gestured at him sharply. "This is what I mean. Two contract killers arrived at SFO the day before yesterday and Cherlenko neutralized them."

Rollin didn't bat an eye. "He made that up."

The ground shifted as a blip of vertigo slapped her brain. She hadn't even considered that Cherlenko lied. "Are you sure?"

"Yes, I would have known. He's manipulating you. Made you do what he wanted, didn't he? Don't trust him, Emma. If he wants you, he'll do anything or say anything to make that happen."

"Yeah, but who says you're telling me the truth? I can't tell, okay? I'm not psychic. And right now I've had so much crap happen to me, I'm almost psychotic. All I've heard from both of you is how the other one is going to get me killed."

He took a deep breath. "Here's the deal with Burke: he doesn't think what he's doing is wrong. He actually thinks he's moral. And he's really convincing. Believe me, I got caught up in his rap. He is fucked up. And he'll fuck you up."

"He didn't make a move on me. He even offered to leave."

"Of course he did. He can read you. Finessing his game. He's good."

"But here's my dilemma: you're working me, too."

"But I actually like you, and not in a narcissistic, freak-of-nature, obsessive way. I just want to take care of you and be with you."

"You have no idea how much I want to believe you. But neither of you guys have left me alone long enough to figure out who to trust. And I am exhausted. I don't think well when I'm exhausted."

"I'd love to give you two weeks in Hawaii to figure out which one of us is lying, but by that time, you'd be dead. What part of this don't you get? You are in danger. They will kill you. We have no time left."

"Well we're gonna make the time," she proclaimed in her no-nonsense tone. She crossed her arms over her chest and held her head high.

He finally looked away. "I'm just trying to keep you alive."

"Stop manipulating me and help me figure out where I can take a safe breather and think."

His gaze went fiery. He started to say something and stopped. He sighed heavily and shook his head. Walking over to the bed, he plopped down looking agonized. His face drawn, the pain lines creased deeply on his forehead and around his eyes. "This is so frustrating. You make me crazy. Blinded. And Burke's like the Big Boss at the end of the video game. Whole scene is like a test from God devised to drive me out of my mind. I should have more distance, more detachment and I don't. I want to tie you up and throw you in the back of my Jeep and lock you in a bunker somewhere. And that is crazy. Especially for me."

His vulnerability sucked her in. She wished she could believe him.

He ran his hand through his hair. His anger faded. "I'm sorry, Emma. Forgive me. I know you. You're a good person. You're doing your best under some of the most extreme circumstances I've ever witnessed and here I am yelling at you and accusing you of behavior you're not capable of. I'm not a jealous guy, either, but with Burke… Anyway, can we start all over?"

Her center warmed, her heart opened and she smiled. "Yeah. Please. Let's. I can relate. All this emotion is screwing with my head. I felt like I was cheating on you with Cherlenko and you'd only kissed me once."

"Three kisses."

She laughed. "Okay, three. Look, I still need a few hours to sleep and meditate on this whole thing. Where can I go that's safe? He's watching me here."

"I know. I'm surprised he hasn't sicced his toadies on me. He must be testing you to see if you still like me. Which means he likes you more than I thought I did. Which means you're in even more danger. I know of a place, but it's going to be a thrilling ride to get there. I'm gonna have to lose your tail."

This actually sounded like fun. Even if she was hung over. "Okay."

He got up and walked over to her. Grabbing her by the hands, he held them in his and inspected them. "You've got the prettiest hands." His gaze traveled up until he met hers. He looked deep inside her. "I really like you, lady."

His attention dropped to her lips, he leaned in and kissed her. A burst of energy buzzed through her. He took her face in his hands and deepened the kiss.

She breathed in his scent and reveled in his taste. He was so different than Cherlenko. So solid. He warmed her whole being.

Powerful emotions welled from within her. She never wanted to stop kissing him. Why did this guy feel so right?

He ended the kiss, smiled at her and moved some hair off her brow. "Let's get you some rest and somewhere safe and somewhere less creepy." He gestured around the room. "What? Did you look in the yellow pages under Flea Traps? Places Most Likely To Be Crime Scenes?"

"Motel Hell."

"Motel Yuck. The fabric of that chair isn't just gross, it's greasy."

Someone knocked on the door.

Adrenaline fired through her.

Rollin had a pistol drawn in a heartbeat. Slinking to the doorway, he hid behind it.

Her heartbeat quickened and her muscles readied for escape. She checked the room, fast. Where should she hide?

"Who is it?" he demanded.

"Fed Ex for a Miss Holsten."

Emma and Rollin exchanged wary glances.

Rollin moved the curtains apart, peered out, and nodded. He turned to Emma and whispered, "Answer it, but step back, I'll cover you."

Her heart beating hard, she hesitantly opened the door.

A young Asian Fed Ex guy handed her an electronic gizmo with a stylus. "Sign there, ma'am."

Expecting to get shot or attacked, she signed it, her hands shaking. The delivery guy gave her a small Fed Ex box and left. She eagerly shut the door and locked it.

Rollin put away his gun and glared at the box. "What the hell is that? Who knew you were here?"

She handled the box like it carried the Bubonic plague. "I don't know but this is creeping me out."

"Maybe it's a bomb."

She set the box on the floor and stepped back. "Comforting thought."

"Wait here. I've got some bomb swipes in my Jeep."

Then she saw the return address. Shit.

"Never mind. It's from Cherlenko. That was quick." She picked it up and shook it.

"What?" Rollin hovered an inch away from her.

"I don't know." She carried the box over to the beat-up old wooden desk in the corner and opened it. There was a small card inside. She tossed it aside to see what was under the wrapping.

Her throat constricted. A 1960 Namura Moon Car, in box, in perfect condition. She opened the card and turned away from Rollin.

E: Happy belated birthday. And sorry about Goofy.

Call me, B

P.S. Rollin is leading you into a trap.

A stab of doubt knifed her gut. Was he? She decided not to make eye contact.

Rollin seemed more fixated on the toy. “He’s trying to buy you.”

She laughed. “I cost a hell of a lot more than nine grand.”

“That cost *nine grand*?”

“Yes.”

“Shit. It’s a toy.”

“Welcome to reality. Vintage Japanese space toys command big bucks.”

Without asking, Rollin took the card from her. She reached for it and he sent her a sharp warning glance. She withdrew her hand and shrugged.

He read the card. His face went steely and his jaw tightened. His dark gaze flickered to her, full of suspicion. It was plain on his face, he wondered if she believed Cherlenko. “He’s playing you.”

Emma made sure not to react. She didn’t want him to know that she was shaken by Cherlenko’s warning. But she didn’t trust Rollin. When was the last time she had a relationship with a man who wasn’t a liar? Never. “I’m sure he is.”

Rollin tossed the card down in a nonchalant move, but his other hand, resting on his hip—with his long fingers digging into his side—told the real story. “So what did you guys talk about, anyway? What did he find out last night?”

“Adam didn’t say “Jenn’s goofy song, he said *Gem’s* goofy song.”

Understanding came over his rugged face and he nodded. His shoulders relaxed. “His pet name for you, of course. Don’t know why I didn’t make the connection. So?”

“I don’t know. I sang them all for Burke last night when I was drunk. He recorded it and has some guy going through them.”

“You’ll need to write down all the lyrics for us.”

“I can do that. But he’s got a head start on that.”

“What else did he find out? Did you tell him where you went that day?”

"No, I didn't. He tried to get it out of me. Thank God, I kept my mouth shut."

Rollin's focus turned penetrating and intense. "Why thank God? What did you find?"

Her stomach contracted and a stab of fear knifed her. Damn the guy, he got her to lower her guard and whammo, he goes in for the kill. Just like Cherlenko.

Turning away, she walked over to her backpack. "I didn't find the money."

"You found something else."

She was too hung over to lie.

He practically jumped on her. "What was it?"

"Nothing."

Moving into her field of vision, he examined her face carefully. "It scared you."

He knew. He knew about the nuke. Damn him. He was just manipulating her. She had to get away from both men. Her heart was clouding her judgment.

"I don't want to talk about it," she bit out, her eyes on the peeling harvest gold and avocado green wallpaper.

He grabbed for her, but she walked over to the concave bed and sat. It squeaked hideously then made a clank sound.

"Emma, you have to level with me. You don't know these guys. The buzz says there's something else besides the money at stake. Something big."

He was playing her and she still didn't know whose side he was on. She'd never forgive herself if the bad guys got that stupid bomb.

Was it possible he didn't know about the nuke?

"I knew it," he exclaimed, pacing away. He spun and faced her. "Adam must have accidentally wandered into that deal. There was a huge bad scene that happened recently. A transaction gone bad, tons of people killed. They sent me after the money, but skipped right over what was being sold. What was it? What was the money for?"

She stared at him, trying to read him.

He seemed intent, upset, worried, furious and exasperated. No duplicity.

He didn't know?

"Why are you looking at me like that?"

"Trying to figure you out."

"You're worried about whatever this is. You think I might be a bad guy. What the hell is it, Emma? Tell me."

"Not yet."

"I don't have time to earn your trust. I'm not kidding, Emma. This could be ten million times worse. I knew a couple of those guys. They deal in the worst, most high-level stuff. Was it computers? Some sort of weapon? Bioweapon? Anthrax? Drugs? Cocaine? Heroin?"

Was he playing her? "No. Stop guessing."

"But where did he hide it? I've checked every place associated with Adam."

"I'll tell you, but not now."

He stared at her, hands on hips, his eyes dark.

She stared back.

Shaking his head, he walked away from her. "Okay, okay. I gotta relax. Sorry. This is stressin' me out." He turned back, his face pained. "I think a client is playing me."

"You need to back off. I'm ready to walk."

He walked over and grabbed her hand. Electricity shot up her arm and his energy encompassed her. She wanted to pull away, but couldn't. Caught in his intense gaze, she could only stare at him. She wanted to trust him so badly.

"Please don't," he said, his eyes full of raw emotion. "I have to protect you and I can't if I don't know the whole story."

She pulled away, stood and walked over to a chipped and stained Formica table in the opposite corner of the room. "I said no."

"Emma, look—"

Fury torched her. Glaring, she pushed by him and stormed off to the bathroom, slamming the door behind her. She turned the lock and the knob came off in her hand. Swearing under her breath, she pushed it back on and almost punched the door.

She turned to the cracked mirror and was instantly alarmed. She looked horrible, especially under the flickering green light of the bare fluorescent. Freakin' bags under her eyes were so big, she'd have to check them through at the airport. The craziness was aging her. Rapidly.

Hawaii. She could take her cash stash, change her name and open up a little boutique in Lahaina. Rent an ocean view condo and learn to surf. Tempting.

But unfortunately, she had the idea she was on a train that wouldn't stop until the money was found and the bomb was in the hands of the authorities. Well, if there was money.

Thanks, Adam.

What should she do about these two crazy men? Rollin was still the most normal of the two. But with the nuke at stake, believing him was too risky.

When she came out of the bathroom, Rollin was standing right outside the door with a tired look on his face. He smiled and shook his head. "I got an idea. Why don't you tell me to back off and I won't listen again? I know you love it in that bathroom."

She chuckled, relieved.

"Sorry, Emma. Burke and I are playing ping-pong with your head, it's no wonder you're messed up. You're smart to hold back. Let's get you somewhere safe where you can rest."

Adorable. The way he said it, what he was saying, it was exactly what she needed to hear.

She walked up and squeezed his hand. "Thanks."

He sent her a heart-melting smile and put his hands on her shoulders. "You'll be okay, Emma."

He gave her a nice hug. When he pulled away, time stopped. A bolt of energy shot from his gaze, annihilating her. A dark hunger in his eyes, he kissed her like his lips were pulled to hers by a powerful magnet.

Something clicked inside her. Like a plug in a socket, he connected with her perfectly, electrifying her. Waves upon waves of buzzy, tingly energy raced through her, heightening the connection.

He manipulated her tongue sweetly, then masterfully, but it all came from deep within him. He kissed her like he loved her. Like he cherished her.

Cherlenko kissed her like he was playing an instrument, with much thought and precision.

Rollin kissed with his heart.

All the voices in her head told her that this man was real and his emotions were authentic. She'd been blinded by all the craziness from Mr. Satan, but Rollin was sincere. Rock solid and genuine.

He pulled away and grinned at her. With his sexy dark eyes, his soul patch and his kissable lips, he was the hottest guy she'd ever been with. Damn, she was falling for him. Fast.

He ran his hand down her face in a tender gesture. "You are so cute. Japanese space toys. Everything about you is cute. The way your eyes light up when you get excited, the way you laugh, the way you dance. I just think you're the most special woman I've met." He leaned in and placed a peck on the end of her nose.

She couldn't resist and kissed him. She got lost in him, relishing the feel of his tongue in her mouth, his taste and the amazing power that lay at his core.

He took control of the kiss and she nearly swooned. Roaming his hot body with her hands, she latched onto his nice, tight little ass.

He groaned into her mouth and ended the kiss. "Wow!" He stared at her, his eyes wide. "That's crazy. You—holy God, woman. We have to stop." He laughed and hugged her tight, then started to drag her toward the bed, but pretended to fight with himself. "The bed has got its own gravitational force and is pulling me over there."

She laughed.

He stopped and pushed away again. "Oh, God. You need sleep and I need to…" He looked down at his crotch. "Uh, get a fire extinguisher."

She sent him a saucy grin. "You get off on fire extinguishers?"

He stood taller and put on a comic, yet serious face. "Oh, yes, I've had many explosive relationships with them."

She laughed.

He brought her close. "I got a good feeling about you, girl. The best in a long time."

"You rock. It's a fact."

He laughed, pure joy radiating from the depths of his dark eyes.

She gave a dreamy sigh.

Emma packed up her stuff and Rollin loaded it into his Jeep while she checked out. She'd never been happier to leave a place.

Once in his car, she tried to put on her seatbelt, but somehow got it completely twisted up.

He looked over, raised an eyebrow and pulled himself up in the seat. "Little did Emma Holsten know that mild-mannered Rollin Hanson was in actuality," he said, doing a booming announcer voice, "Seat Belt Man. Fear not, fair maiden, I can save you." He struck a silly pose with his arm extended and cocked at the elbow.

She giggled and gestured for him to help her.

Behind Rollin, a man in a ski mask appeared in his window holding a gun.

Adrenaline flooded Emma's system and her heart leapt into overdrive. "Rollin! Gun!"

TEN

The masked man shattered the window with his pistol. Rollin reached out so fast she didn't see his hands move and grabbed the guy's arm and slammed it down on the window frame. The assailant screamed and dropped the weapon inside the Jeep.

The door opened behind her, someone grabbed her and yanked her out of the car. A tanker-truck full of adrenaline swamped her body.

Screaming, Emma kicked back into the guy's knee, wrenched her body sideways and ripped out of his grip. She sprinted off and got a few steps away before solid steel arms crushed her in a bear hug and she was in the air. Her heart almost burst from terror.

"Emma!" Rollin shouted.

The guy holding her jerked forward, yelled and let go. Dropping to the ground, she ran.

She glanced over her shoulder. His fists a blur, Rollin knocked all three men to the ground. Another round of kicks, punches and slams, and they were completely out. Two had lost their masks: a blond guy and a Hispanic hulk.

She stopped and stared, astonished. Holy God, the man was a freakin' death factory.

Rollin ran up to her, breathing hard. He seemed bigger somehow. "Quick, we gotta get out of here, they won't be the only ones after us."

A van screeched up to them. Two guys in ski masks and black military garb jumped out.

Rollin advanced on them. Right as he reached them, one of the attackers tased him. He screamed and his body jerked.

She couldn't leave him like that, but she had to.

Terrified and feeling guiltier than she ever had, she ran as fast as she could the other way. She tore past the three guys on the ground—two were stirring—and went around the side of the motel, heading for the street.

Footfalls came from right behind her. Her pursuer grabbed the back of her sweatshirt and yanked her to a stop.

Two men grabbed her, immobilized her and dragged her to the van, stuffing her through the open back door. She didn't see Rollin anywhere. She kicked and screamed and flailed her limbs as best she could, but she was no match for them.

They thrust her onto a seat and threw a dark hood over her head. A guy nearly twisted her arm off and she bellowed in pain and fear.

"You keep screaming, I'll make sure you earn it. Now shut it," he hissed.

She shut up. He eased off. He yanked her hands behind her back and tied them with cable ties.

"Why are you doing this to me?"

A hard punch to her shoulder. Dull, horrible pain radiated out from her shoulder blade.

"You don't ask questions," he bit out, punctuating his reply with a powerful slap to her head.

Her head jerked sideways from the blow and her right ear and scalp seared with pain. She cried out, then cowered.

Fuses blew out all over her brain. Tears stung her eyes. Terror overload. She concentrated on staying alert and tried to pay attention to where they were taking her. They turned this way and that, but there was no way she could determine where they were going.

But who had kidnapped her? Couldn't be Cherlenko, she'd just seen him. And he didn't need to kidnap her to get access. Both

Cherlenko and Rollin had said there were others after her. How horrible that they'd been right.

They drove for about an hour. The van stopped, but kept running. Someone got out and a gate squeaked open. They drove forward, then stopped. The gate closed. The person got back in the van and they drove longer than she anticipated, but finally pulled up and parked.

The door to the van opened and she was pulled outside. She felt the warmth of the sun on her and the material of her hood brightened, then a door opened and they pushed her inside a dark, cool, echoing place. Smelled like motor oil and machine parts.

They walked for a bit, then she was shoved down hard into a chair. Felt like a cushioned office chair with arms. They untied her, then retied her arms, wrists, legs and ankles to the chair.

People moved around her. A table or chair legs screeched close. She jumped from the sound.

She caught one of the men's cologne. Strong. Smelled like he just put it on. Familiar somehow.

"You want the pliers?" came a deep voice.

"Yes," answered a guy with a smoker's voice and a very slight French accent. "We'll start with those, shall we, Mrs. Ramsay? Or maybe you'll tell me where the money is without the pliers. Maybe you'll talk after I cut off your little finger? Would you like that?"

Someone touched her right pinky. She screamed.

Boisterous laughter.

"Oh, she's going to be a fun one, isn't she?" the Frenchman drawled.

"I'm not Mrs. Ramsay and I don't know where the fucking money is."

He tsked. "That's a shame. Because I'll have to do quite a lot of damage to you to find out if you're telling me the truth about that. Wouldn't it be terrible if you'd just told me the truth?"

"I am telling you the truth!"

"I think the drill might be fun with her. Pierce those nipples. You want to be pierced, honey? Are you a wild girl? Do you already have pierced nipples? Well, even if you do, those holes are going to be much, much bigger before I'm done with you."

"Will you stop?"

He cackled with noxious laughter. "Oh, my dear, we're going to have so much fun together. I hope you don't tell me. I like to make the pretty girls scream. Of course, they're not so pretty after I get through with them. Pity, really. They'll be saying, 'she was so pretty, it's such a shame.'"

She burst into tears.

"And since no one knows where you are and your friend is…well, Rollin won't be coming to your rescue, I'm afraid. He's a bit busy. Screaming and dying."

Rollin. Gone. Her gut hurt like she'd swallowed a revving chainsaw.

And now she was next.

Tears poured down her cheeks and pooled at her neck where the black bag was loosely tied. She was beyond fright. Beyond thinking. These guys were going to torture her for information there was no way she could give up. No one was there for her. No one would rescue her. There was nothing she could do to protect herself. Her whole body shook.

"I wish I knew where that stupid money is. Don't you think I would have taken it and run by now? Do you honestly think I'd be hanging around if I'd gotten my hands on five hundred million?"

"Darling, you *will* tell me where the money is. And until then, I'm going to have some fun with you. Take off her shoes. We'll start with her feet."

"No!" Sobbing from sheer terror, she stopped trying to be brave. She couldn't. She was all out of strategy, all out of everything.

The assholes untied her shoes and ripped them off her feet. Her socks came next, cool air rushed over her bare toes.

"Pliers, yes."

A guy grabbed her foot and cold metal clamped on her little toe. Expecting horrible pain, she screamed so loudly her ears rang.

But weirdly enough, the guy didn't hurt her. What the hell?

"Where's the money? You see I have your little toe and I'm going to hurt you very, very badly. Unless you tell me what I want to know."

"I honestly don't know, I've been looking all over for it."

He pressed harder, terrifying her.

"Stop! I don't know!"

"Where did you go the other day? Where were you?"

"I went for a walk along the Baylands! I promise I did!"

The pressure built. She imagined horrible pain. "Stop!"

She couldn't divulge the whereabouts of that nuke. She'd never forgive herself. Ever.

She thought of Lizzie and Mary. Sam and Diane and Peggy and Cathy. All the people she loved who could be blown up by that fucking thing.

Besides, if she told them, they'd probably kill her anyway. Knowledge was her only bargaining chip. Somehow she had to stay strong. She prayed she'd pass out.

Abruptly, her toe was released. She slumped with relief, weeping quietly.

Why hadn't they hurt her? She almost wished they would just to get it over with. The anticipation was frying her nerves.

"These pliers are bullshit. Get me the torch. Let's see what happens if we burn off her big toe."

Overwhelming fear engulfed her and she strained against her bonds. "No!"

A clicking then the whoosh of a blowtorch. A flash of heat across her toes.

She screamed bloody murder. And kept screaming.

"Shut up! I haven't even burned you yet. But I will. I will hold this torch to your toe until the flesh burns off and hangs there. Until I see bone."

Out of her mind with terror, she bellowed.

"Shut the fuck up!" he yelled over her.

She quieted as best she could, not wanting to incur the man's wrath.

"Now where did you go when you disappeared the other day? You thought only Hanson and Cherlenko were watching you, didn't you? Well, we were there, too. Where. Did. You. Go."

"I went on a walk to the Baylands. Please don't burn me!"

Heat on her toe. It didn't hurt exactly, but it would any minute. She shrieked. "I went for a walk! I did! I swear I did! Stop, please, God, stop!"

More heat on her toe.

Frenzied in fear, she let out the longest and loudest scream she had in her. As if the force of her yell could stop them, she screamed until she choked. Until her throat was raw. Until she couldn't scream anymore.

"Fuck this," the Frenchman said. "It's going take too long to cause the pain I want to inflict. Where's the acid? Oh, and get me the drill. Or maybe the bone saw. We could just take off a few toes. I'd chop off her foot, but she'd bleed too much."

"No!"

"You could always cauterize it with the blow torch," said the deep-voiced creep.

"I could…couldn't I?" The smile in Frenchy's voice escalated the terror.

She sobbed harder.

Scraping of metal across the floor. Something clanged against the wall of the warehouse. She jumped.

"What the fuck was that?" the Frenchman demanded. "Go check it out."

"It wasn't anything. Here's the acid, make her scream. I want to hear her scream again."

A *thunk* sound came from far off.

"Okay, did you fucking hear that? Go—"

A loud explosion rocked the building and the concussion changed the air pressure. A wall of air and little pieces of debris blasted her left side.

Her ears rang and her heart almost stopped. What the hell was going on?

A heavy wave of sulfuric odor encompassed her.

"They're coming through the door, get the guns!"

"Motherfuckers!"

Gun blasts echoed in the warehouse. Men screamed.

Shaking and crying, there was nothing she could do to protect herself. They were going to kill her and she couldn't stop them. She could only bow her head a bit.

She said good-bye to Lizzie and Mary and wondered who she'd see waiting for her in the Light. Mom or the Dad she never knew. Hopefully not her stupid stepfather.

A scuffle took place next to her and her chair was pushed sideways. She clamped her mouth shut to halt a scream.

She needed to play dead. Pretend that she'd passed out so no one else took over the torture. At this point, she almost hoped someone would shoot her clean through the head, she'd much rather die than have her feet chopped off.

But who was attacking them? Was it someone rescuing her?

She couldn't hope that. More than likely it was another party kidnapping her to get the information out of her.

The battle went on for a while. Would she die in the crossfire?

Someone picked up the chair and began carrying her. Tears streamed down her face, but she forced herself to stay quiet. The ropes bit into her wrists and legs as she was jostled along. Screams and crashing sounds came all around her. The sounds quieted, the heat of the sun hit her again and the sound of a sliding van door opening came from in front of her.

Set down inside, the vehicle took off, but she didn't roll or topple, someone had hold of the chair.

Someone untied her and removed the hood. The bright light made her wince and the air felt cold on her sweaty, tear-stained face. She blinked.

Banana sat in front of her, grinning. “Burke’s behind us, taking care of those assholes, he’ll be right here. You okay, Emma?”

“Holy shit,” she rasped. Her throat toasted from her screams, she could barely speak. Bursting into tears of relief, she threw her arms around him.

The big galoot laughed and hugged her. “You should be huggin’ Burke, he’s the one who got you out of there. I haven’t seen him like that before. He must really like you.”

“Well, I’m—” She coughed.

Banana handed her a cold bottle of water.

She eagerly drank the cool liquid, delighting in the feel as it slid down her hot and parched throat. “I’m liking him a lot right about now.” Her voice was clearer, but it still felt like she’d deep-throated some sandpaper. “Before we stop, do you know what happened to Rollin?”

“No. He’s not here, the guys were looking for him.”

Black gloom swirled in her mind. She couldn’t think the worst. Rollin was smart and well trained for these situations. “I hope he’s okay. Don’t tell Cherlenko I asked.”

“I won’t, don’t worry.”

Numb, she rubbed her wrists and inspected her toes. Nothing. Not even a mark. Well, if it weren’t for Cherlenko, they’d be bloody stumps. Shit.

She might be falling for Rollin, but she hadn’t felt this level of gratitude in her entire life to anyone. Cherlenko zoomed up to near god-like status.

* * * * *

Burke's gut hurt like someone sucker-punched him. He wiped his brow and fought to get his bearings. He concentrated on surveying the warehouse for damage and tried to detach from his wild emotions. His wild unexpected emotions.

How could he have misjudged his feelings for Emma that badly? He'd never get her scream out of his head.

He forced his mind to the task at hand: cleaning up his stage set. Not too much damage. At least that part had gone well. He'd call in a crew to replace the part of the wall that was blown out and that should do it.

Dubois walked up to him, grinning. "Did you get what you wanted?"

Burke straightened his shoulders. "Yes," he said with confidence he didn't feel.

"I thought we were going to scare her some more. Do you really think she was telling the truth?"

"Yes, I do." Hopefully, he'd at least scared her enough to bond her to him. She was tougher than he thought. He expected her to confess to everything right away.

Was it possible that Adam hadn't found the nuke? Just found the money?

If so, where the hell was the bomb? There was no buzz whatsoever on any channels. And there certainly should be by now.

Dubois laughed. "Did I sound menacing enough?"

"Yes. A very convincing job. I loved the acid addition to the script."

"You told me to improvise to make the dialogue my own. To make it sound more real."

"She believed you." Burke brushed debris from the explosion off his black sweater.

David walked up to him. "Banana took her back to the apartment."

"Are you sure he doesn't know?" Burke asked.

"Positive. He thinks you're the great White Knight, saving your damsel in distress." The dark-haired muscleman shot him a grin.

"Good. We need him for a while longer. Assign Banana to work outside the City again. Once he drops off Emma. It's easier that way."

"You bet. You headed to the apartment?"

"Yes. It's time to close the deal. If this doesn't do it, nothing will," Burke said as coldly as he could. "But first, I need to take a shower to get this bloody cologne off and put on my own. I hope she recognized it as Rollin's."

David grinned and nodded. "She's gonna fall for you like a rock, boss."

Burke smiled. "I think she already has, but this should definitely push her over the cliff. Dubois? Can you finish up here?"

"No problem, Cherlenko." Dubois turned away, grabbed the torch and pliers and headed outside.

"Good."

Burke and David left the building and got into his SUV.

Burke sat in the passenger seat and pulled on the seatbelt. "Let's go to my club, I'll shower there."

"You got it."

Burke frowned. Why wouldn't Emma talk? Would she face torture to protect the location of the money? No.

Damn. She must have found the weapon. No other reason fit.

Still, she hadn't been the problem with the operation, he'd been the problem. He'd completely underestimated her impact on him. He hadn't even gotten halfway through the planned scene.

Did he…? He felt guilty. Rotten, actually.

What was wrong with him? Why did this woman affect him so much? His attraction to her went beyond the physical. She drifted into his thoughts constantly of late.

He normally considered his women interchangeable. But not this one. Emma had buried herself under his skin like a tick.

He wanted more from her. He wanted her mind. Her devotion. Her love.

That thought hit him like steel baseball bat across the head. He stared out the window, floored.

Love. Could it be? Was it possible?

Damn. It had been so long he'd forgotten the signs. He'd thought love wasn't possible for him.

How shocking. And extraordinary.

He laughed. Wasn't the worst thing that could have happened to him. At this moment in time, a relationship with Emma was fairly convenient. Fit in well with his plans.

As they pulled up in front of his club, he chuckled to himself, took the black ski mask from his pocket and stuck it under his seat.

Never saw himself married. But Emma was not a woman to use and discard. And if he wanted to possess her forever, marriage was the only way to keep her.

She was everything he imagined in a wife. Smart, strong and pure dynamite.

A spring in his step, he walked up the steps of the club.

* * * * *

Cherlenko's men took Emma back to his apartment. While she hated the idea of killing, she hoped Cherlenko murdered those jerks in the warehouse. Animals.

As soon as she walked inside his glass mansion in the sky, she wanted to bolt. She felt too exposed, too vulnerable. The openness of Cherlenko's place, the floor-to-ceiling windows, being that high up with all of San Francisco below her, suddenly bothered her.

Banana seemed to be a nice guy, but she wanted away from everyone. What she really wanted was to hide in her bedroom closet. Her old bedroom closet. Crawl in there with a blanket and disappear.

She retreated to the only place in Burke's penthouse that felt comfortable: the bathroom she'd used that morning.

That morning. Yea Gods, seemed like fifty years before. Fifty, long, horrible years.

She washed her face, but even being near the mirror made her nervous. Too much space around her. Even though the marble-tiled bathroom was warm, she shivered. Grabbing a large bath sheet, she wrapped it around her upper body, sat in the corner next to the two-person shower and hugged her knees to her chest.

Raging terror ate at her belly. She wanted to flee. Anywhere. But there was nowhere safe to go.

She couldn't get that Frenchman's voice out of her head. *Rollin's busy, screaming and dying. We'll start with her feet.*

Teetering on the precipice of sanity, a black inky bottomless pit of horror pulled on her, threatening to suck her in whole. She wanted to sleep, but knew only nightmares awaited her. She fought for control. What would make her feel safe?

Emma thought of Lizzie holding her when she was a kid when Daddy was in one of his rages. Lizzie had held her and sung to her. Emma closed her eyes and pictured Lizzie's arms around her. She sang quietly: "If you wish upon a star, it makes no difference who you are. Anything your heart desires, will come to you—"

Someone knocked on the door. She jumped violently, hitting her head on the wall. She broke into sobs.

"Emma? It's me, Burke. Are you all right?"

"No," she cried, rocking in place.

"Can I come in?"

"I don't know."

"I'm coming in."

When Cherlenko saw her, pain lines grooved deep on his handsome face. But he didn't rush right over. He wanted to, that was clear, but he didn't want to freak her out. His hesitation calmed her.

"Hey." He took a slow step toward her.

"Hi," she said, her voice cracking.

"Can I get you anything?"

"No, I'm fine." A part of her heard what she said and she chuckled through her tears. "Okay, that's clearly a load of bullshit. Wrapped in a towel in a ball in front of the shower, totally normal."

He smiled, his shoulders relaxing. Then his expression went haunted again. “I’m sorry I didn’t get there sooner.”

“Me, too. I appreciate it like you can’t believe, but I ran from you, Cherlen—Burke. Look, I’m happy you showed up at all.”

“The kidnapping shouldn’t have happened.”

“Well, it did. And I’m not handling it well, apparently.”

“You’re handling the situation fine.”

“You’re not me. I’m on the edge here. I’m freaked out. That colossal hangover, no sleep, the kidnapping, the torture, the rescue—I’m wasted and crazy and I’m fucking losing it.”

“You’re stronger than you realize. Anyone who goes through what you went through—even people who’ve had training—have issues. Get some food in you and some rest and you’ll be fine.”

“I don’t feel like anything would work. I’m just so terrified.”

He moved down next to her and held out his arms. “Let me hold you, Emma.”

She didn’t want to move. But she yearned for comfort. The sympathetic look on his face and the pain in his eyes drew her to him.

She finally nodded.

He scooched in next to her and took her in his arms.

She stiffened, unsure. A part of her wanted to run.

But after a few moments, his warmth and inner calm began to melt her fear. He was far stronger than her. And he’d protect her.

She leaned into him. He held her tighter.

His tenderness touched her. Her shields slipped and she wracked with sobs. He said quiet, soothing things, rocked her gently and kissed the side of her head. Her tears subsided, but she couldn’t stop trembling.

“You’re safe here.”

“I’m not safe anywhere.”

“You are here,” he said, his voice stronger.

He must have gotten nasty and sweaty during the rescue because he smelled like he’d just taken a shower and his cologne was fresh. Heavenly.

"I'll have to take your word for that."

"I won't let anything happen to you, I promise."

"Good," she heard herself say. But she didn't believe him.

"Let's go lie on my bed and let me hold you where it's more comfortable. That sounded terrible. I didn't mean—"

She let out a chuckle. "I understand you, don't worry."

Burke helped her up and her legs gave out. He supported her, guiding her into his bedroom. Sitting back on his king-sized bed, he pulled her into his arms. She clung to him. A good half hour later, she stopped shaking.

She almost asked about Rollin, but didn't want to upset him.

He squeezed her. "I can't stand what happened to you. And as much as I have issues with Rollin…" His body went rigid. "I'm so sorry about that. I didn't get there soon enough to save him and I'm sorry. We found his body at the motel."

A sledgehammer to her solar plexus. Rollin. Gone. *Fuck.* She burst into sobs.

He stroked her head and back until she calmed. "I should have kept my big mouth shut. I'm sorry."

"Don't be. I needed to know. I'd rather have all the information now."

"I know you have feelings for him, I'm so sorry."

"Wasn't your fault. It just sucks. This whole things sucks."

"I'll agree with you there."

"Do you know who kidnapped me?"

"We're in the process of finding that out. I didn't recognize any of the men in the warehouse."

"Maybe the same people who hired those hitmen. Rollin said you made that up to get me to do what you wanted, but I didn't believe him. Sorry, I don't mean to piss you off."

"I'm not. I would expect no less from him. And you may be right. And I need to find out who else is after you. I mean, I've been trying, but clearly not fast enough."

Felt so good to be in someone's arms. Even Satan's at this point. And he'd saved her from an unthinkable fate. She met his gaze, wiping away her tears. "I can't express my gratitude to you. I've never been happier to see anyone in my entire life."

While his face remained serious, his eyes dilated slightly. Clearly loved hearing it. He nuzzled her and kissed her on the cheek. "I want to take care of you. I want to make you safe."

All she could see was Rollin's face. She felt like she was betraying him by being in Burke's arms, but if he was gone, there was no one left to watch out for her.

"Let me take care of you, Emma. And protect you."

She hugged him closer. "Okay."

"Promise me you'll stay with me."

She nodded. "I promise."

He kissed her cheek. "Good."

While she couldn't deal with the thought of Rollin dying and knew she hadn't accepted the loss, at this point, it was all about self-preservation. She'd be stupid not to accept Cherlenko's comfort and protection.

Even though she still didn't trust him.

ELEVEN

Rollin awoke in blinding pain being flung around in a car trunk. The car hit a bump and he smashed against the top of the trunk, then crashed back down on a tire iron. A fire-hot blast of agony from his ribs. He moved the iron, but kept it close. He'd be needing that soon.

His heart pounding, he tasted blood in his mouth and some trickled down his forehead. He moved, and for some lucky reason, he still had all his limbs and they weren't broken.

Emma! Guilt ripped his insides. He should have been smarter. He should have been able to protect her better. He should have saved her.

The car dipped, then launched in the air. Smacking his head, a line of pain cracked across his scalp. The car came down hard and he slammed to the floor of the trunk. His ribs cried out in agony.

"Well, this is pleasant," he muttered to himself.

Feeling around for the security latch, he found it and popped it, but held on to the trunk lid to make sure not to alert the driver.

Golden rolling meadows with redwoods in the background. They were in the country somewhere on a paved single lane road.

He knew this place. "Pescadero," he whispered.

On Cloverdale Road heading southwest to be precise. The car slowed and made a left turn onto Gazos and went down a steep grade, braking toward the bottom.

He pushed open the trunk, grabbed the tire iron and jumped out before the car accelerated. The driver slammed on his brakes. Adrenaline pumping through him, Rollin ran back up the hill for Cloverdale.

Late afternoon on a Sunday, someone should be driving by. Campers from Butano State Park normally headed home around now.

He ran up the road, the driver spun a U-ie and came after him. Rollin dove off the left side of the road and took cover under the brush. The driver skidded to a halt and fired several shots. Little puffs of dirt exploded near him as the bullets hit the ground.

Rollin's pulse thumping in his ears, his body jerked with each gunshot. Sweat poured off him.

The sound of a car came from down the road. The gunfire ceased.

Rollin peeked up just as a huge truck came around the corner and almost hit his assailant. Honking and swerving, the driver yelled. The gunman waved his gun out of the window and flipped the guy off.

With the gunman distracted, Rollin scrambled toward the man's car, staying low.

Just as the assailant turned back toward him, he flattened to the ground.

"Fuck!" the assailant exclaimed with a hint of a New York accent.

Rollin knew that voice.

The guy opened his door and stepped out. Rollin launched off the ground and kicked the door as hard as he could. He sent his assailant flying back. Rushing him, he smashed the man in the head with the tire iron.

He recognized the guy instantly. Clyde Welsh, some local hired muscle. Square, ugly face, boxer's nose, cauliflower ears, beady brown eyes, shaved head. Not bright, but brutal, the guy would kill him as soon as look at him.

Clyde, barely dazed by the blow, came at him.

Rollin slammed the iron down onto Clyde's gun hand. The pistol flew out of his grip and skittered away.

"Welsh, you're getting slow!"

Clyde dove for the gun and Rollin brought down the tire iron on the back of his head.

Clyde collapsed to the ground, blood seeping from his head wound.

Rollin retrieved the gun, turned back to Clyde and his face exploded in pain and his vision streaked with white lights. Clyde's meaty fist felt like a solid chunk of wood.

Rollin staggered back, trying to keep his focus on hanging onto the gun.

Clyde came in and took another swing. Rollin ducked, got a better hold on the gun and shot the big man in the shoulder and both legs. Screaming, Clyde fell to the ground, holding his right knee.

"Who hired you? And where's Emma?"

Clyde threw himself forward and knocked Rollin to the ground. The gun sailed out of his hand, hit the pavement and slid down the hill and out of sight.

Clyde came for him, half crawling, half dragging his legs. Terrified, with no time to get to his feet, Rollin scrambled backwards like a crab as Clyde closed in on him.

Rollin smashed his hand on a large rock and dull aching pain shot through his fingers. He grabbed the rock and just as Clyde reached him, he slammed the bastard across the jaw with it.

Clyde's head jerked to the left, but the man's skull was made of granite, the blow barely stopped him. Panic juiced Rollin's body. He hit Clyde again, even harder.

Blood streaming down his face, the monster recoiled, but kept coming.

Who was this guy? The Terminator?

Rollin whaled the rock back and forth across his ugly mug, splattering blood everywhere.

Finally, the ex-boxer fell to his side. Rollin leapt to his feet and tackled him.

Dazed, Clyde smiled at him, blood smeared on his teeth.

"Who hired you?"

Clyde came back to life and pummeled his jaw with a left cross.

Rollin mind went gray for a second. Adrenaline powered through him and he slammed into the guy's head with the rock in a series of the hardest blows he could manage.

Finally, he dazed Clyde. The ugly thug's head lolled, his gaze went unfocussed and his arm fell to his side.

"Who hired you?" Rollin demanded.

Clyde's lids fluttered and he moaned.

"Damn you, who the hell hired you? Where's Emma?"

Clyde's eyes rolled, but he laughed. "Dead…killed your stupid girlfriend..."

Anger exploded deep from Rollin's belly, his vision went red and he bashed the guy's face with the rock with everything he had.

Clyde's eyes closed and his body stilled.

"Shit!" Rollin got off the asshole and kicked him. Clyde could have said that to piss him off. He was like that.

He pressed his fingers to the guy's massive wrist, searching for a pulse. Strong as hell. Of course. Nothing could kill Clyde.

He dragged the man from the side of the road and hid him in some tall scrub brush. Searching his pockets, he found his wallet but no cell phone.

Taking his wallet, Rollin jumped to his feet and raced down the hill where he saw the gun disappear. The pistol lay in a dried-out pothole. Grabbing it, he turned and ran for Clyde's car. He had to get out of there before someone saw him.

He did a quick search of the car, but couldn't find a cell. Who doesn't carry a cell phone? Damn it! He was hoping to find a familiar number and find out who hired Welsh.

Emma. His gut contracted hard. Could she be dead?

Why would they kill her?

Maybe someone knew where the money was stashed and wanted to make sure she didn't tell. Or find it.

He checked his own pockets. When his fingers touched his cell phone, he couldn't believe it. They left it on him? He still had his wallet, too. *What the fuck?*

He started the car, pulled onto Gazos and headed for Highway One.

But why did they send one guy to get rid of him? Talk about underestimating him. Maybe they didn't expect him to regain consciousness. Still, a stupid error on someone's part.

He opened his cell and couldn't believe it still worked. But no signal yet. Gazos Creek Road cut through a couple high mountains.

When he finally cleared the hills and hit the ocean and Highway One, all the bars came back on his phone.

Bobby's relieved voice came on the other end of the line. "Thank fucking God, I heard you were dead."

"The news of my demise was greatly exaggerated. Is that the quote? No, wait. I'm not dead yet!" he said in a high English accent, quoting *Monty Python and the Holy Grail.*

"Will you stop and tell me what the fuck happened to you?"

"Sorry. I'm on my way to you now. Have Jose get ready for a car pickup and clean. And call an ambulance for a man dying of gunshot wounds at the corner of Cloverdale and Gazos Creek Road in Pescadero."

"Got it. Banana just called. Emma's okay. Burke's got her."

Relief flooded his body and his neck and back loosened. "Thank God, she's still alive." Then alarm attacked him and all his muscles went tense again. "Wait, Burke has her? Wasn't he the one behind the kidnapping?"

"Not according to Banana. He wasn't brought in on the deal, if it was Burke. He got a call, Burke told him to meet him at a warehouse in one of their vans, they were going to rescue Emma. Burke was frantic. Banana drove up and heard gunfire coming from inside the warehouse. Two of Burke's guys, David and Angelo, came out and handed him Emma, tied to a chair with a black bag over her head."

"Shit. How is she?"

"Upset, but not too hurt. They hadn't tortured her yet, but were gonna use pliers and a blow torch on her."

"Fuck!"

"Burke rescued her before she got hurt."

"If it wasn't Burke who kidnapped her, who was it?"

"Working on that right now."

As Rollin passed by Pigeon Point Lighthouse, Highway One turned west and the sun hit his face. A whole new wave of pain coursed through his head and he squinted. "I'll bet it's Burke. Pullin' some game. Trying to get her loyalty by pretending to save her. He was probably the one holding the blowtorch. But there's a definite possibility it was someone else. Call Doc Woods. I'm gonna need some painkillers and x-rays." He tried to move into a more comfortable position and a jolt of agony shocked his ribs. He groaned.

"You okay, old man?"

"Could you please start calling me something other than that?"

"Okay, middle-aged man?"

"I don't know if I like you anymore."

Donkey laugh.

* * * * *

Faceless men in black were beating her. One put his hands around her neck. "Tell me where the nuke is," he hissed.

Emma screamed and sat straight up in bed, her heart racing.

Someone touched her. She bellowed in fear and leapt out of the bed. It took a long moment to realize where she was. Cherlenko's bedroom. Her heart sank. Second bloody morning in row she'd woken up there.

Lying in bed was the evil pin-up boy himself—bare amazing pecs and all—seeming very concerned about her.

Rollin. Grief gripped her and her mood plummeted. She pictured his dead body lying in that pitted and cracked parking lot of Motel Hell. Tears welled in her eyes and a sob caught in her throat.

"Emma?" Cherlenko asked. "Are you okay?"

More memories of the day before attacked her. The masked assailants surrounding her. Grabbing her, forcing her into that van. Her body shuddered violently and she held herself.

He got out of bed and took her in his arms. "Easy, easy, it's just me. You're okay, Emma."

The Ambien he'd given her the night before made reality very fuzzy, but she finally realized that she was out of danger. While Rollin was dead, Cherlenko had rescued her. And had held her all night. Even though he was the Devil, she was safe with him. She breathed a sigh of relief.

"Come, get back under the covers." He guided her gently toward his soft, expansive bed.

Trembling, she got back in, and pulled the comforter over her. The warmth felt inviting and soothing. She calmed a bit.

Cherlenko got in beside her and took her into his arms. "Let me take care of you, Emma. I'll make sure nothing bad happens to you ever again. I promise."

She couldn't think about the future. Or "ever again". She could barely deal with the present. She had no idea what Burke's intentions were, and at the moment she didn't care. She had to heal and get strong again. That was her only priority.

They were quiet for a long time; he held her and stroked her head and back. She finally relaxed. His body warmth, the feel of his arms around her and his scent centered her.

After awhile, he pulled away, turned her face toward his and kissed her.

Her brain scrambled a bit more, but heat spread throughout her. The guy could kiss. He tasted great and smelled wonderful. His arms were so buff, they felt like flesh-covered titanium.

She melted into him, grateful for the comfort. Maybe he wasn't such a bad guy. Maybe he was okay. Maybe he could help her.

But he wasn't Rollin. She couldn't feel his heart. Burke had a completely different energy.

And she wasn't in love with him.

Dear God. She loved Rollin.

A knife of pain pierced her heart. Inconvenient timing for that little realization.

Burke pulled away. "Morning, gorgeous."

She forced herself to smile. "Flatterer. You're the one who always looks perfect. I probably look like I washed up on a beach somewhere."

"Uh, no. You're a very beautiful woman, Emma. No matter what time of the day I see you, no matter in what condition, you're always strikingly beautiful."

He might be the Dark Lord, but he sure knew what to say. She hugged him. "Thanks for that."

When she lay back down, he ran a finger down her face. His touch sent chills down her back. "I want you more than I've wanted any other woman, but I'm going to take this slow. I can't have you confused. I'm not interested in a three-way with the memory of Rollin."

Her gut contorted. *Rollin gone.* She fought back the tears and concentrated on keeping up a front for Burke.

"I'm selfish that way. I need to be the only man on your mind. But until then, let me take care of you. Breakfast?"

Her shoulders relaxed and the knot in her stomach eased. Her defenses came down. "Thanks, man. You're the best."

He sent her a wicked grin. "I hope to hear that again very soon."

She grinned back, even though she wasn't sure about sleeping with him. She liked him, but her feelings couldn't compare to the love she had for Rollin.

But with Rollin gone and being thrust into this very scary world, she may have to trust Cherlenko. She had to get the nuke out of her storage unit. And she had to trust someone.

Shit. Great. Making friends with Beelzebub. Had not been on her To Do List.

After breakfast, she was remarkably exhausted and Cherlenko suggested she spend the day in his bed. He hit a remote control and a panel in a wall opened up revealing a large plasma screen. He received every channel in the universe.

She couldn't argue that she needed the rest. She alternately slept, grieved for Rollin and watched *CSI* and *Law and Order* reruns. Thankfully, Cherlenko had retrieved her backpack from Rollin's Jeep. Wearing her own pajamas made her feel more centered.

At around five, Cherlenko came into the room. "How's my girl?" he asked with a bright smile. "Would you like to go out to dinner?"

She stretched and yawned. "Love to, but all I've got are jeans and t-shirts. And a totally wrinkled skirt and top that I wore to Escapade. But unless we're going to a burger joint or a pizza parlor, I'm completely unprepared."

He flashed her a grin, stepped outside the door and brought in several large shopping bags. He walked over and handed her one with *Prada* printed on the side. Freakin' Prada.

She got out of bed and withdrew a darling little black number from the bag. Sleeveless with a dramatic drop in the back, mid-thigh length, fitted and shimmering. "Are you nuts? This is—oh, of course, you'd pick this."

His grin widened. "I think it'll bring out the best of your features. Those long legs, your gorgeous back. Can't wait to see it on you."

"Really cool." She laid it on the bed.

"Something else." He offered her a long, red velvet box.

"Please don't."

"I insist." He pressed the box into her hands. "I treated you horribly. I ruined your birthday and destroyed your entire tasteless collection of Goofy memorabilia."

She arched a brow and pursed her lips. He shot her a teasing smile. Dude got more charming by the minute.

"Open it."

She lifted the box lid and gasped. Inside was a gorgeous necklace unlike anything she'd ever seen. An oval-shaped pendant ringed with diamonds on a gold filigree chain. In the pendant's center were two clear glass panes that created a chamber. Inside the glass chamber were a ton of small, loose diamonds. She shook it this way and that, the diamonds sparkled and shined as they rolled around.

"Wow. This is stupendous. Stunning. I've never seen anything like it."

His grin widened and his eyes grew bright. "You like it."

"I looooove it. Here, help me put it on."

"Gladly. I found it at one of my favorite jewelers, Steiners in San Mateo."

He fastened the necklace, his smooth fingers lightly touching the back of her neck. A jolt of lust rocked her. If things kept progressing like they were, she might just end up in his bed.

"Steiners? Wow. My father or stepfather used to buy my mom jewelry from there. They've got gorgeous stuff."

"Yes, they do. I want to see the necklace with the dress. Here," he said, handing her another bag. "There's some shoes in this and I picked out some undergarments for you as well."

"You think of everything."

He shot her a sexy grin.

Her heart danced a little jig. She wished she were immune to his charm.

She slipped into the bathroom and changed.

The pendant looked dynamite with the dress. He'd guessed her size perfectly. He'd either measured her while she was asleep or knew women's clothing. He'd even got her bra, panties and shoe size right. The black leather pumps weren't just comfortable, they made her legs look great. Well, despite the bruises from her ordeal.

She rummaged through her backpack and found her make-up. After a quick application of mascara, blush and eyeliner, she brushed her hair. She examined herself in the mirror. Not too terrible.

When she emerged from the bathroom, Burke's dark gaze raked over her.

"You look stunning," he said, his voice husky. "Simply stunning."

"My legs look like sale table bananas."

He laughed. "No, they don't. If anyone asks, tell them you fell on your mountain bike."

"Good plan. Better than, hey, I was kidnapped and tortured. Well, almost tortured. Thank God, you got there. Those guys were gonna burn off my toes."

His lusty expression fell. "I'm so sorry about that." He took her in his arms and kissed her forehead. "That shouldn't have happened."

Damn, he smelled so good. She loved the feel of his arms around her.

Rollin's arms felt better.

A pang of grief twisted her heart. No emotion in front of Burke. She gave him a smile.

His deep brown gaze grew troubled and he looked away.

"What?"

When his eyes met hers, there was pain deep within them. "I don't want to ask, but I have to. Yesterday…"

Her back and shoulders stiffened and her stomach tensed. No, she didn't want to talk about it. But he'd saved her. He deserved whatever he wanted to know. "Yeah?"

He ran his hand down her back in a reassuring manner. "Sorry. I have to know. What did you tell them?"

"Nothing."

"You didn't reveal the location of the nuclear weapon?"

Walloped, she stammered something unintelligible. The room swirled around her and her knees went rubbery. He increased his grip on her. She couldn't breathe.

"Emma, don't worry. Of course, I know."

Fighting for mental clarity, she tried to push him away, but he held her firmly.

"Emma, please. No more secrets between us. I have to get that weapon into the right hands. For obvious reasons."

She took a deep breath and finally looked into his eyes. Intense, dark, yet strong and self-assured, there were so many thoughts going through his head it was difficult to distinguish if he was telling the truth. "I want to trust you."

"You can. Where did you find it?"

She steeled herself. No emotion. This was about millions of lives. Not her stupid heart or wacko life. "What are you going to do with it?"

He pulled away and his face went cold. He slipped into his calculating Badass Businessman Mode.

A shiver of fear raced through her. She forced herself to center.

His mouth went ugly. "You still don't trust me."

She straightened her shoulders. "This isn't about me and you. This is way beyond that. This is about the lives of millions of people."

His gaze flared, his jaw twitched and he took a few steps away. His brow wrinkling, he shook his head. "Your honor is why I'm falling for you, I don't know why your stubbornness is making me angry now. Sorry. I've just been out of my mind since that disappeared. You can't imagine my sleepless nights. I'd just gotten control over it when some very bad people attacked my men and murdered them all. I should have been there. No matter. Emma, I've spent two years tracking that weapon. I finally almost get my hands on the device and it vanishes. I have to get it to people who can dismantle it."

She studied him. "You're not going to sell it?"

He sent her a sharp look and seemed hurt. His lip curled slightly. "How little you think of me. Still."

"Look, wait. I'm sorry. You just…seemed like…"

Anger flared in his mahogany gaze and his face went hard. "Someone who would sell a nuclear weapon to a foreign power and put my country at risk?" he demanded. "I'm a decorated veteran. I served this country for fifteen years. I was an officer in the Marines and the Navy and a SEAL. I love this country more than I love life itself."

While a bit afraid of his boiling emotions, she held her ground. "I knew you were in the military, but I thought you turned your back on all that."

"Emma, I know I appear to be some sort of criminal to you, but I assure you, I am just a businessman who cares about this country and has found a different way to serve." His expression was full of righteous indignation.

Could she have misjudged him this much?

He'll do anything, say anything to get his objective.

She studied him and watched the varied emotions flit across his handsome face. The US flag seemed to be waving madly behind him. If this guy wasn't telling the truth, he was the best actor in the world.

"I apologize if I've misjudged you," she finally said.

"So where is it?"

She bit her lip. "This is too big. If I trust you and you're lying to me, I've just put millions of people at risk. If I don't trust you and you're telling me the truth, I've put millions of people at risk. I need time."

His gaze scorched her. "We don't have the time."

"We have to make the time. Give me a few more hours with you. Can we do that? Can we go out and just hang tonight?"

"Is the weapon safe?"

"Yes."

"Where the hell did Adam—" He threw up his hands and paced away, then came back to her. "God, this is frustrating. Okay, at least you know where it is. And it was safe the last time you saw it."

She shrugged. "It wasn't damaged."

"Was it in a black plastic case about six feet long by three feet wide?"

"Yes."

"What did it look like?"

"Like a bomb. Long, white, like four feet long. Had a radioactive symbol on it. But there was no money with it."

"Adam must have taken that elsewhere. He probably didn't even know it was a bomb."

"It was pretty obviously a bomb. But Adam was a bucket of stupid."

A slight smile broke his serious expression. Then his face went stony again and he leveled an intense stare her way. "Will you tell me later?"

"Look, Cherlenko—Burke, all the time we've spent together has been pretty intense. I can't get a consistent sense of who you are. I need that. You just gave me some information I didn't know. I thought you were a criminal overlord. You pretty much admitted that."

"No. I merely didn't correct you. The opinion amused me, I didn't realize how badly it would come back on me."

"Let me get my head around the new you. I'll take you to the weapon after our date, okay? I promise."

He rubbed the back of his neck. He slowly started nodding and angled a glance at her. "This is why I like you. This strength. You have a power about you, woman. You would have let those creeps torture you to death, wouldn't you?"

She looked him in the eye. "Damn straight."

His gaze warmed, he smiled, walked to her and took her in his arms. He kissed her. When he pulled away, he said, "You're one hell of a woman, Emma Holsten. Let's go out. You're right, you don't know me. And I want you to. But please, the second you decide I'm not a threat, you have to tell me where that nuke is. I have to alert my old military contacts. Ever since I mentioned the thing, they've been all over me."

"Okay."

He smiled a sweet, almost loving smile. Admiration shone in his deep brown eyes. He leaned in and kissed her. He tasted nice and his strong sexual energy encompassed her, derailing her mind. She found herself drawing him closer, found her hands on that magnificent ass of his. He deepened the kiss, then stopped.

He laughed. "No. I'm going to take this slowly and seduce you properly. All I can think about is throwing you down and pumping you into the middle of next year."

She sent him a flirty smile. "Sounds like fun."

What was she saying?

His gaze and mouth went hungry. "I am going to blow your mind."

The look in his eye sent a thrill through her. He probably would.

Rollin's face popped into her mind and guilt blistered her insides.

But he was gone and it was all about self-protection now. If she had to mate with the scary alpha male, she'd do it. She needed Burke's protection.

And as guilty as her attraction made her feel, she wanted him.

Once in Burke's Mercedes SUV, they drove toward the Golden Gate Bridge. They'd gone six blocks when his phone rang.

He answered it and frowned and his gaze went dark. "Excuse me, I have to stop on the way. Idiots couldn't tie their shoes without my help."

He drove into a three story parking garage and parked on the second story. "Stay here, I won't be long. Will you be all right?"

"Sure."

"I'll be right back."

Burke locked the car and walked off, unhappy. She hoped she never made him that angry. He still frightened her.

An itch tickled her nose and she sneezed. No purse, no Kleenex. She searched his car for some. None in the glove compartment. She reached under her seat. Something soft. She pulled it out.

A ski mask.

Adrenaline shocked her system, followed shortly by blind fury. The truth hit her like a dump truck of lead bricks unloading on her head. She almost puked.

Cherlenko was behind her kidnapping. He wanted to get information out of her and bond her to him. He wanted to know where she'd been. He wanted her to trust him. And she'd played right into his hands.

The fucker. Atomic hatred blasted through her. How dare he do that to her! She ripped off the necklace, stuck it on the ski mask and left it on his seat. She couldn't get away from there fast enough.

Slamming the door, she ran for the stairs.

Christ, if he was capable of kidnapping her and terrifying her, he was capable of anything. Thank God, she hadn't told him where the nuke was!

Panting with fear, she raced down a flight of stairs and headed for the street.

Coming out of a doorway that led to an adjacent building were Banana and a distinctive bald man. Her heart went into tachycardia as she ditched behind a Lexus.

"Have you found Rollin?" Cherlenko asked.

"Uh…no."

"Don't tell Emma he's alive, okay? She's very fragile right now."

What? Rollin alive? Her mind did a one-eighty and almost spun out of control. The clouds parted and light shined on her heart. She wanted to leap in the air and scream for joy. He was alive!

That jerk Cherlenko lied to her! She was going to kick his ass!

"Why does it matter?" Banana asked.

"Because I think he might have been behind her kidnapping."

Emma almost fainted. Her vision tunneled and her stomach wrenched. She gripped the bumper of the Lexus.

"Rollin? But he's…wow."

"Yes. Some of the men we killed at the warehouse were old contacts of his. I recognized them. I don't want Emma to know. I want her protected right now. She's been through enough."

Emma hung onto the Lexus, reeling. Rollin? Behind her kidnapping?

No, it couldn't be. Had to be Cherlenko.

Her mind blew apart like someone took her brain and stuffed it full of dynamite and detonated it. Vaporized it. Was Cherlenko behind her kidnapping or not?

Rollin wouldn't do that.

Or would he?

Should she catch up with Cherlenko? Maybe he'd taken the ski mask from one of her assailants and stuck it in his pocket or something. Shit.

Now she didn't know what to do.

But Cherlenko *had* lied to her. He hadn't seen Rollin's body at all. Which meant Cherlenko was untrustworthy, which was her answer. He was not a man she should be with or hand a nuke. No matter how cool he'd begun to appear, she wasn't putting her safety and the safety of the world in his hands.

Nor Rollin's.

Rollin. The cologne! In the warehouse! It had been his.

But it hadn't exactly smelled like him. His subtle personal odor was so distinct.

But it had been his cologne.

Had someone worn his cologne to fool her? And how come Cherlenko didn't know for sure if it was Rollin?

The thought of Rollin hurting her made her so sick. She would have pegged Cherlenko as the type to stage a kidnapping, not Rollin.

Which proved one point in spades. It was time to go it alone. First, she needed to find somewhere safe to hide. Second, she needed money. She'd left her wallet at Cherlenko's—so her next stop was home to retrieve her cash stash and emergency credit cards.

She fled out of the parking garage and spotted a BART station a half a block away. Racing for the stairs, she dove down them.

Emma hopped the turnstile and thankfully, no one noticed. She got on a BART train and headed for Millbrae. She'd switch to the regular train there and go on to San Mateo.

She'd never felt more alone, nor more scared. Hugging herself, she forced her mind to calm and focus. She had to keep it together.

As the train pulled out of the station, a thought occurred to her. If Adam found the nuke he would have found the cash as well. If the nuke existed, the money existed. That money would save her ass. She could pay for Lizzie to get back on her feet and afford to disappear in style.

Where would Adam have hidden the cash where she hadn't checked?

Gem's goofy song. So many of them. However, most didn't apply to a location. Which ones were specific to a place?

As the train rocked and the cement walls of the tunnel flashed by, she thought through the litany of songs she used to sing to torment Adam and amuse herself. Sniffy Butt Song. Neutered Pooter. Probably not cat songs. Naked Man Song. Toilet Paper Man—that one originated at the cabins at Lake Shasta, Adam's favorite summer place. Adam loved to fish and waterski. Loved boats.

Would he have hidden the money there? He'd been staying at the resort since he was a kid. He'd brought her up to Lake Shasta a couple times and where she'd come up with the Toilet Paper Man song. Damn, he hated that song. He'd gone to fetch some TP from the resort office and when he returned, she'd tormented him with her spontaneous performance. She laughed at the memory of his pouting face. Adam was fun to tease, she'd give him that.

The BART train slowed and stopped at the San Francisco airport. She wished she had her ID. She wished she could take a plane somewhere. Anywhere.

Yeah, driving up to Lake Shasta sounded better and better. Not only would the cabin be a great place to hide the cash, the trip there would get her out of town. Put some distance between her and the Bay Area.

And she loved the drive up. May help clear her head. She could rest a bit, then come back and dispose of the nuke.

Wait a minute, how would she drive there? In her car? Might as well attach a giant fireworks display to the top of her head. They'd be on her in a second.

And they could trace a car if she rented it.

Shit. She'd have to buy one for cash. There went a big chunk of her stash.

But whatever she had to do, she'd do it. She had to get that money and make sure the nuke got into the right hands. And keep herself safe at the same time.

A hell of a test, but one she'd pass.

If all that abuse at her stepfather's hands had proven one thing to her, she could withstand a lot of shit.

TWELVE

Exhausted and cold in the nasty little Prada dress, Emma snuck through a neighbor's yard and hopped over her back fence, glad there was no one around to witness Emma's Underwear Show. Quietly, she crossed her patio area and peeked around the corner of her cabana at the house.

Her heart thumped so hard, she had trouble breathing.

Lights were on in her bedroom.

Cherlenko paced her room, yelling into his phone. Sounds were too muffled, she couldn't hear what he was saying, but it didn't take a rocket scientist to figure it out.

She retreated and went into her cabana. The wood shelter creaked. A spike of adrenaline buzzed her. She stopped to listen but heard nothing from the house.

She reached behind an outdoor couch, through the cobwebs. A rat scuttled away. She clapped her hand over her mouth to quiet a scream. Shivering, she moved aside a floorboard, feeling around for the small metal Band-Aid box she had hidden there.

The tin was there! But was the cash still inside? Grabbing the box, she pulled it out and flipped open the lid. A huge roll of hundreds plus her mother's credit cards were still there. Hope warmed her. Thank God!

Snapping the top closed, she carefully walked to the back fence.

Outside lights on the back of the house flooded the yard, trapping her in the long shadow behind the cabana.

She nearly choked from terror. Sweat broke out all over her body.

Careful to remain calm, she threw the can over the fence. Clank!

Shit!

"Did you hear that?" came Banana's voice.

"Emma?" Burke called out.

She jumped up on the fence, knocking over a chair, making a hideous amount of noise.

"Emma!"

Loud footfalls.

She threw her leg over and hopped down onto the other side.

"Emma!" Burke called out, sounding frantic. "I didn't kidnap you! It wasn't me! I had that mask in my pocket from rescuing you! Don't run away! I can't protect you! Please, Emma! I care for you!"

She crouched next to the fence, her pulse insane, all her limbs frozen with fear. What should she do?

"Emma!"

Without another thought, she grabbed the money and ran.

"Emma! Wait!"

Her shoes were slowing her, so she kicked them off and kept running.

A loud scrambling of feet on wood came from behind her as someone climbed the fence.

She sprinted to the end of the driveway, hung a right, ran across the street and down a little alley that led to a shortcut to El Camino Real.

From the far end of the alley came a large SUV. Shit!

Panicked, she searched her immediate area for escape. Directly next to her was a gate to a backyard. She kicked it open, jumped inside and shut it, just as the SUV passed.

Blood pounding in her ears, she stood frozen to the spot. The SUV kept going. A second later, footfalls raced past and faded off.

Relief flooded her and she finally breathed.

The lights came on in the backyard. "Who's out there? Identify yourself or I'm calling the police!"

Her heart leapt into her throat. She clutched her chest in fright and spun toward the voice.

Mrs. Lilly, an old family friend. Of course, this was her yard.

Emma let out a long sigh and tried to get her heart to calm. "Mrs. Lilly, it's me, Emma Holsten."

"Emma? What are you doing out there?"

"Looking for my cat," came out of her mouth. "I…locked myself out of the house and my car's in the shop and all this horrible stuff has happened to me. Sorry, I thought I heard my cat's cries, but I think it was…um…someone's dryer vent."

Terrible lies!

"You look freezing in that little dress. Come on in and get warm, honey."

Thank God! "Good idea." Just the break she needed. Burke's men would be back any second.

She went inside and Mrs. Lilly, a diminutive Irish woman in her eighties, shut the door behind her. Her duplex looked like a set for a 1970's film, all harvest gold and avocado green. From the couches to the rugs to the wallpaper, nothing had been changed in years. A time warp.

The place smelled like fresh-baked cinnamon rolls and Mrs. Lilly's perfume. Emma relaxed even more. For some reason, the homey scents made her feel safe.

"It's great to see you, Mrs. Lilly."

Bright blue eyes examined her from behind big pink square-framed glasses. "Would you like some tea dear? I just made some rolls. You must be so cold in that…oh, you've got a rip there." She clucked. "Let me just sew that up for you."

"I really don't have the time, Mrs. Lilly. I'll change when I find a locksmith to get me back inside my home. Could I use your phone? My car's in the shop and I'll need a taxi to go looking for the cat."

"What's that can you're holding?"

"My emergency money I had stashed outside. It was the only thing I could get to. Then I realized the cat was gone and I've been looking all over for her."

"Oh, my dear, you poor little thing. Why don't you take my car? I can't drive anymore. It's just sitting out there. My nephew comes by and runs it for me occasionally. I don't know why I keep it. Probably reminds me of George."

"How sweet. But I couldn't impose."

"Oh, please," the older woman said, waving her liver-spotted, bony hand. "It needs some exercise. Take it for as long as you need it. You and your mother did a lot for me when I broke my leg six years back. I'd love to return the favor."

A free car! Joy erupted inside her and she stifled a relieved giggle. As if the heavens opened up, here was her car! Wow! *Thanks, God!* "You have no idea how much this means to me."

"And aren't you freezing in that shift? Are you sure you don't want me to fix it?"

"Yes and yes."

"I've got an idea." She pointed to a collection of bags sitting in the corner of her tiny living room. "I was going to give those clothes to the Salvation army, maybe you can use them." A hideous orange sweater lay on top.

"Oh, no thanks, I—wait. Yeah, yeah, I'd love to." Emma walked over and began perusing the offerings. She coughed back laughter at some of the garish outfits.

Mrs. Lilly gave a satisfied nod. "Sensible. My daughter's too good for my old cast offs. They may be a bit dated, but they've still got a lot of life left in them. I don't understand all this needless waste of time on fashion. Clothes are clothes."

"I couldn't agree more."

The only thing that fit was a high-water lime green pantsuit. Emma topped it off with a raspberry-colored sweater and white orthopedic shoes. And, just her luck, in one bag she found a gray bubble wig and a pair of old cat-eye glasses.

Mrs. Lilly pointed to the wig. "You're taking that? That was from my cancer."

"A friend is in a play and can use it."

"Well, good. Glad someone can use that stuff."

After thanking her old friend again, she went out into Mrs. Lilly's garage and knocked the lenses out of her glasses. She slipped the old frames on, got into Mrs. Lilly's powder blue 1978 Buick Regal—with forty thousand original miles—put on the bubble wig and headed for the freeway.

Emma came to the intersection for El Camino Real and hit a red light. In the McDonald's parking lot to her right sat a big dark SUV. She recognized the large square jaw and long blond hair of Banana in the driver's seat.

Adrenaline slammed her body and her heart jumped to light speed.

Act old!

Hunching over, she squinted and leaned closer to the window.

She turned onto El Camino very slowly, drifted into the left lane, then overcorrected sharply back into the right lane. Staring into her rear view mirror, her throat tightened. She didn't take a full breath until she hit Highway 92.

No one followed her.

As soon as she was clear of San Mateo, she let out a yelp of glee.

Thank you, Mrs. Lilly!

* * * * *

"Emma *what*? Why?" Rollin demanded, leaping out of bed. Pain shot through his cracked ribs, he held his side. Pinning the phone to his ear with his shoulder, he turned off the TV.

"Banana said that Burke told him she found a ski mask in his car and assumed he'd been the one behind the kidnapping," Bobby said in a rush. "Burke said he'd picked it up at the warehouse when he saved her and stuck the thing in his pocket. Then he'd dumped it in his car. When she found it, she took off. They went to her house, almost caught her, but somehow she escaped. Burke's crazy upset right now and has everyone out looking for her."

"He must be lying to Banana," Rollin said, kicking some dirty jeans out of his path.

"I don't know. Maybe."

"Fuck! I should have gone straight over there! I left a million messages on her cell."

"Her phone was still in the Jeep when we recovered it," Bobby reported. "I have it here, but the battery's dead." Slurping came over the receiver.

"Shit! Of course! I should have gone right to Burke's after seeing the doc. I should never have listened to that quack! God, she has no idea where I live. I hope she's trying to find me."

"Um, I don't think so. She thinks you're dead."

Rollin's head nearly blew off his shoulders. "*What?* Dead? She thinks I'm *dead*?"

"Yeah. Banana said Burke suspected you of the kidnapping and—"

Rollin stopped mid-stride. "Wait. Back the hell up there. I was behind the *what*?"

"Burke thinks that you were behind the kidnapping," Bobby enunciated carefully. "And he didn't want Emma to know because she's too fragile to handle it. He said he wanted Emma to think you were dead to protect her."

Rollin's jaw dropped to his knees. A rocket of urgency blasted off inside him. He had to get to her! If she thought he was dead, who knows what she'd do? "What the hell? Burke thinks that? He's not behind this whole thing? But he's gotta be," he said with a wild gesture.

"Don't know," Bobby said, crunching.

He stormed across the hardwood floor of his bedroom. "So who the fuck kidnapped us? This is crazy. Damn it!" He kicked a boot and sent it flying across the room. "If I'd gone over there as soon as I left the doc's, none of this would have happened! Shit!"

"You better calm down, old man. Doc wouldn't have sent you home without a good reason."

Rollin barely heard a word. "Burke has to be working Banana," he said, rubbing his throbbing forehead. "He's gotta be. He wanted Emma's information and to get her to trust him. We have to assume from here on out that anything Banana says is what Burke wants us to think. Shit, we have to find Emma and now."

"Already on it and already got a hit," Bobby reported, a smile in his voice.

God Bless that kid! "So?"

"On a gas card in Dolly Holsten's name just a few minutes ago in Pinole. Emma's headed out of the Bay Area on 80. Only places she went outside the Bay Area in the last few years were Lake Shasta and Reno. Reno to gamble and Lake Shasta for boating. She and Adam rented a cabin there. Place is remote and Adam went there within the last month of his life. He knew the place and he had the time to hide the money there."

Rollin went to his dresser and pulled out a clean pair of jeans. "I'm on my way."

"No," Bobby replied firmly. "You need to rest. Doctor's orders. Let me send someone else."

"I'll rest on the drive up."

"Rollin, it's fucking eleven at night. Go in the morning."

"I'll go tonight and stop in Redding at a motel. Will that make you feel better?"

"No. You're on Vicodin, aren't you?"

He toed the bottom of the dresser. "Maybe."

"Rollin!"

He made a cell phone static noise. "Uh…you're breaking up…I can't hear you…"

"Goddamn you, old man!"

"I told you to stop calling me that." He quickly hung up, tossed his phone onto his bed and headed for the shower.

The phone rang as soon as he turned on the water.

* * * * *

At two the next afternoon, his back killing him, his ribs sore as hell, Rollin left Lakehead, gloomy and exhausted. According to Bobby, Dolly Holsten's gas card had been used in Lakehead at one-thirty the morning before. But the owner of the resort where Emma had stayed with Adam hadn't seen her.

However, the owner/manager reported that a pair of large men wearing suits and sunglasses had been there two weeks before asking questions about Adam Ramsay.

The tall, lanky resort owner also revealed that a weird old lady had been there earlier in the day and had asked to tour Cabin Two. Which just so happened to be where Adam Ramsay stayed each year. The old woman had explained that the cabin was where she'd had her last anniversary with her husband, that he'd passed away and she'd wanted a few minutes of quiet time there to remember him.

Sounded phony as hell.

What the hell were they after? Rollin wished Emma had trusted him.

After the resort, he'd checked every other recreational facility and motel in the area, but came up with nil.

His gut burning with frustration, he finally gave up and drove to Redding and stopped at a Raley's for some water, snacks and ibuprofen.

He sat in his SUV, munching on some Pringles, wondering where the hell Emma was.

An old lady wearing bright colors pushed a cart up to an old Buick Regal parked across from him. Should he get out and help her? With just one bag of groceries, she was probably fine.

The old woman loaded the bag, then slammed the trunk. Suddenly, she erupted in a stream of expletives and shook her hand violently. Sounded familiar and not very old.

On second look, something was off about the woman. Her face wasn't lined. And there were no lenses in her glasses.

She was in disguise. And not a great one.

His heart rate kicked up and his body readied for trouble. She could be following him. Working for Burke. Or whoever else might be after them.

Or maybe she was the old lady who'd visited the resort that morning!

He'd find out.

Rollin stepped out of the Jeep, his hand on his pistol. "Excuse me, ma'am, can I help you?" he asked in his most cordial tone.

The woman looked like he'd hit her. She gasped and blinked and stared at him with her mouth hanging open.

Then she took off running for the street. Talk about a dead giveaway. She sprinted away from him like a track star.

He gave chase. His ribs and injuries slowed him, but finally, he got near enough to grab her.

"Let me go you asshole!" She fought him like a wild woman. Attacking him, she slapped his face and punched his gut.

Excruciating pain shot through his stomach.

"You kidnapped me, you jerk! You pig! You lied to me!"

Emma. It was Emma!

His heart surged with joy. He'd found her! And she was okay! Dressed freaky, but okay. "Emma? It's me, Rollin."

"I know, that's why I'm hitting you!"

He grabbed her wrists and got her in a quick hold. "Stop, Emma. I didn't kidnap you. I wasn't behind it. They almost killed me."

"So you say, you big jerk!"

He pushed away from her and lifted up his shirt to show her his injuries. "Would I have done this to myself?"

She gasped, her eyes went wide and she put her hands to her mouth.

"No, I wouldn't have," he answered for her.

"Is there a problem here?" came a deep voice from beside Rollin. He looked up into the angry face of a very tall cowboy. All squared shoulders and balled fists.

Emma stepped forward, her hands up. "No, but thanks so much for your concern. I'm fine."

The cowboy gave Emma a small smile. "Looked like you were holding your own, but I wanted to make sure." With a blistering glare at Rollin, the large man turned and walked away.

As soon as the man was out of hearing distance, Rollin swung on her. "I was kidnapped, too. And beat to shit. Why the hell did you think I did it?"

She gestured around vaguely, seeming completely confused. "I overheard Cherlenko say you kidnapped me. And I smelled your cologne. Granted, it didn't exactly smell like you, but someone was wearing your cologne and a hell of a lot of it."

His gut tightened and his back stiffened, causing a new wave of pain to rip through his side. "Ow. My cologne? Who set me up for this? And what the hell is it about? It's not just the money."

She bit her lip and her brow wrinkled. "Now I don't know what to think."

He examined her, caught between wanting to kiss her and laugh. She looked like his grandmother with the big round hairdo and glasses. Not to mention the orthopedic shoes. Gross. "Are you okay? Physically, I mean?"

"Yeah. Tired, but I'm okay."

"Bastards. Watching them grab you was one of the single worst moments of my life. I was so glad Burke got you out of there. Unless he did it. I'm—"

"I'm not sure. I mean, I thought he did until I overheard him. After I found that ski mask—"

"I heard about it. Burke's goin' nuts looking for you."

Her face went hard. "Yeah, I know. I had to go to my house for some money and almost got caught by him and Banana."

"He fell for you. He thinks he's in love."

She shuddered and wrapped her arms around herself. "That's not good."

Warmth spread through him. The best reaction he could have hoped for. She didn't love Burke back and she wasn't caught in his spell. Thank God, she was a smart woman. Actually, he'd never known any woman who could stand up to Burke. Emma was the first.

But no one could be that strong. Her beautiful face looked drawn and there were bags under her green eyes, but it was the haunted look behind her gaze that made his gut hurt. He wanted to throw his arms around her and kiss all her worries away. She'd withstood more trauma in the last week than most people endured in a lifetime. He had to get her somewhere safe where he could take care of her.

"Emma, it sucks what happened to you. You have to be wiped."

"I am."

Rollin gave a quick check of the parking lot. People coming and going with grocery carts, but nothing seemed out of the ordinary. Still, he needed to get Emma back to the Bay Area and quickly. "We have to get you somewhere to rest." He turned back to her and her outfit stopped him. "And I have to get you out of that get-up. It's creepin' me out here. I still want you and you're wearing an mmmmm lovely green pantsuit." He burst out laughing. "Damn, girl, where did you get that?"

"Miss Lilly, a neighbor. I'll tell you all about it." She looked around the area like someone was about to jump out and kill her. "I don't feel safe talking to you in the open like this." Her attention went to his Jeep. "Let's go talk in your car, okay?"

"Good."

And then she sent him an intense stare as if she were trying to determine if he posed a threat to her. She held up her hand. "Wait a sec, okay. I want to trust you, but I'm afraid to."

"I won't hurt you, Emma. I couldn't." Fucking Burke! Filled her head full of all kinds of crap. He wanted to punch his old buddy. Hard. Several times. Until he bled.

She examined him for a moment, then looked away. Her brow furrowed and she worked her mouth. Closing her eyes, she took a deep breath. She nodded and her expression went neutral. "Okay," she said, opening her eyes. "My gut is telling me to trust you. So I will." Her gaze sharpened and she pointed at him. "But if you fuck with me, I'll cut your balls off."

He chuckled. "I would expect no less."

Still on the wary side, she followed him back to his car.

They climbed up into his Jeep and rolled down their windows.

Rollin turned to her. "Emma, I didn't kidnap you. I'd never do anything like that to you. I couldn't."

She rubbed her forehead and sighed. "Everything's so messed up and Burke screwed my head up so good, I can't tell what's going on. Give me a minute here. I mean, I thought you were dead, I'm all cryin'—"

His heart lifted and he took in a short breath. "You were crying?"

"Yes. Of course." Her green eyes warmed and she smiled.

Happiness powered through him, giving him a half-shaft. She liked him!

God, he hoped he could be with her. Feeling her gorgeous breasts, sliding inside her. He wanted her so much it hurt. He'd never been this crazy about a woman.

"…then I overhear him say that you were behind it. And with your cologne…how the hell am I supposed to know what's going on?"

"You're not. I'm sorry."

"I'm sorry, too." She frowned. "I can't tell if being with you is going to protect me or get me killed." Then she softened and gave him a smile. "But I'm really glad you didn't kidnap me. I really like you."

I love you. All of you. All of me loves all of you.

"I like you too," he said, trying for a reasonable tone, inwardly thrilled he didn't blurt out that he loved her. "Are you okay? How are you, really? I've been worried."

"Oh, I'm damaged. But I'll recover. I'm tough."

His body went hard and his jaw clamped. "Who hurt you? What kind of damage?"

"No, not physical damage. Mental damage. But I'll be fine."

"Sure you will. But we all have limits." He took the chance, leaned over and gripped her leg, hoping he seemed reassuring and not like he was coming on to her. "Jeez, Emma. I want to take you to a private island and take care of you. Make things normal for you."

She settled down into the seat and didn't pull away. Did she still want him?

Her gaze went to the dashboard. Her expression still pained, she nodded. "Sounds heavenly."

Rollin took her by the hand. "Don't worry, Emma. Burke's probably given you all kinds of bullshit about me and my abilities. But I can take care of you and I will."

She nodded, but bit her lip. "It's certainly more in Burke's character than yours to set up a phony kidnapping to get me to trust him. You've been the most honest with me by far."

His insides contracted to the point of pain. Honest. Hardly. In no way did he want to admit what he'd done to her, but he had to. If their relationship was to work, he had to come clean. And he wanted a future with this woman. More than anything.

His muscles tensed solid and he let go of her hand. "Speaking of honesty, before we go any further, I have to level with you. I've held back some stuff from you. Stuff that won't make me look good. But I want to tell you now. Because I'm in love with you."

Fear gripped his belly, he nearly screamed.

Shit! How the hell did that slip out?

She didn't scream or choke or look angry. She seemed stunned, but not displeased.

Quick! Keep talking to smooth over your stupid admission! "I really knew I loved you when I saw you being dragged into that van. But you need to know some stuff about me, what I've done to you."

Some of the light went out of her eyes and her mouth went hard. "To me?"

Just that look on her face made him want to slam his head on the steering wheel. "Yes."

She twisted her mouth to the side. "Now you're worrying me."

"I didn't know who you were. I gotta tell you, Adam Ramsay isn't really high up on anyone's lists—"

She gave a slight nod. "Guilt by association."

"Sorry."

"So what did you do?" She sent him a dark glare. "You planted the fucking murder evidence on me, didn't you?"

Her words hit him like a right cross from a professional boxer. He could only stammer.

Her green gaze reddened with fury. "You did, didn't you?"

He wished he had something to beat himself with. "And I am really sorry I did. And I'm so glad you found the baseball bat."

She narrowed her eyes at him, but she didn't seem as angry as she should be. "I want to punch you, but you're already so hurt, it would be redundant."

Rollin gave a short barking laugh. "You couldn't possibly hurt me as much as I'm beating myself over it. When I started watching you and listening to you, I knew you were cool and that I'd blown it. But over the past few weeks, it's been torturing me. That's why I had to tell you. And…"

"There's more?" She gaped at him.

He hated this. His stomach burned like he'd swallowed a case of hot sauce. "I brought Adam to Cherlenko that day."

Her face paled. She aged ten years. "You mean the day—holy shit. You? Did you know what they'd do to him?"

His face went hot with shame and he picked at his leather steering wheel cover. "Didn't expect them to frighten him to death. I tried to help him. But fuckin' Adam was such an asshole. I told him to just give up what he knew. That the guys knew he was hiding something. I tried to reason with him. But God, what a prick. He started puffing up his chest and threatening me, bragging about all his Mafia contacts, I just…" He shrugged.

"He pissed you off," she finished.

"Big time."

She snorted and let out a long breath. "Sounds like him. Like I said, a whole dirigible of stupid. Never knew when to keep his mouth shut." She shook her head.

"I felt terrible. I thought Burke would just scare him some."

"He did that all right."

"Did you know Adam had a heart condition?"

"If I had I would have been following him around trying to scare him all the time," she said with a smirk.

He broke up and the tension eased from his belly. Thank God, she still had her sense of humor. "I'm sorry, Emma."

She didn't look that mad. Did she love him, too? She'd said she'd cried over him. Maybe she did love him!

Emma shot him a glare. "You should be." Her anger faded a bit. "But thanks for telling me. I'm not happy with you, but…" She waved her long slender hand. "I'll get over it. So can we get some food? I'm starving." Most of the anger left her face.

He let out a sigh. She wasn't ordering him to leave. She wasn't punching him. She looked more sad than anything, which made his gut feel like it got caught in his Harley's drive belt, but at least she wasn't splitting.

Rollin nodded at Emma's outfit and sent her a crooked half-smile. "Yeah, but I don't think I can eat with you in that get-up."

"Too bad. This is my clever disguise. Besides, I don't have anything else to wear but a ripped up million-dollar Prada dress."

"That would be a hell of an improvement."

"Burke bought it for me."

"You know, I think green might be your color."

She chuckled and the sparkle returned to her emerald eyes.

Then her expression became intense. Emma opened her mouth, then closed it. She stared at her lap and pursed her lips.

His stomach tensed. She was about to order him out of her life. She'd come to her senses and realized she couldn't be with someone who'd done such horrible shit to her. "What?"

Emma twisted her full lips in a half-pout and looked out the window. "Nothing." She snapped back to him. "Okay, I just have to clarify this. Do you really love me? Did you say that?"

"Uh-huh," he said, putting the key in the ignition.

"You do…" Her dark brows knitted and she gave him a small frown.

She didn't believe him.

He laughed. "What? I didn't say it right? I didn't bring my violin section with me? Oh, Emma," he said in a falsetto, "how I love thee." He batted his eyelashes. Then he broke his comic expression and shot her a grin. "How was I supposed to say it?"

She laughed, her gaze twinkling, warming his heart and dick. "I don't know. You seemed sort of casual about it."

"I'm very comfortable with my emotions." *And I couldn't shut my mouth in time.*

"Apparently."

In his mind, her costume disappeared and he saw his darling Emma. Goosebumps raised on his arms. His body shivered with lust and an electric pulse went through his cock. God, she was so beautiful. Even in the granny outfit. Her turned-up nose, that strong, yet feminine jaw, those full, luscious lips. He couldn't wait to get her out of the wig. And out of all her clothes…

Rollin caught her hand. "I know you're too confused to give any kind of a response. And I don't expect one. I just wanted you to know."

She nodded and blinked rapidly, taking in the information. A slow smile grew on her lovely face, but then her brow furrowed. She finally shrugged. "You're right, I can't process this right now. Let's go eat."

Pulling her close, he kissed her. Bubble wig, strange glasses, green polyester Grandma clothes and all.

Her sweet taste and the feel of her in his arms sent him flying. His whole body cried out for her.

After a moment, she swooned in his arms and he gripped her tighter.

And then she came alive. Gripping his head, she kissed him back hard.

Hot energy flooded him and his heart burst open with love for her. He crushed her in a hug. He'd been worried he'd never kiss her again. He never wanted to let go. He needed her next to him, with him forever.

When was the last time he felt like this? With his ex-wife when they first met, eighteen years before.

But the connection with Emma seemed even more powerful. He wanted to make her part of him. Take her into his soul and keep her there.

And fuck her every which way for years on end.

They pulled apart and grinned at each other.

A young couple stood at the car across from them, staring.

"Yeah, Grandma, it's great to see you, too," he said in a loud, bright tone.

Emma broke out in belly laughs.

Damn, he loved her.

THIRTEEN

Emma watched Rollin as he drove them to a nearby steakhouse. Dude was so strong and centered. The lines on his face told her he'd carried and continued to carry heavy loads, but with ability, grace and courage.

And he was such a dish. His intense dark brown eyes, his crooked nose, his cut cheekbones and prominent jaw. That cool little soul patch. So handsome, so cool, so sweet.

But what gave him the edge over any other man she'd been with, by far, was his emotional availability. When he kissed her it felt like he was kissing her soul.

And then there was that other shit to contend with. The murder evidence. Aiding in the death of her ex-husband. Even though the latter was gift to mankind.

She had no idea how to sort out the two warring concepts.

Rollin signaled for a left and turned into the parking lot for Cattlemen's. Grinning at her, he said, "Ready for some food?" He glanced over and winked at her.

A little rush of joy zipped through her. Damn, she loved him.

"Past ready." She wanted to hug him and kiss him and jump in bed with him.

Rollin's behind the kidnapping.

And run the other way as fast as she could.

Emma perused her menu at the old west themed restaurant, so hungry, she couldn't begin to make a choice.

Out of the corner of her eye, she noticed Rollin pursing his lips at her. "I can't believe I kissed you in that outfit. Even though Burke bought you that dress, I could handle a ripped black dress better than this, *Grandma*."

"Shush. I want to get the senior discount on this steak. Look, I'll save five bucks."

"I'm paying."

"So you'll save five bucks."

"I'll pay you five bucks just to get out of that outfit."

"Tough beans. Besides, the dress is too ripped."

"After we leave here, we're headed straight to a mall."

The waitress came by and Emma ordered a steak in character, old lady voice and all. Terrible acting, but the waitress didn't give her a second glance.

"So how tough are your steaks, dearie?" Emma said, suddenly feeling emboldened. "Worried about my teeth, you know?"

Rollin stifled a laugh.

"They cut like butter. No worries, ma'am."

"Oh, good. Now make sure I get extra vegetables. I have to make sure I get my fiber."

The waitress nodded absently. "Extra veggies."

"My son doesn't need as many veggies, he's regular," Emma added.

Rollin turned bright red and kicked her under the table.

"What, honey?" Emma patted his arm. "Now don't get embarrassed, I'm sure the waitress has heard it all before." She turned to the fifty-something blond. "My son, he thinks he's the only boy in the universe with a talky mother."

"You remind me of my mother," the waitress said with a quirk of her lips.

"Oh? Isn't that nice. I'll bet she's a wonderful person."

"I don't know, I haven't seen her in years," the waitress reported in a flat tone, her gaze cold. "I'll be back with your drinks."

When the waitress was out of earshot, Rollin exploded with laughter.

"I don't think she liked me," Emma said with mock upset.

Rollin wiped the tears from his eyes. "Stop making me laugh. My ribs are killing me. You are terrible. Why haven't I seen this side of you?"

"I had to wait until after you told me you loved me."

He cracked up even more. "You are a very bad woman. Holy hell, I hurt."

"Teach you to laugh at your mother."

Soon, their waitress brought them steaming platters of steaks, baked potatoes and fresh sautéed vegetables. She practically threw Emma's steak at her. Rollin coughed to cover his laughter.

The food looked enticing. The aroma intoxicated her and made her salivate. Seemed like years since she'd eaten.

Emma took a bite and waited for Rollin to notice her. Then she faked losing her teeth and pantomimed putting them back in.

He busted up, then jabbed a finger her way and sent her a fiery stare. "As soon as we get out of here, I'm getting you out of that costume. Christ, I can barely eat."

"I'm getting even with you for screwing with me." Her gut tightened. Why had she brought that up? "I shouldn't joke, you almost got me thrown in jail for life."

All humor left his face, he looked her dead in the eye and put his large, warm hand over hers. "Emma, I would have made sure you were cleared. The people I send to jail belong there. I thought you were in on it with Adam. I had no idea who you were." The spark deep within his dark eyes radiated honesty.

Seemed like even her bones relaxed. This guy was rock solid and man enough to own up to his mistakes. Another first in her life. She squeezed his hand. "I can see how you'd think that way. I mean, I'm still working through it. But I can tell that you're telling me the truth."

"I am."

"It'll take me some time here, but I'll get over what you did. Still, this is the strangest relationship I've ever had with a man."

"It'll get a lot more normal when this is all over," he said with a confident nod.

He assumed they'd be together. While she agreed, she still had to wade through all his ugly information.

She knew he'd been hiding something from her. Wasn't a complete surprise, in retrospect.

Still, she should be angrier. She should be furious. Certainly, she was angry. But Rollin made so much sense. He wasn't spinning a tale to manipulate her, he simply told her the truth. And it was hard to get angry at that.

And it was certainly hard to stay mad at him when she wanted to screw him so badly it took all her strength not to leap across the table and attack him. Ever since they'd sat down, she'd had a whole subprogram going on inside her head devoted solely to a prolonged sex session with Rollin including every position imaginable.

WARNING! Your track record with dead sexy creatures is abysmal!

Shut up, voice, I have to trust somebody. And I pick Rollin.

Good choice. A proven liar.

Not listening!

Rollin escorted Emma out to the parking lot and opened her door for her. He couldn't wait to get her out of that old lady outfit. He wanted his hot girlfriend back.

Girlfriend. A rush of lust and love powered through him and he went hard. Damn, was this a dream or what? A woman like Emma as his girl? Life couldn't get better than that.

Rollin scanned his immediate area. Clear. He closed Emma's door and climbed in the driver's side. "We'll go back and move Miss Lilly's car to a side street so she won't get towed. I'll send someone to pick up the car and deliver it back to her."

"Thanks."

Emma smiled at him, warming his whole body. Her sweet oval-shaped face. Those amazing green eyes of hers. Her full lips. He couldn't wait to get her alone in a motel room.

He left the steakhouse parking lot and headed back to Raley's.

Crash! His heart rate tripled, Rollin smashed against his door and Emma flew toward him. Someone had rammed into the driver's side of the Jeep!

Rollin slammed on the gas and launched them forward. He checked his mirror. A large, dark SUV rode inches behind him.

His body primed for action, Rollin slipped into Warrior Mode. Everything slowed down. The Jeep's engine quieted. Red mini-van in front of him. A guy getting into his truck by the side of the road. A crow flying low over the road. A side street coming up on the right.

Perfect choice.

"Hold on, I'm getting us out of here!" he yelled at Emma.

The SUV charged them.

"Watch out!" she cried.

Smash! The black SUV clipped the back of his Jeep and suddenly they were spinning. Up close and personal view of the front of the pursuing SUV with two dudes in sunglasses, a big one and a small one. And then they were facing a red Bug with a screaming woman driving, then a light pole before coming full circle.

Rollin's side window exploded, glass sprayed the interior of the car and a searing line of fire blazed his scalp. He nearly had a heart attack. Shit! Bullet missed killing him by a fuckin' quarter-inch!

"Emma! Get down!" He grabbed her head and shoved her to the seat.

Sweat pouring down his neck, he put the gas pedal to the floor. The tires squealed and the Jeep sped forward. Almost past a side street, he yanked the wheel to the right.

The back of the Jeep slid out, but Rollin maintained control and hit the street at a good clip.

The SUV roared after them, its engine so loud it sounded like a jet.

His first choice for escape gone, Rollin quickly downloaded several alternate routes. He knew Redding, thankfully, and had lived there once upon a time.

"Emma! Reach under the seat, there's a pistol under there!"

She pulled out his shiny silver Kimber 1911. "Got it. Is this a picture of *The Punisher* on the grip?"

"Yeah, love *The Punisher*. Know how to shoot?"

"No, but I'm pretty motivated to learn! Holy crap, you're bleeding!"

"I'm fine it just grazed—"

A loud crash. The Jeep hurtled forward. Rollin's head slammed hard back against the headrest.

The Jeep fishtailed, but he quickly got control and accelerated.

Rollin hit the button for the secret panel in his dashboard. A hidden door popped open, revealing a cache of ammo and more guns. He shuffled through but couldn't find his armor-piercing bullets. Shit! He grabbed a couple clips of regular ammo and handed them to Emma.

He barked out instructions on loading the magazine into the chamber. "Shoot those assholes, Emma!"

She hung out the window, her wig flew off, and she fired at the SUV. Her hands jerked back from the kick.

Rollin checked his rearview. She'd hit the windshield, but only small spider webs appeared on it. Bullet-proof glass. Of course. But damn, she'd hit her target on the first shot with a gun? Amazing! "Aim for the engine!"

"I was!"

The SUV got bigger in their rear view. A guy leaned out of the window and fired. Rollin's back window exploded. He flinched and another injection of fear blasted through him. Emma screamed and shot her gun, her hands tipping back from the force.

"Watch it, I'm taking this next corner!" Rollin yelled.

He had to get all this shooting away from as many people as he could. He headed for an industrial area, hoping he could lose the assailants there.

More gun blasts. Bullets pounded into the metal body of his Jeep.

Rollin flashed on Iraq. Inside a Humvee, bombs exploding. Ceaseless gunfire. Sand everywhere, unbearable heat, guys screaming. Oceans of blood.

"You sons-a-bitches!" Emma bellowed, wrenching him back to the present. "Take this!" She fired off the gun, emptying the magazine.

Awesome woman!

"Ow!" she exclaimed, getting back in the car.

"Are you hurt?" He quickly examined her. No blood.

"No." She reached for another magazine. "The kickback hurts, this gun is a monster. Watch out!" She pointed frantically out the front window.

A huge semi pulled out of an industrial yard, directly in Rollin's path. Another super injection of adrenaline dumped into his system. "Hold on!"

He hit the brakes. The Jeep went into a spin and the back just barely missed the semi. Rollin stepped on the gas and took off down the street.

Tires screeched. The SUV braked and spun too late and smashed into the semi with the passenger side of the vehicle.

Unfortunately, the SUV wasn't very damaged. With the semi's horn blasting, the SUV pulled away and came after them.

Emma slipped in another magazine, turned around and fired at the SUV through the back of the Jeep, deafening him. His ears rang. The assholes fired back.

Rollin's side mirror shattered. His heart rate jumped and he jerked away from the window.

Midway down the block, he hung a left and skidded into a giant parking lot for a group of industrial businesses and warehouses. He knew he couldn't outrun the fuckers and the lot was filled with SUVs, trucks and Jeeps. Tons of places to hide.

Emma loaded another magazine into the chamber of the pistol.

"Don't, too many people around. I'm gonna hide and ambush the assholes!"

She held the silver 1911 in her lap. Her sweet face pale, her dark hair stuck to her sweaty brow, she managed a weak smile. “Good. Annie Oakley I am not.”

Rollin raced down the long lines of parked cars, turned a corner, tires squealing, and circled a warehouse, looking for a good place to park. He came around the far side of the long metal building and saw his opportunity. He dove into a parking place between two large vans. He turned off the car and took his foot off the brake. “Get down!”

He ditched down into the seat, nearly smacking his head on Emma’s.

The SUV roared by them.

“They’re gonna be back in two seconds. Get out and hide, Emma. Keep the gun with you. I’ll get rid of these dickheads.”

“Are you gonna be okay?”

The frantic worry on her oval-shaped face tweaked his heart. He sent her a grin. “You bet, babe. Now hide!”

She leapt out of the car, hunched down and disappeared.

His body fired up to maximum war mode, his heart beat a hard fast rhythm. He withdrew a partial arsenal from the special compartment in his dashboard. Two more Kimbers and a Lugar, plus all the loaded magazines he had, about ten. But where the hell were his armor-piercing bullets? Sloppy. Hopefully, the mistake wouldn’t cost him.

Rollin opened his door, dropped to the pavement and shut it. His limbs and belly buzzing like he’d shot up straight caffeine, he moved into the thin strip between the two rows of parked cars and searched for signs of the SUV.

Within about a second, the dark SUV with the spiderwebs in the windshield returned, moving slowly through the lot. His breathing ragged, Rollin waited for it to pass. Keeping low, he slipped out behind the vehicle.

Right as he reached it, the SUV gunned the engine and raced away. He checked to see where they were headed.

Emma, now a bright green dot, sprinted for a building.

Fear engulfed him, making his body even harder. He'd told her to hide! Damn it!

He tore off after her.

But why hadn't the gunmen stopped and shot at him?

The SUV's brake lights came on. A guy leapt out of the vehicle and aimed a gun at him.

Question answered.

His heart thumping so hard his whole body pulsed, Rollin dove for cover behind a white Taurus.

A gunshot and a simultaneous *pank* sound came from the Taurus. He flinched and covered his head. Paint chips flew everywhere. The shot echoed through the parking lot.

Men yelled from the building nearest to him.

Crouching low next to the Taurus, he scrambled for the median, then dove behind another car.

He rose and peered through the windows of a red sedan.

The assailant—he looked familiar—scanned the area for him. Tall and skinny, he had gray hair, a black mustache and goatee. Kent Cooley, a mercenary he'd worked with in Iraq. Not good. Guy was ruthless.

And unfortunately, no way to know who hired him. The man worked for anyone who paid him enough. Kent was on no one's side but his own. Hopefully, Zane could find out who'd hired him. Better yet, maybe Rollin could wound the guy and get him to talk.

The other assailant must be Yori Blevnakov. Another sadistic, malicious jerk. The two often worked together. There'd been rumors about them being a gay couple, but no one in their right mind would dare to ask.

"Rollin!" Kent called out. "How long we gonna play this game? And how long you think we've got before the police arrive?"

Rollin didn't answer, he moved quickly away. He'd double back and ambush the asshole.

Blam! Ping! He dove to the ground. A bullet hole in a gold Malibu appeared no more than a few inches above his head.

Rollin's heartbeat wild, he stayed down and watched for Kent's feet.

About three cars away, Kent dropped on his side on the asphalt and fired at him from under the car.

On pure instinct, Rollin fired back while scrambling for cover.

If Kent was working with Yori, Emma didn't stand a chance. Rollin had little time left.

Hunching low, he darted behind a large van. A loose brick sat near a back tire.

He stood behind one of the wheels to hide his feet and grabbed the brick.

Footfalls approached him. He threw the brick as far as he could. The hard object hit a truck and made a loud *clank*. Rollin lunged out.

The gunman was no more than six feet from him, aiming toward the sound.

As Kent saw him out of his peripheral vision and swung toward him, Rollin fired.

Kent yelled, clamped his hand to his neck and reeled back. Blood splattered his shirt and arm, and trickled out from beneath his fingers. But he managed to keep control of his gun and fired back.

A bullet zinged by Rollin's ear. He aimed and fired his Kimber just as Kent's eyes went unfocussed, the gun dropped from his hand and he crumpled to the ground, still holding a bloody hand to his neck. His face ghost-white, a red stain seeped out from his shoulder soaking his light blue collared shirt.

Rollin rushed him and grabbed his gun. He stepped on his chest with his booted foot. "Who hired you?"

Blood running out of his mouth, Kent choked, groaned, then laughed. "Fuck you, Hanson."

Fury fueled his limbs and Rollin stomped on him as hard as he could.

Kent yelled, then moaned in a rasp, "Not gonna work. I'm gonna die and I'm not telling you anything."

"What the hell does it matter?"

"I want you to die. If I tell you, you'll protect yourself from him."

Him.

"Tell me and I won't kill your boyfriend."

"You're no match for Yori."

"Who the hell hired you to kill me and kidnap Emma?" Rollin demanded, kicking him. "Was it Burke?"

Kent frowned through his grimace of pain. "Burke? I thought he was your buddy buddy." He coughed, spraying blood on his shirt.

"Well then who? Who fucking hired you? Was it Frank Bortolli?"

Rollin was so focused on Kent's face, he almost missed the movement.

Kent pulled out a gun from his jacket and Rollin ducked just before he fired.

Without a thought, Rollin nailed Kent in the center of his forehead with his 45 ACP. Blood and brains sprayed the area and what was left of Kent's head slammed against the pavement. His dark eyes went vacant and his breathing stopped.

Rollin let out a sigh of relief, but nausea roiled his gut. His mouth filled with bitterness. He hated killing. Even assholes. And he wished he could have kept Kent alive just a bit longer. "Shit!" Well, one question answered. Burke hadn't hired them.

Which comforted him and scared him all at the same time.

Maybe Burke wasn't behind Emma's kidnapping. But who else would be after them? Who else knew about the money?

Same man who hired Burke and Rollin for the job. Was Frank Bortolli behind all this?

He had to find out and fast.

Rollin raced off to help Emma.

Tearing into a warehouse for cover, Emma glanced over her shoulder. The SUV had parked and a big monster of a blond dude was getting out, all his focus on her.

Her heart beat as fast as a rabbit's. Terror propelled her faster.

Still clad in the hideous lime green pantsuit, she felt like she was wearing a neon sign with huge letters on her back that read: "Follow Me!"

She hoped Rollin was okay and that earlier volley of gunshots didn't mean he was dead.

Emma! Stop it! Concentrate on escape!

She needed to find cover and kill the asshole chasing her. In retrospect, she should have done that outside. Too late now.

Even though her lungs seared and her leg muscles burned, she ran faster.

As she raced through what appeared to be a machine shop, acrid metallic smoke from an arc welder burned her nostrils. Several guys manned large industrial grinders and welders. Sparks flew. The loud whining from the machines must have masked the gunfire because none of them glanced up.

Light spilled in a small square patch from an open door at the far end of the darkened warehouse. She ran for it.

A couple of the men finally noticed her and stopped working.

"Hey! Lady! You can't be in here!"

She reached the door, spun and pointed at the blond man. "Stop that man! He's trying to kill me!"

The Blond Bruiser pulled out a gun. "Anyone stops me, I'll stop them permanently. This is between me and my wife!" he shouted in a heavily accented voice. Sounded Russian.

"He's lying!"

The men in the warehouse looked between the two of them, their mouths open. But no one moved.

She couldn't fire at the Russian, she was too unsure of her aim and the workers were too close to her target. "Shit! Call the cops!"

Dashing out the door, she hung a right and ran around the side of the building, heading back toward the parking lot. As soon as she reached the front, she'd use the building for cover and kill the bastard.

"Emma Ramsay! I won't hurt you! Stop and I won't shoot!" the guy shouted from far too close behind her. "My boss just wants to talk to you, that's all!"

She knew just what kind of "talking" they'd be doing. With pliers and blowtorches.

Without looking, she pointed the gun behind herself and fired.

"Bitch!"

She fired again, but was too terrified to turn around to see if she'd hit him.

Just as she reached the edge of the building, the man grabbed her shoulders and yanked the gun out of her hand.

Screaming, her pulse bonkers, she elbowed back into his gut with everything she had. She hit solid steel. Like a kitten batting at a gorilla.

The massive man locked his arms around her, crushing her, picked her up and carried her toward his SUV. He had such a tight hold on her, she couldn't breathe.

Overwhelmed with terror, she kicked and flailed with everything she had, but nothing she did had any effect on the man. She felt like a toddler in the man's gigantic arms.

"Stop fighting me," he ordered. "You already pissed me off. My orders were not to hurt you, but I can cause you a lot of pain without leaving a mark."

"I can't breathe!"

"Good, maybe you'll pass out for a while."

"Big dumb jerk!"

He quickly reached the SUV. Gripping her with one pillar-sized arm, he opened up the back of the SUV. Just as he cracked it, the door burst open, knocking them both to the ground.

Raw pain ripped across her elbow and she lost most of her breath. Gasping for air, she pushed away from the hulk, got up and dashed away.

A thundering gunshot came from behind her, nearly deafening her. Her heart stopped. She expected to feel horrific pain and die. When she glanced over her shoulder, Rollin was standing over the body of the Russian, holding a shotgun.

Her body loosened a bit. She slowed to a stop and turned around.

The Russian groaned and held his stomach.

“Emma! Get in the SUV!”

Sirens whined from far away.

She didn’t need any more encouragement and ran for the SUV, slowing when she reached Rollin.

The Russian writhed in agony on the blood-splattered asphalt, an ugly hole in his side. His white shirt soaked with blood, more pumped out of the wound. The blond clamped his hand over the gunshot and blood seeped through his thick fingers.

The world swirled in front of her and she almost barfed.

“Emma, in the car!” Rollin barked.

Staring at the injured Russian, she moved toward the front of the car, unable to look away.

“Who are you working for? Is it Frank?” Rollin demanded.

“Go to hell, Hanson,” the wounded man moaned.

Rollin kicked him where he’d shot him, hard. The guy screamed.

Her stomach twisted, her whole body jerked, and she had to clutch the SUV door for support.

“Did Frank hire you guys?”

“Fuck you!”

Rollin kicked him hard, several times. The Russian howled in agony.

She almost passed out.

“Emma! Get in the fucking car!”

Finally, she managed to climb inside. Pulling on the seatbelt, she lay back, closed her eyes and hugged herself.

A soft thud and another scream.

“Was it Frank?”

“Yes! Okay, yes! Fucking call an ambulance!”

“Cops will be here shortly, asshole. I see you again, you won’t survive the exchange, get me?”

Rollin slammed the back door shut and leapt into the driver's seat. He threw the car in gear and sped away. She finally opened her eyes.

He was so different, she couldn't get her bearings. His face grooved with anger lines, his dark eyes were cold. Completely transformed into a soldier. Frightened, she held herself.

He tore off the opposite way from the street.

Rollin looked so scary, she was afraid to ask questions. But she finally couldn't stop herself. "Aren't we going the wrong way?"

"No, cops are coming in the way we came in. I got a good feeling there's another way out of here."

He raced along the road between two sets of buildings.

Sirens whined closer. She checked the entrance to the parking lot. Blue and red flashing Christmas lights.

Blood whooshed in her ears and her gut knotted so hard it hurt. "Cops are here!"

At the end of the row of buildings was a fence. But no gate anywhere.

"Rollin, where the hell is the way out?"

He slammed on the gas and headed straight for the middle of a long expanse of chain link fence. "I'm makin' one!"

"Are you nuts?"

He flashed a grin at her. "Brace for impact!"

She held onto the door handle and put her hand on the dash.

A second later, they blasted through the fence. She lurched forward, but the chain link didn't slow them as much as she'd expected. With parts of fence flying everywhere, they landed in the middle of a dead end street.

Rollin turned left and sped down a short street and made a right onto a main thoroughfare, narrowly missing a dark sedan, which honked loudly.

He zipped down the road, blew past some people in a bike lane, and suddenly, they were on the entrance to Highway 5, heading south.

He checked his rear view mirror. "No one following us, good." He let out a long breath, his shoulders relaxed and the coldness left his face. "Well, that was exciting. Next on our tour of Lake County, we'll proceed onto Corning where hopefully we won't be shot at and chased."

She stared at him. Maybe joking was how he dealt with the trauma. There was no way she could distance herself from this hell. She couldn't stop shaking. Her body had transformed into one quivering giant mass of nerves. "They must have gotten the license plate. Besides, how many SUVs have bullets lodged in the windshield?"

"No worries, little lady, I've got that all covered. Including getting you out of that green nightmare."

"Good plan."

Rollin's phone played a Star Trek communicator sound and he answered it. "Bobby? Where the fuck have you been? Sorry, I was in a dead spot. Zane saw what? That would have been nice to know. No, my fault, shouldn't have eaten where there was no reception. No worries, we met a pair of lovely gentlemen and played a nice little game of hide and go shoot. We won. I need a cleanup in Redding on Caterpillar Road. No, I'm fine. No damage except for my Jeep. Tell Zane to stop his search. Frank Bortolli hired them."

A loud exclamation came over Rollin's phone and he winced. "Ow. Yes, I know what that means. But I want to keep this quiet. I need to know what's going on. Yeah, Emma's fine, too." He glanced over at her. "Well, relatively fine for someone whose life has been thrown into a food processor and turned on high. Anyway, tell Zane and the rest of the guys. We need to know who Frank is working for if anyone. Yeah…no. It's getting late, I'll probably crash somewhere on the way down…will you stop? Yes, I'm doing what the doctor said to do. I'm fine. Awwwww. Don't worry. I plan on torturing you for a lot longer. I'll call you later."

He hung up and shook his head. "Guy is like my own personal mother hen."

"What's going on?"

"Bobby's been trying to get hold of me for the last hour. Zane saw my picture and the make and license of the Jeep on an IM between some high level assassins he's tracking for another job. He also saw a picture of you. They had orders to kill me and kidnap you."

She wrapped her arms around herself. "Nice."

"Shouldn't have eaten at Cattlemen's. No signal inside. Wish I hadn't had a beef jones." He looked over at her and grinned.

Emma returned his smile, but couldn't get the image of the fallen Russian out of her mind. Nor the look on Rollin's face as he interrogated him. She'd never seen such a complete transformation, from his happy-go-lucky smiling self to this hard, immovable chunk of granite. Emotionless. As if he were almost dead inside.

So different than the guy sitting across from her now. Normal Rollin. Albeit with a hyped-up edge. At least his sweetness had returned.

But aside from what was going on with Rollin, she felt terrible. Her stomach in revolt, that steak was threatening a return. She couldn't get her heart to slow down, nor stop her limbs from trembling.

This crazy drama was sucking her soul from her. All she wanted was to go somewhere quiet, have a couple beers and sleep for a year. Actually, no. She wanted to crawl into her bedroom closet and hide in a pile of blankets.

But probably not even rest was on the schedule. More than likely another heaping helping of horror would follow, ending with her torture and/or death.

She couldn't remember when she'd put Endure Endless Horrible Violent Dramas on her agenda, but it was time to check it off the list.

FOURTEEN

The normality of the traffic on Highway 5 compared starkly to the action/thriller movie Emma had experienced seconds before. Big rigs hauling hay and cattle. A camper van full of a happy family of six. Grandma and Grandpa in their huge boat of an American car.

Her stomach did a flip and twist combo. Bet none of them had been kidnapped recently. Or been chased through a warehouse by a gun-wielding Russian thug. And she was fairly certain none of them had found a nuke in their storage unit.

Emma concentrated on slowing her breathing and getting her heart out of the Attack Zone.

Rollin took an exit onto a two-lane highway and eased down into his seat. He glanced over at her and did a double-take. Rolling his eyes, he shook his head. He slowed, turned off the road and parked in an orchard, out of sight from the highway.

She turned toward him. "Why are we stopping?"

He unbuckled his seat belt and held out his arms. A sympathetic look on his face, he said, "Come here, baby."

"I'm fine."

"I'm not. Come here, I need a hug."

She chuckled. A half second later, the tears practically shot out of her eyes. She'd had no idea how close she'd been to the edge of sanity. She ripped off her belt, moved over and collapsed into him.

Sobbing, she clutched him and tried to keep a lid on her emotions, but her filters were broken.

He wrapped his arms around her and kissed the side of her head. His unique scent, strong arms and solid inner energy enveloped her, making her feel safer. "You're okay, honey. I'm here and I won't let anything happen to you."

The edge came off her emotions. The man knew what to say. She'd rarely had anyone care enough about her to comfort her. After a few moments, she calmed. Rollin brought her closer to him.

The horror was over. They'd escaped.

She took in a deep whiff of his scent. Why did he feel so right? So familiar? She got the sense her connection to him went beyond the present. If she believed in past lives, she'd say she'd been with this man forever.

Now that was a crazy thought.

Yes, brought on by extreme stress. She needed a nap.

Emma pulled back a bit, but stayed in his embrace. "Thanks."

"No, thank you. Thanks for being so cool, thanks for forgiving me, and thanks for listening to me. I'm sorry you had to see that. What I had to do to that guy. I…"

"It's okay, Rollin. It was him or us."

"Well, it's not okay. I'd do anything to transport you out of here. I promise we'll stop soon and get some rest. And some alcohol."

"Sounds great." She pulled a tissue out of the pocket of her lime green pants and blew her nose.

"You got guts, lady. Most women, hell, most men would have broken by now. But you're a rock. I love you."

She was just about to tell him that she loved him, too, when he tilted her head toward his and kissed her tenderly.

Under his spell, she got lost in his warmth, his strength and his caring.

All at once, her body came alive. She wanted him. Wanted to be with him. Wanted to feel his skin on hers, the warmth of his breath on her neck, his steely tool inside her. She didn't know if it was the danger, but her feelings went beyond anything she'd experienced before. Their sexual chemistry was off the scale, but the connection went beyond the physical.

Rollin made her feel like she'd come home.

A vision of them at seventy years old sitting in front of a fire, drinking wine and laughing while playing footsie popped into her mind. Seemed so right. So possible.

He ended the kiss and wiped her tears away. His dark eyes were alive with emotion and lust. "God, lady. You are something special," he said in a husky voice.

"I love you, too, Rollin."

His eyes dilated and his mouth dropped open. Blinking fast, he shook his head. "Did you just say you loved me?"

"Yeah."

He gasped and burst into a supernova of a smile. "Really?"

She giggled. "Really."

His smile faded, his shoulders relaxed and his gaze softened. In a near whisper, he said, "Thank God." He drew her close, moved some hair off her brow in a tender gesture and looked at her with the most love she'd ever seen on a man's face. His attention dropped to her mouth and he kissed her.

Reeling, she had the sensation of falling. Her heart opened so fast and so powerfully, it hurt. Jubilant and terrified, she clung to him.

He pulled away and bestowed little kisses all over her face, then hugged her tight. "I wish we were anywhere else. We have to get back on the road and all I want to do is love you."

"Me, too."

Rollin ran his hand down the side of her face. "You gonna be okay for a while? Until I get you to a good place to rest?"

"Oh, yeah." She sat back, feeling remarkably better.

Soon, they came to a juncture with Highway 5 and entered the town of Anderson. Rollin pulled into a parking lot for a group of clothing and shoe outlets.

Rollin drove slowly by the stores, checking them out. "I'm going to let you off at…where?"

"Gap is fine."

"Can you get some clothes in a half an hour?"

"Yeah."

"I'll meet you at the entrance, right over there. I don't know what vehicle I'll be in. Be ready to jump inside, okay?"

Her stomach did a three-sixty and her muscles tensed solid. "Okay." She bit her lip. Stealing a car? Even though she trusted him, she hated this. When would this stupid drama end?

"You'll be fine, Emma. We'll be fine." He leaned over and put his large, very bruised hand over hers.

The confident look in his eye calmed her. "Okay."

Rollin handed her a few hundred-dollar bills and dropped her off at the Gap.

Twenty minutes later—after some very strange looks from the salespeople at her old lady clothes and orthopedic shoes—she was in new jeans and a t-shirt. She'd grabbed a hoodie for nighttime and underwear. After leaving the Gap, she spotted a shoe store and picked up a pair of trail runners and some socks. Back to normal, she felt a tad more sane.

When she arrived at the entrance, she didn't see Rollin anywhere.

Emma stood there for probably thirty seconds, which seemed like thirty hours, when a silver Mercedes Benz sedan pulled up in front of her. The tinted window rolled down revealing Rollin, now wearing cool wraparound sunglasses.

"Emma, get in!"

She inspected the sleek, new vehicle. "A Mercedes?"

He grinned. "Well, as long as I stole a car, I figured I ought to get one with style."

She laughed and ran around the car and got in, feeling bad for the person who owned the car. "Don't expensive cars have a tracking system with an engine shut-off?"

"They do." Rollin took off, got on the freeway and headed south. "Took care of that. Don't worry, Emma. We won't hurt the car and I'll make sure they get it back. Besides, they've probably got great insurance. And this is about our lives. I don't steal from people without good reason."

"Okay." She ran a hand over the plush leather and admired the inlaid dark wood on the dashboard. So different than her utilitarian Prius.

"You look great, by the way. Now I won't feel all *Harold and Maude* when I kiss you."

She nodded. "Being stuck in a lime-green pantsuit for a day was worse than being shot at. Well, close second."

He laughed, leaned back in his seat and drove, casual and relaxed. He felt safe, so she felt safe.

She watched the olive orchards of Corning go by, then gazed at her companion. A surge of energy rushed through her sex. With his crooked nose, masculine carved features and long dark hair, he was so handsome. So hot. So scrumptious.

Beyond that, he'd saved her life. His talents at self-defense astounded her. She'd never been with a guy who had such skills before.

She smiled at him. "I'm sorry about the circumstances, but I'm glad we're here together. I feel like I can handle my life with you in my corner. Especially with that thing in my…" She choked and began coughing. She almost said nuke in her storage unit!

Her pulse ratcheted higher and she clutched the door handle. While she loved the man, she clearly wasn't ready to trust him with the nuke yet.

Rollin's focus on her sharpened. "What thing?"

There was only one way to approach giving Rollin the bomb. She had to keep the truth from him until she showed him the nuke. His reaction would tell her whether or not he was still manipulating her. As much as every cell in her body cried out to believe him and be with him and love him, she had to stay on guard. Her heart had never been a good judge of character.

She crossed her arms over her chest, then noticed a stray thread on her new jeans. She removed the blue strand and rolled it between her fingers.

"Emma? What thing?"

Erk. She blanked on an excuse. Damn this exhaustion!

He honed in on her and appeared to be attempting to read her mind. "What thing in your where?"

She stared off at the expansive brown fields of freshly turned soil. "I can't. Damn, why didn't I just make something up? I can't even lie to you anymore. You've gotten to me. All the way."

"Good. Because I need to know what you found. I've been double-crossed by the guy who hired me to find you and recover the money. It's time, Emma. What else did Adam steal? What was it that you found and where did you find it? Please tell me."

A plan came to her. Not denial, just obfuscation. "Uh, I don't know what it is."

If he failed the test, she'd call the cops. And run. And then throw herself off a cliff for falling for yet another bad boy/charlatan.

Rollin clearly wasn't satisfied with her lame answer. His attention darted between her and the road. "What do you mean, you don't know what it is? You didn't see it?"

"It's in a box. I opened it and I can't identify the object," she said as simply as she could.

Rollin looked even more disturbed. "Could you describe it for me?"

"How about I show it to you?"

His expression brightened. "Great. Where is it?"

"A storage unit in Redwood City." She hoped she wasn't blowing this. She hoped she could trust this man. She hoped her heart hadn't lied to her yet again.

"You have a storage unit? That didn't come up anywhere."

"My mother's storage unit. Under her maiden name."

"Shit, of course. I'm surprised no one found it. I'm surprised we didn't run that last name. I'll have to get on Bobby about that. Damn, a storage unit? Here I thought you went through some huge machinations, broke into a building you both used to frequent or something. An old house we didn't know about."

"Nope."

He sent her a penetrating stare. "So you can't even describe the thing?" He swung his focus back to the road.

"I want you to look at it. I'm not sure. I don't even want to speculate. Some electronic gizmo."

"Really? Okay. Worrisome, but okay. Shit, I wish I wasn't so tired, I want to go there now. But I'm about to drop. This looks good."

He exited Highway 5 in Willows and drove to a Best Western. He didn't even ask, he got them a room with two beds. Even after their amazing kisses and proclamations of love, he still respected her enough to give her space.

Such the gentleman. No pressure, no expectations, all his focus was on her well-being. He was the best. She relaxed even more.

They found their room. Very clean, very nice. Emma felt even better.

Rollin stood in their room near the door. "You rest or take a shower or whatever you want, I'm gonna get us some food and beer." He smiled, walked to her and took her in his arms. "You gonna be okay alone for a bit?"

"Sure."

"Good girl." He leaned in and kissed her.

Emotion and lust welled up inside her, she felt like a volcano about to erupt. All the day's events and the danger made her want him more than she'd wanted any other man.

He ended the kiss and stared at her, looking stunned. "I don't think I've ever felt anything like this, Emma."

"Hurry back."

He broke into a huge smile. "Will do." With a peck on her cheek and a quick hug, he left.

She had no idea what would happen between them, all she knew was that she felt stable when in his company. Which seemed definitely at odds with the situation.

Emma walked into the bathroom and turned on the water in the shower. She hoped it worked out with Rollin. She wanted to believe she could have a long-lasting relationship with a good man.

But she wasn't taking any shit, either. If Rollin panned out, as her gut told her he would, great. But if he proved to be a liar, good-bye.

Maybe she was finally growing up. Maybe all this adversity had taught her something. Maybe she was learning to rely on herself.

Either that or she was completely deluded.

FIFTEEN

Emma took a shower and put back on her new clothes. As she was brushing out her hair with her fingers, a knock came on the bathroom door.

"Who is it?"

"Brad Pitt," came Rollin's reply.

She opened it and he gave her a dazzling smile. Her heart beat faster and hot energy buzzed through her, starting at her feet and bursting out the top of her head. He made her so happy. She hoped he wasn't lying.

He held a large grocery sack. "I got us some sandwiches and beer."

"All I want is the beer."

"Me, too."

She sat back on one of the beds and he relaxed on an overstuffed chair next to her, his long legs stretched out with his feet propped up on the end of the bed.

Munching on a club sandwich, she drained a beer in about ten minutes.

He tapped her foot with his. "Easy there, girl. That's going to hit you hard."

"I'm counting on it."

He rolled his eyes and sent her a grin that lit up his whole face.

A warm tingle went through her.

She loved the way he looked at her. Like he could see her; all the way inside her and loved everything he saw. Like he cherished her. Amazing.

As they ate, he moved his feet next to hers and started playing footsie, just like in her vision. "I wish we'd met under different circumstances. I want to be planning a trip to the Bahamas with you, not holed up here worried about getting killed."

"Me, too. So you were double-crossed by your boss?"

"Not my boss, a colleague. An ex-colleague. I don't have any bosses now. Just friends I do jobs for. Frank Bortolli hired me to find the cash that Adam stole. Then he and Burke double-crossed me. At least, I think Burke did. Does Burke know what's in the storage unit?"

"Yeah. He knows. He didn't tell me what it was, but he asked about an electronic thing."

Rollin's expression darkened. He moved his feet from the bed and sat up. "Shit. So Frank and Burke *were* working together. Damn him." His mouth went tight and the line between his eyes deepened. "Burke might not have kidnapped you. It could have been Frank. But if the kidnappers were associated with Frank, Burke should have recognized the guys in the warehouse when he rescued you. Maybe Frank's been playing me and Burke off each other. I hope Bobby and Zane can find out what the hell is going on." He tossed a beer bottle into the trashcan and reached for another.

"Who's Zane?"

He popped the top off an Anchor Steam beer. "A friend of mine. Good friend."

"Is he in the same business as you?"

"Yeah." He took a swig of beer. His brows raised and his anger lines smoothed out. He put the beer down and pointed at her. "I have something for you, if it's still in one piece. I've remembered and forgotten ten times to give it to you." He dug around in his jacket hanging off the back of his chair and withdrew a Scooby-Doo Pez Dispenser.

She gave a little gasp and her heart sped up.

He handed it to her. “Here, happy birthday.”

She checked the markings and yipped. A bona fide original. “I don’t have this one. This is super rare. Like it costs over a few hundred bucks.”

He smiled. “I know.”

“How did you know I didn’t have it?”

“You keep a list on your com…pu…ter. Sorry.” He sent her a sheepish smile.

She gave him a mock frown and burst into a wide grin. “No worries, I get it. Both you and Burke probably have copies of my whole hard drive.”

Her stomach tightened and her face warmed. Holy crap. Then they knew how much she’d spent at *Good Vibrations* last month. Christ. She hoped they hadn’t read those damned sexually explicit emails between her and Adam. She should have deleted them.

He picked up his beer and leaned back, stretching his legs on the bed again.

She admired the plastic treasure. So thoughtful. “Sweet. Where’d you find it?”

He gestured toward her with his beer. “Pez store in Burlingame. They’ve got them all.”

The twinkle in his eye sent a tingle through her. She returned his grin. “You didn’t have to do that.”

“I wanted to. I helped destroy your birthday. Besides, you’ve got a whole chunk of space above your toilet that doesn’t have any.”

She’d been hoping to fill that area soon, but her Pez budget had run out. Envisioning the wall covered in prized Pez trophies, she clapped her hands and bounced on the bed. “This is so exciting!”

Rollin laughed.

She joined him. “Wow, I almost get killed, watch a guy get shot and now I’m all happy about a stupid Pez dispenser.”

“They aren’t stupid.” He nodded at her. “I finally figured out why you love them so much.”

“Yeah?”

"Lizzie. She started giving them to you, right? When you were a little girl?" His dark gaze sparkled with warmth.

A glow overtook her. "Yeah. She gave them to me when things were bad in the house. The collection grew until I had to put them all somewhere. How did you know?"

"Ran across a note she wrote to you when you were a kid when I was searching through your house. Again, my apologies."

"It's okay. God, Lizzie." A wave of guilt washed over her and her stomach wrenched. She frowned and picked at the bedspread. "Damn, I hope she's okay."

"She's fine."

Her attention snapped to him. "How do you know?"

"I got her in a nice place and I've got people watching her. Along with Scary Mary."

"Are you kidding me?"

"No," he said in a matter-of-fact tone.

"Can I call her? Can I talk to her?"

He grinned. "Sure."

Her heart lightened with hope. "God, I've been so worried about her. I lost my cell phone and can't remember Mary's number. I've been going out of my mind."

"Babe, you can use my phone anytime. But they got an early bedtime at that place. Probably better to call in the morning."

"Okay. Wow." Her head swam with the implications. He cared about her and her sister this much? Unreal. "Damn, I didn't think people like you existed."

Rollin sent her a bright grin. "I'd do anything for you and your sister, Emma."

She set aside her beer and went to him. Sitting on his lap, she hugged him, then kissed him. A blast of over-the-top desire destroyed her thought train and she forgotten why she'd kissed him, all she could think was what a good idea it'd been. And how she wanted more. How she wanted all of him.

She pushed away. “If I don’t have you inside me within about a second, I will expire.”

Chuckling, his expression turned lusty. He got a hungry, predatory set to his eyes and mouth. “Wouldn’t want *that* to happen.”

She jumped up and ripped off her shirt.

When he saw her breasts, he gasped and stopped and stared, an expression of awe on his rugged face. No man had ever given her a greater gift.

As if drawn to them by a gravitational force, Rollin took her breasts in his hands. He touched them as if he revered them. He massaged them gently, then tweaked the nipples lightly between his thumbs and forefingers. Bolts of sexual energy blasted from her breasts and bombarded her clit and sex, setting her whole body on fire.

His gaze dark, he looked at her mouth as if he might eat it, then leaned in and kissed her lightly, then hard, thrusting his tongue into her mouth. She attacked him right back, thrilled with the feel of him, her senses filled with his scent and taste.

Her body roared for more. She explored his steely pecs, his ropy shoulders, then grabbed the back of his head and deepened the kiss. He moaned into her mouth.

They broke apart, breathing hard, their gazes locked in lust as if he were already inside her.

She tore off her pants and he stripped.

At the sight of his ripped, naked body, it was her turn to gasp. The hard planes of his musculature made him look like a classic Greek statue—if the statue was painted with nasty bruises and carved with scars. The man had seen some action. But his dick was the prize. Oh. My. God. Fully erect, it stood a good eight inches. Where the hell had he been hiding THAT?

“You have the most beautiful cock I’ve ever seen,” she said in a whisper. Then heard what she said and her face went hot.

He sent her a lop-sided grin. “Don’t be embarrassed, Emma. Be yourself with me. Say whatever comes to mind. I love it. I love you. And thanks for that. Men love hearing that shit.”

"Well, you probably heard it before a bunch," she said, moving to him and taking him in her hand. Hot, silky smooth skin over hard metal. A wallop of lust made her dizzy with longing. She couldn't wait to have this gorgeous tool inside her.

His eyes closed, he took in a huge gasp of air. "No…actually. I haven't. Oh, God, Emma, I love you touching me."

"I love touching you," she said, stroking him.

He kissed her hard and roamed her body with his hands. Her skin came alive with every place he touched, sending licks of hot sexual fire burning through her. She moved her hand up and down his shaft, relishing the feel of him.

With a growl, he grabbed her, pushed her onto the bed and climbed on top. When his hard body touched hers, his skin felt so good her brain whirled, the bed spun, she wanted to laugh and moan and holler. She latched onto his tight, round buns and pulled him closer.

He explored her mouth, then pulled away and laid beside her, dropping down to take a breast in his mouth. His hand traced her belly and settled between her legs.

She cried out and spread wide for him.

He groaned deep in his throat. Gently parting her tender folds, he slipped his finger inside her slick sex. Tickling at first, he slid further inside and hit the magic zone.

She drew in a sharp breath. "Oh, God, that feels so good."

Rollin nibbled her nipple then kissed his way down to her abdomen. Withdrawing his hand, he moved between her legs, pushed her further apart and gazed at her sex like it was the most beautiful sight he'd ever seen.

With a wicked glint in his dark gaze, he leaned down and slid his tongue over her clit.

Squealing, she nearly launched him off the bed.

Laughing, he took hold of her hips, pinned her to the bed and lightly ran his tongue over her nub again. She grabbed the sheets in both hands and gritted her teeth to stave off the orgasm.

He made little circles around the head until she nearly fainted. Powerful waves of exquisite hunger rushed through her. Curling her toes, her body sizzled with sexual energy.

Gradually, he increased his pace, teasing, tormenting and pleasuring her.

Flashes of red and orange light zapped through her mind and her body detonated in a massive orgasm. Her sex spasming, she grabbed his head and held him to her while she thrust her hips up to meet his tongue. Rollin stayed with her, causing her to rip into a series of earth-shattering orgasms. A succession of dynamic explosions rocked her sex.

Rollin was a master at oral sex.

She finally pushed him away. "Too much, too much. Besides, I need you inside me *now*," she growled, pulling him on top of her.

"Comin' right up."

He guided himself inside and his dick slid into place like it belonged there. Click. No cock had ever felt this perfect.

Two thrusts in and her thoughts blew apart. Moaning and flailing against him, she wanted to come and never stop coming.

Every thrust with his diamond-hard dick sent her higher. She howled and fought him until he grabbed her wrists and pinned them above her head. Sending her into a wild frenzy.

She came so hard, she thought her heart would stop. She couldn't breathe, couldn't see, all she could do was come.

His thrusts got harder and deeper, his body jerked and he cried out loud and long, sending her even higher.

Images of his pecs, his cock and the dark look in his eye flashed through her mind as he powered into her g-spot, launching her into an epic, mind-blowing climax. Coming so violently, she felt like the center of an atomic reaction.

And then they became one.

His love encompassed and lifted her. She floated, clinging to him, adoring him, relishing him. Her heart soared.

As she came down, tears streamed from her eyes. She gripped his hard, sweaty body, releasing her emotions, never wanting to part from him.

No one had ever moved her like this.

He pulled away and kissed her tears. "I hope those are good tears."

"The best."

"Good. Hell, Emma, I thought I was in love with you before. That went beyond beyond. I want to bottle you up and sell you to the masses as the best product ever on the planet. If everyone felt the way I did during that, everything would be perfect."

She kissed his shoulder, then nipped it. "That was the first time I've made love to someone who knew what they were doing. I always thought I was kinda frigid."

He burst out laughing and pushed away to examine her face. "Frigid? Are you crazy? You're so hot, you're freakin' Kilauea, lady. Who were these assholes you slept with, anyway?"

"Assholes."

"Bastards. They didn't know how good they had it. I'm never letting you go. You're mine, baby. All mine." He hugged her tight.

Joy radiated from deep within her belly. "Happy. Wow, this has been a while. I haven't been happy in…forever. Thanks, Rollin. Thanks for finding me. Thanks for coming into my life. I'd almost given up on humanity."

"Me, too." He kissed her thoroughly, then kissed his way down to a breast. "Mmmm, these taste good. Kinda orange lemony." He shot her a cute grin and she giggled.

He hugged her hips, pressing the side of his face to her abdomen.

Her body tingled with warmth and satisfaction.

A giant dose of fear slammed her. They'd had unprotected sex! Holy shit.

"What?" He turned and examined her face.

"We didn't use any protection. I completely forgot."

"Jesus," he said, paling. "I'm sorry."

"Don't apologize. I'm equally at fault."

"Well, I'm clean. I just got tested a month ago."

She relaxed. "I got tested right after Adam dumped me, and you're the first person I've been with since him."

"What about…um..." He gestured awkwardly.

"Pregnant? Not possible. Part of the reason my first husband left me. I can't have kids." A huge bomb of terror engulfed her and she went rigid. She quickly checked his reaction. She hadn't meant to blurt that out.

He seemed surprised and concerned, but not unhappy.

"I hope that's not a deal breaker with you." Her brow furrowing to the point of aching, she examined his face carefully. Would he dump her even before they got started?

He waved away her concerns with a flip of his hand. "Emma, don't worry about me, I don't care. Never had many paternal instincts. And in my line of business, kids are a liability."

She let out a long sigh and squeezed him.

Then, of course, her mind began to torment her. What if they weren't on the same page? He said he loved her. But how far did that go?

"So…" She ran her hand through his soft hair.

The look in his eye sharpened. "Uh, oh. Is this the part where you tell me you're a lesbian?"

She laughed. "No, this is the part where I try to get you to commit to me."

His muscles relaxed and he kissed her belly. "Done. Next?"

Chuckling, she hugged him. "Okay, that was easy."

He ran a hand over her hip and down her thigh. "Good. When do we move in together?"

"We seem to be living together right now."

"I like that idea." He scooted up to embrace her in a full body hug.

Her sex swelled with need. She'd never get enough of this guy.

He kissed her neck. "I want you with me always. You and your Pez dispensers," he said, giving her butt a squeeze. "By the way, Scooby isn't the only one I got you. I bought about fifty more."

"Fifty! I hope they weren't all rare. Those cost way too much."

He laughed and kissed her shoulder. "I have money, Emma."

She checked his face carefully. "Really?" With that nasty old Jeep and beat-up leather jacket?

"Just because I don't show it, doesn't mean I don't have it."

"So like how much?"

"More than Burke."

Her head jerked back against the pillow. She examined his eyes. "Really?"

He shrugged. "I'm not into spending much. I don't really care. I mean, I got a tricked out surfboard, a dozen choppers and a big ass boat, but that's all. I'm not into stuff. No judgment on you, either. I know it's your thing."

She hadn't even considered the prospect of Rollin having money. "If you're rich, why the free drinks at Embassy Suites?"

Laughing, he replied, "Because it's fun. And besides, I've spent enough time in those hotels, they already have enough of my money. But mostly? Just to get away with something."

"You are a bad boy."

"Bad boy gonna getcha, baby." He tickled her.

Giggling, she pushed his hands away.

He kissed her, pulled back and smiled. "So…" He traced her shoulder with a long finger, his dark eyes twinkling with affection. "What would you do if you were rich? Buy more Pez dispensers?"

"No, I think I can call that collection complete. But if we find that five hundred million and I get a percentage—kinda figured I'm owed after all this crap—I'd move my shop to Union Square and sell super high-end antiquities. Then I'd hire a knowledgeable staff, pay them a lot to run the place while I traveled the world, searching for treasures. That would be a blast."

"Sounds fun."

"Better than scraping by in my little joint. Even though I love it. I hope after all this drama, I get to keep it. And get rid of Jerry."

"Consider it done," he said with certainty. "Get that worry off your mind."

"Good."

He smiled. Sweetness radiated from his core.

Her whole body heated. Finally, someone in her corner.

And something about the man made her feel normal. Centered. Just being around him relaxed her. Well, when they weren't getting shot at and attacked. His inner energy was constant, he believed in himself. He didn't put on any airs. Everything about him was honest.

Even those awful confessions of his. Still, he'd come clean with her. And that was something no man in her life had ever done before. Talk about scoring huge points.

Finally, a man worth the effort.

Not to mention the hottest lover ever on record. She ran her hand over his ripped belly. Yum.

But what about their future? Would he always be getting himself in crazy situations?

She examined his tanned face.

He raised a brow. "Now what?"

"Um, so now that we're in a committed relationship, what have I gotten myself into? What kind of a life do you have? I should have asked before, but I couldn't help myself and had to have you." She hugged him. "I mean, is your life all about danger? Killing people, almost dying yourself?"

He stretched out his neck, then laid back against the pillows. She nestled beside him and he put his arm around her.

"Uh…nope. Well, yes and no."

"That was clear." Jesus Christ. What *had* she got herself into? She got a flash of living in a camouflaged bungalow surrounded by a white picket fence topped with razor wire. Tank in the driveway. Her stomach squirmed.

He stiffened. Then sighed and relaxed. She could feel him thinking.

"I think it's time," he said, his voice rumbling deep in his chest.

"Time?" She pulled away to look at him.

"Yeah. Time to tell you more of what I'm doing." He had reservations about telling her. A slight brow furrow, a pensive twist to his mouth. He finally nodded and looked her in the eye, dead serious. He transformed into yet another man. His professional persona. Strong, competent and confident. Even sexier. "I'm with a group of guys—well, and Catherine—called the Patriots."

"Who are the Patriots? Who's Catherine?"

"A group of friends, all ex-military, most of us SEALs. Catherine was a Marine, girlfriend of another woman Patriot who died. But she's tougher than the rest of us. We fight crime."

"For the government?"

"Sometimes. For friends. But we mainly fight government corruption."

Dangerous and scary, but courageous. And exciting. She didn't think she could want to fuck him more. Wrong. She had to hold herself back from attacking him. "Very interesting."

And crazy.

A cloud of dark doubts squelched her bliss. Secret Crime Fighter was exactly the occupation she didn't want to be married to. Christ. She must have an *I Like Drama* sign tattooed in invisible ink on her forehead that only men with dangerous jobs could see.

Of course, it was way too late to turn back now. Unless Rollin was lying about the nuke, being with him was a done deal. Maybe her lesson was that she'd never be able to avoid bad boys as mates, but she could pick one on the right side of the law.

Rollin shifted, grunted and rubbed his side. "We go by the code of honor the military taught us to uphold, but then never came through on their part of the bargain." His gaze darkened. His muscles tensed and his jaw clamped hard. "They used us. Used good soldiers to do their fuckin' evil shit. Told us that it was for our country when it was only for the rich assholes of the world. Still burns my ass."

She wanted to heal him and get even with those jerks for letting him down.

"Started in Iraq. Captain, Ty, Dino, Roman, Zane, bunch of guys. When we saw what was really going on over there, we couldn't turn a blind eye to it. So we said, fuck them, we'll do our own thing," The tension eased from his face and body, he gave her a squeeze. "Correct some of this bad shit. Show those corporate bastards that they can't always have their way. They hurt someone, they're gonna get hurt. And we hurt 'em where it counts. Their bank accounts."

Dark vengeance filled his eyes, his shoulders straightened. He glowed with power. Scary, but he clearly felt good about what he did.

She lightly massaged his superb pecs. "That sounds awesome. And so reassuring there's someone out there trying to balance things."

Rollin smiled, seeming proud. "Exactly. We got hackers, computer geniuses, and warriors like me. And spies. I mainly want to be a behind-the-scenes spy. I'm getting sick of this hand-to-hand shit. Hurts." He gave a chuckle, brought her closer and nuzzled her.

"So doesn't the government get pissed off at you and want to shut you down?"

"Yeah, but our network goes far and wide. We have a ton of friends. When the bad guys in the government try to shut us down, we know way ahead of time. We've got solid contacts in the CIA and NSA and FBI. We do jobs they can't get caught doing."

"Huh. So you guys are like Batman or something? The Justice League?"

Chuckling deep in his belly, he kissed the side of her head. "Pretty much. Without the tights and superpowers." He let out a long breath. "Makes me feel good. A great group of guys." His smile broke and a shadow passed behind his eyes. His face dark, he fiddled with the sheets.

"What? Are some of them assholes?"

"No. I shouldn't be talking about him." His gaze hollowed and the pain lines deepened on his chiseled face. "But Burke was one of us until six months ago. I still can't believe he turned on us. And we need him, too. He can work a computer like no one I've ever seen. He taught Bobby everything he knows. And he can handle a gun with the same ease. He went on this stupid ego trip about how we didn't trust him and couldn't see his brilliance. He wanted to run this one operation and none of us agreed with his assessment of the situation nor his crazy fucking solution and he lost it. We had this huge fight and he quit and went off on his own."

This did not add up with the Burke she knew. She couldn't picture him as anything but a smug criminal. "That's weird."

"Yeah, and then he decided we were all enemies or something." He shrugged and pushed some hair out of his face. "I still don't know what happened. Zane says he was always that way. Captain liked him, but I was his closest ally. I thought he had the same values. Now I'm not sure he ever did."

"Damn. I wonder what happened."

"Who knows?" His body tensed. "So can I ask you something? I don't want to sound like a jealous fool, but how do you feel about the guy?"

She gave a short laugh. "He's a Machiavellian creep who's incapable of telling the truth."

He chuckled. "I know you like him."

"And I know you do, too. He's charming." *Kissing Burke. His smile. Waking up in bed with him.* Her belly did a spin and her neck tightened. The man disturbed her to the core. "But I could never love him or trust him. He builds his life from the outside in. He choreographs every movement he makes. Controls his every emotion and action. He's definitely not doing what his heart tells him to do. It's like he's ignoring all the voices in his head and choosing to be this badass crime boss moron. I think he gets off on the power. It's almost like he's created a Frankenstein creature and feeds on it. But the monster isn't who he really is."

Rollin nodded. "Exactly. You articulate that so well." He sent her an admiring grin.

"You were right when you said he believes his own lies about himself. Which makes him dangerous."

"Yeah, it does. You're a very perceptive woman, Miss Holsten."

She pulled the covers over her. “You get beat enough by people like that, you figure it out. Burke is just like my stepfather.”

“Nasty.”

“Tell me about it.”

She moved the pillow and her bladder sent her an alert. “Damn it, I don’t want to get up, but I have to. I’ll be right back.” She sat up and stood.

Rollin gasped behind her. “Emma? What the fuck?”

She turned around, his face was white as the sheets, and his eyeballs were popped out of his head.

Her heart tripping into a fast beat, she looked around the motel room, fast, expecting to see an assailant or a fire or something. Nothing. “What?” His line of sight went to the tattoo on her back. Relaxing, she said, “It’s just a tattoo, honey, nothing to be afraid of.”

His alarmed expression didn’t change. He took the covers off and turned around. On his lower back was a very similar tattoo. In fact, a near dead copy.

Emma’s body went cold and all the hair stood up on her arms and neck.

SIXTEEN

All the blood drained from Emma's head. The floor waved and she put a hand on the bed to support herself. "What the hell, Rollin?"

"Holy shit." His dark eyes wide with shock, his mouth open, he blinked fast, like an avalanche of epiphanies were bombarding him.

She snapped her fingers. "This is what Burke meant. He saw my tattoo and said he'd seen another like it. When did you get that?"

"I was ten and I remember it like it was yesterday. Oh, my God, Emma…" He stared at her as if she were a ghost. "You were one of those kids. I know you!" He put his hand to his mouth. "*I know you,*" he whispered into his fingers.

Her legs went wobbly. "I'm getting terrified right about now." She sat on the bed.

He pointed at her, his gaze still wide. "You were adopted by your stepfather—oh, my God, your real last name was Gallagher." He slapped himself on the forehead. "I ran across the name, I just didn't connect…Franklin, your dad's name was Franklin—your dad was Frankie Gallagher!" He gestured at her sharply. "Fuck! I met you a couple times. You guys came to our house—before the tattoo nightmare—you came for dinner one night around Christmas. You latched onto my Rudolph the Red-Nosed Reindeer snow globe and wouldn't let it go. Mom finally gave it to you."

She gasped and shuddered. "Holy moly. I still have that snow globe. It's in my Christmas stuff. I had no idea where I got it, I've always had it. Okay, this totally spooks me out."

"I remember you, Emma. This little thing with dark hair and amazing green eyes. Jesus, Emma. Our dads, they were in the Bayside Crew. Holy fucking—excuse me, I have to stand up and pace now."

Running his hand through his hair, he walked the room, the muscles of his hard body seeming even sharper in the light cast from the brass bedside lamps. "I can't believe this. This freaks me out. I thought everyone got killed. My mother told me that we were the only survivors. We took off. We went back East. I went through hell trying to get clearance to get into the Navy because of my father. Because of that whole mess."

Cold, she slipped back under the covers. "But why the hell did they tattoo us?"

"I don't know." Rollin shrugged. "Dad said he lost a bet and I had to get tattooed." He walked back and stopped at the foot of the bed to face her. "He comes into my room and wakes me up and says I have to come with him and be a man. I'm like, what? I just watched a Dr. Who marathon and he rips me out of bed and drags me to this…horrible place." He rubbed his forehead. "I'll never forget it." He put his arms around himself. He suddenly appeared much younger. "Someone's basement. Like they couldn't have picked somewhere less creepy? And the fuckers held me down and tattooed me. When I cried, Dad said I shamed him." His gaze and face went hard. "Fucking dick. My mom said if anyone saw it, they'd kill me. I didn't take my shirt off to go swimming for years."

Emma sat up and hugged her knees. "My mom said the same thing, that Dad lost a bet. She always made me wear a one-piece bathing suit. She didn't say anyone would kill me, she pulled the modest card. That only bad girls who wanted to get knocked up wore bikinis. Then she had to explain to me what knocked up meant."

He gave a quick laugh and sat on the bed. "Model parents. I remember all these other little kids being tattooed, I was the oldest."

His gaze went haunted. “Man, the screaming. Those guys were brutal. Didn’t matter how much you cried, they just kept on.”

“And they tattooed all eight of us?”

“Yeah. Sick scene, man. I still have nightmares about it once in a while. That room was so horrifying.” His handsome face etched with disgust.

“Why would they do this?”

Rollin rested all his weight on an arm. “The only thing I heard them say was ‘copy that right, man, don’t miss a letter, a lot’s riding on this.’ At the time, the only thing I could think is that all of our tattoos combined led to a stash of cash or something. A treasure map, I guess.”

“You think that’s true?”

He shrugged. “They were killed for a hundred million in loose diamonds, sapphires, emeralds and rubies they stole from a jewelry broker in a hotel in Sacramento. It was the Mob’s job, too. Our dads’ gang got wind of it, scooped the deal and got massacred for it.”

“Damn.”

“We split fast. When they had the investigations and stuff, we were miles away, living at a cousin’s.”

“And the jewels were never found?”

“Nope. Well, who knows? Mob could have got them back the day after the massacre. Or they could be out there somewhere. We could be a quarter of a treasure map. Mind-blowing, huh?”

“A little past that. I can’t get my head around this.”

“Let me see yours.”

She moved the covers off her and turned around.

Rollin traced the tattoo with his warm strong fingers, sending a rush through her. God, she loved his touch. “Yeah, it’s more distorted than mine because you were smaller when it happened. But I can make out the name and numbers: 0-2-Charles-0-0,” he read. “And mine says: C-4-Miller-35. What the hell?”

She turned back around and wrapped the sheet around her. “So we’re the only survivors?”

“Yeah.”

"Well, there goes the treasure hunt idea."

He waved a hand. "We have other treasure to find, something that's concrete, that I know for sure exists."

"Yeah. If I could only figure out which stupid song of mine Adam was talking about." Weirdly enough, she was relieved to be discussing something else rather than a creepy past she didn't remember. Even if it was another creepy situation.

"We will." He looked at her and smiled, then an expression of awe came over his face. "Wow. Emma, we're like almost related or something."

Instantly, she felt their bond strengthen and cement. They knew each other. Their fathers were friends and business partners. Even though their business had been crime.

"Puts a whole new spin on things, doesn't it?" she said in wonder.

He crawled across the bed and took her in his arms. "Damn, Emma, all this time you were that little girl with the huge green eyes." He hugged her, hard. "I feel like I just came home."

Her entire body abuzz, her heart blazed with love.

He kissed her and she melted into him.

After a nice, long exchange, he pulled away and lay back on the bed. "Can I have my snow globe back?"

"We'll talk."

He chuckled and hugged her tighter.

She'd found him. After all this time, she'd finally found her soulmate. With this new connection, it was past clear to her. This was the man she belonged with.

Emma had never been happier.

* * * * *

The muscles in his neck tight to the point of pain, Burke paced his penthouse, gripping his phone so hard his hand hurt. "What do you mean you just missed them in Redding? Why are you fucking calling me? Find them! Check all the motels between there and the Bay Area off of 5. Good idea? Do I have to fucking draw a map for you? What the hell do I pay you for? Now don't call me again until you find them!" He clicked off and kicked a living room chair. "Idiots, fucking imbeciles!" His gut knotted so tight it burned. He wanted to beat his men bloody.

He had to get to them before Rollin slept with her. He couldn't stand the thought of him getting his hands all over his woman. Not again. And not Emma.

Damn it, Rollin must have convinced her somehow that he hadn't kidnapped her. That cologne should have done the trick.

Goddamned Bortolli trying to double-cross him. He'd pay for that.

Burke's phone rang. He checked the number. Speak of the devil.

He forced himself to calm. He had to make sure Yori had told Rollin the truth. "Bortolli, what can I do for you?"

"Hey Burke," the man drawled in his normally lazy tone, "I was wondering about, uh, that thing. Whether you had any luck finding it yet."

His body heated and his muscles went harder. His hands itched to strangle the man. As if he needed this asshole shoving his failure in his face. He pushed his fury deeper and took control. The pressure on his neck eased. "No, I told you I'd call you when I found it. By the way, you have any idea who else is interested?"

"No, why?"

"Because Rollin and Mrs. Emma Ramsay were ambushed and nearly killed in Redding about two hours ago. By Kent and Yori."

"Really? I didn't know they were in town."

Frank was behind it. Just a slight pause. A tense quality to the inflection in his voice.

Burke's jaw tightened, his fists balled and hatred filled him. Time to get rid of Mr. Bortolli. He'd kill him not only for double-crossing him but for trying to hurt his woman. "Yes, I just heard from my people that Kent's dead and Yori's in the hospital under heavy guard."

"That's too bad. They were good workers."

"That's right, you've used them before."

Bortolli coughed. "Wait. You don't think I was behind that, do you?"

"No. Why would I? Furthest thing from my mind, actually. But come to think of it, I guess I wouldn't blame you." Burke ran his hand over the blade of a samurai sword on the wall of his living room. "I'm certainly not getting the results I wanted as fast as I expected them. Rollin hasn't been much of a help to you, either."

"Look, you guys are my guys," Frank said quickly, sounding worried. "I know you and Rollin had a falling out, but I don't care about that. I didn't bring Rollin in on the nuke deal because he's too much of a goody-goody. But he's great at finding stuff."

"What if he finds the weapon before we do?"

"That wouldn't be good. I wouldn't feel right about it, but you know what I'd have to do. He wouldn't let it go to those guys."

Burke nodded. "No, he wouldn't."

"But I told you, we're in this together. You get that thing and all I gotta do is make one phone call and you can go make the drop."

"I should have it shortly."

"But you don't know where Emma Ramsay is."

"It won't be long before I do."

"Well, let me know the second you know something."

"Will do."

Burke hung up and wanted to spit, but he wasn't ruining his carpet. Once he got the deal set up, he'd take care of Frank. Bastard.

Now all he had to do was find Emma. And turn her against Rollin. This time, permanently.

Once Emma got a look at his evidence, she'd be convinced. She'd believe everything he wanted her to believe.

Power surged through him. He grinned and his dick went hard.

He'd have the nuke and a new life with a very beautiful, very loyal woman.

Rollin and Frank thought they could play with him.

Underestimating him would be the last mistake they made.

SEVENTEEN

The next morning at around eleven, Rollin had the lock on the storage locker undone in two seconds flat.

"Why did I bother?" Emma said with a shake of her head.

He shot her a grin. "Not everyone has my particular talents."

"You can say that again," she said, giving his hard butt a good grab.

A quick image of him naked above her, pounding her into rapture ran through her mind. That morning he'd woken her up with more amazing sex. God, he was addicting.

He sent her a sinister smile and gave a little growl. "Oh, baby. I'm gonna get you later, yes I am." He turned back to the locker door and opened it. "But first, let's see what Adam stole."

They walked into the fifteen-square-foot room and flicked on the overhead light.

Emma's heart rate jumped and her stomach went squiggly. Here was the final test. Even with the revelations about their shared past—plus their emotional connection—there was a teeny part of her that hadn't been convinced. Didn't completely trust him.

She tuned in on his face completely. So far, nothing. Once he saw the bomb, she'd know if he'd been lying about it. And if he'd been scamming her, she was out of there. Sweat broke out on the back of her neck.

Rollin examined the giant pile of boxes, then walked over and checked out the piano, pressing a key. “What is all this crap?”

“My mom’s stuff.” Emma couldn’t stand the wait, so she went straight for the plastic case. If he didn’t react right, her whole future with the most awesome man in the universe would be yet another Big Fat Lie. “It’s under here, help me.” Her hands trembled as she moved an old whiskey case labeled Beads and Beading.

Rollin helped her move the rest of the boxes, revealing the long plastic box covered with a quilt. She stepped back and fixed her gaze on his face and body reactions.

He sent her a sharp glance, but was so focused on the box, he didn’t seem to notice her intensity.

He flipped off the quilt and his brow furrowed. “Why the vests? Russian. Why does this make me nervous?” He sent her a worried glance, pushed off the vests and flipped open the plastic box.

For a half a second, he just stared at it. Then all the color left his face, his mouth dropped open and his eyes popped wide. Yelping, he leapt to his feet, stumbled back, tripped and fell against the metal wall of the unit, clanging his head.

She slumped with relief. He hadn’t known. Her defenses came down, the last shield dropped from around her heart.

Thank God. Her true love. Finally. After all these goddamned years.

Rollin didn’t notice her reaction. He was too busy freaking out.

“Holy fuck—that’s a—Emma! Jesus Christ, do you know what that is? Fuck!” He lunged forward and shut the lid and sat on it. Then he jumped off the box as if it had burned him. “Holy God, we are fucked. I mean, *fucked*. I have to call in the big guns. I have to call Zane. Why didn’t you tell me? Holy shit! Emma, you have a fucking nuke in your storage locker,” he whispered vehemently, gesturing violently toward the box.

While he was losing his mind, his reactions made her happier than hell. “I know. That’s why I didn’t tell you before we got here. I’m sorry. I had to know you were absolutely telling me the truth. You couldn't fake that reaction. Burke knows it's a nuke. He knows I know where it is. I almost brought him here. It's not going to be long before he figures this out."

"Holy fuck, I gotta call Zane." His hands shaking, sweat pouring off his forehead, he punched the keypad of his phone. "Fuck! Blew it!" He canceled the number, then pressed the button again. "Zane! Dude! Priority Alpha, no, bigger than Alpha! What's crazier than Alpha? Like quadruple fucking mega Alpha, dude! I need you now! I am calm! Drop whatever it is you're doing and get here as fast as you can. I'm in Redwood City off of Spring Street at a storage place. Get here now and bring your new Hummer! Yeah, the Hummer!"

Hanging up on Zane, he pushed another button. "Bobby! We're in deep shit, my friend, I just found out what Adam took. A fucking nuke, man, a fucking *nuke*! Scramble the team. I already called Zane. Tell Captain America I need him. I'm gonna need everybody. This is huge! What? Don't tell me that! Fuck! I gotta calm down. Zane will be here, we'll get out of here in time. Don't tell Banana anything. No, tell him we're still on the road, that we had car troubles. Make Burke think we haven't gotten to the Bay Area yet. Shit!" He clicked off and stared at the case like it was about to jump up and eat him.

"What? Is Cherlenko on his way here?"

"He's tracking us. Found out we were in that motel last night. Shit. He could be here any minute."

He sent her a frantic glance, then his gaze went back to the box. "Where the hell did this come from? And who the hell was selling it? I have to find out who the players were. Burke must know. Jesus Christ, when that guy falls, he goes all the way. But what the hell is he gonna do with this?"

"Sell it, is what I think. Going for Badass of the Year."

"No. Not Burke. He may be an opportunist, but he couldn't have changed that much. He's a snake, but he would still die for this country."

"You're the one who told me what a creep he was, that he was going to kill me."

Rollin waved his hand dismissively. “I only said that to keep you away from him. He wouldn’t kill you.”

A flicker of anger burned inside her. “But you—”

“I’m sorry, okay? But look, he may not kill you, but he would mindfuck you. He would hold you against your will for as long as it took for you to accept the situation and stop fighting him. He’s a Svengali with women. A total control freak. Some of his morals aren’t very moral, but when it comes to this country, he is pure. But that doesn’t mean he didn’t come up with some hare-brained scheme that could backfire on him, either.” He sighed. “I gotta get calm here. Sorry, I don’t usually freak out. This—this shocked me.”

“I wasn’t too happy when I found it.”

“I saw you right afterwards, how did you keep your mouth shut about this?”

“Duh. The lives of how many millions of people are at stake? I get the seriousness of the situation, Rollin. Believe me.”

He relaxed a tad, came over to her and hugged her hard. “Of course, you kept this to yourself. Sorry. I’m…”

“Freaked out.”

“Yeah. Fuck, I don’t want to leave this thing. Could you go outside and look for a Humvee? My friend Zane should be here any minute. No, wait. Burke might be sniffing around, I don’t want him seeing you. Shit.”

“I’ll babysit the bomb.”

“No. Just do me a favor and go out and see if there’s a black Humvee in the parking lot.”

“Okay.”

She opened the storage door and gasped. Her heart pummeled her ribs. Towering above her was the scariest man she’d ever seen in her life. Nearly seven feet tall and dressed in black, the man had long black hair and big glowing green eyes. With a heavy black brow, goatee and long sideburns, wearing a military beret, he looked straight out of a horror movie.

She screamed and reeled back, right into Rollin.

He clamped his hand over her mouth. “That’s Zane, Emma.”

Zane quirked his mouth to one side. “Pleased to meet you, too.” His voice was so deep, it rumbled.

“Th-that’s—you’re Zane?”

“Yes, ma’am. At your service.” His hard expression broke, she saw shades of a gentle person underneath. But he still frightened the hell out of her.

Rollin motioned for Zane to enter the room. “Come in, dude, fast. Did you see anyone in the parking lot?”

“Nope. So what’s up?”

“Check this out.” Rollin walked over to the box.

Zane shut the door and crossed to Rollin. The overhead light dangled dangerously close to his hat. Rollin flipped open the lid.

Zane’s thick black brow went to his hairline. He blinked a few times. His mouth opened a bit. But that was his only reaction. His face relaxed almost instantly. He nodded. “A nuke, very nice.” He gave a quick check of the entire unit. “Goes real well with the piano and Mom’s Sewing Projects. Whose storage place is this, anyway?”

“Mine.”

He cocked a giant dark eyebrow at her. “I don’t even want to know what you keep in your bedroom closet.”

“Where can we take it?” Rollin asked.

“Greg’s warehouse,” Zane said with a confident nod. “Got a call from him on my way here. Bobby’s got everyone notified. We’ll make some calls and get it to Johnny or Zipper.”

“Yeah, yeah. Good.” Rollin’s shoulders loosened.

Zane smiled and clapped him on the back. His hand made Rollin’s back look petite. “Dude, I know nukes flip you out, but we’ll take care of it. So who are we up against? Whose was this? This can’t be what Adam stole.”

“Yes, it is.”

Zane laughed from deep in his belly. “That fuckin’ idiot? Did he even know what he had?”

“Doubtful. He was more focused on the cash.”

"That five hundred million?" Zane asked.

Rollin nodded.

Zane glanced at the bomb. "Well, now we know what a nuke costs on the open market. Have you found the cash?"

Rollin shook his head. "Nope. And this is beyond Burke's reach. Beyond Frank. They must have stumbled on the deal. We gotta know who was selling it and who was buying it. And we have to know what Burke's plans are."

"Somethin' that will benefit him and fuck other people over," Zane said with his lip curled.

Rollin gave a grim nod. "Speaking of which, Burke could be on his way here. He's stepped up his game. I think he might kill us for this."

Zane's gaze went cold. "Told you that bastard was no good."

"So did everyone. I still can't believe he'd use this on American soil or sell it to the enemy."

"You got more faith in him than I do, pal. He turned."

"We'll see."

Zane looked over at her, then back to Rollin. "So you gonna introduce me to this nice lady?"

Rollin gave his head a quick shake. "Sorry. Emma Ramsay or Holsten, this is Zane Black."

Zane's head jerked back a bit and he seared her with his intense gaze. "Ramsay? You were married to—"

Emma held up her hand. "Please don't judge me for that. It was a bad four-month hormonal lapse that ended in a two-minute marriage."

Zane's serious expression broke. He sent her a sympathetic half-smile. "Sorry. I get it. And so does Rollin." He turned to Rollin and raised an eyebrow. "Don't 'cha, pal?"

Rollin turned red, coughed and looked at the ground. She'd get the story later.

She held out her hand, Zane's completely covered hers. She felt like a baby shaking hands with King Kong. But his hand was warm and smooth and his grip was gentle.

When he flashed her a white-toothed grin, his entire face changed. The man was actually very good-looking. Even features, sweet internal energy. She finally relaxed.

"So, dude, you got here fast, where were you?" Rollin asked.

Zane laughed and rolled his eyes, shifting all his weight to one leg. "Johnny Petrini's. Shit, you can't believe the job he's on. Get this: he has to sift through two hours of some really weird and irritating songs sung by this drunk woman. Some kinda code's embedded in the lyrics."

A weird feeling roiled Emma's stomach. Couldn't be.

Zane continued, seeming astonished and not in a good way. "Dude's losing his mind. And you can't believe the songs. Something called the Sniffy Butt Song about two cats sniffing each other's asses."

Emma's face burned hot with humiliation. She wanted to sink inside her Nikes and disappear.

Neither man seemed to notice.

"…a Toilet Paper Man song that's annoying as hell. At first Johnny laughed and thought it was funny, but by the time I left he wanted to murder the chick just to make sure she never sang those stupid songs again." Shaking his head, Zane glanced over at her and did a double-take. "What's wrong?"

Emma hid behind her hands and wished she were anywhere else.

Rollin took her arm. "Emma? Why are you hiding?" Understanding came over his face. "Oh." He burst out laughing. "Honey, don't worry."

Zane shot her a look. "Don't tell me."

"I plead the fifth. Don't we have to get this nuke out of here?"

Zane continued to stare at her, his green eyes wide.

Rollin smacked the behemoth on the upper arm. "Dude? The nuke?"

"Oh, yeah." Zane turned to the black case. But then he gave her one last long wary look before his attention returned to the bomb. He tapped the case with his Frankenstein-sized boot. "How heavy is this thing? Let's get a move on, I'll back up the Hummer to the door."

"Okie-doke," Rollin said.

"Artichoke," Emma said automatically.

"In awhile, crocodile," Zane said with a cute smile as he opened the door.

Very charming.

The tall man ducked through the door and shut it behind him.

"That is the biggest man I've ever met."

"He's a kitten."

"Pretty kick ass kitten."

"Well, you don't want to get on his bad side…"

"I'll bet."

Emma sat in Rollin's stolen Mercedes and waited for the men to finish loading the nuke into Zane's Humvee. She wiped her sweaty hands on her jeans, her heart thumping hard. She kept her focus on the corner of the long storage building and wished there was another way out. If anyone came around that corner, they'd be trapped.

Rollin got in the car. "We'll let Zane lead us out of here. He said something about adding some trick weapons to his Hummer."

"Okay."

Zane's black Humvee pulled out and Rollin followed. They turned the corner and Zane slammed on his brakes.

Emma's heart went wild and she yipped in fear.

Two black SUVs blocked the front gate of the storage unit. Four armed men took cover behind the vehicles. None, however, were bald. Cherlenko's hired guns.

Rollin's expression went grim. "Fuck. Get down, Emma! We're gonna shoot our way out!"

As she ducked, she caught movement on the top of Zane's Humvee and stopped. A small door opened on the roof of Zane's Hummer and a weapon raised. Looked like a rocket launcher or something. Very surreal. Very scary.

Emma's stomach twisted, she hunched down and held herself.

The armed thugs' mouths dropped open and they scattered.

A small rocket blasted off the top of the Hummer and blew the SUVs into the street, turning them into giant fireballs.

The concussion rocked their Mercedes and a blast of heat came through the windows. The air smelled of sulphur, burning tires and plastic.

A rush of excitement powered through her. She gasped and clutched her hands to her chest. She couldn't believe her eyes. Who the hell had a rocket launcher in their Humvee?

His weapon retracting back into the roof, Zane roared out of the gate, drove between the two burning vehicles and disappeared into a cloud of smoke.

Rollin followed into the smoke and they drove blind through the middle of the burning tangled masses of ex-vehicles. Emma grabbed her seat cushion in a death grip and prayed they made it.

Within a second, they cleared the smoke. Zane's Humvee was right in front of them.

Rollin shot her an angry glance. "I told you to keep your head down."

"I'm glad I didn't. Did you see that?"

Rollin's serious expression broke and he laughed. "That fucker gets more badass everyday. But those guys will be back and with bigger guns."

"I feel like I'm in a movie."

"Let's hope it's a movie where the good guys triumph in the end."

"We will. You heard Zane."

Rollin flashed a big grin at her. "You're awesome, Emma."

As soon as Zane reached Woodside Road, he slowed and turned right onto the six-lane thoroughfare, heading west, probably to the 280 Freeway. Rollin followed. Two blocks later, sirens filled the air and three cop cars came flying down Woodside going the opposite direction.

Her heart rate spiked and she hugged herself tight, but Rollin didn't seem worried.

Zane drove another few blocks, then veered right onto a side street without signaling. Rollin continued on another block, then hung a left.

After the fifth turn down a residential street, Emma looked over at Rollin. "Are you trying to lose someone?"

His dark eyes intense behind his sunglasses, he nodded. "Yeah. Gotta go into an underground garage to make sure the satellites can't track us. Burke's got a war room and he's probably watching us right now. There's a shopping mall right ahead I've used before."

"Do you think anyone got Zane's or our license plate number?"

"That happened so fast, I don't think anyone really noticed us. But we'll act like we've been compromised. One of the rules. Zane's plates will be different, the Hummer will be a new color and his VIN changed by this afternoon. And I'm dumping this car in about a minute."

"But won't it be reported as stolen?" Panic seized her limbs. "Oh, shit, the storage unit has cameras!"

Rollin sent her an easy smile. "Took care of that, no worries. And I swapped license plates early this morning at that motel, so it'll be awhile before they track this."

She took a deep breath. "You think of everything, don't you?"

"That's my job, babe," he said with a smug grin.

Well, she may be in the middle of a war, but at least she seemed to be in the right camp. And she had the best protection she could imagine. With Rollin and now Zane on her side, she became more and more certain that things would work out. They'd get the nuke into the right hands and maybe, just maybe, recover that cash.

She smiled and her mood brightened.

A new man, a huge stash of cash and a great future.

Almost too much to hope for.

But it was time things worked out. She'd paid her dues.

She hoped the Gods agreed.

EIGHTEEN

After driving through two malls and on umpteen highways and streets, Emma and Rollin arrived at a complex of warehouses and construction supply wholesale outlets in an industrial area of South San Jose.

They passed a few machine shops and a plumbing supply place. At the far end of the complex sat a very large warehouse marked San Jose Custom Cycles. A door rolled open and Rollin drove the Mercedes inside. It closed behind him. He parked next to Zane's Humvee.

Oil, gas, machines and metal filled the air of the cycle shop. A niggling terror ate at the edges of her mind. She flashed on the warehouse where those men tortured her. This cycle shop smelled just like it. Shuddering, she pushed the memories away.

Motorcycles in various stages of assembly were clamped into vises at stations around the vast shop. However, no one was working on the bikes.

A group of men, two women and Zane stood around the giant's Humvee. Wearing somber expressions, all were in their late thirties, early forties. Their appearances ran the spectrum. A few of the guys and a pink-haired woman dressed like bikers. Another woman with short blond hair wore a suit and high heels, the consummate corporate careerwoman. A tall blond surfer guy in a Hawaiian shirt stood next to Zane. On Zane's other side, two military-looking guys with square-shaped heads and close-cropped hair inspected the bomb in the back of the Humvee.

As she and Rollin approached, each member the group examined her carefully, head-to-toe.

Her stomach clenched and her skin tingled uncomfortably. She wanted to sink inside her skin and hide.

All wore hard faces and their emotions were closed off. Despite the difference in their exteriors, they were all hardcore fighter types. She felt like Bambi wandering into a den of wolves.

No one said anything.

She turned to Rollin to nudge him into introducing her and breaking the ice, but all his focus was on the back of Zane's Hummer. His gaze hollow, he seemed like he was ready to run at any moment.

The group shifted their focus to one another. They exchanged glances and then broke apart. Without glancing at her, the executive woman and one of the military-looking guys walked right by her and left.

What? Did she smell bad or what? What was wrong with these people?

The pink-haired biker chick and a brawny bearded biker with a shoulder-length hair started working on the motorcycles. The blond surfer and another burly balding biker disappeared into the office of the warehouse.

Zane spoke in low tones with a silver-haired military guy. The man glanced up at her and nodded.

Breaking into a smile, he walked over to her. Her stomach did a flutter. Dude was raging hot. Tall, with very short salt and pepper hair, he had pale blue eyes and a symmetrical tanned outdoorsy face. Looked like he was in supreme physical condition, his muscles bulged against a black t-shirt.

"Is this the famous Emma Ramsay?" he asked with barely hidden smile.

She relaxed immediately and a ripple of giddiness swept through her. So charming! And at least one of these people seemed to like her.

"Captain, I mean, Carter, this is Emma Holsten," Rollin said, gesturing toward her. "She was divorcing the idiot."

Captain Carter seemed to ignore his remark. He gave her a reassuring nod. "I've heard a lot of good things about you, Emma."

Zane and Rollin seemed to defer to this guy. This Carter man. He had the aura of an Admiral.

Emma smiled. "Despite the fact that I had a stupid attack and married Adam Ramsay. I appreciate that there's some other information about me out there."

"What you've done for your country in regards to that nuke shows your true metal. Good job." He shook her hand.

Her cheeks glowed with warmth. She'd rarely been recognized for anything she'd done. "I probably should have trusted Rollin sooner."

"Don't second guess yourself. You had to be sure."

"Yeah, well I wasn't sure about him until I saw his reaction to the weapon."

Carter's silver brows raised. "I think we all had the same reaction. And you never found out where Adam recovered it, correct?"

"Nope. I was completely oblivious about his nefarious activities, even while we were married. I found the bomb last Wednesday. Shit, it's only been a week. Feels like a year. I know you guys have probably thought of this, but does Cherlenko know about this place?"

None of the men reacted. She let out a sigh.

Rollin ran a hand down her back. "No, worries, hon. Greg set this up after Burke split." He examined her face and his brow wrinkled. Like he'd just noticed she might be having emotional issues. He threw his arm around her and hugged her tight. "We know him. We can take care of him."

She relaxed a bit.

"I just wish we hadn't been put in this position," Zane said.

Carter nodded, grave. "Disappointing. Had a lot of hope for that guy."

Rollin pulled away, but kept his arm around her. "Who are we using to dispose of the nuke?"

Zane said, “Zipper. He’ll be here tonight, after dark.”

“Good.” Rollin’s worry lines eased. “The sooner this scary thing gets to the Navy, the better.”

Her stomach dropped. “Navy? But they’re going to want to know where this came from and that leads right back to me. I have to take care of my sister and—”

Rollin brought her close again. “Emma, it’s okay. We’re not tellin’ ‘em anything about the nuke. And they don’t want to know. Ever heard of plausible deniability?”

She checked his face carefully. “Really?”

“They trust us,” Carter said.

Zane nodded. “We do things they can’t.”

Carter straightened his broad shoulders and nodded. “We have friends in high places who appreciate our talents.”

“Okay,” Emma said with shrug. “It’s your world. I’m just a visitor here.”

“And such a lovely visitor you are,” Rollin said, and gave her a quick peck on the cheek.

Rollin ordered pizza. He, Zane, Carter, Rollin and Emma sat around an old beat-up metal table in an assortment of office chairs clearly rescued from Dumpsters. The men, even Rollin, slammed the pepperoni, but Emma could barely choke it down. Her stomach was still twisted as a pretzel, her neck hurt from being rock-solid tight and her heart was uncomfortably open.

She wished she’d gotten involved with Rollin after this whole ordeal was over. New relationships were hard enough to handle, but with her brain so scrambled, the emotional impact was fifty times stronger. And this wasn’t the best time to be vulnerable. Or nervous about her future with him.

Rollin tipped back in his chair, his manner relaxed and self-assured, his expression open and affectionate with Zane and Carter. This was his world. And he was fine with it.

But she wasn’t. Given his dangerous job, how long was the guy going to live?

Probably not a question she should dwell on for the time being.

Actually, dwelling on any questions regarding this craziness was futile. She couldn't quite believe any of it could be happening to her. Ever since the day Burke Cherlenko walked into her shop, nothing had seemed real.

She had no background, no frame of reference, no previous experiences from which to draw upon to handle the current situation. She floated free in a sea of confusion with only her new man for an anchor.

Which was no sort of anchor at all. She'd learned long ago never to fully depend on men. While she loved Rollin and intended to have a future with him, she wasn't deluding herself. She still had to watch out for number one.

But at this point, the only thing she could do was take the ride. Step back and try not to freak out too much.

Emma gestured toward the group with her half-eaten slice of pepperoni. "So the ladies, everyone here, you guys are all Patriots?"

Rollin chewed and nodded. After swallowing, he said, "Most of us went through the academy together, were stationed together. All of us served together."

The whine of grinding metal filled the air.

Emma indicated the warehouse with a sweep of her arm. "Is this motorcycle shop a front?"

"Yes and no." Rollin talked louder, over the noise of the machine. "Greg loves his motorcycles and also does improvements for our cars and takes care of all our mechanical needs."

Carter sat directly across from her. With his silver buzz cut and tanned carved face, the man reeked Good Guy. Most of the Patriots looked like they belonged in a motorcycle gang, Rollin and Zane included. Carter stuck out as the All American Soldier. He had a saintly quality about him. She pictured him as the chaplain more than commander.

"So, Carter, were you the Captain of these guys?"

The three men laughed. Zane's rang out, deep and booming.

Carter smiled and shook his head. "Uh, no."

Zane said, "I named him Captain America. Because he's so…" The green-eyed giant examined Carter, narrowing his gaze and gesturing at him, searching for words.

"Perfect," Rollin finished.

Carter threw a wadded napkin at Rollin, his cheeks reddening.

"Captain America," Zane said, with a wide grin. "Just a joke that stuck." His white teeth set off against that black goatee and mustache gave him the air of a rogue. Maybe it was the beret that crowned his waist-long black hair.

Carter rolled his eyes. "Didn't it though."

Emma couldn't get over the Patriot's awesome gene pool. She'd never been around such a healthy, good-looking group of people. She gestured at Carter. "So were you a Captain?"

"For about a minute," Rollin teased. "Our Carter here went further than any of us. He was a fucking rear admiral."

Carter smirked. "Until I couldn't take it anymore."

"Whoa!" Rollin exclaimed, fumbling with a piece of pizza. He lost the slice and it landed face down on his thigh.

They all cracked up.

Rollin gave a sheepish laugh. "Damn it. Never did like nukes. Got me jittery."

"Well earned jitters," Carter responded.

"Damn, all over my best pants." Rollin used a napkin to clean up the mess. "Gooped it all over."

Emma immediately launched into, "*The Goops they lick their fingers, the Goops they lick their knives*—"

Zane's green eyes sparkled as he chimed in. "*They spill their broth on the table cloth*."

Emma grinned at the hulk.

"*Oh, they lead disgusting lives*," they said in unison.

A lightning bolt of realization zapped her and her muscles went hard. Humiliation burned through her, making her face go red hot. He'd listened to those damned tapes of her singing!

"Christ, what didn't I sing that night," she muttered.

Zane's thick black brow flattened over his green eyes. "What?"

"You heard me singing drunk on those tapes. I must have done the Goops."

"No. My foster mom used to read that to me when I was a kid."

"Oh." Her face burned with embarrassment. "Sorry."

Zane grinned, revealing a mouth of straight white teeth. "No worries, girl." His smile faded and he sent her a teasing smirk. "But I do hope you never get that drunk around me."

"Don't worry. I won't sing. And I'll never be that drunk again."

Rollin sent them questioning looks. "What are the Goops?"

"*Goops*," Emma explained. "A Victorian kid's book about manners. My mom used to read it to me. Her mom read it to her."

"My foster mom loved that," Zane said. "She may have been a cold bitch, but she gave me a love of books."

Emma gave up on the pizza and set it on a paper plate. Leaning back in her chair, she held a coke in her hand. "I used to recite it to Adam all the time because he was such a pig. He thought it was a song although I never sang…the—shit." She sat straight up. "He called it my Goopy Song! Adam wasn't saying Gems' Goofy Song, he was saying *Gems' Goopy Song*." Her heart rate jumped five times faster and thrills of excitement rushed through her.

Rollin's focus on her intensified. "Really? You think that's what he meant?"

"Yeah, the Goops!" She leapt to her feet and jumped in place, gesturing wildly. "I have the book on my shelf! I have to go home! The clue to the money is in that book!"

Rollin took hold of her arm and pulled her down into her chair. "Hold on, cowgirl. You're not going anywhere. And especially not to your house. Not until we dispose of the Thing."

She bounced on her chair. "Come on, you're just waiting for a pick up. We could sneak in the back, get the clue—don't you want the five hundred million?" She was so excited she wanted to jump all over the warehouse. Run in all directions at once. This was so awesome!

No matter what those guys said about the Navy not asking questions about the bomb, with that money she could hire enough firepower to protect herself from anyone. A rocket of joy burst inside her. She could take care of Lizzie for life with that money! All her problems would be solved!

Rollin's eyes crinkled with amusement, but his mouth twisted with exasperation. "Emma, calm down."

She grabbed his arm and squeezed it. "Rollin, this is what we've been looking for. Let's go get the money!" She pulled on him.

He held out his arms, his hands flat and pointed them toward her head. Narrowing his eyes, he made a really weird buzzing noise. "Mind control!"

She finally got his reference. From the movie *Time Bandits*. "No, really."

He waved a hand over her face. "You do not want to go back to your house until we've disposed of the nuke," he said, doing a dead-on impression of Alec Guinness as Obi-Wan. "You want to stay here."

She giggled, but was not dissuaded. "I could—"

Rollin's face went harder. "No, definitely not. Burke probably has the whole place rigged with cameras and sensors. He wants you. He loves you." A bit of pain marred his handsome features.

Carter sat up in his chair, alarmed. "He loves her? Burke loves her?"

Zane seared her with his green eyes, his face transforming to stone.

Burke was clearly a touchy subject with these guys.

She sighed. "Yes. Insert eye roll here. He thinks he does, anyway."

Carter's ice blue gaze hollowed. "That's not good."

"I know that, but I don't care what Burke feels, I want the money!"

Rollin increased the grip on her knee. "No, we wait," he ordered, his face and eyes steely. "End of discussion."

She pulled her knee away from him and frowned. "Who put you in charge?"

Rollin held himself taller, his shoulders straighter. “Me,” he said, his voice deeper and more commanding. “And you when you told me you loved me.”

While she was turned on by his power, he was still deluded as hell. “I told you I loved you, not that I will obey your every command. Don’t you get who I am yet? I am uncontrollable.”

Rollin’s jaw and lips went tight. He narrowed his dark eyes.

Carter nodded at her. “Listen to him, Emma. Burke is not someone to play around with. And if he thinks he loves you, he’ll be more dangerous to you than you can imagine.”

With a grave expression, Zane jerked his head toward her. “Girl? That dude kept a guy hostage for a month alone in a cave in Afghanistan. All by his lonesome. Both he and his prisoner were half-dead by the time we got to them, but he was still in control.”

She leaned back, crossed her arms over her chest and examined the three impediments. “Do you guys practice this kind of tag teaming?”

“Yes,” they answered in unison.

Her shoulders slumping, she nodded. “Okay, okay. But I still think I can work Burke.”

Rollin’s face turned somber and his gaze took on a haunted quality. “You get near him again, Emma, and he’ll find a way to turn you against me.”

She snorted. “Oh, come on, Rollin.” She took his hand and squeezed it. “Have more faith in me than that. Not after what we shared. Everything’s changed.”

Neither her words, nor her gesture had any effect on him. His expression remained fixed. “You still don’t understand him. He *will* turn you against me. And it won’t be your fault.”

She let go and turned her attentions to her coke. “This is a pointless argument. Okay, okay, I’ll wait. I’ve waited this long.”

Rollin studied her.

Her nerves flamed. “I mean, it,” she said. “I capitulate. Okay? Relax.”

"Good." He finally softened, he reached out and hugged her, kissing her on the cheek.

Her red-hot love for him momentarily derailed her. She melted into him, adoring the feel of his arms around her and his scent. But as soon as he pulled away, all she wanted to do was run out of there, jump into a car and rush home.

The *Goops*! The location of the money must be hidden inside! This was so exciting!

A stocky, balding biker guy with earrings and a black beard came flying out of the office, his face red. She thought she heard the men call him Greg. "Zipper's here, but he's not alone. Not two blocks behind him, four Humvees loaded with Stillwater guys."

Everyone at the table leapt to their feet.

Carter jerked his head at Greg. "How do we know this?"

Greg replied, "Just broke a coded message on a new band that Burke is using. Burke's running the show from his War Room. He ordered Stillwater to do whatever it took to get the nuke short of killing us."

Zane waved his hand in a quick, violent gesture. "But Stillwater's been itching to get back at us because of that Iraq deal. They'll wipe us out. Doesn't Burke know that?"

Rollin gave a quick shake of his head. "Maybe not. He was stuck in the cave in Afghanistan. I told him when I saw him, but he was loony by then."

Greg ran for his office. "We've got two minutes. Go!" he called over his shoulder.

Adrenaline swamped her and her heart thudded hard against her breastbone. She wanted to bash Adam's face inside out. He'd shoved her right in the middle of a fucking war zone. She hoped there was a Hell. And that her ex was Satan's favorite whipping boy.

The Patriots worked like a finely tuned machine, heading calmly but purposefully to different areas of the warehouse. Rollin grabbed Emma and pulled her toward the back of the metal building.

A high window broke in one of the front walls. A small, metallic can landed inside on the concrete floor with a loud clank. White gas began spewing out.

Her system revved higher. Rollin and she broke into a run.

"That was a fast two minutes!" Rollin yelled.

They passed the biker Patriot woman with the pink spiky hair. She held a huge weapon and already wore a gas mask.

An explosion rocked the building, nearly deafening her. As they reached the back wall, she had no idea where Rollin was planning on hiding her. There were a couple old cars in the far right corner, but they didn't seem like they'd provide any kind of shelter.

He leapt up and kicked an old poster on the wall which turned out to be a hidden door. It popped open.

Rollin shoved her outside to a small strip of asphalt behind the huge warehouse. A tall chain link fence stood in front of her. On the other side was a drainage ditch and beyond that, a residential neighborhood.

He pointed to the row of back fences. "Emma, go hide! Hop this chain link fence, go through the neighborhood and stay concealed. In five hours, at six pm sharp, meet me at Paul's Diner. You know where it is by Hillsdale?"

"Got it. But I don't want to leave you!"

"You'll die if you stay! Run, Emma, run!"

Searing pain blazed her gut and her heart cried out for him. She couldn't lose him! She grabbed him by the ears and mashed a big one on him. Pushing away, she quickly said, "I love you, take care of yourself."

"I love you too, and ditto. See you in five hours." He turned and dashed back into the warehouse, closing the door behind him.

She ached to stay with him and protect him. Thankfully, her logic was in control. Jumping up on the fence, she scrambled over and then hopped the ditch.

Gunfire erupted in the warehouse. The noise echoed off the inside walls.

Her heart beat so hard, she could barely breathe. She climbed over a wooden fence and landed in a manicured backyard with a large statue of St. Francis in one corner surrounded by zoo of small cement animals. No one was around and thankfully, there were no dogs, just statuary. She ran through the pristine yard, pushed open a wrought iron side gate, hit the sidewalk, and kept running.

A few blocks later, her lungs burned and her legs were on fire. She finally ran out of breath and slowed. She took a casual glance around the housing tract. A postman delivered the mail. An old lady deadheaded her roses. A young Mexican guy rummaged around in the back of his truck. No one gave her a second glance.

She reached a bus stop right as the bus showed up.

Shit! She had no money! Her belly contracted and she held her head with both hands to prevent it from blowing apart.

Wait. She dug around in her pockets and found a wad of bills. Her whole body went loose. The change from the Gap when she ditched the lime-green pantsuit! She paid, found a seat and slumped down, trying to appear tired rather than freaked out.

Damn, she almost loses her marbles when she doesn't have bus fare? She had to toughen up. This ride wasn't over yet.

Images of a huge war inside the warehouse bombarded her. Panting, her body shook with fear. She saw Zane getting shot. Rollin reeling back against the metal wall of the warehouse, blood running down his face.

Stop it! She gave her head a shake. Not helpful. She'd go meet Rollin at the appointed place at the appointed time and try not to visualize any more catastrophic outcomes.

Of course, it would be her luck to find true love and have the guy die on her.

Emma! Positive thinking!

Good plan. She'd think about the five hundred million dollars.

Because if she thought of Rollin and what he must be enduring, she'd go out of her mind.

NINETEEN

Blood pumped fast through Rollin's veins. His muscles tightened and readied for battle as he raced into a cloud of tear gas. He tried to hold his breath, but started coughing. His nasal passages closed, his lungs went into retreat, and his eyes stung and watered.

Carter appeared next to him in a gas mask and handed him one.

He quickly put it on, relieved for the metallic-smelling, canned air. After a few seconds, his lungs and nose cleared.

Carter gave him two fully-loaded Kimber 1911s and a wad of loaded magazines. He shouted over the gunfire. "Zane's Humvee has been compromised, he's down! Stefans's down, hope he's not dead. Catherine's holding off the guys at the front, along with Ty and Dino. We need to get that nuke out of the Humvee and get Zane! Cover me!"

"Go!"

His body hard, his senses heightened, Rollin followed Carter, who partially disappeared in the gas.

Gunfire blazed from in front of them. His heart beating at maximum, Rollin took cover behind some oil drums at the same time as Carter. Stopping for a second, they continued on, making their way to the front.

The fog got brighter. One of the roll-up doors was open.

Shouting and a scream. Bullets whizzed overhead. Rollin hit the ground and scrambled toward the action.

His body acting on pure instinct, he breached the gas and came into the daylight.

Zane's Humvee was on its side far across the parking lot, in between two trucks. Looked like he'd plowed right into them. Smoke poured from the Humvee's hood.

The back of the Hummer was open and the nuke was gone. Fuck!

Below the Humvee on the ground were two motionless legs.

Zane's.

His stomach dropped and panic fired through him. Then a boiling rage overtook him. He'd kill those bastards for hurting Zane.

Two dark SUVs with tinted windows backed away at high speed. Smoke billowed from a third SUV, parked in front of the garage, then erupted into flames, engulfing the vehicle. A bleeding guy lay on the ground below the burning mass.

Firing with both guns at the fleeing SUVs, Rollin ran abreast of Carter and rushed forward. He just caught sight of Catherine's pink head as she leapt into her Jeep to follow.

Tires squealing, Catherine took off after the assailants with Ty riding shotgun. The SUVs and Catherine's Jeep disappeared from sight.

Carter surveyed the area quickly. "I'll make sure the warehouse is secured, you go check out Zane!"

Rolling ripped off his gas mask and holstered his weapon. "I'm on it." He raced over to Zane.

The giant lay crumpled on his side, bleeding from his head.

Rollin's gut wrenched. He'd already lost Burke, he couldn't stand the thought of losing his last close friend. "Shit!" He dropped to his knees and checked Zane's neck for a pulse. Strong. A short wave of relief rushed through him. "Zane! Wake up, dude!"

Carter ran up to them. "Warehouse is secure. Is he okay?"

"He's alive and breathing and his pulse is good, but he's unconscious."

Carter said, "Stay with him, I'm going inside to see if I can help Dino and Stefan. Both got shot, but Stefan looks bad."

"Okay, go."

Carter rushed off.

Rollin lightly slapped Zane's face. "Zane, man, please wake up."

The giant groaned, his eyelids flickered open and he reached up and rubbed his head. "Fuck. What did I drink?"

The tension in his body eased and he laughed. "Shit, dude, are you okay?"

"No," he growled.

"Be careful. Don't move your—"

Zane turned his head, rolled onto his back and looked up at him. "Don't move my what?"

Rollin made a face at him. "Your head."

Zane moved his neck, and then each body part in turn. "I think I'm okay."

Rollin let out a long breath of air. "Thank fucking God."

Zane's attention went to his vehicle, his green eyes popped wide open and he sat up. "Shit, they got the nuke. Fuck!"

"Don't worry, we'll get it back." Rollin clapped him on the shoulder.

"How's everyone else?"

Rollin stood and gave him a quick report of everyone's status.

Zane motioned for his hand. "Help me up."

Rollin took his dinner-plate-sized hand and got him on his feet. Zane wiped his head, then noticed the blood on his palm.

Rollin wanted to check his head wound, but Zane was too tall. "Is your head okay?"

"Yeah. I'll live. Unless you think I should put a tourniquet around my neck."

Rollin smirked and nodded toward the warehouse. "Let's go see what the damage is."

When they walked into the warehouse, Carter came up to them. He pointed to Stefan, lying in the corner on a sofa. "Stefan's messed up with a broken arm and a gunshot wound to the knee, but he'll live." He indicated the opposite corner of the large room where Dino stood. "Dino got grazed in the shoulder, but it's not serious."

"Speak for yourself," Dino said, walking up to them. As he rotated his shoulder, the tall Italian grunted. "Hurts like a mofo."

Carter said, "All the Stillwater guys escaped, but we hurt a few of 'em." He scanned the warehouse with a grave expression on his weathered face. "Has anyone seen Greg?"

Dino picked some debris out of his curly black hair. "No, he disappeared."

Carter looked out through the open front door to the street beyond. "I hope Catherine and Ty will be okay."

"They're fine," came Greg's voice.

The balding human fireplug had appeared out of nowhere, completely undamaged. His black leather jacket didn't even have any dust on it. "Their engine was shot dead, they're stranded a few blocks away, they're walking back now."

"Where were you?" Carter asked, peeved.

With no apology on his face, Greg pointed to the ground. "I never got around to showing you guys my new computer room. It's underneath the building. I'm tracking the two SUVs."

Stefan groaned and waved at them. The lanky blond was lying on the front seat of an old car that served as a couch. The bandage on his knee had bled through. "I got two of those tracking devices on the SUVs. I was putting on the third when they cut me down."

Carter nodded. "Good job." He turned to Greg. "Where are they now?"

"On their way to the airport." Greg backed up toward the office. "We gotta roll and try to cut them off. I'll run the operation from here."

Sirens sounded from a few blocks away.

Rollin motioned for Greg to stop. "Problem is we don't have any working vehicles left that haven't been stolen."

Greg shot him a grin. "Hell we don't." He pointed toward the side of the warehouse with a long, beat-up finger bearing a silver skull ring.

"I got three new Denalis around the corner I was improving for a customer. Take those."

After making a brief battle plan, they all left. Rollin and Zane in one Denali, Carter in another. Dino took Stefan in his own car to a doctor colleague of the Patriots in the City. When Catherine and Ty got back, they'd take the last Denali. That was if the cops didn't get in their way.

Rollin asked Carter over his headset, "Greg knows the Chief of Police of Redwood City, doesn't he?"

"Yeah, his dad served with the guy in Vietnam. And he knows what Greg's doing. Covered for him before."

"Good. Really don't like fighting on our home soil."

"Me, neither. But Burke started this one," Carter replied.

Rollin's gut hurt like he'd been punched. How could Burke have gone this wrong?

He followed Carter's SUV onto 101 and they headed north. "Doesn't make sense. Burke knows we'd take care of the nuke. Why take it?"

"Wish I knew," Carter said. "But despite what Zane says, I don't think he'll try to sell it. Knowing him, he cooked up some elaborate plan that has good intentions, but'll wind up starting World War 3. I'm hanging up. We'll get back on when we get close to the airport."

"Roger that," Rollin said, clicking off his headset.

Emma's sweet smile. Those firm breasts. He smiled.

The masked assailants grabbing her.

His back went rigid and his brow furrowed. A shot of pain went through his forehead. He rubbed the tension from his face, pulled his neck to one side to stretch it and noticed his hand was white from gripping the steering wheel so hard. "I hope Emma's okay and she stays away from her house. I sent her to Hillsdale, I should have picked Gilroy. She's gonna be tempted."

Zane's face hardened. "She just doesn't get it yet."

"She should," Rollin bit out. His blood pressure rose so fast, his face went hot and his pulse thumped in his ears. "She's been kidnapped three times, beaten and terrified by the bastard."

Zane shrugged. "Burke's got some magic with women."

"Tell me about it," Rollin spat.

The hulk stared at him. "You in love with her?"

Emma in his arms with her face buried in his chest. Her flowery scent. He ached for her like he hadn't seen her in months. "Horribly. Badly. I've never felt anything like this before."

Zane smiled and grabbed him by the shoulder with his humungous hand, nearly covering the whole thing. "Good for you. She's a nice girl."

Rollin covered his wild feelings with an eye roll and changed lanes to get around a large tractor-trailer. "A little too crazy."

Zane laughed. "Sounds like your perfect mate."

The spark in her green eyes. The saucy twist to her full red lips. The arousing noise she made in the back of her throat when she came. "Yeah…"

Past perfect. Too good to be true.

When they reached the airport, they found two transponders lying on the ground in a parking lot and no SUVs.

Rollin's head pounded and he bit back a scream. Once back in the Denali, he punched the steering wheel. Zane wore his Death face.

"Greg? What the fuck?" Rollin demanded over the headset.

"I don't know, Rollin," Greg said, his gravelly voice tinged with anger. "I got access to all the cameras at the airport, but they don't cover every single square foot. The Stillwater fuckers must know where they are and skirted 'em. I haven't seen the SUVs, anywhere."

His gut turned to fire. "Shit!" Rollin stomped his boot against the floorboards. "What about Burke's plane?"

"Burke's jet's ready to fly and the pilot's been called," Greg replied. "But knowing Burke, that could be a distraction."

"Agreed," Rollin said with a sharp nod. He rolled his shoulders and twisted his torso. "We'll check out the jet and the ground to make sure. Carter? You there?"

"Yep." Captain America sounded as down as Rollin. "How about I take the south, you take the north. And Catherine and Ty can check the parking lots. Catherine? You hearing this?"

"I'm here," Catherine's high raspy voice came over the com. "Ty and I are in Long Term Parking now."

"Stay on the coms and let's find these assholes." Rollin started the vehicle and drove off, wishing he didn't have to obey the speed limits.

"You bet," Captain replied.

After an hour-long intensive search, the Patriots found no sign of Burke or the Stillwater guys.

Rollin's belly hurt and he glowered at the passing airport transportation buses. They were better than this. He was better than this. He spat out the window to rid himself of the bitter taste. "So what now, Captain?"

"Catherine and Ty, you stay and watch the airport," Carter said.

"Roger that," Catherine replied.

"Rollin, you and Zane and I will go back to Zane's to discuss overall strategy. Zane's got that bunker of weapons in case we need them."

Rollin chuckled. "Remind him to show you his new tank."

"Tank?" Captain and Catherine exclaimed in unison.

"Yeah, his tank. He got it last week."

Zane smacked him on the upper arm. "Don't be sayin' nothin' about my tank. It's cool."

"It's overkill," Rollin shot back.

"At any rate," Captain said, "Greg, keep on running the operation from your control room."

"Great plan," Greg said with a sarcastic edge. "Since I can't leave because my warehouse is crawling with cops."

"We'll contact you when we get to Zane's. Carter out."

Rollin clicked off his earpiece. Emma's lovely breasts. The milky white, soft skin. "I gotta get to Paul's Diner by six. Emma's supposed to meet me there." He yearned to hold her. To take care of her. To make her safe. "I hope she's okay."

"She's fine. She got out of there in time, right?"

"Yeah. But she'd better have listened to me and stayed out of sight." Rollin blocked the images of Emma being tortured and killed from his mind and pictured her that morning, waking up in his arms. He wished he could drive right to Paul's to see if she was there.

If they got through this okay, he would marry her. Straight away. He wanted her forever.

A half an hour later, they arrived at Zane's place, a ten thousand-square-foot mansion on a fifty-acre estate in the Woodside hills. Rollin and Carter stood in Zane's expansive wood-paneled office, facing a large plasma screen displaying Greg via webcam. The hefty, balding biker wore square-framed glasses and sat in his underground lair amidst a roomful of computers, screens and refrigerator-sized data storage devices.

Rollin pulled up an Aeron chair and sat. He tapped his feet on the floor and drummed his fingers against his knee. His mind wrenched between being freaked out about the loose nuke and worried about Emma's safety.

Zane leaned on his huge blond wood desk, sucking down a Diet Dr. Pepper. Behind him on the wall hung a collection of original Clint Eastwood movie posters. "Should we alert the Admiral?"

Carter shook his head. "No, too tempting, too big of a feather in his cap. He's running for office. He'd be all over us. And a complete distraction. I don't want him to even get a whiff right now. That's all we'd need."

Rollin took a long breath and stretched his back. "So we got jet or car or semi-truck. What other ways would he try to get the thing out of the country? By boat? And Greg? Can't we just hone in with that nuclear detection satellite?"

The square-jawed biker nodded. “Yeah. That was if I had a better idea of where the damn bomb is. There’s so much nuclear noise in the Bay Area, you can’t believe it. I mean, the computer should have picked it out, but so far, no go. And I thought the Homeland Security improvements were supposed to negate the idea of a nuclear surprise. I gotta tell you, I don’t have a lot of confidence right now.”

Rollin’s head ached and he was nauseous from having his stomach in knots. He probably needed more food. He kicked a cat toy across the carpet to one of Zane’s two Siamese cats. “Too many security agencies nowadays and all they do is fight each other.”

The cat eyed him, defiant, and didn’t make a move toward the bell-in-the-ball. Even Zane’s pets were too cool to react. Rollin wished he was that calm.

Carter ran his hand through his short silver hair. “Everything’s a pissing contest.”

“You got that right, pal,” Zane said. He picked up a fuzzy ball from his desk and tossed it to the cat.

The animal came alive, leapt up from its lying position and pounced on the ball. Grabbing the pink furry mass in its mouth, the cat trotted out the door, apparently to murder the toy in another room.

Zane shot a grin at Rollin. “Fang hates bells. Loves fuzz. Go figure. His brother, Killer, is the bell lover.” His deep smoky baritone voice rumbled in his wide chest.

Carter gestured toward them. “Okay, if the jet is a ruse, how else? We’d better station people at the ports. And at all the airports, not just SFO. Darn it, I wish Jake hadn’t taken some of the guys for that deal in West Africa. Could really use him and Cruz and Roman, especially.”

“Yeah, and they’re in deep,” Zane said. “Haven’t heard dick from them.”

Greg said, “I heard from Cruz this morning. They’re okay, but their situation is tense. We may need to send back up.”

Carter’s brows went to his silver buzz cut. “We’re stretched too thin as it is.”

“Need some fresh meat,” Zane said.

"Agreed," Rollin said. "Need to look into that."

Greg gestured toward the webcam. "I've got Bobby online. I told him to monitor the ports and let us know if there's any action there. Burke can't have gotten too far."

Rollin swore. He dug his fingers into the armrests and used his feet to twist in the chair. "I wish David hadn't turned on me. He'd know what Burke's plan was. Or maybe not. Something like this, Burke's probably playing his cards close to his vest." He forced a hand off the armrest, grabbed his can of coke from the floor and finished it. "He could already be on the way to LA or something by now."

Longing for the old Burke tweaked him. Rarely had he found a buddy that compatible. They spent months together, working side-by-side, their only arguments were about movie plots.

Not only had he lost Burke as a friend, he'd gained him as an enemy. Had that month in the cave in Afghanistan permanently warped his brain? Or was it the massacre? Probably a combination of the two. They'd been a real one-two punch to his sanity. He'd never forget the look in Burke's eye when they found him. Never seen anyone that crazy. He'd thought Rollin and Zane were hallucinations.

"He'll probably have it out of the country by tonight." Carter rubbed the back of his neck, his pale blue eyes hard.

Zane flipped a length of his long black hair over his shoulder and shifted on the large desk. "If he's selling it, he'll need to meet with his buyer. But where?"

Rollin shrugged. "I don't know. Wait a minute. We did a deal a year ago and he was all hot to complete the transaction out in the middle of the Pacific Ocean between here and Hawaii." Followed by a surf holiday in Hawaii.

His gut roiled and his fists wanted to bash some sense into his old friend. Burke had been so animated when he revealed the plan to Rollin. He'd been practicing surfing and wanted to show off his new tricks. Afterwards, they planned on tag-teaming some local surfer chicks. Rollin had never caught more women than when he was with Burke. Damn, they'd had fun together.

"Greg? You hear that?" Carter asked. "Where is his boat?"

"Bobby says its in Hawaii," Greg said over the computer. "He's got all the dope on every vehicle the man owns or has rented. I have all his aliases. We're processing all that now. Oh, just got another IM from Bobby. He says he might have got false intel on the whereabouts of Burke's boat—"

A rush of energy forced him straight up in his chair. He snapped his fingers. "I knew it!"

"Bobby also says he's got another hit he's following up. Cherlenko rented nine limos this morning. Damn, Bobby's good. I checked all the rental places no more than fifteen minutes ago and came up with nil. That guy just gets better and better, Rollin," Greg said.

Rollin's chest swelled with pride. "Love that boy."

Zane snorted and sent him a teasing grin. "Don't let NAMBLA hear you say that."

He almost barfed. Rollin threw his coke can at him. "If you weren't already hurt, I'd slap you one. NAMBLA…" he grumbled. "Don't get me started."

Zane laughed, his green eyes sparkling with mischief.

Carter squinted. "Why would he need nine limos?"

Rollin's head hurt just thinking about it. Burke had the biggest computer in the world between his ears. "I don't know, but I'll bet we find out." He rubbed his temples to ease the tension.

"Wish he was still on our team," Carter crossed his arms across his chest. "This will be interesting."

His throat tightened. "I'm going to kick his ass," he pronounced, still massaging his head.

Zane grinned. "I'll help."

"Whatever happens, I have to meet Emma at six in San Mateo." He checked Zane's office for a clock. "What time is it now?"

Zane pointed to a grandfather clock behind Rollin. "Three."

His back tensed and he tapped his foot harder. "Shit. Now I get to worry for three fucking hours. Should have put a GPS on her before I let her go."

"She's a survivor, friend. No worries," Zane said with a confident nod.

"You're right," Rollin eased the worry lines from his face to fool his friends. But this was going to be the longest three hours of his life.

* * * * *

Emma took a series of buses to the train station in downtown San Jose. She arrived at the Hillsdale station in San Mateo with three hours to kill before meeting Rollin.

As she walked to Hillsdale Mall—a block from the station—a vision of Rollin making a silly face popped into her mind. She laughed. He'd better be okay. She already missed him. And was so worried about him. She wished she had her cell phone, Rollin said that Bobby had it at his place. She could get a prepaid phone, but she didn't even have Rollin's number. Stupid.

She hit the pedestrian signal at El Camino Real and waited for the light. A picture of the Russian lying wounded on the pavement flashed through her head. She shuddered.

If she and Rollin survived, would their lives stay this crazy? Was this a window into her future? Waiting for him, not knowing if he was alive or not?

Yes.

But she loved him. Deeply, wholly, fully. She felt like she'd finally met her match. Someone smart, funny and super hot.

Speaking of hot, the sun was blazing. No surprise in late September. Fall was normally the hottest season in the Bay Area. As she crossed El Camino, she took off her hoodie and wrapped it around her waist.

Once inside the mall, she got a latte and wandered around, looking in the windows of the shops. The scent of fresh chocolate chip cookies wafted by. Normally, she'd be making a beeline to the bakery, but today the smell made her nauseous. No room in her tight stomach for anything but a little coffee.

Emma walked by a kid's clothing store. In the front display, a child mannequin sat in a small chair, reading a book.

She pictured her *Goops* book on a shelf in her bedroom.

Her heart skipped a beat. The money. Think what it could do for Lizzie. And if something happened to the Patriots—her heart lurched and she shoved the thought away.

No, she had to deal with the possibility. This was about her and her life now. That cash would protect her.

Her stomach hollowed and she had to gasp for a breath. Cherlenko with that money. If anyone other than her or the Patriots got hold of that money, the results could be apocalyptic. The bad guys could buy a nuke or any number of horrible weapons.

For her sister, for her and for her country, she had to get that money and do it fast.

What time was it? Three o'clock. Three hours left. Plenty of time to go there, retrieve the book and meet Rollin.

But how could she get into her house without anyone seeing her? She formed and rejected several options.

Damn, this wasn't like foiling her parents when she was a kid, fooling Burke was like trying to outwit a freakin' Bond villain. A professional spy. A man far out of her league.

She groaned, punched her palm and left the children's clothing store.

Emma stopped mid-stride in front of the Disney store. Burke was busy attacking the Patriots and trying to recover the nuke. He would need all his resources to defeat them. No matter how good he was, he had to be stretched at the moment.

Her pulse sped like she'd had fifty espressos. She rushed to the nearest exit and hailed a cab.

After circling her block twice, Emma ordered the cab driver to pass by the house one more time. Her heart rate increased with each moment. She carefully checked out all the parked cars, but no one seemed to be watching her house.

A storm of doubts and ugly images pounded her brain. She gave her head a shake and took a deep breath. *Focus on the goal, not the obstacles.*

She had the cabbie drop her off in the bank parking lot next to her house. Lots of cars coming and going, no one should notice her.

Her heartbeat accelerated. Her body buzzing with flight-or-fight juices, she quickly and quietly walked down her driveway. She retrieved the back door key from cement frog and went in through her back door.

The house was cold, dark and dreary as a tomb, and smelled like garbage. Fruit rotted in a bowl on the kitchen counter, the dirty plates in the sink had turned into giant Petri dishes and bread molded in the breadbox. She resisted the urge to start cleaning and raced for her bedroom.

Tracing her finger along the spines of all her kids' books, she finally came to the large yellow book. *Goops and How To Be Them,* by Gelett Burgess. Her hands trembled. Her pulse pounded in her ears. She opened the book.

Nothing. She fanned through the pages. A dark spot caught her attention near the back of the book. She opened to the page.

Gasping, she broke out in a full body sweat. A metal key nestled inside a hole that had been cut into the pages. It was a safe deposit key with a number written on it in permanent marker. She recognized the number. Hers.

Her interior went hot and a delightful tingle raced through her. She jumped in place. The key to the money! She knew where the cash was hidden! Whoo-hoo!

But wait a minute. She and Adam had cleaned out the safe deposit box the same day they filed for divorce.

She thought back to that day. She'd wanted to close out the box out completely, but Adam suggested that she hang onto it for a bit longer because the bank had a waiting list for safe deposit boxes. She'd been so distracted, she hadn't thought much about it.

They'd left the bank and Adam had told her he'd meet up with her later to divide their belongings back at the apartment in the City.

The jerk had gone right back into the bank and made sure he stayed on the account. He probably paid for it in cash. The box was in her maiden name, nothing that could be traced to him. A perfect place to hide stolen valuables. He probably had no idea that he'd be using it so soon.

But five hundred million wouldn't fit in a safe deposit box. Unless it was in diamonds or something.

Still, she'd found a biggest clue yet! She was on the right track! She would find that cash! Yippee!

Emma finally realized she was celebrating when she should be fleeing. Tucking the key inside her bra, she headed for the backdoor.

After taking a quick check of the backyard, she dashed out, locked the door, hid the key back under the frog and took off up the driveway.

Her body one solid nerve, she expected to be attacked. But as she cleared her house, she saw nothing suspicious and no one followed her.

She headed for the bank downtown, about twelve blocks away. A half hour walk. Seemed like fifty miles and twenty hours away.

After a few blocks, she finally breathed. No one had grabbed her and no one was paying an inordinate amount of attention to her.

She took some shortcuts through parking lots and alleys and stayed off El Camino Real, the main drag.

Her heart rate escalating with each step, she increased her pace. Soon, she was full on running. She probably should have taken a damn cab.

Breathless, Emma arrived at her bank and was soon in a little locked room, facing her very heavy safe deposit box. Her chest was so tight, she could barely breathe.

She opened it up with a shaking hand and gave a little yip.

Her heart rate leapt higher. Her body pumped with adrenaline.

Scads of hundred dollar bills. The box was crammed with them.

She wanted to hoot and laugh and jump and dance around the tiny room. She found it! She found the money! Yes!

But no way was it five hundred million worth.

Stuck down along the side of the box was an envelope. She withdrew it and opened it.

Inside was a set of keys, a note, and a receipt for a truck storage place. The storage yard was right by Highway 92 and the 101 freeway, not five minutes from her. She opened the note and recognized Adam's handwriting.

If you're reading this, Emma, then I'm dead. Which pisses me off because I should get this fucking money, not you. And even though you don't deserve it, I'll tell you where I hid the rest of the five hundred million. There's a chunk of this money at your house under the insulation in a backpack, almost to the front of the house. I also put some in your mom's storage unit in Redwood City on Spring Street in that fucking piano that I almost broke my back moving.

"Holy crap, I was right next to that! And some in my attic? Hell."

But the rest of the cash is in a storage container in a red semi-truck marked Bob's Produce. The keys will fit the five locks on the outside of the storage container and the truck itself. The semi runs fine and is full of gas.

But you'd better lay low. Maybe even change your name and move to another state. Plastic surgery might not be a bad idea. Give yourself bigger tits.

Her gut twisted and her ears went back. "Fuck you, asshole."

Because if I'm dead, then you're probably next.

Her stomach hollowed and her heart thumped hard. "Thanks for the warning, jerkoff."

And watch out for the thing in the big black plastic container in your storage unit. I think it's a bomb.

"Ya think?"

If I were you, I'd dump it as soon as you can. But watch out, there's some guys after that bomb and the money. If I'm dead, they probably killed me.

I found the bomb and money when I ran into this really bad scene. I overheard this guy Burke Cherlenko talking about a big deal at a warehouse out in the middle of nowhere near Hollister. Sounded good. I found a tractor-trailer full of cash surrounded by dead guys, all shot up.

Fuck, I hope this is me reading this. That would suck if you get to spend all that cash for doing nothing for me. Hey, make sure my new girl Jenn gets some of the money. She's a nice girl. Nicer than you were to me. I know I lost you that hoity-toity director job at the museum, but it was only a job. You made way too big of a deal about that in my opinion.

Adam B. Ramsay

Burning rage scorched her nerves. She gripped the page, almost ripping it. "Asshole! Even dead you're an asshole."

Holy shit. Emma was now five hundred million dollars richer! She jumped up out of the chair and did a little victory dance in the room.

She stopped, mid fist-pump. What if the truck was gone? She had to go check!

What time was it? Three forty-five. She had just enough time to take a cab to the storage area before she had to meet Rollin. She had to see the money for herself.

But did she want to risk getting caught with the keys? No. First she'd establish that the truck was still there. The keys were safer in the safe deposit box. No way did she want to hand the rest of the money to some attacker. Especially Cherlenko.

Emma grabbed a wad of cash and stuffed it in her jeans pockets. After memorizing the address for the storage yard, she closed the box and bamboozled the bank clerk into letting her use to the bank's phone to call a cab.

She waited in the bank until the cab arrived, then ran out, got inside and gave the storage yard address to the cabbie. As they drove, she thought better of it. What if she was being followed? What if someone was tracking her and questioned the cabbie?

"Uh, cabbie? Could you drop me off at the YMCA on Grant instead? I think I'll work out."

"Yes, ma'am," the older Indian man said.

After the cabbie drove away, Emma walked along Grant, went under the Highway 92 overpass and took a left onto 19th Avenue. Lots of traffic on 19th. Too much, it was making her nervous. She checked around as casually as she could, but didn't want to attract attention.

A half a block later, she slipped into the storage yard through an open gate and was immediately concerned. It would take nothing to steal a truck from these guys. There was no guard at the gate and there were a ton of vehicles in the parking lot.

Adjacent to the lot stood a large metal warehouse. Inside were a few auto repair bays. A tow truck was up on a lift with two Hispanic guys working below.

Where the hell was the truck?

As she walked further into the complex, she finally spotted a separate fenced-off area at the back of the property. Inside were many parked trucks and boats.

Her mood picked up, a little buzz started in her belly.

A guy who resembled a human Basset hound sat on an old metal folding chair at the entrance to the fenced lot in front of a little wooden kiosk with peeling white paint.

"Can I help you?" he asked in a gruff smoker's voice.

"Yeah, I'm thinking about storing my boat here. Can I have a look around? I'm not sure about your security."

He frowned, his jowls nearly touching his chin. "Lady, we haven't had one theft in ten years. But you can look around if you want."

"I can look through the fence, that's okay. I don't want to be a bother."

His expression softened and he beckoned her closer. "Oh, come on. Little lady like you shouldn't be in this part of town alone, anyway."

"I'd be much obliged. My husband is super picky about his boat."

The man slid the gate open and let her in. She wandered up and down the lanes, nodding, as if she were inspecting the area. Emma tried to appear relaxed—not ready to combust—and walked purposefully. She came around a row of trucks and boats, and shortly came upon a red semi. She casually walked by it.

Bob's Produce was clearly marked on the door.

Her heart thumped so hard, it sucked all the blood from her head and she almost fainted. But she forced herself to focus and kept walking the same pace. Took all her inner strength to avoid whooping. With wobbly legs, she circled the entire yard, then went back to the front.

She smiled at Mr. Basset Hound. "This might work. I'll tell my husband what I found. Thanks for your trouble."

"No trouble, lady," he said, opening the gate for her.

She left the yard and could barely contain herself. The money! *She found the money*. Not Rollin, not Burke, not anyone else, but her. She found a freakin' shipping container full of cash!

Casually glancing around the area, no one seemed to notice her. She allowed herself one fist pump. Yay! She was rich!

Now she had to meet up with Rollin—fuck. What if he was dead? Her stomach turned in on itself and she rubbed a fist. He went back into that fight…

She mentally threw a glass of cold water in her face. She couldn't think the worst. Until she heard otherwise, she'd believe that Rollin was fine. That all the Patriots were okay.

Her throat tightened and her stomach did a sideways jump. Rollin would kill her if he found out she'd gone to the house. What would she tell him?

She stopped and made an exasperated noise. Why the hell was she worried about what he thought? Damn, no more giving her power away to men. She could take care of herself.

Speaking of which, she took a slow glance around her area. Cars zipped by on 19th, a bicyclist on a recumbent rode past, but no one gave her a second look. Still, she had to get to cover. Walking around

San Mateo when she had a huge target on her back wasn't smart. She'd head to a strip mall on Grant and call another cab.

She picked up her pace, hit Grant and took a left.

Rollin smiled from her memory and a rush went through her. Damn, she loved the guy. Despite the fact he was overprotective at times, he was the best man she'd ever been with. She hoped he was okay.

Emma walked by several manicured yards and perfect little ranch homes, wishing she were one of the normal people living inside. Boring would be great right about now. She longed for mundane. Go to work, come home, fix dinner, watch a bit of TV, fuck her husband's brains out and go to sleep. Heaven.

Her therapist would never believe a word of this. Meg would probably commit her once she started telling the tale. She'd just omit the part about the money and the nuke.

But damn, she'd give anything to talk to Meg. Or Sam. Or Diane. Or Cathy or Peggy. Someone who knew her. Someone from her old world. Her safe world.

Emma shook off the doubts. She had to keep her head together. Just for a while longer. Then she'd commit herself to an institution.

Of course, at this point, she'd settle for a few quiet nights in Motel Hell.

All at once, steel-banded arms wrapped around her.

She screamed. Her mind vaporized in a cloud of terror.

TWENTY

Emma bellowed and fought as hard as she could, but the man holding her was built like a rhino. A limo pulled up beside her, the door opened and Mr. Rhino threw her inside. A monster-sized man from inside—she didn't see his face—grabbed her and hauled her onto his lap, the door slammed shut and the car sped off so fast, she was thrown back against the man's chest.

All of it took less than a second.

Her mind wild with fear, she flailed, but the guy had her in a death grip. Someone else sat in the backseat.

Still yelling, she turned to see who.

Cherlenko. Smoothly shaved head and face, meticulous black Italian suit, penetrating dark gaze and all.

Fuck!

Her vision shifted, her entire body contracted, then she exploded in an atomic blast of fury and let loose with a deafening roar.

The guy holding her clamped his hand over her mouth.

"Sorry, boss, that was killing my ears."

David. While a hired goon, he wasn't a bad guy.

She stopped fighting and seared Cherlenko with the most hate she could muster. Something about the perfection of his sculpted features and his neat appearance pissed her off even more. So unruffled and relaxed while he terrorized her all to hell. Dick.

"You must see something."

She turned to David as much as she could given his tight hold. "I won't yell." Which came out as "Mmm, mmm, mmm."

David took his hand from her mouth.

"I won't scream," she assured him.

"Okay, Emma."

"And you can ease your grip, I'm not jumping out of a moving car."

David complied, but still held her firmly.

She turned to Cherlenko and scorched him with another glower. "Okay, you bastard, give me your worst. But know this, you hold me against my will and I will make your life a living hell. And I don't care if you beat me or kill me or torture me, I will not comply and be your subservient bitch. Get me?"

He tried to hide his smile.

"Fuck, I want to smash your face in," she growled.

"I only ask your attention for ten minutes. Then I'll let you go. I'd never hold you against your will, Emma. That's Rollin's view of me. And I think you know that. Will you please look at this video?"

"Well, since David won't let me go and I'm stuck in this limo with you, okay. I'll just bet it's not *America's Funniest Videos*, either."

Cherlenko said nothing, but sent her a wary glance, his worry lines deep. He didn't seem concerned about himself, but about her. She'd have thought he'd be piling on facts to prove his case, trying to turn her around. From what she knew about his objectives, he was acting weird.

"I'm genuinely sorry about this, Emma." He pressed a button underneath a large screen on the back of the front seat.

What the fuck?

On screen came a grainy, shaky handheld shot of the interior of a large, nearly empty warehouse.

A woman cried in the background.

The camera swung down and focused on a person tied to a chair with a black bag over their head. She recognized the shirt.

Her shirt.

Walloped like someone smashed her with a solid steel door, she couldn't breathe. A crushing weight pressed on her chest.

The camera panned up. Two men stood in front of her. A short wizened one with a buzz cut and a tall gaunt ghostly-looking man with long dark hair.

The camera moved to the right and revealed a table of torture devices. The blowtorch, pliers and an array of horrible-looking tools that looked like surgical instruments. Emma almost passed out.

The camera returned to her. Her body shook so hard, the black bag vibrated.

Her gut hurt like she'd sent it through a meat grinder. The screen seemed far away, like she watched it from out of her body. Like she was sitting beside herself, watching this horror movie featuring someone who looked remarkably like Emma Holden. Her, but not her.

The person holding the camera set it down. And then he walked in front of it.

Rollin. Wearing his hatchet face. No emotion. His gaze was dead.

Her life popped like a balloon.

Her stomach went into spasms of pain. The car stopped moving and everything went silent.

But she couldn't take her eyes from the screen.

Rollin's expression chilled her to the bone. Her body trembled uncontrollably.

Of course he'd lied to her. What man in her life hadn't? How stupid to think she'd find someone who truly loved her.

"I wish I knew where that stupid money is," came her tearful voice. "Don't you think I would have taken it and run by now? Do you honestly think I'd be hanging around if I'd gotten my hands on five hundred million?"

The wizened one leaned toward her. "Darling, you *will* tell me where the money is. And until then, I'm going to have some fun with you. Take off her shoes. We'll start with her feet."

The Frenchman!

"No!" she screamed on screen.

Emma fisted her hands and dug her fingernails into her palms. Her innards twisted and burned.

The two guys laughed like hell, but Rollin didn't crack a smile. He had the creepiest look on his face.

Was it really him? How could that horrible man be her wonderful tender lover from this morning?

Her worst nightmare had come to life. She'd never experienced anything more horrifying. The memories flooded back. Tears streamed down her cheeks. Crushing.

Rollin disappeared from view. He stood again with her shoes in hand and pointed to the table.

"Pliers, yes." With a delighted grin, the short Frenchmen handed the pliers to Rollin.

Rollin's expression remained dead. He bent down until she could just see the top of his head.

Next came the most horrible sound she'd ever heard in her life.

Her screaming, half-mad with fear.

"Turn it off! Turn the fucker off!" Emma cried, turning away from the screen.

Her entire body in agony, all she could see was darkness. Gut wrenching sobs ripped from her as she broke out in a full body sweat. Why did it have to be Rollin? She expected that kind of shit out of Cherlenko, but not Rollin. Why the duplicity?

So that she'd lead him right to the nuke. She had handed it to him.

Whatever he'd done, it'd worked.

Her body shook violently and her stomach collapsed in on itself, sending bile raging up her throat. She swallowed hard and panted to control the sickness.

"Let her go, David," Cherlenko said.

David set her on the seat beside him, but she was hardly aware. Her life was over. She had no more fight left. No one to trust.

She gasped and cried out. Rollin was watching over her sister for God's sake! Could she have screwed herself any further?

The limo stopped, David got out and went up into the front seat. Her mouth flooded with spit, her body went hot with nausea. She was going to puke.

"Wait," she said to Cherlenko. "I'm not going anywhere, I have…" She put a foot outside the door and threw up on the pavement. She stumbled all the way outside the limo and barfed until there was nothing but dry heaves left.

After awhile, she became aware that Cherlenko stood behind her. He handed her some tissues. She gratefully took them.

"Are you through?"

Nodding, she got back in the car and slumped in the seat. The car started off again. She and Cherlenko were alone.

He handed her a cold bottle of water. "When you can, this might help."

Taking it, she pressed the bottle against her forehead and closed her eyes.

She concentrated on breathing and tried to put the whole situation out of her mind so she could stop being sick. After a few minutes, she took a sip of water. The cool liquid soothed her flaming throat.

Emma noticed Cherlenko out of the corner of her eye, examining her.

"Are you all right?"

"No." All she could see was Rollin, smiling, telling her how much he loved her spliced in with images of that Death Mask he wore while he tortured her.

"…Hawaii…"

She finally realized that Cherlenko had been talking to her. "Wait, what?"

His lips quirked. "You missed that whole thing, didn't you?"

"Yeah, what? Hawaii?"

He leaned in. "I know this is not the right time, but I must ask you. I'm leaving for Hawaii in two hours on my jet. You're welcome to come. You'll have your own room in my villa. No pressure. It will just get you out of here. And…" His gaze grew troubled and he frowned.

"What?"

He pulled himself up taller and his face hardened. His powerful gaze seemed to penetrate her defenses. Like he could see into her soul. "I'm very concerned about your safety."

His intensity was too much. She faced the front of the limo. Guy never stopped wanting something from her. And right now, she was too shell-shocked to play his games. Too open and too vulnerable.

She turned her attention out the window. The driver had turned off onto Woodside Road from 101 and headed west. She had no idea where they were going, but wherever they ended up, she was getting out of that car and leaving Cherlenko behind.

"I know you don't trust me, but I care a great deal for you and besides that, I want to offer you protection. If you come with me, I'll make sure none of those idiot Patriots comes near you. You'll be a target for some time. I think you know that. Especially if you found the money. That fist pump couldn't have meant anything else."

Her muscles tightened to the point of pain and hopelessness engulfed her. Burke brought up an excellent point. She'd thought that the money would provide her with all the protection she'd need. But the money wouldn't help her, it had only painted a bigger target on her chest.

She punched the seat and tears flowed into her eyes. She wiped them away in a violent motion. Because she didn't have network of criminal toadies to deploy or a hoard of bodyguards to protect her, she was screwed. Instead of freedom, her new knowledge had just put her in more danger. That five hundred million was as helpful as a cement wetsuit to a surfer. *Fuck!*

"You found it, didn't you?"

She ran her fingers through her hair and rubbed her head, which ached like hell. Her thoughts dissolved into a black, murky nothingness. "All I wanted to do was to protect my sister. But that money won't help me, all it will do is get me killed."

"No, it won't. I won't let any harm come to you, Emma. Or your sister. We'll arrive there shortly."

"Where?"

"Where your sister is."

His words made no sense. She blinked the tears out of her eyes and tried to read his face. "Wait, what? My sister?"

He nodded and smiled, his expression open. "Yes. Lizzie. We're going to see her right now."

"But Rollin has her."

"No, he doesn't. I've been watching over her."

She shook her head. The darkness abruptly cleared. She had to hold herself back from leaping across the seat and attacking him. "Lizzie? You know where she is?"

He smiled. "Yes. We're on our way there now. It's where I was going to leave you. Unless you accept my invitation, that is." The lines between his mahogany eyes deepened. "I'm concerned about protecting your sister as well. We need to make this visit short. I don't want anyone else to know where she is."

She couldn't believe it. Lizzie! Her hopes soared and her heart lightened. "No, that's okay. But seeing her, Cherlenko—Burke. You don't know how much this means to me."

He smiled and his dark eyes twinkled. His old familiar warmth returned. "I have a good idea."

She found herself even more stunned. In all this foggy hell, finally, a beacon of light. And fucking Burke was holding it.

He'd taken care of her sister. He'd saved her ass how many times? And he hadn't been the one to kidnap her and torment her. In fact, what wrong *had* he done to her?

Just that crap in the beginning. Which he kept apologizing for. And ever since, he'd rescued her and taken really good care of her. He'd even cooked for her.

She looked over at him and saw completely different person. Satan transformed into Superman before her eyes. Burke? A nice guy? Emma fought hard to get her center back. She'd been so convinced of his evilness.

So should she go to Hawaii with him? Pros? Protection and really nice fuck you to Rollin.

Protection was the key. Rollin wasn't the only one after her, there were others. Burke was a master of that world.

And since she had no idea how to protect herself without professional help, nor did she have the resources to take care of her sister outside of her home, what other option did she have?

Um…none.

But what if Zane and Rollin and Carter's allegations about Burke were true?

That video did not look faked. It looked real. She had smelled Rollin's cologne. It didn't smell like him exactly, but what if he'd tried to disguise himself somehow?

But why pick his own cologne?

Maybe subconsciously he wanted her to know. Maybe he did care for her. In his own twisted way.

Her heart tore like Rollin ripped it in half. He'd been so tender with her. So fun. So protective. It didn't make sense that he'd torture her.

And why hadn't Burke found him in the warehouse when he came to rescue her? And how had he got hold of the video?

Good questions all, but she was too exhausted to think clearly. Which answered her question. She was better off on her own.

She turned away and inspected the back of her hand. She swallowed to get the sour taste out of her mouth. Damn it, she still wished Rollin was seated beside her.

He'd probably known all about her tattoo and went out and got one to match hers to cement their bond. Asshole. He was meticulous that way.

Did Burke get the nuke? She turned to him and considered asking him.

He raised a brow. "What?"

"I probably don't want to know," she said, realizing it as she said it.

"Ask anyway. I don't want anything between us."

"Did you get the nuke?"

He patted her on the knee. "All taken care of. All done. I'm celebrating with a trip to Hawaii."

"Good." She relaxed a bit, but her mind was so tied in knots she was afraid she'd never unravel the mess. A subprogram of terror ran beneath all her thoughts. She rubbed her temples and sighed.

"You'll be fine, Emma. You'll be strong again. You just need to rest. You must be exhausted."

The tender look in his eye nailed her. A sob caught in her throat.

A sympathetic sweet expression on his handsome face, Burke reached out and brought her to him. She resisted for about one second, then leaned into him. His warmth and scent and kindness touched her. So comforting, just like when he'd taken care of her after he'd rescued her. If the drama stopped, hanging out with him might be okay for a while. Maybe. Sure felt good to be in his arms.

"Thanks, Burke. I know I haven't made it very easy on you to be nice to me, yet you continue to, despite my rabid attacks."

He chuckled deep in his chest. "Your spice is part of the reason I'm attracted to you. But I am glad that you're finally letting down your guard and trusting me. While I like my ladies to be spicy, I appreciate the attribute in bed more than out. But I've understood every one of your reactions. You don't create drama for drama's sake. All your outbursts have been firmly rooted in logic."

"Thanks for recognizing that. You're the first male in my life to do that."

"I understand you, Emma."

"And that makes me feel good."

"I'm so glad." There was a pause. "So you found the money?"

She pushed away to meet his gaze. "Yeah. It's yours. I don't want anything to do with it. There's some in my purse."

He smiled widely. "Where was it?"

"God. Well, it's in several places, actually. Safe deposit box, some at my house, some in the storage unit where I found the nuke."

"Your house? Really? I tore that place apart—sorry."

"I'm over it. Yeah, Adam knew that house better than I thought he did. Some of it is in the attic under the blown-in insulation."

"I had a man check all through that. He coughed for a whole week."

"It's up in the front of the house."

"When I return from Hawaii, you can help me recover it."

"You bet."

"And don't worry, there's a finder's fee."

"It's okay."

"I insist."

She finally chuckled. "Pretty stupid to turn down free money."

"You earned it." He gave her a squeeze and let out a long sigh. His body relaxed.

The guy really liked her.

Burke's driver parked in the Redwood City hills in front of a pretty estate surrounded by colorful lush gardens with a fountain in front. A purple bougainvillea-covered trellis ran the length of the walkway up to the front glass double doors. Morgan House, stated a large carved wooden sign.

"This is where Lizzie is? Wow."

"I think you'll like it."

David opened the door for her. Burke escorted her up the walkway and through the doors to the reception desk.

"We're here to see Elizabeth Holsten," he said.

"Room 7A. Down the hall, on the left," the young red-haired woman answered. "She's doing so well. We're so proud of her progress. And her nurse is a kick."

Emma's heart lifted. Through her battle-weary mind, a clarity took hold. Lizzie. She'd see her sister. The one constant in her life. No matter how crazy Dad and Mom had gotten, Lizzie was there for her. Her true mother. Because Dolly sure as hell hated parenting. All she wanted to do was dress up and go to fabulous cocktail parties and pretend she was Audrey Hepburn.

But Lizzie had always been there.

They walked down a pink-carpeted hallway with ivory walls and fresh flowers set on gleaming wood tables.

Her heart drumming her ribs, energy bubbling in her belly, she found 7A and approached the wide doorway. Laid out before her was a spectacular, airy room done in the same pinks and ivories as the rest of Morgan House. The far wall was floor to ceiling windows with a sliding glass door that led out to a tropical wonderland of an inner courtyard.

She stepped in further and her eyes filled with tears. Lizzie was sitting up in a queen bed with a canopy. While the bed still had rails and was motorized to enable Lizzie to sit up, there'd been a lot of effort put out to disguise the hospital equipment as normal furniture. The management had taken great strides to make the room a home.

Lizzie looked great. Back to normal. She wore makeup and her long white hair was trimmed and framed her youthful face beautifully.

Mary sat in the corner reading a magazine in an overstuffed chair. Lizzie perused a large children's picture book.

Emma's lip quivered and a sob caught in her throat. "Lizzie?"

Lizzie looked up, her mouth dropped open and she screeched with joy. Throwing the book aside, she reached out her arms and her smile lit up the room like a solar flare. She bounced in place. "You! You!"

Emma flew to her bedside and they crushed each other in a hug.

"You!" Lizzie repeated. "Exciting! You!"

Lizzie pulled away and touched Emma's face, then kissed her on the cheek, then hugged her again. "Happy. Happy. You."

"I've missed you so much, Lizzie. I…this is the greatest gift ever. You're doing so well."

Mary came up to her and held out her arms. "Emma!"

Emma let go, stood and embraced the Filipino fireball. "Mary, it's so good to see you."

They pulled away and Mary's eyes went wide. "What happened? Where have you been? Can we go home soon? I mean, I'd rather have her stay here, but it has to be expensive. How can you afford this?"

“Uh…” She turned back to Burke, but he was gone. Sweet. He wanted to give her time alone with her sister. “A…a friend helped me out.”

“That man that was with you? The bald one? But he got you to confess to that murder! He’s the one who’s paying for this?”

“Turns out he wasn’t a bad guy, he actually saved me. It’s a long story.”

Lizzie held out her arms again and bounced on the bed with anticipation and excitement.

She sat down and took her sister in her arms again. Momentarily lost in Lizzie’s sweet scent—a combination of lavender and her own—a thousand memories of her sister holding her flashed through her mind. When she was kid hiding in her closet with Dad screaming out in the living room. In her poster-filled bedroom after her first boyfriend dumped her. In the living room of her home after Mom died.

Emma felt centered and whole again. “Anything I have to do to keep you safe, Lizzie, I’ll do it.”

“God, I hope this is over soon,” Mary said.

“Me, too,” Emma said, pulling away from her sister. “So what’s the status here with her recovery?”

Mary gave her the quick run down. Lizzie could walk further each day and her speech was improving. The day before Lizzie cooked a meal in the home’s kitchen and she’d done really well.

Mary smiled. “So they think one more month and she can go home. With some help, but she can go home.”

Emma leapt to her feet with joy. “Home? The doctors said she’d never be on her own again!”

Lizzie laughed and grabbed Emma’s hands. “Home. Home, I go… home.”

Astonishing progress. “This is the best news, ever. I’m blown away.” A dream.

“Emma?” came Burke’s voice from behind her.

She turned to him.

He nodded, a solemn look in his eye. "If you're going with me, you need to come now. And if you stay…" His face clouded and the line between his eyes grooved deep. "I can't guarantee your sister's safety. Or yours. Or Mary's."

Her bubble of happiness popped. She choked back tears. Massive guilt weighed on her like a fifty-ton backpack. She should be by her sister's side, not running off to Hawaii with people trying to kill her. Her life had become utter craziness.

Emma's insides wrenched in pain. Both options terrified her. If she stayed, she put Lizzie's life in jeopardy. If she went, she could fall into a La Brea Tar Pit of a relationship with a criminal.

She examined his face. She only saw kindness and caring. He'd saved her ass, he was taking great care of her sister, there was only one logical conclusion. "I'm coming with you."

His features softened and his eyes smiled.

She turned back to Lizzie, who looked at Burke and not in a super friendly way. Mary was beyond unfriendly, she outright glowered at him.

Emma laughed at their fierce expressions. "Lizzie, Mary, I know you don't think he's fine. But he's fine. He's a friend. He's helping us out right now." She motioned for Burke to come closer.

Thankfully, the man was excruciatingly charming. And respectful. He came forward and nodded at Lizzie.

"Burke Cherlenko, this is my sister, Lizzie."

Burke smiled at her. "Pleased to meet you. Your sister has said some wonderful things about you. And I can see that beauty runs throughout your entire family."

The guy was amazing. That line coming out of anyone else's mouth would have seemed trite and obsequious. But he carried it off.

Lizzie's expression completely changed. A slow smile grew on her face and she nodded at him.

Burke turned to Mary and gave her a little bow. "Mary, I have rarely heard of someone with your kind of loyalty and devotion. I admire you. Lizzie and Emma are blessed to have found you."

Mary tried to stay mad at him, but smiled. She quickly wiped away her grin. Her eyes narrowed and she pointed up at him. "You hurt her and you answer to me."

Burke worked hard to stifle his laughter. He managed a serious acknowledgment. "I'll take that under consideration."

Emma turned to her girls. "Okay, honeys, I have to go."

"Where? When will you be back?" Mary demanded.

"No…no. Stay." Lizzie grabbed her hands and pulled her back down on the bed.

Her heart cleaved in two. She steeled herself. "Soon."

"Two weeks to a month," Burke said.

She looked deep into Lizzie's dark brown gaze. "I wouldn't if I didn't have to."

Lizzie made a sad face, then broke into a smile. "Soon."

Emma nodded. "Soon." She gave Lizzie one last long hug. When they pulled away, both had tears in their eyes. "I love you, Lizzie."

"Love…love you."

She reluctantly stood and gave Mary a quick hug. "Thanks, Mary. My gratitude to you goes beyond anything I've felt for anyone."

Mary waved a hand. "Don't worry about it. Besides, he's paying me a lot. And I got a nice apartment next door."

A bomb of information. Wow.

"Still. You're a champ."

Mary grinned. "That's what you do for family."

After another round of hugs, Burke escorted her out to the car. She walked along in a daze.

They got into the back of the limo and took off.

Overwhelmed by Burke's kindness, Emma had no words to express her gratitude. She turned to him and crushed him in an embrace. "This goes deep, Burke." She pulled away and lay her palm on his cheek. "You're a good man and I'm so glad you came and found me."

His eyes dilated, he nuzzled into her hand and kissed it.

Then he reached out and took her face in his hands and kissed her gently, tenderly and full of emotion. His kiss quickly turned passionate.

Instantly, he had her hormones steaming. His taste. His scent. His strength. But mostly what she felt was gratitude.

Rollin. Why hadn't he been the one to save her? Why was he the one who betrayed her? Why wasn't he the one kissing her?

Burke pulled away. "I've missed you, Emma. More than I thought possible. I'm not pushing, I don't expect anything from you. But I'm in love with you."

Her center slid out from underneath her. Reeling, she stared at him and fought for clarity.

Emma examined his face more carefully and saw vulnerability in his mahogany gaze for the first time since she'd met him. She sensed his heart. His passion for her. She hadn't thought love was possible for him, but she knew she wasn't misreading him. He wasn't lying. And he wasn't trying to manipulate her. He just wanted her to know. Shocking.

So this was what lay underneath the polished, badass criminal exterior. A sweet, kind and strong person. For some reason he was playing the role of underworld overlord, but it wasn't who he really was.

Maybe she could bring out the good person and get rid of the wannabe criminal. What he'd done for her sister and her showed his true nature.

She didn't love him, but she'd stay open about the possibility. Maybe she'd fallen in love with the wrong man. Maybe she could heal the guy. Maybe Burke was her future.

She hugged him tighter. He kissed her on the side of the face and stroked her back.

Her heart cracked open and her defenses came down. Anyone who'd done this much for her deserved her loyalty and devotion. No one had ever come through for her like this. Not even her parents.

While there was a small part of her that couldn't quite adjust to the new Burke, the rest of her decided to go with him and see where the path took her.

She prayed he was who he appeared to be. Because she was sick of duplicity. If this guy lied to her…she couldn't go there. She might commit murder. If this guy was manipulating her, he was dead meat.

But for the present, she'd trust him. Until he proved himself a liar again, she'd believe what he told her.

Basically, at this point, it was the only way to stay sane.

And, more importantly, alive.

TWENTY-ONE

Rollin exploded. His stomach hurt like Emma used it for a punching bag. "No! Don't tell me that, Bobby! She couldn't be kissing on Burke! And why didn't the fucking guard stop them when they left Morgan House?" He paced across Zane's expansive office, cell phone in hand, narrowly missing Carter and Zane with his wild gestures. "Fuck! Where are they now? I have to get her out of there, he'll fucking toxify her mind!" He inadvertently hung up on Bobby. But he didn't care. He had to get to her. He had to convince her that Burke was manipulating her.

Zane held up his huge hand. "Dude. Be calm. You might want to take a step back there."

It took all of Rollin's strength not to run out the door. "You don't get it! I have to find her, Zane."

"We'll find them, don't worry," the giant said. "But we have to plan things out, man. We can't just go in there all Dirty Harry."

"But he'll fuck her mind if I don't get to her fast!"

Zane didn't react. "So what? You'll unfuck it. Burke always blows it when he lies. And we'll probably find them before that. But I do have one tiny question—what about the fucking nuke, man? Your little head has taken over. What is our priority? Dick or nuke?"

He tried to make sense of his swirling mass of conflicting thoughts. He blocked images of Burke fucking Emma and fought to concentrate on the moment. "Well, nuke, of course. But shit, the longer she's with him—"

"The quicker she'll figure out he's a big fat liar," Zane replied acidly. "That's her lesson. She'll be back. Don't be insecure."

His self-image warped and his belly contorted. He'd been called many things, but never insecure. "I'm not." He ran his hand through his hair and paced the huge office. "But Burke wants to keep her. I know he does. You know how good he is. Could be years before she figures him out."

Zane looked at him like he had midgets dancing on his head. "No, hours because we're gonna find Burke. And Emma's with him so why don't you calm the fuck down?"

"Because I have to stop him!" Rollin practically screamed. Zane's words finally penetrated his brain. His stomach hollowed and a small flash of fear went through him. "I sound stupid, don't I?"

"Extremely," Zane said, his mouth drawn down in disgust.

Were his emotions really derailing his logic? Apparently. His mood went even glummer. "Shit. She does make me crazy."

Carter's lips pulled tight over his teeth, he shook his head. "Never seen you like this, Rollin. Not even Maggie did this to you."

And Maggie had made him really crazy. "Damn."

"And I hate to bring this up," Carter said, "but if she's chosen Burke at this point, maybe she wants to be with him."

The room tilted, Rollin's throat closed up and he choked out, "No way!"

Carter's face went hard. "Rollin get a hold of yourself. However she made the decision, if she's there by choice there's not a lot we can do for her. The nuke is the priority. Keeping Burke and Emma alive isn't."

Rollin stomach convulsed and he had to hold himself back from attacking Captain. "No way am I gonna let her die! There has to be a way to get the nuke and save Emma! Has to be. Don't tell me anything else right now, I'll fuckin' spontaneously combust."

Carter and Zane stared at him. Even Greg stopped what he was doing to gape into the webcam.

"What? Are you, like, fourteen?" Zane asked. "Dude. She's a chick who picked Burke. Who has a nuclear weapon in his possession. Get your priorities straight."

They were wrong about her. They didn't know her like he did. Burke was probably holding her against her will. She kissed him for self-preservation only. "Look, all I need is ten minutes alone with her. Then I can turn her around and get her out of there. We can make this work. Don't be pullin' the trigger on her just yet."

Carter and Zane sighed and shook their heads. Greg pushed away from the screen.

"This adds some challenge to an already difficult situation," Carter said.

Rollin stood taller, held his shoulders straight and made his face harder. "I know, but we can do it. I can do it. And you guys are going to help me," he said forcefully.

Zane and Carter turned to him, their mouths slightly open. "We are?"

Hands on hips, Rollin glared at them. "You are."

"Check his coke for LSD," Zane said to Carter, pointing at Rollin's half-empty can of soda.

"I'm going to save Emma. Period. End of discussion."

Zane shot him a sharp look. "No guarantees, pal. You could blow it for us."

"I have to try to get through to her."

Zane's massive shoulders relaxed a bit. "Let's see what happens. No promises. But you're not in charge of this gig. Captain is. Then me. Then you. All your decisions go through us."

"Fine. I'm still talking to her."

Zane seared him with his powerful green gaze.

"I am." Rollin looked him dead in the eye. "She's true blue, I know it. We were kids together. Our dads were partners. She's almost family."

Zane snorted and his eyes went dark. "My father abandoned me, and after my mother died, I went to live with my uncle who beat the shit out of me and dumped me in foster care. Family don't mean shit."

"You know what I mean."

Zane rolled his eyes and sighed.

Carter turned to Greg, still on the computer screen. "Greg? Any idea yet on Burke's location?"

The balding biker shook his head. "Frustrating. We got all eyes and ears out lookin' for 'em. But after they left Morgan House, they disappeared. Not a peep. Burke hasn't been seen at his place since yesterday." On screen, Greg briefly checked a monitor to his left. "Wait. No way. I just got a text from Banana."

Rollin almost jumped out of his skin. His heart rate shot higher. "What's he say?"

"Burke and Emma are heading to San Francisco Airport. They're stopping for dinner at 231 Ellsworth in San Mateo."

Rollin's attention flew to the screen. "Dinner?" he demanded, rushing up to the monitor. "When he has a personal chef in his private jet?"

Greg gestured toward the screen. "I asked Banana that. He said something about Burke needing some extra time to break down Emma's defenses. Besides, he couldn't get a departure time until 8."

"Shit. All right, I'm on my way." Rollin grabbed his black leather jacket and headed for the door.

Carter blocked his way. "Did you just miss that whole conversation? Banana's been compromised. The only reason we have that intel is because Burke wants us to know he'll be there. And why would he let us know his location when he's trying to hide a nuke from us? It's either a trap or wild goose chase."

Rollin's jaw went tighter. "Captain, I know that. But I have to go check it out. I won't blow it. If I can get to Emma, she might know where the nuke is."

"No, soldier, you will stand down until we figure out a plan. Sit. And that's an order."

His body screaming at him to run to Emma's side, Rollin made an exasperated noise and sat in the chair. He seriously considered rushing Carter, but Zane would capture him in a minute.

Zane's brow wrinkled. "So what's Burke's motivation for drawing us there? He doesn't do anything without good reason. Can't just be to break down Emma's defenses. And if she's with him in a public place, it means he's already Svengalied her. Maybe he's planning to take us out there so we can't stop him."

Carter stroked his chin. "Is Burke so far gone that he'd put a bunch of innocent people at risk? I can't imagine he wants a shoot-out in downtown San Mateo."

"He sent the Stillwater guys after us. I think he's gone-o," Zane said.

"He wants me to see her," Rollin said as the idea occurred to him. "For some twisted reason, he wants me to go there and talk to her—shit. He wants to know beyond a shadow of a doubt that she's chosen him. He's testing her. Fuck. This is about Emma, not us."

Zane gestured with his Dr. Pepper. "And he wouldn't let us know where he'd be if he didn't have an exit strategy."

Carter pointed at them. "But if he is doing this to see if Rollin and Emma still love each other, it means his hormones are clouding his judgment. Which means we may catch a break. Especially if Rollin can talk Emma into leaving him. That would really mess him up. And that's when we'll get him."

Zane slowly nodded. "Good one." Then he grimaced. "So what is up with this woman, anyway? I mean, she's cute, but two of you guys losing your mind over her? What? She's got a magic pussy?"

Rollin flashed on Emma's amazing naked body. He gave a sheepish smile.

Zane burst out laughing. "Jesus Christ. Glad I'm not caught in her spell."

"Me, too," Carter said.

Good thing they weren't, too. Burke was enough competition.

Zane turned to the monitor. “We need to consider all the avenues of escape from Ellsworth. Greg, can you pull up maps of the area? Maybe some schematics of the restaurant?”

“Yeah, comin’ right up.”

Carter walked up to the computer. “Greg, have Catherine and Ty found anything at the airport yet?”

Greg leaned over, almost off camera and rubbed his black goatee. “No, according to Ty, Burke’s jet is still ready and nothing’s been loaded yet. Catherine’s team is checking everything with Geiger counters. Nothing so far. But Banana says here that the nuke is at the airport, waiting to be loaded on the jet.”

Zane shook his head. “Which means that’s bullshit.”

“So all we know is that the nuke disappeared at the airport,” Carter said. “Makes sense they stashed it somewhere nearby. Greg, have Catherine send her team out on a wider sweep.”

“She’s already on that.”

Rollin massaged the tension out of his forehead. “Burke wouldn’t let that thing out of his sight for long. Wherever he ends up is where we’ll find the nuke.”

Carter stood tall and gave a sharp nod. “Right. So let’s make a plan and not lose him after he leaves the restaurant. Let’s hope you can talk her into going with you, Rollin. For your sake and ours. We need him unbalanced.”

Rollin’s frustration eased, but tension curled in his gut. “I will.”

Captain could be right. Emma could have picked Burke.

He couldn’t figure out how, after that amazing sex. He could have sworn she felt the same way about him. But he’d been wrong before. Very wrong.

And that mistake cost him the life of a dear friend. No matter how much he loved her, he wouldn’t make the same mistake again.

* * * * *

Burke's driver parked the limo in front of a swanky downtown San Mateo restaurant.

Emma turned to Burke. "Why are we here?"

He smiled. "I'm starving. Aren't you?"

"I thought we were flying away."

"We are. Departure is at eight. Plenty of time for a nice meal."

Emma had been so caught up in all the excitement, she'd completely forgotten about food. "What a great idea. I'm famished. The last time I ate was at noon. A half a slice of pizza. And then I promptly lost that." *Rollin.* Her heart twisted and her mood took a nose dive. She shoved the creep out of her mind.

They went into the restaurant and were seated in a quiet corner. She wanted everything on the menu.

Burke leaned in. "If you go with the three or five course meal, make sure you order it with the wine, it really adds to the experience. They pair them perfectly."

"Okay."

Once they ordered, Emma excused herself to go to the bathroom. Burke shot her a wary glance.

"I'm not going anywhere. Stop worrying."

"Can't blame me, you've disappeared on me before. Several times."

"Those days are over. I'll be right back."

He caught her hand and brought her in for a nice kiss. She sighed. He made her feel about a thousand times better. Thank God for this guy.

She found the ladies room and spruced up her hair. In her jeans and t-shirt she felt outclassed in the restaurant. Burke's poor relation all over again.

When she walked out, Rollin appeared in front of her.

All the air got sucked from her lungs. Her heart ripped apart like he'd plunged a steel bar deep inside her chest. She wanted to cry, puke, and scream, all at the same time.

What the hell was he doing there? Emma glared at him and forced her arms to her sides so she didn't hit him. "Get the hell out of my way before I beat you to death."

His expression hardened to granite and his gaze went volcanic. Such a contrast to the dead look in his eyes in the video. "I told you he'd do this. What'd he tell you?"

She sneered and tears burned her eyes. "Don't. Just stop it. I saw you torture me. I saw you on the tape. You kidnapped me, stop denying it. Now get out of my way or I swear, I'll strangle you."

Slack-jawed, he stared at her like her head had transformed into a cabbage.

"Great performance. Now get away from me." She made a move to pass him and he grabbed her arm.

She bared her teeth at him. "Let go or I'll make a scene."

He narrowed his gaze and his lips went tight. "How the hell could I mean this little to you? How could you believe his bullshit?"

Her gut wrenched. She ripped out of his grip. "How dare you do that to me?"

"I didn't do anything. He's fooled you."

"Liar." She wiped the tears from her eyes.

"You don't get it, Emma. He's lied to you and turned your head around. You stay with him and you'll die. He's got twenty targets on his back. He almost killed Zane and left him for dead. Is this the kind of guy you want to be with?"

"A lot better than the guy who kidnapped me and terrified me."

Rollin pulled himself up taller and his dark gaze fired into her. "How could you believe that? After what we shared? Were those all lies you told me?"

Glaring, she put her hands on her hips. "You couldn't fake what I saw."

"Well, Burke did fake that video, because I didn't kidnap you. I showed you my bruises, you think I did that to myself?"

"Yeah, and the tattoo was a real nice touch."

Rollin gaped. "Fuck, Emma, how could he brainwash you that fast?"

Hatred boiled deep in her gut. She glanced at a wine bottle behind the bar and considered bashing him over the head with it. "Your dead expression in the video convinced me, Rollin. Now get out of my way before I call Burke's goons."

He snorted and his mouth went harsh. "Tapes can be faked. He's a master at it. I told you he was good. I told you he'd turn you against me."

Her blood turned to ice. "You must get real tired of being right all the time."

"How can you be this cold?"

"I've had some good teachers. Are we through? Will you get out of my way?"

He blocked her way, but the anger left his face and he took a deep breath. His expression calmed, but his muscles were so tight, she could feel the heat coming off his body. "Emma, listen to me. Aside from what happened between us, he will get you killed. He has the weapon. Which makes him dangerous as hell."

"He doesn't have the weapon, he's already taken care of it. I'm in no danger from anything but drowning in the bullshit you're piling on me."

Rollin's eyebrows shot to his hairline. He honed in on her, examining her expression carefully. "He told you that? That he doesn't have the weapon?"

"Yes."

"Do you believe him?"

"Yes. I believe everything he's told me," she snapped.

His eyes went wild with fury and his face reddened. "Then you're more of an idiot than I thought you were."

"Fuck you, Hanson." She pushed by him, but he grabbed her and shoved her back.

Her vision went blurry and she took a swing at him.

Rollin reached out fast and caught her wrist. "Wait, Emma." He let her go, but still stood in her way. His gaze went haunted and the pain lines on his face deepened. "Shit, I'm saying stuff just to piss you off and this is way too dangerous for that. Look, I know you hate me. I know you don't believe me, but he's lying to you. He will get you killed and it could be us that kills you."

She glared up at him, her jaw tight. "Thanks for the warning. Now will you get out of my fucking way?"

His expression darkened and his mouth twisted. "Burke set this up, too. He wanted me to see you. He let us know he'd be here. You're playing right into his hands."

"And you are such a reliable source of information. Go to hell, Hanson."

Tears in his eyes, Rollin shook with rage.

"Tears are a real nice touch," she said with as much loathing as she could muster.

His expression turned so angry, so fast, she saw shades of the man in the video. Her belly clenched, her limbs and back went tight, but she forced her face to stay neutral.

She brushed by him, several voices in her head screaming at her that he could be telling her the truth.

But she'd seen that film. Smelled his cologne. She'd handed him the nuke. And slept with him.

Her brain was so thoroughly destroyed, none of this made sense anymore.

Her gut hurt like she ate a bowl of habaneras. She stopped at the doorway to the dining area. She couldn't handle seeing Burke just yet. She checked the front of the restaurant. Rollin had left, thankfully. She slipped back into the bathroom and cried like hell.

God, what a bastard. He'd used everything against her. She'd been so blind to his games. She gave him her heart and he'd filleted it and served it back to her. That dick! She wished she'd landed that punch. Maybe she'd feel better.

Tired of crying, Emma finally took her anguish and set it aside. This was no time to deal with all her crap. She had to stay strong. She had to make it through a month with Satan. After that, who knew what her life would look like?

After washing her face, she put on a public-friendly mask and rejoined Burke.

He tuned into her like a heat-seeking missile. “Are you all right?”

Burke *had* set up the meeting. The fucker wanted to make sure she wanted him and not Rollin.

A hot wave of anger burned through her, hardening her body and twisting her stomach. While Burke seemed sweet and generous, underlying his perfect exterior was a master chess player. And he never tired of the game. Exhausting. She wanted a boyfriend, not an opponent. “I know you know who I was just talking to. And I know you set it up so I’d run into him. Well, I passed your test. I’m here, so let’s just let it go.”

She’d surprised him, but he wasn’t upset, he seemed relieved.

But he still eyed her with suspicion. “He denied it all and said I faked the film.”

“Burke, I wouldn’t be here if I didn’t believe you. And if things work out between us and I commit to you, I don’t want you second-guessing me. I’ll give you this one pass, but hear me now.” She pointed and shot him a fiery look. “Don’t ever test me again.”

His shoulders and face relaxed. He reached over and gripped her hand tightly. “I’m sorry. I had to be sure. You’re one hell of a woman, Emma.”

She shot him a grin and he chuckled. But Burke’s contrasting worry lines showed how disturbed he was inside. Jealous. He didn’t even like the fact that she’d spoken to Rollin. Even though Burke had set up the meeting, the idiot.

But his emotions were his problem. Her problem was forgetting about Rollin and trying to get some food in her stomach. She took a sip of water, grabbed her napkin and spread it on her lap.

As soon as she took the first bite, she knew she'd been lying to herself about eating. She couldn't unclench her stomach. She could only get down a few spoonfuls of asparagus soup, one bite of duck and a half a slice of sourdough. Plus three beers.

But even that much alcohol on an empty stomach couldn't silence the voices in the dark reaches of her mind. What if Rollin was right? What if Burke had faked that tape?

Then why had he taken care of her sister? Why was he being so nice to her?

Easy. The nuke. The money.

But he hadn't needed to profess his love for her.

Or do the myriad things he'd done for her. He could have just tortured her for the information. She would have broken eventually.

No. Burke loved her. He cared about her. He wouldn't hurt her like that.

Fuck Rollin. Fuck the Patriots. Fuck the whole thing.

The only reasonable choice was to go with Burke. At this point, she needed somewhere safe to lay her head. Until she could reassemble her brain into something useful. No matter what doubts she had, Burke was her best bet.

The sun was low on the horizon when Emma and Burke stepped out of the restaurant. Instantly, they were flanked by two giant men in suits wearing sunglasses and earpieces. Her body coiled for action and her heart beat faster. The guards made the danger seem more real. Emma recognized David's curly hair, but didn't know the other hulk, a Pacific Islander dude the size of a small building. The bodyguards escorted them the three steps to the curb, where Burke's limo awaited. Burke opened the door for her, but something down the street caught his attention.

A Hummer was parked halfway down the block.

Burke smiled. "Wave to the Patriots, dear."

A blast of fury blew through her. She had half a mind to storm down there and punch the big dumb jerk. She sneered and flipped them off.

Burke's grin widened. "Good girl."

Emma got into his limo. "They aren't going to let us leave the Bay Area, are they?"

Chuckling, Burke slid in beside her and shut the door. "The games have only just begun. David?"

"We're all ready, Boss."

After Burke fastened his seat belt, he turned to her. "I'd advise you put yours on, too. We may not need them, but it's always best to be prepared."

She grinned and belted herself in, a little excited buzz racing through her.

David drove the limo slowly down Third Avenue, headed for the freeway, keeping an eye on his rear view mirror. He appeared to be in communication with someone besides the big bruiser in the passenger seat.

They hung a right onto Delaware and an identical limo pulled in front of them. They took a left on Fourth Avenue. A block later, another black limo pulled behind them.

Emma turned to Burke. "Some sort of shell game?"

"Something like that."

All three limos pulled onto the 101 Freeway and headed south.

"Aren't we going to the airport?" she asked.

A smile played at the corners of his mouth. "Eventually."

The limos shuffled positions until theirs was in front.

All three limos signaled for a right at the Highway 92/Fashion Island interchange.

At the last minute, one limo headed east on 92 and one headed west. Burke and Emma took the Fashion Island Boulevard exit in the middle. Instead of turning onto Fashion Island, they went straight through and got back on 101 headed south.

As soon as they were on the freeway, two more identical limos appeared and flanked them.

Emma laughed. "Are there two limos following each of the others?"

"Oh, yes." Burke beamed, clearly proud of himself. "David?"

"We still got one. Rollin."

"Good."

All three limos took the Holly Street exit, pulled up and over the freeway and got back on 101, heading north toward San Francisco.

Emma examined Burke's face. "So there are nine identical limos driving around the Bay Area?"

"Yes."

She laughed. He was inventive, she'd give him that.

They hit Highway 92 and turned off, heading east toward Hayward. The two other limos kept going toward the airport followed by Rollin.

"Aren't we going to the airport?"

Burke sent her a wicked grin. "Apparently not."

A tremor of lust shook through her. "Cunning bastard, aren't you?"

He leveled his smoldering gaze at her, took her hand and kissed it.

For the first real time, she considered a relationship with Burke. A real one.

Demented. Dramatic. Unstable. Zero trust.

She let out a chuckle. Perfect foundation to a lasting, fulfilling relationship.

Forget it. She'd fuck him and that was it.

Maybe.

"Fuck, how many goddamned limos are there?" Rollin spat, his gut taut.

"Nine, remember?" Zane growled.

All of Rollin's instincts told him to run the two limos off the road. But that was his anger and jealousy talking. Still so furious he could barely concentrate, he wanted to bash Burke over the head, throw Emma over his shoulder and take her somewhere for deprogramming. How could she do this to him?

And how could he still love her so passionately after all that shit she'd said to him?

Greg came over his headset. "More good news. Burke has two jets at SFO. Both are ready. Catherine just called me to tell me."

Rollin blew out a long breath of air and tried to calm down. "Jinkies, that's great," he said in a cold flat tone. "So one of these limos has to have Burke and Emma in it. Tell Catherine that Zane and I will be there shortly. We're at the south edge of the airport now. Captain's with Dino following two other limos south on 880 toward San Jose. Does Burke have a jet in San Jose?"

Greg said, "I'll check." There was a pause. "Shit. He's got one chartered, yes."

"Damn it, we need more people." A bitter taste in his mouth, Rollin grabbed a pack of peppermint Lifesavers from his ashtray, popped one in his mouth and handed the roll to Zane. "And that bullshit he told Emma, that he'd gotten rid of the nuke, now we know he's lying."

With a flick of his thumb, Zane flipped a Lifesaver out of the pack and into his mouth. "You expected him to tell her the truth?"

"No."

"Damn it, we knew he had an escape plan." Zane shoved the candy back in the ashtray. "And we knew about the nine limos. Should have put it together better. I wish those guys weren't in Africa."

Rollin nodded. "Jake and Cruz would have been very helpful right about now."

"Damn Burke, he knows all our strategies," Zane grumbled, "he knows exactly what to expect. Okay, the limos are leaving the freeway. Nice of them to signal." His thick black brow furrowed. "So why are they signaling unless they want us to follow?"

Rollin's stomach felt uneasy. "Yeah. What *are* they doing?" He took the exit and followed the black stretch Cadillacs onto North Access Road. "Greg, patch me through to Catherine."

"She's there," Greg replied.

One limo took a turn off for the chartered jets area. This time without signaling.

Rollin's attention darted between the two limos. "Shit, which one do I follow? Catherine, are you there?"

"Here," she said, "I see it. Follow the next one."

"Okay."

The second limo continued along North Access Road and turned a bit further on, but headed to the same general chartered area.

Rollin's heart rate jumped and his mind sharpened. He surveyed the area as he drove. A few lines of parked cars. Several people milled about. Four private jets sat parked, with their doors open and ready for loading.

Something was off about the scene. If Burke were defending a nuke, he'd have more firepower there.

"This isn't right," Rollin said. "We should have more company by now. Catherine? What've you got?"

"Limo just drove right by Burke's plane," she replied. "Let's hope you've got him."

"I think we're screwed," Rollin said. "He'd have more Stillwater guys here."

"Yeah, I don't see anything," Zane agreed. "But maybe he's throwing us off. What better way to confuse us than to have only a few good snipers here to protect him?"

"Could be."

The limo in front of him suddenly zipped forward, heading for a jet that was set apart from the rest. The small Lear jet's door open, there was a black Humvee parked below.

Zane loaded a magazine into his 1911 and got ready to jump out.

Adrenaline fired up Rollin's muscles. He reached under his seat and withdrew his semi-automatic. He popped a magazine into the chamber. "Catherine, do you see this?"

"We're on our way."

The black stretch limo skidded to a halt. Four big guys jumped out of the Humvee and flanked all the limo doors.

Burke and Emma got out of the limo and the guards surrounded them.

Emma! His heart cried out for her.

The group ran for the jet.

His pulse thudding in his ears, Rollin raced up to the limo, slammed on the brakes and skidded to a stop. Zane leapt out, took cover behind the door of their Rover and aimed his Kimber. Rollin opened his door, jumped down and got into position.

Catherine and Ty flew up in their truck and lay down a stripe of rubber as they stopped.

Rollin's body coiled for action, he aimed his gun. "Hold it!"

Burke and Emma hustled up the stairs.

Why weren't the Stillwater guards drawing their weapons?

Zane fired off a warning shot.

The four big guys hit the ground, but didn't return fire. No sign of any guns, either.

What?

Burke and Emma disappeared into the plane.

Rollin signaled Catherine, Ty and Zane.

They executed a simple attack plan. Weapons drawn, they trapped the bodyguards.

Three of the guards were strangers, but Rollin recognized one. McCarthy, a moving-van-sized Stillwater jerk with short blonde curly hair and a round head. Had the unpleasant experience of making his acquaintance a year before on another job. Total asshole.

Instead of defending themselves, the mercenaries burst into laughter. None were armed, but they all wore body armor.

"What the fuck?" Rollin demanded.

Rollin and Zane exchanged perplexed glances with Catherine and Ty.

McCarthy seemed particularly amused.

Rollin's mind went black. Anger ravaged his gut and his jaw clamped so tight it burned. A fucking distraction. Misdirection.

Their faces hard, Zane, Catherine and Ty lowered their weapons.

Rollin put on his safety and tucked his weapon into his jacket. "Fuck."

A bald guy poked his head out from the jet. As expected, not Burke. "Burke has a message for you. Fuck you, I think was his direct quote."

Burke's flunkies howled.

Rollin's temples throbbed with anger. He balled his fists, digging his fingernails into his palms, turned and walked away.

McCarthy called out to him. "You guys need to go back to pre-school. Four-year-olds are smarter." His companions laughed so hard, they held their sides and gasped for air.

Rollin kept his cool until he reached his Rover. He bashed the door panel so hard, he put a huge dent in it. Searing pain blazed his knuckles, but he didn't care. He envisioned his hands around Burke's neck, squeezing until the bastard's eyes popped out of his bald head.

He flung open the door and climbed inside. "Greg?" Rollin growled through gritted teeth into his Bluetooth. "Burke faked us out."

"Shit," came Greg's reply. "Let's hope that Captain has better luck."

Rollin glanced over, Zane looked like an executioner. A perfect mirror to Rollin's mood.

He hoped he got a chance at Burke before Zane pulverized him. Once you pissed off Zane, there was no going back. Not until many, many bones were broken.

Burke deserved to be beaten for what he did to Rollin's relationship with Emma alone.

Greg rattled off a stream of expletives over the headset.

Rollin's jaw and neck tensed to rigidity. "Please don't tell me we lost him."

"Sorry. San Jose Airport was a bust, too. Burke, Emma and the nuke are gone."

His mind blew apart with rage. He punched the steering wheel in a series of hard blows. "Fuck! That bastard!"

Zane's mouth went ugly. "We'll get him."

"We'd better. We have to."

Rollin hit the gas and headed back to Zane's.

He'd kill Burke. No one betrayed him like this and got away with it. Eighteen year friendship or no, Burke was going down.

TWENTY-TWO

Rollin opened the false wall of Greg's warehouse office—hidden behind a bookcase—and went down a steel circular staircase. His body trembled with aftershocks from Burke's game. Emma's angry face went through his mind and his heart wrenched. He walked into Greg's war room with Zane right behind him. "Any news anywhere?"

The walls were filled with plasma screens and underneath, the balding biker had his own Mission Control with about twenty computers. Gaze fixed on a screen, Greg shook his head, seeming perplexed. "Nope. Captain is on his way back here. Catherine and Ty stopped for some dinner."

"Shit. Okay, so if he's not taking the nuke out by plane, how else?"

"Boat?" Zane asked.

Greg shook his head. "We've got watches on all the major ports. Nothing so far. Burke hasn't chartered any boats and Bobby is still trying to track down his Sunseeker. Wait. I've got a text coming in from Banana."

Frowning, Rollin snorted. "Great, more misdirection. Let's see where Burke wants us to go next."

"Banana says he was wrong," Greg reported. "He just overheard a conversation between David and another one of Burke's guys at the apartment. Something about a boat at Alameda."

"Next he'll send us to Disneyland," Zane grumbled. "I should have grabbed that Dr. Pepper out of the Jeep. We're in for a long night."

"We'll go get some food shortly," Rollin said. "Fuckin' Burke."

Greg hit some keys on his computer and inspected a screen to his right. "I'm checking with the US Nuclear Surveillance Satellite. Let me put in the coordinates."

"This is so futile." Rollin collapsed in an old office chair.

Zane sat across from him and stretched out his twenty-foot-long legs far past Rollin's chair. "I can't believe we let that nuke slip through our fingers," he muttered.

"Holy shit," Greg said. "Bingo. It's just pulling out."

Rollin's heart rate kicked high and he leapt out of his seat. "What?"

Zane sat up, his green eyes alive.

Greg indicated a screen in front of him. "There's a small, well, probably big boat, leaving Alameda, headed for the Golden Gate. Got the right signals coming off it."

Rollin grabbed his coat. "Find out if it's Burke's Sunseeker and send me the plans. Tell Captain and the others to meet at my boat in Redwood City ASAP. Thank God, I just got prepped for that diving trip."

He rushed for the stairwell with Zane right on his heels.

His priority was supposed to be the recovery of the nuke, but all Rollin could think about was Emma.

* * * * *

Burke's boat, The Roxy, was like nothing Emma had ever seen before. She'd never been exposed to such luxury. At 121 feet long, the "Snapper" model made by Sunseeker was astounding its appointments. Four decks packed full of expensive. Vast living room, three sun decks, crew's quarters and four guest cabins. The galley was stainless steel and granite, and the adjacent dining room, huge. The master suite was astonishingly large and sleek with dark wood ceilings and its own deck.

Burke introduced her to the captain—a stately Dutch man with a gray trimmed beard and piercing blue eyes—and the boat's four-man Filipino crew. Also on board was Burke's muscle: David, a big red-haired goon named Max, plus two thugs she didn't recognize: a buff, wiry Hispanic guy and a blond dude who looked like a WWF wrestler.

Burke led her to her room and she marveled at its space. She ran her hand over the smooth polished wood of the inset desk.

He clearly enjoyed her reactions. "You like?"

"I'd have to be incredibly stupid, vapid and spoiled not to. You've got style, boyfriend, you've got style."

He took her in his arms and kissed her. As usual, at first, some voice in the back of her head asked why the hell she was kissing The Dark Lord. Then Burke's spooky and potent sexual energy overwhelmed her and her entire body came alive. Guy knew how to kiss.

Would she ever trust him? No. But every time she kissed him, she felt like she was high on an illegal drug. Sinful.

When he pulled away, his gaze shone with admiration. "I'm so glad you're here with me."

A tingle raced through her. He even made her toes feel alive. "I'm pretty damned glad myself."

He gestured toward the room. "This is your cabin, but I want you to know, you're free to stay in mine anytime you wish," he said with a wicked sparkle in his mahogany eyes.

What a great idea. A cleansing screw with a hot man on a killer boat. What better way to get Rollin out of her system?

She looped her arms around his neck and took in a deep breath of his heady cologne. "God, I want to fuck you. Oh, dear. I'm sorry. That should have stayed in my head and came out rather crudely."

He laughed and kissed her, hard and hungry.

She'd do anything for this guy, especially if he could exorcise Rollin from her heart.

Rollin. Why wasn't she kissing him?

Her heart twisted hard and her hormones evaporated, but she kept up her horny act for Burke. Stupid Rollin asshole. Ruining her moment with Satan.

Someone knocked on the door. "Boss?" David.

Burke pushed her away with a tortured and pained expression. "Damn." His gaze went fiery. "Whatever it is, can't it wait?"

"No, sorry. That guy is having some trouble with the cargo."

Burke's face went dark. "Fuck." He closed his eyes and took a deep breath. When he opened them, he ran his hands up her arms. "God, I want you, woman. I'd rather chew off my arm than stop. But this is important."

Perfect escape. "I'll be asleep in twenty minutes."

His expression softened and he rubbed her back in an affectionate gesture. "I know. We have all the time in the world, Emma. And I want to make our first time special." The look in his eye made her want to rip all her clothes off.

His incredible sexual prowess derailed her mind. "Damn, you are the most seductive man I've ever encountered. You're like sex personified."

His grin widened and became predatory. "I've pictured what it will be like so many times."

"Me, too."

His expression turned sweet. "I need to work. You sleep. I'll see you tomorrow. Or later tonight if you wish. Just come find me."

"Okay."

They kissed one more time, just a quick one, and he left her. As he closed the door, a wave of exhaustion flattened her. She barely made it to the bed. The rocking of the boat, the super soft mattress and the confidence that Burke was protecting her, allowed her to fall into a deep sleep.

She screamed at Cherlenko. "You liar! You lied to me!" He'd lied about everything. About Rollin, about the videotape, and he had the nuke in the belly of the boat and was selling it to the Taliban. She'd picked the wrong man. Again. She was angrier at herself than she was at Burke.

Emma awoke, her heart pounding, her body covered in sweat, her body on fire with fury. That asshole! She'd kill him.

Wait. Where was she? And why was her bed rocking?

Oh.

Burke's boat.

Holy shit, she *was* with Cherlenko.

She'd come to hate waking up lately. She was either startled awake *from* a nightmare or had woken up *to* a nightmare. And this one just wouldn't end.

And somehow, deep in her bones, she knew her dream was true.

Rollin's devastated expression in the restaurant popped into mind. Like she'd reached into his chest, taken his heart out, threw it to the ground and stomped on it with thick-soled boots.

The wreckage was so profound, she could only laugh.

Rollin had been a hundred percent right. *He'll turn you and I won't blame you. He's that good.*

God, Cherlenko was good. And smooth. And rotten to the core.

And he loved her?

No, he was obsessed with her. He wanted to own her. Like one of his ships or antique weapons or his Pollock. She was just another acquisition to him.

A soft knock came on her door. "Darling, wake up. It's me, Burke," he said as he pushed open the door.

She found herself staring at the Devil. Before she could stop him, he rushed to her side and kissed her.

Emma pushed him away with a violent shove. Letting out a scream, something broke loose inside her and a flood of emotion poured out. Adam, Mom and Lizzie flashed through her mind. Rollin. The kidnapping. The black bag thrust over her head.

Her gut hurt so badly, and she felt so stupid for trusting Cherlenko, she cried like hell, held herself and rocked back and forth. Stuck on a fucking boat with her enemy!

Burke stepped back, slack-jawed, his eyes wide with shock.

Of all the things that had happened to her, why was it Burke's betrayal that set her off? Damn it. She liked him far more than she'd realized. She'd wanted to believe him. Wanted him to be honest.

"Emma, what's wrong?"

She started laughing through her tears. "Oh, God, what isn't, Burke? I can't believe it, but I was falling for you." Gritting her teeth, she punched the soft top of the mattress. "You bastard. There is no word for this kind of betrayal. I was right. You are Satan. My personal demon from hell."

"What are you talking about?"

She saw it in his eyes for the first time. Fear. Even more telling, he stepped back and crossed his arms across his chest.

Her rage spiked. "Don't. I know you fabricated the tape. I know you were behind my kidnapping—" A wallop of pain slammed her. He reached for her and she pushed him away. "No, you don't get to touch me anymore. Stay over there!" She pointed toward the door. "If you care about me at all, tell me the truth."

He looked away and shrugged. "I don't know—"

Her body shaking with rage, she threw aside the bedcovers and leapt out of bed to face him. "Stop it! Just stop it! You kidnapped me. At least have the balls to admit it. Or I swear, I'll lose all respect for you."

He stopped and stared at her with a look that was as good as a confession. But he didn't seem apologetic. His face went harder. Sighing, he turned away and ran his hand over his smooth head. When he turned back, his eyes were colder, darker. Almost emotionless, he gave a nearly imperceptible shrug. "You had my nuke. And technically, I didn't hurt you. I made sure of that. And I punished the guy who hit you. My orders were first and foremost not to hurt you."

His simple admission punched her hard in her stomach. She'd still held out hope that it was all a bad mistake.

She broke out in a full body sweat, her heart beat wild. She glowered at him and pointed. "You gave me PTSD, you asshole!"

A fleeting raise of his brows. "You wouldn't have told me any other way. I won't apologize for that. Like you said, that was about the safety of a million people. Not about us."

She clutched her chest. "Oh, don't even go there. Don't justify the torture."

"It was the best decision at the time."

He seemed completely unaffected by her anger.

She felt like she was screaming at an inanimate object. "You say you love me, how could you do that to me?"

"I didn't love you. Well, I did. I didn't realize it. Not until you started screaming. That's why I cut the fake torture session short. I was planning to go on a lot longer. But I couldn't take it. That's when I knew I'd fallen for you."

"Oh, please."

"I didn't want to, believe me," he said, shooting her a sharp look. "Fuck you, yes. Love you, no. It's totally screwed up my head and my plans. Well, some of them."

She wondered if her dream had been completely true. "But not the one where you're selling a nuke to the Taliban. What the hell is wrong with you?"

He looked a bit surprised by the information, but then he pulled himself up to his full six feet and his face went stony. "Don't judge me when you don't have all the information."

She could barely comprehend his admission. Every bit of her wanted to jump off the boat and swim for it. "Fuck! I just guessed that! You fucking creep! Selling a nuke to the Taliban? Have you lost your mind?"

His gaze went fiery and his jaw tightened. "I would never do anything to put our country in danger."

"Bullshit."

"I'm not lying."

"You wouldn't know the truth if it came up and gave you a blow job."

"I have reasons for everything I do. At this time I'm not at liberty to divulge them. You'll just have to trust that I have the country's best interests at heart."

"Trust you? Are you insane? As soon as we hit Hawaii, you'll never see me again."

"That remains to be seen."

Her muscles seared from being so tight. Bastard was so sure of himself! "I'm not getting over this. You crossed all the lines with me. All my boundaries. You didn't just decimate our relationship, Burke, you obliterated it. Vaporized it. Murdered it."

He chuckled and sent her a patronizing, smug grin. "You'll learn to trust me again. I know you. And I know you still want me. You suspected me of all this and still came back to me. On some level, you knew. It's only your ego that's hurt. You'll get over it."

Her mouth dropped open. This guy's audacity knew no bounds. "You are mental."

"If you really loved Rollin, you would have listened to him in that restaurant. At least own up to your choices. You chose me."

"I chose the Burke you wanted me to see. Shit. Rollin put my sister up in that place, didn't he?"

"I arranged to take over the payments when I was there," he said like there was nothing wrong with what he'd done. Very matter-of-fact.

Crazy. She could not get her bearings. "Holy Christ. You actually believe this crap, don't you? Look, I'm not staying—"

Burke talked over her. "Rollin can't make you as happy as I can."

Her body went rigid and her head flamed with heat. "Oh, yeah, you've made me so happy so far. Fucking kidnapping me, lying to me, manipulating my emotions?"

Burke's gaze shone with confidence. "I would not have begun this relationship like this had I foreseen where it would take me. Take us.

But I'm serious about you. From here on out, there will be no more secrets between us with the exception of my work. That I will never share with you. To protect you."

"Burke, you're not hearing me—"

"We belong together, Emma. I know you can't see the whole picture now, but I can," he said with an eerie serenity.

She never met anyone more arrogant. "I'm not going to forgive you."

He raised one brow. "If you'd just told me where the weapon was when I asked, none of that would have happened."

She held up her hands. "No, wait. I'm responsible for my kidnapping. You're just about to blame me, aren't you?"

A small shrug. "I tried to get the information out of you very nicely."

"Nicely? I can't believe you actually used that word."

His cheeks flushed red and his mouth went tight. "How many times did I ask you directly?" he demanded. "I tried everything I could think of before kidnapping you. Do you remember Escapade? I poured enough Cosmos down your throat to get a football team drunk." He softened. "But I understand why you didn't tell me. For the same reason I faked that kidnapping. We both have this country's best interests at heart."

She made a dismissive noise, crossed her arms and tapped her foot violently.

"And I didn't hurt you physically. I'm sorry you ended up with the nightmares, but they will pass."

"What about the nuke? You're a decorated veteran. What the hell is wrong with you?"

"I'm not going to tell you my plans. All you need to worry about is what color bikini you want to wear on the beaches of Maui."

She snorted. "You are such an asshole."

"You're painting me as the villain here, but you seem to forget how many times I've saved you recently. Do you think you would have fared better if the government found out you had a nuke in your storage unit? With your ties to the criminal world?"

She looked down at the comforter and straightened out the corner. "I'd be in a goddamned black prison somewhere in Jordan."

"You would have been made to disappear. I've protected you. I know I ruined the trust between us. And that's something I'll have to live with. But this country is worth more than you and me. More than our love. More than you trusting me."

This guy should have a boombox blasting the national anthem. "Problem is, Burke, you're a lie factory. How do I know which lies to believe?" She turned away from him.

He took a step toward her. "You're angry and I don't blame you. But I am offering myself to you. My loyalty, my devotion, my love. Once this mission is complete, I'm leaving the business entirely. I can offer you a life rich with travel, culture and exploration."

"Oh, please."

"Rollin is never going to grow up. He needs that adrenaline rush. I'm ready to move onto something else. I can offer you security, stability and love. He can't."

She busted up laughing. Rollin was right. Burke believed his stories. "You're delusional."

"Clearly when I fell in love with you."

"You don't even know what love is."

"Unfortunately, I do." His brow furrowed and his face went dark. "And I missed all the signs until it slapped me in the face when you were tied to that chair. It's been a long time for me, Emma. I've had many women."

She gave a harsh laugh. "I'll bet."

"But I've only been in love three times. One left me, I left the second when she betrayed me, and now there's you." A haunted shadow passed behind his eyes.

"At this point, I don't care if you *are* telling me the truth. I'm gonna leave this boat when it docks and you'll never see me again."

He held her gaze, unmoved. "Feelings change. Yours will. We have something. It goes beyond these events. Beyond the nuke, Rollin, your husband's death—speaking of which, did you ever wonder why Adam's chest was so bruised when they found him?"

"Because you beat him up?"

"Because I tried to save the idiot. I only hit him a few times before he went into cardiac arrest. I hit him more doing CPR. I wasn't going to kill him. I just wanted my weapon back."

"You had Rollin plant the murder evidence on me."

Finally, some actual sorrow in his gaze. He looked away and then turned back to her, his pain lines deep. "Okay. *That* I regret. That is the only thing that's happened between us that I truly wish hadn't."

Tired of the game, she slumped on the bed and tears welled in her eyes. "I don't know how I can say this so you'll actually understand me. Fuck off?"

A small, patronizing smile.

She wanted to punch him.

"You'll feel differently soon. Until then, I'm sure you'll understand why I need to lock you in here. I'll have some food brought to you shortly. Call me if you need anything," he said nicely.

He left, shut the door and locked it.

Emma let out a roar of frustration and kicked the closet door, which burst open. Slamming it shut, she knocked a chair across the room. Jesus, the guy had a five-inch thick iron skull. No information could squeak past his impenetrable shield of denial.

Unreal.

She went to the door and worked on the handle, but couldn't open it. She paced her room, getting angrier and angrier with each step.

Damn this! If Cherlenko thought she'd be a good little girl and stay locked in her cabin, he was nuts.

Her head throbbed and a stab of pain knifed her neck. She massaged her sore muscles. There was no way she was gonna sit there and let him sell a bloody nuke to the Taliban.

She looked closely at the door hinges. Her heart lifted, her mood soared, she laughed. All she had to do was get the pin out, then bust the door open. Easy peasy.

But if she got out too soon, he'd just lock her in another cabin and probably put a guard on her. She'd have to wait until the boat stopped or slowed. Then she'd attack those hinges and get out and create havoc. Yes!

That bastard thought he had her where he wanted her. He had no idea how much trouble she could be. Once she was done with the jerk, he'd regret ever meeting her.

TWENTY-THREE

Juiced and nervous, Rollin paced the bridge of his ship. The engine was holding. Even at top speed for the last twenty hours, the sucker kept chugging away. He knew he was pushing the boat's limits, but he had to save Emma.

Oh, yeah, and get that nuke.

Shit. They should have done a drop. He almost scrambled a plane, but wanted more equipment at the site. He checked the radar. Burke and another boat at the edge of his equipment's range seemed to be heading for one another. They'd reach each other soon.

Sipping on a Dr. Pepper, Zane sat at the far end of the controls, his mile-long legs stretched out across two seats. "You okay, buddy?"

"No. Goin' out of my mind."

Greg, sitting on the other end of the bridge, waved his hand dismissively. "Check it out," he said, indicating the radar display. "Burke's slowed way down. We'll be on him in an hour, way before the other boat. Plenty of time to set the trap."

"Okay, but what if Emma's already found out the truth? She always does. He'd better not hurt her."

Zane leaned back further in his chair and stretched. His arms almost reached the ceiling. "Burke's a lot of things, but he's never hurt a woman. He's in love with her. He'll protect her."

Rollin's gut and heart hurt like they'd been squeezed through a wringer. Burke would protect her by fucking the hell out of her. He kicked the bulkhead. "Yeah, great protection taking her with him when he's selling a nuke. Which I can't get my head around. How could he change that fast?"

Zane shrugged. "I don't know. But he's lost it."

"Way lost it," Greg echoed.

"If he's so crazy he can sell a nuke, he could hurt her." Rollin gestured broadly, hitting his hand on the wall. Pain radiated from his knuckles, but the adrenaline rush erased his discomfort fast.

Zane raised a dark brow. "Dude, calm down. Besides, she dumped you for him."

"No, he showed her a videotape and she believed it. Her head is fucked up. And if I get my hands on that bastard, I'll beat him to death." Rollin punched Burke's imaginary face.

"You *will* get your hands on him. Right, Greg?" Zane asked.

"With the engine holding strong like it is, we'll get there for sure on time," the balding biker quickly said.

Rollin's straightened into battle posture. "We have to." He suddenly couldn't stand the confines of the small bridge. "I'm gonna go down below and get the equipment ready. Zane?"

"Yeah?"

"I want to go over the plan one more time before we go. Where are Catherine and Dino?"

"With Captain and Ty, checking out the diving equipment." Zane held up his monster-sized hands and rolled his eyes. "Don't worry."

Rollin stopped and held his head. "You're right, I'm driving myself nuts. I gotta make sure this comes off right. Aside from Emma, I'm worried about that nuke. And whoever they're selling to—"

Fixated on a screen, Greg gave a low whistle. "Al-Qaeda."

Rollin turned to him so fast, he pulled a muscle in the back of his head. "Al-Qaeda?" he demanded, rubbing his neck.

The balding biker nodded. "Message from Bobby." His face went grave as he gestured at his screen. "He's monitoring all of Burke's communications. He busted an encrypted message between the two boats. Al-Qaeda for sure."

Rollin's heart hammered his breastbone. "Fuck. What is wrong with that asshole?" He gave his head a shake. "Okay, now we really can't make any mistakes."

Zane shot him a wry grin. "We always make mistakes. It's how we handle the mistakes that makes us the best."

Exactly an hour and a half later, in the pitch black of night, his blood pumping fast, Rollin slipped into the ocean wearing full battle/dive gear. Zane, Dino and Catherine followed.

Rollin shivered. The water, while technically warm, still chilled him. Been awhile since he'd done this, and it brought back a thousand memories. Most of them unpleasant, yet thrilling.

Took a full twenty minutes to reach the enemy boats. Rollin and Dino would attack from the stern. Zane would take care of the small boat loaded with the nuke, and Catherine was headed for the bow to capture Burke's crew.

Captain said in his earpiece, "We secured the homing device to the Al-Qaeda boat. We'll watch for the signal. Out."

Rollin treaded water while the other Patriots got into position.

Catherine and Zane gave the signal over their coms.

His body super-charged, his pulse pounding in his ears, Rollin motioned to Dino and swam up to the back of the boat, Dino right by his side.

Two guys were directly at the top of the stairs, on the main deck.

After darkness fell, the boat slowed.

Time to rock and roll.

Emma grabbed the butter knife, pressed her ear to the door and listened. Nothing but the ambient noise of the boat. She went to work on the hinges.

She dug the tip into the space between the hinge and pin, and pushed down, but the knife slipped. Not as easy as she'd first thought.

Sweat trickled down her forehead and she wiped it away. She pressed the edge of the knife into the hinge again and budged the pin up a bit.

The boat stopped.

A rush of adrenaline surged through her. She had to hurry. She peered through her porthole. A boat the size of Burke's had anchored nearby. Shit!

She worked faster and finally slid the top pin out. She dove for the bottom hinge. After a few tries, she removed the pin and dropped the knife onto the floor.

Her pink shorts and white tank top caught her attention. Not spy clothes. She grabbed her black sleep shirt and pants, the only dark outfit in her backpack. After adding her white sneakers, she checked her reflection in the mirror. She looked like a Stealth Yoga Instructor. She shrugged.

She'd go up to the next deck and hide either in Burke's cabin or the galley. Then she'd get out onto the deck and see what kind of trouble she could cause.

And hopefully not die in the process.

Emma picked up the knife and stuck it in between the door and the frame and wedged it open, but only by about an inch. The doorknob's lock held firm to the jamb.

She grabbed the edge of the door with both hands and wrenched it open, splintering the frame, making a hideous amount of noise.

Her heart slammed her ribs. Her breathing shallow, she jumped out into the tiny hallway and strained to listen for anyone coming.

Nothing.

All her attention focused on the stairwell and the Main Deck above her, she slowly crept upwards. She reached the top and found the area clear. The sky was inky outside.

She peeked around the corner into the living area. Her legs went rubbery and her head felt so light she was afraid it might float away.

Beyond the vast room, a group of men stood outside at the stern of the boat, talking. A distinctive bald guy was turned away from her.

She ducked back into the stairwell and took a breath.

She checked again. The men were engrossed in conversation.

Her body hyped, she counted to three, strode onto the deck and quickly scanned her area. No one in her vicinity. But floating just a couple football fields across the water was the Taliban's boat.

Beyond the two boats, she couldn't see anything, not even the water. The cloud cover blocked the moonless sky.

Her blood rushed in her ears. She crouched down and tried to figure out what to do. She snuck closer to the stern and the action. Right below her on the water was a small empty boat.

Looked like a small ski boat with a windscreen.

On second look, it wasn't empty at all. A long black box lay in the back.

A blast of energy erupted inside her. The nuke!

But why wasn't anyone guarding the boat? And why was the skiff tethered by a skinny little rope? You'd think they'd have better protection.

She knew what she had to do. She hoped this wasn't the last crazy thing she ever did.

Emma said a quick prayer, launched herself over the side of the yacht and landed hard on the deck. Sharp pain shot up both legs and they gave out. She fell forward on top of the bomb, her legs screaming in agony.

Hurry! No time for pain!

She pushed off the bomb case and hurled herself toward the end of the boat. She untied the rope, pivoted and flew for the controls.

She sat in the captain's chair and turned over the engine. Pulling back on the gas, she grabbed the steering wheel and roared off into the blackness.

Rollin's focus on his target, his body shook with hard heartbeats. He raced up the stairs, Dino right behind him.

He leapt onto the deck, surprising a crowd of guys including Burke. Two men attacked him: a red-haired guy in his forties and an olive-skinned kid in his twenties with curly black hair. He slammed

Red in the face with the butt of his MP 4. Red reeled back, tripped and fell to the deck. Dino punched the black-haired kid so hard, he knocked him flat. Rollin hit Red again and he slumped to the ground.

Burke ran for cover inside the boat. Two Mediterranean-looking guys headed down the stairs toward the water.

In the background, a loud roar of a boat's engine cut through the night. Zane had the bomb.

Three more thugs came rushing out from where Burke had disappeared, guns blazing.

Rollin flattened behind a bench and fired back.

Dino took out one of the guys and Rollin nailed another. But the last had excellent cover behind a bulkhead.

Blam! A bullet shattered the edge of the molded fiberglass bench above Rollin's head. He ducked, his heart crashing in his chest.

A volley of gunfire came at him. Rollin covered his head and searched for Dino.

He spotted the tall Italian hiding behind a large barbecue. Dino signaled him and pointed toward the inside of the boat. Rollin acknowledged him, leapt to his feet and blanketed the area with bullets. Dino slipped down the deck and disappeared inside the boat.

The assailant popped out. Rollin dropped behind a chair. Bullets tore into the metal chair and its cushion. Bits of foam rubber went everywhere.

A flurry of gunshots, a bloody hole appeared in the man's forehead and he crumpled to the deck.

A wave of relief and revulsion washed through Rollin. *Thank you, Dino.* But fuck, he hated killing.

Dino came out from the interior of the boat, stepped over the bad guy's body, and rushed up to him. Water still dripped from his black mustache.

Rollin said, "Help Catherine below, I'm going after Burke."

"You got it." Dino turned and raced down the stairs.

Rollin ran to the aft, searching for Burke. He'd studied the plans of the large yacht, Burke was more than likely retrieving weapons from his cabin.

He found the main cabin door locked. No problem.

Rollin shot all around the door handle and kicked it open. His weapon ready, all his senses tuned for danger, he cautiously entered the room.

Her muscles so taut they shook, Emma steered the boat away from Burke's yacht. Gunfire pierced the night air. Screams. Men shouted. More gunfire.

Hopefully, they were shooting at each other and not her. So far, no bullets had come her way. Maybe she was home free.

The windshield of the boat exploded and glass showered her.

She screamed and dove for the floorboards, her pulse zooming higher.

She reached up high to the steering wheel and piloted the boat blind.

Bullets pounded the boat's dashboard within inches of her head. She flinched and cried out with each explosion.

Searing pain lit up her lower leg and she screamed. She reached down and her hand came away wet. Another vat of adrenaline unloaded into her system. She'd been shot!

Tears blinded her and she wiped them away with her forearm. She grabbed her wild fears with both hands. She had to keep her head together or she'd die for sure.

Her whole body shaking, she stayed down while her boat roared away from the larger yachts. She pressed the wound hard to stop the bleeding.

The gunshot didn't feel like it penetrated her leg, just grazed it.

Well, hopefully. She couldn't see it properly in the dim light coming from the boat's running lights.

A few long minutes later, the gunfire ceased. She hesitantly looked up and the two boats were far away from her now. Small.

She slumped against the side of the boat and caught her breath. Christ, that was close.

As she congratulated herself for surviving, it occurred to her that she had no plan. Alone in a tiny boat with only a nuclear weapon for company, she had no idea what to do next and she was bleeding.

Her stomach gnarled and her mood went grim. Great. Now what?

She pulled herself up and a sharp pain stabbed her leg from her bullet wound. She brushed the broken glass from the pilot's seat, sat down and slowed the boat. Reaching down, she flipped off the running lights.

She steered the boat away from where she'd been, went a distance, then cut the engine and let the boat drift. If they started shooting at her again, at least they wouldn't know where to aim.

Quick plan: stop the bleeding. Challenging, since she couldn't see anything. She ripped off her t-shirt and wrapped it around the wound. But her hands and body shook so hard, it took several tries before she could tie the shirt to her leg.

Shouting and more gunfire came across the water.

She held herself and tried to stay focused. One of the boats headed away from the other, fast. What happened? Was the boat coming toward her?

She watched carefully, but the yacht went the other way.

Which ship was left? Burke's or the Taliban's? And who'd fired the weapons?

Shit.

What if Burke had taken off? What if only the Taliban was left? All they had to do was wait until daylight and they'd find her floating there like a platter of victim served up with a side of nuke.

Flashes of light came from the remaining boat's deck as more gunfire cracked the night air. Men shouted. Amazing how the sound carried across the water.

The cool night air chilled her sweaty body and she shook harder. She hugged herself tighter and rubbed her upper arms.

She needed a plan.

If she pushed the nuke into the ocean, the salt water would eventually penetrate the hull and then radiation would poison the whole area.

No other ideas came to her. She'd successfully screwed up the deal for the time being, but battling terrorists wasn't exactly her forte. Despite the pain in her leg, her uncontrollable trembling and the fact that she would more than likely die soon, she started to laugh.

Life had taken a serious turn for the ludicrous.

TWENTY-FOUR

On an adrenaline rush, Rollin burst into Burke's room, weapon at the ready.

Burke sat in the corner of the room in a large chair holding a pistol in his hand. But he didn't point his gun at Rollin. And he didn't seem surprised.

"You are an idiot," Burke pronounced, his lip curled, his eyes dark.

His cool demeanor threw Rollin off. He aimed his gun, but couldn't get his bearings. "I'm an idiot? What the fuck is wrong with you, man?"

"Nothing. You've totally screwed up my plans. Again."

"Yeah, I hope so."

Burke glared at him. "You have no idea what you've done."

"I've got a pretty good idea." He gave a quick once-over of the sleek master suite, but didn't see Emma. "Where's Emma?"

"Locked in her cabin below. I wanted to make sure she stayed out of danger."

Her cabin? She wasn't staying with Burke? None of Emma's belongings were visible. His heart lifted. She must have found out Burke had lied to her. "I don't want to hurt you, Burke."

"So don't. And get off my ship. You've already totally fucked me over and successfully screwed up the deal. So who's with you? I saw Dino. Let me guess, Zane, Captain America and Catherine. Probably more on your ship. I would assume someone swam over and put a tracking device on the Al-Qaeda boat?" He almost sounded bored.

Why wasn't he defending himself? Why was he acting so weird? "Yeah, so what the hell are you doing?"

"You clearly wouldn't believe me." Burke looked away and seemed disgusted.

"Try me."

"I'd rather have you think I've betrayed you."

"Why?"

"Because maybe I'm not done."

What had Burke set in motion? Were more bad guys on their way? Was he going to detonate the weapon? Or was Burke fucking with him? "The other guys will be here in a minute, you'd better come clean with me."

Burke's anger lines deepened. "Fuck you. Turn around and get out or I will fight you."

"I'm taking Emma with me."

Burke's face darkened, his eyes flashed with fury and he got to his feet, his shoulders squared. "She's mine. You lost her. She chose me."

Rollin snorted. "Yeah, because you faked a videotape and convinced her that I'd kidnapped her. I didn't have to lie to her to get her to love me, Burke. You had to put on a whole theatrical production."

"That's because Emma's ego is bigger than her brain. I enabled her to lie to herself long enough to recognize her true feelings. I can give her what she needs. You can't."

Rollin gave a harsh laugh. "Are you out of your fucking mind? She'll hate you when she finds out."

"She found out and doesn't hate me. She loves me."

Rollin's gut lurched. "You are so full of shit."

"You wish. Now get out and leave Emma alone or I *will* fucking kill you."

"No."

"Fine, have it your—" Burke reached out fast and pressed a button on a console in front of him.

Astounding pain exploded in the back of Rollin's head as a large armoire crushed him to the floor. A fucking booby-trap!

Dazed, the room went fuzzy.

Burke lifted the large piece of furniture off, yanked him to his feet and punched him in the face. Searing pain shocked his jaw, his head snapped back and flashing lights streaked his vision.

"You should have stayed away."

Rollin took a swing at Burke, but the bald man easily ducked out of the way and nailed him in the jaw. Harrowing pain rocked his face and a hard jab to his gut nearly knocked all the wind out of him. Then Burke kicked his bad knee. Excruciating pain shot through his leg and he crumpled to the floor.

Fucker knew all his weak spots.

"This brings me no pleasure, old friend," Burke said, kicking him hard in the head.

Fireworks. His skull rang with horrible pain. "Fuck you, Burke." Rollin spat out some blood and slowly picked himself off the floor.

He pretended to be more groggy than he was. While Burke assessed him and prepared to attack, Rollin leapt up and kicked him in the solar plexus, sending him reeling back against his desk.

Jumping across the distance, Rollin slammed him with a right cross, then a left uppercut, followed by a punishing series of hard hits to his gut.

Before Burke could get his hands up to protect himself, Rollin pounded him four more times in the face.

Blood dripping from his nose and mouth, Burke bashed him in the jaw. Sharp pain blasted his face and his head snapped sideways. Burke delivered a series of hard punches to his stomach—pure agony—sending him reeling.

Rollin fell back onto the bed.

Burke came in, his fists raised.

Rollin used the bed as a springboard and popped off, nailing Burke with a right. Another series of punches to his face and a hard kick to his chest and Burke stumbled.

Tripping, Burke fell back and hit his head on the edge of a table, making a loud *thunk*. Bouncing off, he crumpled to the floor. And didn't move.

Breathing hard, Rollin's body pulsed with pain with every heartbeat. He approached him, wary. But Burke remained motionless.

Rollin kicked him. Burke's body moved, but he didn't awaken. He bent down and cautiously felt the pulse in his neck. Strong.

His belly roiling with grief and anger, the bitter taste of betrayal in his mouth, Rollin could only shake his head. After all those years of being there for each other, now there was nothing between them.

"Asshole," he spat.

Rollin examined the closet and all the drawers, but only found Burke's stuff. He ducked into the bathroom, but Emma's toiletries weren't there, either.

What the fuck?

He rushed out of the room and headed downstairs. As soon as he reached the deck below, he saw the busted door, broken outward from the inside. He slipped inside. No sign of Emma. But her stuff was there.

His shoulders relaxed a bit and a rush of hope went through him. They didn't fuck?

Zane stuck his head inside the room.

"Why aren't you with the bomb?" Rollin demanded.

"Emma has it."

Rollin's brain spun out of control. He couldn't make sense of Zane's words. "What?"

Zane made a face and shrugged. "I'd just taken care of the two guards. I turn around and I see Emma flying away in the fuckin' boat."

Terror gripped his belly and all his muscles went hard. His Emma? In a boat with the nuke? "Where the hell is she going?"

"I don't know." Zane made a quick examination of the room. "So she was in here, broke out and took the nuke?"

"Burke said he locked her in to protect her."

Zane looked at the door again and smirked. "Guess she didn't want to be protected."

"Where's Catherine?"

"She and Dino have the crew under guard. I saw Burke," the tall man said with a knowing look. "Feel better?"

Rollin grinned even though he didn't feel good about beating his old friend. "Yeah. But what the fuck is Emma up to?"

"We'll find out."

"What about the Al-Qaeda boat?"

"They turned tail and left five minutes ago."

"Shit. Let's go find Emma and that bomb."

"I'm right behind you, brother."

A humming came across the water.

A boat engine. Emma looked out and saw nothing. But the noise got louder.

Shit! Some kinda stealth boat. Her heart pounded harder.

Oh, God, a third party! Someone *had* come after them!

The Patriots?

Or was it that other guy that tried to kidnap her? Frank Bortolli?

Didn't matter, it was time to run.

She hit the ignition, started the boat and slammed down on the gas, heading away from the sound.

Several pops came over the roar of her engine. She smelled gasoline.

She had no idea where to go, so she just stayed on course.

The engine sputtered and the boat bucked, throwing her forward.

A violent wave of fear hit her, firing up her limbs. Oh, God, no! They'd shot her gas tank!

The engine died and she nearly fainted. She felt like a bunny covered in beef fat surrounded by a pack of coyotes.

Fuck! She needed a weapon. No one was gonna take that nuke away from her without a fight. She felt around for the controls to the interior lights on the boat.

Emma flipped on the lights and frantically dug through the boat's compartments. Maps, life vests—wait. Something metal. She lifted off an orange vest and nearly cried. A rifle!

Her hands shaking, her knees like jelly, she grabbed the gun, cocked it and flipped off the lights again. Hopefully, her eyes would adjust shortly and she could see someone in the dark enough to shoot them.

They wouldn't dare fire on the nuke. She hurried down and straddled the bomb. Aiming her weapon toward the back of the boat, she tuned all her senses into the darkness. She put her finger on the trigger and got ready.

Blam!

Propelled backward, she landed flat on her back on the deck. Searing pain lit up her shoulder blades and butt, and her heart nearly stopped from fright. Stupid hairpin trigger! The rifle's recoil had thrown her onto her ass. Shit! Sitting up quickly, she cocked the gun again.

She strained to hear the engine of the boat pursuing her.

Nothing.

Her boat rocked violently, the rifle got yanked out of her grip and a very large man tackled her to the floorboards.

Terror blasted her brain apart. Screaming, she fought the guy, but within about a second, he had her in a painful hold.

"Emma, stop fighting or I'll hurt you. You're lucky to be alive as it is."

Carter.

"Well, thank God." She slumped with relief.

"Will you stand down?"

"Stand down? I'm not fighting you."

He didn't budge. "You're working for Burke, aren't you?"

Her belly hollowed and a dark sinking feeling overtook her. "What? Are you kidding?"

"You went with him. It's no stretch to think you're working for him."

"You're not kidding. Jesus Christ, I feel like I just stepped into some weird alternate universe."

"Where were you taking the nuke?!"

"Away from Cherlenko. For God's sake! He held me hostage! He showed me a fake videotape of Rollin torturing me. And then I found out he was gonna sell this nuke to the Taliban, so I busted out of my room and screwed up the deal. Okay? Now will you get off me?"

Carter didn't move. "I think you have friends out here. And you'd better tell me how many of them there are and where they are."

This could not be happening to her. Not after everything she'd been through. "You're a tanker truck full of dumb if you think I'm capable of that."

He gave her a shake. "If any of my men die because of you, you won't fare well. Now answer me. Where were you taking the nuke?"

"I refuse to answer on the grounds that the questions are too stupid." He yanked up on her arm and searing pain blazed her shoulder. "Owww! Get off me, you asshole! Owwww!"

He eased the pressure slightly. "Answer my questions and I'll stop hurting you. What was Burke's back up plan? Are you meeting him somewhere? Or are you meeting the Al-Qaeda boat at a rendezvous point?"

"Al-Qaeda? I thought it was the Taliban."

He pulled on her arm and it burned like it was on fire.

"Ow! I'm not a fucking spy, you idiot!"

"Stop cussing, I don't like it."

"Fuck you!"

"Fine, I'll get the truth from you back at the ship."

All the fight went out of her and hopelessness and exhaustion overwhelmed her. How could the Patriots think she'd drunk Burke's Koolaid to the point where she'd betray her country?

Rollin and Zane searched the boat for additional weapons and money, but found none.

Carter came over the com. "Emma still maintains she was just trying to mess up the sale, but I don't believe her. She took off in a small boat headed out to open sea with a nuke. No one does that without a reason."

Rollin chuckled. "Actually, that sounds exactly like something she'd do."

"Sorry, friend, but you're a bit biased," Carter said.

Zane nodded. "She jumped on that boat like she'd practiced the move. She might have been playing you, Rollin."

"Don't let this turn out like Rome, Rollin," Carter warned.

He bristled. "It won't." He wasn't losing Emma. "I'll be there in five minutes. You didn't hurt her, did you?"

Carter hesitated, then said, "A nuclear weapon is at stake, Rollin. I did what I had to do."

"Fuck. She's not some secret operative and I'll it prove to you. Catherine is taking care of the engine so they can't follow."

"Roger."

Rollin clicked off. "Captain better not have hurt her that bad."

"She chose to go with Burke," Zane said. "You can't blame that on anyone but her. And Captain's not an idiot. He might be picking up something you're missing."

In the back of his mind, he heard Burke's voice. *She chose me.* He brushed away the doubt. "Captain is suspicious of all women. Ever since Debby left him, he's been bitter with every chick we encounter. He even snapped at Catherine the other day."

Zane smirked. "She deserved it. She was teasing him."

"She does have a mouth on her. Like Emma. Oh, God, Emma will eat him alive."

TWENTY-FIVE

Every cell in Emma's body screamed with fury. Tied painfully to a chair, she saw double. All she wanted was to beat the shit out of Carter.

The tall weathered military man sat opposite her at a beat-up metal table in what appeared to be the living area on the main deck of Rollin's boat. She'd gotten a quick look at the ship. Bigger than Burke's but older and not as fancy.

With icy pale blue eyes, Carter leveled an intense stare at her.

She flashed back on that horrible interrogation at the hands of Detective McCoy. She couldn't believe she faced the same intolerable situation.

"I'll repeat myself. Tell me about the sale."

"I don't know anything, you stupid idiot!"

Carter's gaze sliced her and his jaw twitched. "Long swim back to San Francisco."

"Fuck you!"

Tears streamed down her face and her body trembled, making her chair squeak. She had nothing to wipe her nose on, she wore only her bra and black sleep pants. Blood trickled down her leg.

Rollin walked into the room, followed by Zane.

When she locked gazes with Rollin, it felt like someone had picked her up and slammed her to the deck, face first. A tornado of emotions grabbed her and spun her mind until her thoughts flew out in all directions. She couldn't figure out whether to laugh, cry or scream. Despite his foreboding expression, he looked so good. His long dark hair wet, he was dressed in a wetsuit, now unzipped to his waist, revealing his tanned chest. He looked like a centerfold. But his gaze was wary and guarded and the anger lines on his face were deep. He looked older.

Rollin glared at her, his face hard. "What the hell happened? Why did you believe Burke? Why did you go with him?"

Her gut scorched in agony. Vulnerable, open and raw, she wished she could jump out of the chair and shake him. Thankfully, her anger helped quell some of her shame. She'd been all set to apologize, but with that nasty look on his face, all she could think about was smacking him. "What do you mean, what happened? The videotape, hello? Are you this stupid?"

"I thought you loved me. Was that all bullshit?"

"Are you deaf? Because that goddamned tape convinced me! I told you this! Now please untie me."

He didn't move.

"Don't tell me you believe this fucking crap about me conspiring with Burke and Al-Qaeda?"

His dark gaze narrowed and his mouth went harder.

She lost it. Screaming, she let loose with a torrent of expletives. So crazy with anger, she almost spoke in tongues. After all she'd been through, to see Rollin looking at her like she was the enemy was too much.

After she began to run out of steam, Rollin rolled his eyes, sighed and took a step forward. "Emma, calm down. Why did Burke put you in that room?"

She made an exasperated noise. "Because he was giving me space to come to him. I collapsed and slept for a bazillion hours, then I had this nightmare…" The story tumbled out of her.

Rollin's expression remained guarded. "How did you get out of the room?"

"Used a butter knife."

"When did you escape?"

"Right after the boat stopped."

"Why then? Why not after he locked you in there?"

"And what would that have done? He would have just locked me somewhere else and put a guard on me. I wanted to screw up that deal. I wasn't about to let him sell a nuke to the Taliban. Or Al-Qaeda. Whoever they were."

His jaw tightened. "You knew that before you got onboard."

A vat of acid poured into her belly. She wanted to punch that expression right off his fucking face. "No, I didn't. At that point, I was buying Burke's crap. He told me he'd already gotten rid of it."

He gave a harsh laugh. "You can't be this naïve."

"Are you out of your mind? He kidnapped me, showed me that goddamned fake video and then took me to see my sister and told me he'd paid for it. I know you did, okay? And aside from everything, thanks for that. She's thriving in that place. But he took credit. And any man who'd take care of my sister deserved my loyalty."

The pain lines on Rollin's face deepened. "Did he admit that I'd set her up there?"

"Eventually. Fucking thickheaded duplicitous bastard. But he doesn't think there's anything wrong with his lies. He thinks he did the right thing. He believed I'd stay with him. It was like talking to a rock. A satanic rock. And then I try to do the right thing and get accused of complicity! You fuckers! You stupid Patriots are starting to make Burke look good! Burke's Hitler and you guys are making him look like Barney!"

Zane coughed into his hand, then glared at her. Had he laughed?

Carter didn't even flinch.

Rollin seemed to expect her outburst. "What was your plan for the nuke? Dump it?"

"And poison the whole ocean? I didn't have a plan. I realized that once I got away. But where the hell were you guys? Why wasn't anyone guarding the nuke? It was just sitting there. It's all your fault I took it! Morons!"

Zane's eyes widened and he gaped at her, then started laughing. "Audacious little thing, isn't she?"

Rollin nodded and turned to Carter and Zane. "I believe her. Her stuff was in the room where she says she was held. And I didn't see any of her junk in Burke's room."

"I believe her, too." Zane said. "The pins were off the hinges just like she said. I saw the butter knife, too. She did some damage to that door."

Carter examined her and his harsh expression softened slightly. He nodded.

"Finally," she bit out. "Now will you untie me already? I have to take care of my gunshot wound."

Rollin's attention snapped to her. "You got *shot*?"

"You think I'm sitting here in my underwear with stage blood dripping down my leg for effect? To get sympathy? Get over here, you bastard!"

Rollin turned to Captain with a scowl.

Captain didn't react. "I checked it. Just a graze."

Emma snorted. "Just a graze, he says, like I got a fucking splinter. I got shot, you bastard, and you fucking attacked me!" she yelled at Carter. She swung her attention to Rollin and glowered. "Get your ass over here, Hanson, and untie me! Now!"

A half smile on his handsome face, Rollin walked over and cut the cable ties. "We had to be sure. You took off with the weapon. You left with Burke willingly."

She rubbed her wrists, rolled her sore shoulders, and wiped her nose. "Christ. I'm trying to save the world and suddenly, I'm Satan's mistress?"

"Calm down, honey, and let me look at your leg." Rollin laughed, but his gaze was guarded. "Cowgirl decided to wrangle the nuke."

Zane busted up, too, his laugh so low, it sounded almost like a growl. "She takes off riding that thing like Slim Pickens in *Dr. Strangelove*. Good plan, girlfriend."

"I screwed up that sale," she replied indignantly.

Rollin snorted. “Yes, you would have. And gotten yourself killed in the process.”

“Maybe, maybe not.”

Rollin shook his head. “You’re nuts.”

“Selling a nuke to Al-Qaeda,” she muttered to herself. “Well, I can check that off my To Do list.”

Carter said, “She’s a feisty thing.”

Zane grinned. “I like her, she’s trouble.”

She narrowed her eyes. “Don’t even try to charm me now. I still want to slap you both.” She turned away from the men and bent down to inspect her wound. The gash had stopped bleeding, but didn’t look great.

Rollin kneeled down. “Jesus, you did get shot.”

“I told you.”

Carter handed him the medical kit. “I’d help but she looks a bit rabid yet.”

“Good plan, Carter,” she fired at him. “You’re gonna have to work really hard to get back in my good graces.”

He chuckled. “Yes, ma’am.”

Rollin ripped open an antiseptic wipe and gently pressed it to the wound.

Her leg burned like he lit it on fire. “Ow! What the hell is that, gasoline?”

“Sorry. This is going to hurt.”

“Thanks for the warning.”

He worked on the wound, which hurt like hell.

Her anger had kept a nice shield between Rollin and her heart. But now that her fury was fading, grief and pain began to take over. There he was, the man she loved right in front of her, and she couldn’t have him. She took in his unique scent and stared at his buff muscles, his awesome bare chest, that crooked nose and those wonderful dark eyes.

Deep sorrow and confusion roiled through her and she wanted to shut her brain off.

Did Rollin still like her? Probably, but after what she'd done to him, he sure as hell didn't want anything to do with her.

A dark fog took over her mind. She'd lost everything. Her mother, Adam, she'd almost lost her sister, and Burke betrayed her and had made a fool out of her. Now she'd lost Rollin, too.

Rollin finished dressing the wound. "Okay. You're done." He stood and turned to Zane and Captain. "I think we're late for a date with the Navy."

Captain nodded. "I think we are, too."

Zane gazed at her thoughtfully, cracked a smile and left. Carter followed.

Leaving her with Rollin. While she finally felt safe physically, her heart had never been in more danger. She wanted out of there. Even if it only took a half a day to get back home, it would be the longest twelve hours of her life.

He said nothing and repacked the first aid kit. After he put it away, he turned to her. She couldn't tell what he was thinking. But he didn't look happy.

Chilled, she crossed her arms. "Well, this is awkward."

"Why did you keep choosing him over me?" Rollin clipped out, his gaze turning hollow and wounded.

Her heart felt like he'd stuck it in a paper shredder. She'd hurt him badly and he clearly wasn't about to forgive her. But there was nothing she could do about it at this point. She hugged herself tighter. "I didn't choose him."

"Is it true you didn't sleep with him?

Anger roared from deep in her belly and she leapt to her feet. She itched to slap him. After all they'd been through, this was all he cared about? "Of course, this is all you want to know. Was I defiled by your enemy? You're an idiot."

He didn't react. His eyes stayed guarded and hard. "You didn't answer my question."

She leveled her gaze at him, her jaw set. "If he were the last man on Earth, I'd become a lesbian."

He finally nodded and his expression softened a touch. "Do you blame me for being mad at you?"

She stood tall and glared up at him. "Yes, I do. You should have understood how vulnerable I was, how exhausted and how confused. And you're giving Cherlenko no credit at all. He put on a very convincing show."

His pain lines deepened and he put his hands on his hips. "You say you love me, but how could you if you believed that tape?"

"Don't bullshit me. It was you in that videotape. Maybe it wasn't me you were torturing, but you were hurting someone."

His attention went to the floor and back to her.

She nodded. "You had that same dead look in your eye as the day you beat the Russian. And I had the information about the nuke. It's not a stretch."

His brow wrinkled. "I'd never hurt you like that, Emma."

"You've been hurting me ever since you came aboard."

"I had to make sure you were on the right side."

"This conversation is pointless. Our relationship is obviously over and I see no more reason to speak to you." She turned and limped away from him and went outside onto the deck.

Emma only got ten feet past the door before he grabbed her by the arm and spun her around to face him. Her body went hard and her fists balled at her sides. He was an inch away from being smacked.

He glared down at her. "I'm not done."

"Well, I am." She tried to pull out of his grip, but he held on tighter. "Let go of me, you jerk."

"You're stuck on this ship and can't get away and you're gonna hear me out. I think you're in love with him."

She finally shrugged out of his grip. "You are such an asshole. Right now I'd love to kick his ass. And yours for believing I could actually love that bastard."

His gaze went darker. Disbelief was all over his face. "Powerful emotions, Emma. I think you're in denial."

Her ears went back. She poked him hard in the chest. "How the fuck would you know? You're so busy trying to hurt me and push me away because your stupid precious ego got bruised. Well, poor you! I got fucking kidnapped about a million times, tortured, chased, beaten, shot and duped by a big fat lying piece of shit that I hate, but noooo, you want to believe that I still love him. You're an asshole!"

He rolled his eyes and motioned downward with his hands, trying to quiet her. "Emma—"

She talked over him. "Go fuck yourself. You're too pig-headed and too jealous to see that I still love you and want you. Well, you don't deserve me. You big, dumb stupid jerk!"

Rollin burst into a white-toothed grin.

Her mind went black with rage. She raised her arm and advanced on him. "You think my feelings are funny? Stop smiling at me or so help me God, I'll punch you flat!"

He grabbed her and pulled her to him. She pushed on his chest, but he held her tightly. "Okay, so I am an asshole. And I am jealous. And I am worried that you wanted him more than me. And I guess I let my worries get ahead of what I want. Which is you."

His gaze dropped to her mouth and he kissed her.

Her body shook with anger. How dare he kiss her! She yelled into his mouth and pushed on his chest.

Emotion welled up inside her like roiling thunderclouds, threatening to blow her mind apart. She clung to him and let loose. Wracking with sobs, a monster-sized ball of pain, love, longing and fear swallowed her. He loved her. She hadn't lost him.

Her heart burst open with red-hot love and hope, setting her body on fire. She laughed and cried and hung onto him.

"It's okay, baby," he said, rubbing her back. "I'm sorry I got mad at you. And I'm sorry I let Captain interrogate you."

"No, I'm sorry for saying that shit to you in the restaurant. I was so hurt and confused, I just wanted to hurt you, too."

He kissed the side of her head. "I thought you loved him. I shouldn't have roasted you like that."

"It's okay."

"No, it isn't." He cupped her face and gazed deep into her eyes. "I lied to you and planted murder evidence on you and did a lousy job of protecting you. I let you down and I let myself down, Emma. It won't happen again. I'm promising you that right now." He kissed her.

His taste and energy derailed her for a second. But she had things to say. She ended the kiss. "Look, it wasn't all you. My problem is that I'm used to being with jerks like Burke. I couldn't believe someone as nice as you could love me. He's an asshole and tailor-made for my damage. And really, in all honesty, that video freaked me out. You can get scary. Like really scary."

He looked away, the line deepened between his eyes. A haunted expression came over his face. "Yeah, I know. And I hate that part of my job. I hate who I have to become. Takes a piece out of me every time I kill or hurt someone."

The vulnerability and pain in his gaze drew her in.

He took her hand and kissed it. "And I know what magic Burke can work with video. I'd probably believe that film if I saw it. Especially given my performance." He met her gaze. "He was there that day, too. He didn't show you his part." He frowned and concentrated on her hand once more. His brow furrowed. "That was a bad day," he said softly.

She rubbed his bare rock-hard shoulders. "Don't worry, Rollin. I can see your heart. You're a really good person. You do what you think you have to do to survive and help others survive."

He crushed her in an embrace. "I love you, Emma."

She pushed him away to make eye contact. "Are you sure? You seemed so cold earlier. When you first boarded the ship."

"Yeah, because it killed me to see you, I had to shut down. Captain thought you might be helping Burke. I couldn't believe you were, but I had to be sure."

"Do you still really want to be with me?"

Squeezing her, he nuzzled her face. "More than anything. I was worried you were done with me."

"Hardly. We barely got started."

Rollin kissed her and hot pulsing energy rocketed through her. She'd never been with anyone like him. No man had ever opened his heart to her this fully.

When he ended the kiss, she let out a huge sigh. "I love you, Rollin. So much. I thought I'd lost you. I thought he'd destroyed out relationship."

He wrapped his arms all the way around her. "We're gonna be okay. Now everything's gonna work out fine."

She settled into his warm embrace and the boat rocked them gently. The moist night air and his scent filled her senses. An intense, yet light and hot energy overtook her. She was safe. Finally, really safe. Then the bomb popped into her mind. She pushed away to look up at him. "What about the nuke?"

He gave her a confident smile. "We're on our way to deliver it."

"To who?"

"The Navy. We'll be there in another half hour."

"Wow, cool, the Navy?"

He shot her a proud grin. "We still have friends in high places."

His attention dropped to her mouth and he kissed her. His strong and magnificent tongue played with hers. His taste and the feel of him sent her sailing. Her body burned with love and lust, and her sex swelled with want. She breathed in his scent, remembering their lovemaking. She explored his ripped chest and back with her hands, his hot skin and hard muscles sent her pulse higher. She couldn't wait to be with him again.

Only after she woke up with him a few times would she believe the nightmare was over.

Rollin ended the kiss and nibbled on her neck. "I love you," he whispered in her ear.

His hot breath sent delightful shivers racing through her and delivered a special zing to her favorite nerve. She hugged him hard.

Cherlenko's smug face came to mind and she stiffened.

Rollin pulled away, his dark brow wrinkled. "What is it, baby?"

"Will he ever leave me alone? Burke knows I found the cash."

Rollin took her by the hips and brought her to him, kissing her forehead. "Don't worry about him. He's got boat troubles. And Navy troubles. He'll be lucky to survive the night."

"I'm surprised you didn't kill him."

His hands roamed her back, touching her sweetly, gently. "He saved my life way too many times. Same reason he didn't kill me when he had us kidnapped. Once he gets over being mad, he'll forget about us."

"Really?"

He grinned. "Really. You're safe. It's over, babe. And I got ya." He hugged her tightly.

Her body on fire, her heart filled with his love. She snuggled against his broad chest. He gently pushed her away, his eyes darkened and the set to his mouth went predatory. "You must be cold in that bra. How about I take you to my cabin and warm you up?"

"Will you use your immersion heater?" she asked and sent him a saucy grin.

He laughed and then his gaze went feral. His focus went to her lips. He kissed her, hard and hungry.

All at once, she centered. The tension left her belly and back. She molded her body to his and something clicked inside her.

This was where she was supposed to be.

In this man's arms.

Finally, she'd found him.

Thank fucking God.

EPILOGUE

Emma retrieved the mail and walked up the driveway toward her house. Shuffling through the letters, she came upon a bank statement she'd been waiting for.

Her pulse shot up and she raced inside the house, slamming the door behind her. With shaking hands, she opened the statement.

When she saw the balance on the money market account, she gasped. A huge wave of relief came over her and she almost collapsed in a puddle. Then a burst of joy exploded in her belly. She was rich! Rollin's magic moneyman had triumphed!

"Hey, Rollin!" she called out. "You were right! Yeah!" She did a fist pump. "The twenty million deposit went through and the cops are not on my doorstep! Whoo-hoo!!! Now if all the other accounts come through like this one, I'll be home free! This rocks!"

Rollin came out of her bathroom, stark naked, toweling his wet hair. From his buff shoulders and pecs to the line down the middle of his belly to the delicious curve of his hips to his long, hard tool, the man was a beautiful specimen. As usual, her mouth gaped open and she devoured him with her gaze.

"I told you that guy's good," he replied, drying his ears.

"Turn around so I can see your ass."

Whipping the towel around his head and shimmying, he turned and wiggled his tight butt, then spun around to face her and waggled his eyebrows. Dropping the towel, he licked the tip of his forefinger, touched his naked ass and made a sizzling noise. “So hot, I’m on fire for you, baby.”

She laughed and dug around in her pockets. “Where are my dollar bills?”

“Well?” he asked, holding his arms wide. “Are you going to take advantage of me before I leave? I’m all clean.”

Despite her love high, her gut twinged with sorrow. How would she make it a month without him?

“What a great idea.” She went to him and stopped just before she touched him. “Damn it. You got me all distracted. I have to call my sister. She’s coming by tomorrow and have to let her know I might be held up and to let herself in.”

Rollin smiled, picked up his towel from the floor and tossed it in the clothes hamper. “I can’t believe how well she’s doing.”

“Yeah. Blows my mind. She’s doing everything now, chopping firewood, shopping, gardening. You know she’s driving herself here tomorrow? First trip by herself.”

He twisted his mouth into a partial frown and his brow came down hard over his dark eyes. “She still can’t talk well.”

“She’s still Lizzie,” she said with a shrug. “No one can tell her what to do.”

“I know. The Holsten Stubborn Streak. I’m very familiar with it.” He smirked.

“Hey, I listen to you…Once in awhile.”

“Brat.”

His gorgeous naked body kept distracting her. “Oh, hell, I’ll call her later, come here.”

He put on a worried face and clutched his hands to his chest. “You aren’t going to hurt me, are you?”

She raised a brow and sent him an evil look. “Oh, yeah.”

“Eeek!” he shrieked and ran to the bed and jumped on top.

She ripped off her clothes and dove on top of him. He wrestled with her a bit and let her take the advantage. Then in one swift move, he had her on her back, pinned to the bed.

His dark eyes gleamed with victory. "Muahahahahaa!" he laughed, throwing his head back. "She fell into my trap. And she's mine, all mine! Prepare to be ravished, wench!" His comical expression faded and his gaze turned predatory and dark. "Goddamn, you are hot," he whispered in a husky voice. He leaned down and kissed her.

After a long and spectacular lovemaking session, Rollin collapsed next to her, sweaty and breathing hard. "Damn, I'm gonna need another shower."

Emma lay on her belly. Hot waves of hormones coursed through her veins. Almost satisfied. Almost. No matter how many times he made her come, she always remained hungry for him.

Angling a glance at her, he grabbed her butt, then leaned over and chewed on her neck. She squealed and pushed him away.

Laughing, he kissed her, then lay back against the pillows.

She snuggled in next to him. "I don't want you to go."

He sighed and squeezed her. "Yeah. Sucks. I don't wanna go, either, but Captain strong-armed me into it."

"He's a persuasive little bugger, isn't he?"

"Very." He kissed her until every muscle turned to jelly. He pulled away and sent her a heavy-lidded look.

"Again?" she demanded.

"I want to wring every last naked moment out of you while I can. I don't know how I'm gonna last a month without you." He kissed her and climbed on top.

She started to tell him she loved him, but was cut off by the amazing sensation of his hard dick sliding inside her. Laughing with pure exhilaration, she got carried away on an ocean of ecstasy.

Later, as Emma toweled off, her mood soured. She missed Rollin already and it had only been a half an hour since he left. How would she last a month?

Mumbling to herself about how stupid it was to fall in love with a mercenary, she dried her hair.

A clunk like a door shutting came from somewhere nearby. Probably the neighbors. Ever since Rollin had installed the state-of-the-art security system, she stopped worrying about intruders.

Wrapping the towel around her damp body, she opened the door and walked into her master suite.

She caught a whiff of masculine cologne. She stopped and sniffed the air. Stronger now and more intense. Familiar somehow. Not Rollin's, more musky.

Weird.

Emma walked past the bed on the way to her dresser when something shiny on her pillow caught her attention. Probably a loose earring knocked off during that outrageous sex session. Grinning at the memory, she rubbed her earlobes, but found both hoops still in place. What the hell? She went around the bed to check.

Her heart leapt into her throat and she gasped. A chill came over her. Pulling the towel tighter around her body, she shuddered.

The diamond necklace that Cherlenko gave her lay on her pillow.

The End

ABOUT THE PATRIOTS

At the time I wrote this book, I didn't know it would be part of a series. *Caught* was going to be a stand-alone work. Then I came up with the idea of the Patriots.

After Judy moved back home, I was watching the news and feeling powerless. I wished I could fight the corruption endemic in our society. I wanted to bring the banking industry to their knees and have them pay for their crimes. Since the only true power I have is over my imaginary worlds, I decided to create an organization of heroes that would fight for the common man. Fight against the small group of greedy bastards who run the planet (the "Cabal" in the series). Like a modern day band of high-tech Robin Hoods meets the Impossible Mission Force. So I created the Patriots. A group of disillusioned ex-Navy SEALS who fought in Iraq, gained firsthand knowledge of the corruption of the war and decided to quit and fight the real war behind the scenes. As one of the characters, Rollin Hanson, describes his group: "We're the Justice League without the super powers and tights."

In *Caught*, you will meet characters and receive clues to the plots of future books. Most of the characters you'll meet in *Caught* will appear throughout the entire series. I have fallen in love with the lot of them. I hope you do, too.

PAYBACK EXCERPT

Chapter One

The barrel of the gun seemed three feet in diameter. Blood splattered all over her white Backstreet Boys sweatshirt. Drenching, sick, warm, meaty-smelling blood. The disbelief and shock in her father's eyes. Larry's psychotic leer.

Her body shuddered violently, breaking her out of the daymare.

"How ya doin'?" Paul asked from below her on the trail.

Samantha Murdock looked around, half-surprised to find herself hiking in a redwood forest, following her date down a steep trail. Covered in cold sweat, she forced a smile. "Great," she said, sounding shakier than she would have liked.

Paul sent her an easy, sexy smile. "Beautiful out here."

"Fabulous." Sam descended the single-track trail toward Paul. Grabbing a root on the moss-covered rock wall next to her for support, she stepped over a small boulder, and tried for some upbeat patter. "I couldn't believe it when we drove past Pescadero and the fog disappeared. In summer, Butano State Park can get as socked in as the beach. We hit a perfect day."

"We sure did." Turning, he continued on.

Thank God, Paul had asked her out on this date. A week ago when she'd accepted his invitation, she'd had no idea how much she would need a nice tranquil walk surrounded by gorgeous scenery—Paul being the best scenery of all. He outshone the entire Santa Cruz Mountain Range. With his steel-blue eyes, aquiline nose and square jaw—not to mention his astounding buff body and broad shoulders—the man was a HUNK. Thank God for the Internet.

And thank God for the distraction.

Ever since she'd seen Ursula the day before to confirm the location of the murder weapon—and then stumbled across that wild evidence against Larry—the flashbacks had been intensifying. Last night, she'd hardly slept at all. She had to relax. Her mind had to be razor sharp to handle the next two weeks.

Sam took a deep sniff of the forest air, catching the musty and muddy hints of the sandy creek bed far below, the piney scent of the trees, and the intense lemongrass-like aroma of the sword ferns, nettles, and oxalis. Blue jays and woodpeckers chattered, the creek babbled, and the wind rustled through the branches and leaves of the tall, majestic redwoods. Stepping into a patch of bright warm sunlight, she let out a long breath and felt more peaceful.

Gunfire pierced the air and echoed off the ridge opposite them.

Sam's heart jumped and her attention snapped across the canyon. "What the hell? There's no hunting allowed back here. Oh, yeah. Probably coming from Ridge Road. I know some guys who like to do target practice up there."

Paul's eyes widened. "Let's hope they stay on target."

A shot rang out. The shale rock wall blew apart right above her head, spraying her with debris.

"Hey!" Sam yelled up toward the ridge. "There are people down here, you idiots! Knock it off!"

Gun blasts strafed the area. Trees splintered and puffs of dirt exploded in the ground near her feet.

Her heart rate quadrupled, adrenaline blasted her system, and she frantically searched for cover. Holy shit! This wasn't any accident! Larry had found her!

Someone heavy tackled her from behind. Screaming, she ate trail. Every muscle bellowed at her to run. Rocks and redwood leaves poked painfully into the exposed skin on her arms and legs while she struggled against the muscled mass on top of her. She turned her head as best she could, but couldn't see her attacker's face.

Paul leapt to his feet and charged with fierce expression. "Get away from her!"

Another volley of gunfire shattered the silence of the forest. Bullets pounded the area around Paul and he dove off the trail behind a small tree.

All at once, she was up and facing the other way and shoved forward.

"Run, Sam! Run!" came a male voice. "There's no good cover here!"

Gunshots blazed. Dirt and a spray of rocks peppered her left side.

The person wasn't attacking her, he was protecting her! Her heart slamming in her chest, her body jacked, Sam sprinted up the hill. "Where's my friend?" she shouted over her shoulder.

"Right behind us! Run!"

Sharp cracks of gunfire bounced off the two tall walls of the canyon above her. Rocks, dirt, and trees were torn apart as she flew by them. She crested the trail and jumped down the rocky path. Ursula must have leaked her identity. Damn it!

But Ursula wouldn't.

Unless Larry had kept surveillance on her old friend. That was it. He'd found out about their meeting. And now he knew Sam was still alive.

She should have brought the Glock. Her peashooter Smith and Wesson 314 revolver was no match for snipers.

Sam came around a corner and was shoved sideways into a clump of brush. The man protecting her tackled her again and covered her with his big and muscular body. Leaves, sticks, and rocks dug into her flesh as the man's weight pressed her to the ground. While he was clearly trying not to squish her, the forest floor against her bare skin hurt. Of course, getting shot would be a lot less comfortable.

"Who—"

He clamped his large hand over her mouth. "Hush."

A barrage of gunshots filled the air. No bullets impacted their area.

"Stay down for another second, then I'll let you up," he said quietly in her ear.

Wait a minute. She knew that voice. But it couldn't be. She turned around to see who it was and gasped.

Burke Cherlenko, a mercenary and ex Navy SEAL who terrorized her best friend, Emma. Notorious and dangerous. All her instincts told her to run and keep running.

She tried to throw him off, but he kept her pinned, his hand tight on her mouth.

But where the hell did Burke come from? And how did he know Larry was after her? She'd only met with Ursula the day before. What the hell?

She elbowed him in the ribs and scrambled to get away, but he stayed with her.

"Stop fighting me. I'm trying to protect you, you idiot."

Idiot? She nipped his middle finger.

"Ow!" Burke pulled away, shaking his hand.

Sam pushed off the ground with all her strength—Burke fell aside—and she jumped to her feet. Throwing herself further into the brush, she leapt bushes like hurdles until she reached a small clearing that seemed safe from attack.

She stopped and spun to face him. "Burke? What the hell are you doing out here?" she snapped in a harsh whisper.

Breathing heavy, he scorched her with his dark brown gaze. A flush raced over her skin and her body prickled with unwanted sexual awareness. She'd forgotten how fine he was. From his symmetrical oval face to his strong jaw and full sensual lips to his muscled, lean body, he screamed man. Real man. But his eyes mesmerized her. Sultry, mahogany, radiating self-confidence and power.

"What the hell is wrong with you? I'm trying to save you and you bite me?"

"Answer my question," she whispered. "What are you doing out here?"

"Who is this guy and why are those people shooting at us?" came Paul's voice from behind Burke.

"Thank God, you're okay." She brushed by Burke to embrace her hard-bodied date.

Paul crushed her in a hug. His warmth and strength reassured her instantly.

He let go and offered his hand to Burke. "Thanks for protecting her, I'm Paul."

Burke took his hand and shook it. "Burke Cherlenko. And you're welcome." He shot a disapproving glare her way before turning back to her date. "I was sent by Sam's best friends—Emma and Rollin—to protect her. Which she doesn't seem to appreciate," he said directly to her with a nasty twist to his lips. "I have to get you both out of here."

Sam stood her ground. "Wait. How did you guys know someone was after me?"

Burke stared at her and his brow wrinkled. "Bobby intercepted a message between a group of contract killers slash professional kidnappers we're tracking. Your picture and name were attached. Their orders were to kidnap you, but apparently, they've changed their minds."

Her fists balled, her teeth clenched, she wanted to scream. Damn it! That bastard! Now he had the money and power to deploy a team after her!

Paul paled and stared at her with his mouth slightly open. "Sam?"

Her insides burned. Holy bejeebus, she'd put her new boyfriend in danger! This couldn't be happening! "Paul, I swear, I—"

"It's not her fault," said Burke.

"But why would someone want to kill her?" Paul gestured toward her in quick movement.

Sam searched Burke's face. Why would he say it wasn't her fault? Unless it had nothing to do with Larry. Could this be about something else?

Burke turned to her. "Does the name Linda Anderson mean anything to you?"

She gaped. "Linda Anderson? This is about *Linda Anderson?*"

Her body flooded with relief and she let out a long sigh. The shooting wasn't about Larry? He still didn't know she was alive? Thank God! She could still bring down that murderer.

Wait a minute. Rollin was cheating on Emma with Linda Anderson. Why were contract killers after *her*? All she'd done was drop by Linda's house.

Her stomach twisted and she got goosebumps. This better have nothing to do with that box the mailman had shoved into her hands. The package addressed to Linda filled with evidence against Larry and several other high level politicians.

Please tell me I didn't just fuck myself.

Burke honed in on her with his laser-sighted gaze. "Who did you think was shooting at you? Is someone else trying to kill you?"

Holy shit. She'd almost let out her most precious secret!

Quick! Cover your reaction, girl!

She averted her attention. "No." She forced herself to make eye contact. "I'm just…shocked, that's all. Hard to imagine contract killers would target me."

"You look relieved," Burke said with a penetrating stare.

The bark on the trees above their heads splintered. Gunfire echoed through the forest. Every nerve ignited and Sam flattened to the trail.

Burke grabbed her and pushed her further into the brush. "Go! And keep down! Paul, hurry!"

She bolted into the dense shrubbery and realized that she was on a very old, overgrown trail. Maybe an old logging road. Keeping her head low, she raced forward, pushing aside branches and leaping over sticks and logs. The men crashed behind her.

The trail zigzagged around massive thousand-year-old redwoods. No one had used the abandoned road in years. Sam's boots crunched through a thick layer of duff. The soft mass slowed her and she picked up her legs higher.

She hopped over a fallen log, landed on a sword fern, and kept running. Twigs whipped her bare legs and arms. Her lungs and muscles burned. Taking a cobweb in the face, she clawed it off.

Burke grabbed her daypack and stopped her. Sweat glistened on his brow. She was happy he was breathing nearly as hard as she.

In full Navy SEAL mode, he surveyed the area. His sharp focus didn't miss a detail. "They can't get us from here."

Paul came up next to her and put his arms around her protectively. She leaned in to him. His scent, warmth, and the feel of his buff body made her feel better. Such a great guy. The way he was handling this whole crazy mess said a lot about his character. Give him a kajillion more points for that.

Burke headed back down the path. "You two stay here, I'll lead them off. I want them to think we're going another way." He disappeared into the brush.

A few minutes later, gunfire.

Her stomach reacted to every shot. Her shoulder muscles were so tight, they felt like a solid flaming mass. Sam sat on a moss-covered log and tried to distract herself by brushing the dirt off her shorts.

But her whole body felt like it was sinking in quicksand. This had to be about that evidence. As soon as she'd seen those photos and checked out the files on the thumb drives, she'd known the information was insanely dangerous.

Shit. Linda must have found out that she had taken the box. And now the woman was trying to kill Sam before the information got out.

Figures that Rollin would be sleeping with another spy.

Fuck! How should she handle this with the Patriots? She couldn't admit that she had the package. If they asked, she'd lie. But somehow she had to get them to keep protecting her from Linda.

Besides, if they found out she had the box of file and photos, they might connect her to Larry. Those guys were so true-blue if they found out she was preparing to destroy the most powerful man in the country, they'd use all their resources to stop her.

Sam picked moss out of her hair and released tension by jiggling her leg. Which barely helped at all.

Paul sat next to her and nudged her. "So who's Linda Anderson?"

As she cleaned off her clothes, she kept a keen eye on their surroundings. She still felt too open, too vulnerable. "Uh, this chick who lives in Seattle. She's sleeping with my best friend's boyfriend, Rollin. My buddy Emma found a bunch of love letters and the woman's address."

"I thought you went to Seattle on business."

"I did. After I picked up the shipment for Emma's store, I went by Linda's place to kick her ass, but she wasn't home." Sam decided not to volunteer the fact that she'd broken into the apartment with keys Emma had found with the letters.

His blue gaze sparkled. "Kick her ass?"

She shot him a grin. "No one screws with my friends."

"Looks like she wants to kill your ass," Paul said with a smirk. "Maybe you ought to find out who you're up against before you interfere."

"Yeah, I tried to find out all I could about her, but came up with nothing other than those letters. I have no idea how she tracked me down." Unless she'd been followed from the apartment. Maybe the woman had seen her with the mailman. Her stomach tightened painfully.

"If Emma's seeing Rollin, why would this Linda gal come after you?"

"Got me. I was just about to ask that same question," Sam said as innocently as she could.

"Ask Burke when he gets back. He seems to know all about her."

A chunk of cobweb was caught on her watch. She tugged at it and the gummy yet whisper light material stuck to her fingers. "I hope so. This is crazy," she said, flicking the spider adhesive to the ground.

"I'll agree with you there." He moved a few leaves off her shoulder, then smiled and gave her a squeeze. "Are you okay?"

She gave a small smile and sighed. "Yeah, but I feel crappy about bringing you into this disaster." Patting his wide, hard thigh, she looked deep into his sexy blue eyes. "I'm so sorry about this."

"Not your fault."

Oh, yes it is.

He rubbed her back and kissed the side of her head.

Despite her heightened sense of danger, goosebumps popped up all over. They had good chemistry. While they'd only kissed a couple times so far, she could tell they'd be a nice match. She'd hoped on this date that they'd ramp up the sexual connection. But at this point, having sex was the last thing on her To Do list.

"Such a great third date," Sam said with a roll of her eyes. "I won't blame you if I never see you again."

"Are you crazy? And miss all this excitement?" His eyes twinkling, he hugged her tight. "You stop worrying. This just makes me want to stay close to you and protect you."

His words stopped her. No man had ever said anything like that to her but her father. All her previous dates and boyfriends wanted her to take care of them. While some of the men had started off promising, they all degenerated into the same, whiny self-centered boy who wanted to sponge off her.

Was it possible? Had she finally found a man?

She smiled and leaned into him. "Thanks for that, Paul. You're a good guy." It was then she noticed that the forest had been quiet for a time. "Gunfire stopped finally. Thank God. Freakin' me out."

Paul ran his hand over her hair and moved a wisp from her face. "We'll be fine. I've got some old military friends who can help protect us, too," he said, massaging the back of her neck. "I won't let anything happen to you. I promise."

She gazed into his intelligent and kind eyes and her heart wrenched open. Mentally using both hands, she slammed it shut. This was not the time to make decisions about relationships. But he was being very sweet. "Thanks, hon. You're making me feel better."

Smiling, his attention went to her mouth.

Her body went warm and fuzzy and she tilted her head to receive his kiss.

"I took care of them," came Burke's voice.

Her hormone bubble popped.

Paul let go, stood, and turned to Burke.

Sam got up and brushed the dirt off her pants with a bit more vigor than needed. Goddamned Burke, ruining their kiss. He could have taken two more minutes. She could use a good kiss right around now.

Burke sent her a pissy look.

Why was he mad?

She gave him a nod. "You think they were fooled?"

"Yeah. We're safe."

Letting out a long breath, her body loosened a bit. "Thanks, Burke."

"You're welcome." He took off his small daypack and set it on a log. "We wait here for a bit, then we'll take another trail."

"Sounds good," Paul said.

Sam slid her backpack off her shoulder and laid it further down on the same log. "Burke, explain to me how breaking into some chick's apart—" She sent a guilty glance at Paul. "I mean, uh, how *visiting* someone's apartment made her put a contract out on me. And how did Linda find out I was there?" *Please tell me this isn't about the evidence against Larry. Please tell me that Linda didn't see me take that box.*

Burke shot her a glare. "Rollin wasn't cheating on Emma with Linda Anderson. There is no Linda Anderson."

"What do you mean there's no Linda Anderson? I was in her apartment. I read the letters she sent to Rollin."

Burke frowned and gave a wary look at Paul. His attention went to the forest floor and he sighed. He briefly raised his brows and gave a small shrug. Then he leveled his intense gaze at her. "Linda Anderson is a false person we created for one of our jobs."

Sam's train of thought veered off the rails and she took a step back. Linda Anderson didn't exist? That explained the anomalies in the apartment. She snapped her fingers. "No wonder there was that weird assortment of food in the cupboards. Didn't feel like anyone lived there, ever. Wait, this means that Rollin isn't cheating on Emma! Wicked cool! I mean, it didn't make any sense, the way the guy treats her, but damn, those letters were convincing." Her muscles went hard and her face heated with anger. "What the hell is he doing, leaving that crap around for Emma to find? She was devastated!"

Burke pursed his lips. "He thought he'd hidden them well. Apparently, Emma is a fanatical housecleaner."

"I still don't understand what's going on." Paul shifted his attention between her and Burke.

Burke said, "Rollin, Emma's fiancée, and I work for a security firm, Rampart—"

All the blood left Sam's head and her knees went weak. She hadn't stolen evidence from a stranger, she'd stolen evidence from her friends. Friends that happened to belong to a large, powerful spy organization. Sam's heart beat so hard, it hurt. She broke out in a full body sweat. Holy fuck.

Paul's eyes lit with recognition. "I know Rampart. I work for DAE, sold you guys some equipment. And you helped out a buddy of mine when you were Consolidated Security."

Burke did a quick double take at Paul, but continued. "A client of ours was in possession of sensitive information regarding a group of high-level criminals."

Here we go. Sam made a great effort to remain standing.

"Information which could expose them and ruin their business," Burke said in a grave tone. "We convinced these very dangerous and powerful operatives that Linda Anderson was in possession of the intelligence, not our client. This professional and well-funded crime organization believes that Linda Anderson is real, that she is our agent, and that she has information that could destroy their operation." He turned to Sam. "And now they've found her."

Sam chest contracted and she couldn't breathe. "Holy shit." How could she possibly keep the information now? How would she put Larry away with hired killers after her? Especially when Larry belonged to the group that had hired them? Great. Now the asshole would try to kill her all over again, only this time without knowing her true identity.

And what about the Patriots? If they found out she had the packet, she'd have to fight them, too. Crazy!

Her pulse thumping in her ears, Sam stared into space, stunned, overwhelmed by how naïve and stupid she was and how badly she'd just fucked herself.

Burke nodded. "*Yeah, Miss Anderson.*"

She fought for equilibrium. Rubbing her forehead, she hugged her body with her free arm.

Samantha Murdock! Fight! Fight with every bit of your soul! God put that evidence in your hands! You prayed for help and He answered!

A crazy confluence of events took place that day in order for the information to land in her lap. Wouldn't have happened if she weren't meant to use the evidence. Right?

Paul's head jerked back slightly and his lips quirked. "Wait. Wasn't this a movie plot? Yeah. *North by Northwest*."

"You're right." Her body trembled and she held herself tighter. "And I'm playing the Cary Grant role. Rollin's a Hitchcock nut. He probably came up with the plan."

Burke nodded.

Paul ran his hand down her back. "Jeez girl, when you step in it, you really step in it, don't you?"

"Unreal," Sam said, shaking her head. So hard to grasp. A day ago, she was safe in anonymity, now she had yet another death sentence on her head.

And if what Burke said was true, that meant Larry was now not only a Senator and Presidential nominee, he was also involved in organized crime. Great.

She gestured toward Burke. "So how did you get involved?"

"I was closest. I happened to be in Half Moon Bay when I got the call from Rollin. And I was in Seattle yesterday. I must have missed you at the apartment by minutes. Did you happen to pick up a package addressed to Linda?"

Her insides folded like Origami and she stopped breathing. Worst fear realized: they'd tied the missing materials to her. Thankfully, she had the wherewithal to hold his gaze firmly. She forced herself to continue breathing normally. "No, I was only there for a few minutes. What was in the package?" she managed to say with an ease in her voice that surprised her. *Good goin', Murdock. Keep it up.*

He looked away. "Something very important." His expression darkened. "Damn it. I was hoping you had it."

"Nope." Sam concentrated on keeping her face absolutely free of movement.

Now it was fifty million times more urgent that she get to Seattle and finish her plan of securing the evidence. But how was she supposed to get there with a team of hired killers after her?

Sam felt like she'd been transported unarmed and naked into the middle of an Afghani firefight. She'd known her life would probably be short, but not this short. Shit, she had to stay alive long enough to deal with Larry.

A spike of pain seared Sam's shoulder like someone had stabbed it with an icepick. "Ow!" She rubbed it out.

Paul massaged the area she worked.

She moved away from him. "Sorry, Let me get this, it's spasming." Digging harder into her shoulder, she eased the pain.

Paul asked, "Are you all right?"

"Fine. Shoulder's hurting from when Burke tackled me. Not that I'm complaining."

Burke sent her a half smile. The green and yellow filtered forest light played across his handsome face and illuminated the spark of playfulness in his dark gaze. How could this gorgeous man be the same evil jerk who kidnapped and tormented Emma?

Then like a glass of ice water in her face, the realization hit her. She had a score to settle with this bastard. Instantly, her belly turned to fire. She'd warned him what she'd do to him if he hurt Emma. "Oh, yeah."

She punched Burke in the face so hard, his head snapped back, he stumbled and almost went down.

Paul gasped and his eyebrows went high. "Whoa."

His eyes flaming with rage, Burke's face flushed bright red. "*What the hell was that for*?" he demanded, rubbing his jaw.

She pointed at him. "That was for what you did to Emma. No one hurts my friend. I warned you that night at the club. You're lucky you saved my life or you'd be holding your balls in your hand right now. Say *thank you, Sam, for not chopping off my nuts*."

Burke made an exasperated noise and gestured violently. "Emma didn't—"

"*Say thank you, Sam, for not chopping off my nuts*."

He squared his shoulders, his dark eyes blazing. "Sam—"

She stepped forward and got into his face. "Say it!" she snarled viciously, ready to kick him. She'd longed to have her moment with this man. Planned it carefully. And boy, did it feel good to channel all her fear into anger at the guy.

Burke's scorching dark gaze didn't waver. He seemed twice his size, all bristling muscles and wide shoulders.

Sam didn't move and kept her sneer firmly in place. No way was she backing down.

After a long few seconds, his fierce expression broke. His body relaxed and he sighed heavily. Fighting a smile, he said, "Thank you, Sam, for not chopping off my nuts."

She gave him a sharp nod. "Good. No one messes with my friends. Damn you. What the hell were you thinking?"

Stepping back, his face went hard. "I was under deep cover. Playing a role. That wasn't me."

"Bullshit. I hung out with you at your palatial penthouse in the City. I'll bet you still have that place and still shop at Burberry." Sam was starting to feel like herself again. Her anger and focus on Emma's defense was centering her.

He held her gaze with no apology on his even-featured face. Which made him twice as hot. "Despite my tastes, I'm no criminal and never was."

"No, but you're a smarmy, showy, smug bastard who uses anyone and everyone to accomplish his goals."

Dude didn't even react. "That was—and still is—a matter of national security. Through her actions, she put the country at risk. And I'm not going to argue the point with you any longer because we both swore not to discuss the situation. *Didn't we*?"

Narrowing her eyes, her mouth went tight. "I'm just about to cut your nuts off."

His anger broke, but his frustration was clear. "I have apologized. Profusely. Rollin forgives me."

"Emma doesn't."

"And I don't blame her. But I was doing my job to the best of my ability. Granted, I pushed her further than I meant to."

"Because you loved her."

"That was…unplanned," he said, looking down for a moment. A hint of pain flashed in his eyes and the line between his brows deepened. "I think that was most of the problem."

Sam's anger faded. At least he admitted to part of his game. "Rollin told me that you were okay and I shouldn't kill you when I saw you. But you deserved a good punch."

Much of the heated emotion left his face and he smirked.

Her fire gone, her beef with Burke aired, it occurred to her that she hadn't thanked him properly. Awkward timing, but so be it. "But you also deserve thanks for saving my life and Paul's. So thanks, Burke. Much appreciated."

He gave a small snort and the corners of his mouth twitched. "You're welcome. Brat. No wonder you're friends. Both you and Emma are trouble. But I knew the moment I met you in that club that you were fifty times worse."

Sam blinked innocently. "Me?"

Burke broke out into a wide smile. Her heart tripped and a zing went through her, electrifying the bottoms of her feet.

What the hell was wrong with her? How could she be attracted to this guy?

And why the hell was she thinking about being attracted to anyone when her life had just exploded into a bajillion pieces?

Burke stared at her for just that extra second longer. Damn, she hoped he hadn't caught the interest in her eyes.

He turned to Paul. "We should go. The assailants will assume they've flushed us out and will be waiting for us at the trailhead."

Paul asked, "What are our options?"

Burke jerked his head to his left. "If we double-back and take the other path, it leads to another trailhead. Earlier, I arranged for men to meet us at the end of each trail. We should be fine. But keep alert."

Sam grabbed her backpack from the forest floor, but had forgotten to zip it shut first and several items fell out. Including, unfortunately, her handgun. She tried to snatch it up before the men noticed, but when she checked their expressions, their eyebrows had shot to their hairlines. Damn it. She didn't want people knowing she carried. Especially these two guys.

Frowning, his focus sharp, Burke came closer and held out his hand. "Let me see that."

"It's no big deal." She stuffed the small revolver inside the pack.

He jammed his hand in front of her face. "Hand it to me."

"For crying out loud, here." Retrieving her weapon, she held out the gun, handle first, with the barrel pointed toward the ground.

He took the revolver and inspected it. Then he concentrated his piercing attention on her. "Where the hell did you get this?"

Sam's jaw and belly tightened. She let her gaze go cold. "The store."

Burke's eyes narrowed.

"Yeah, why did you slip that into your pack?" Paul demanded, coming closer.

She tried to look at them like they were mental. "Protection from mountain lions, hello?"

Burke examined her, his face full of suspicion. "On a busy Saturday? When there haven't been any sightings in a year?" He hesitantly handed the gun to her, butt first.

"I've always had a gun," Sam replied smoothly. "Sometimes I carry a lot of expensive stuff for Emma's antiquities store. I'm her manager, you know."

"I know. Still doesn't warrant a firearm." Burke challenged her with his harsh gaze and the set to his shoulders and mouth. "California has strict laws on carrying a concealed weapon. Do you have a permit to carry that?"

Damn this! She had to keep her cool. Had to be super careful about how she responded to this situation. No one could find out about her past. Maybe she'd blown it by visiting Linda Anderson's apartment and stealing that box of evidence, but she wasn't going to compound her mistakes by letting these guys know the truth about her.

"Of course, I have a permit." Ignoring the two men, she performed a check of the gun.

Paul stared at her little snubbed nose Smith and Wesson. "Sorry, but I agree with Burke. Not only are you putting yourself at legal risk, do you have training to use that, Sam?"

Her body went hot and she squeezed the grip of the gun until her hand hurt. Nothing pissed her off more than being patronized. She wasn't some weak female loser idiot. Glaring between the two, she snapped, "Why? Because I'm a woman?"

"No," Burke replied flatly. "This is not a gender issue, it's an experience issue."

"Exactly." Paul crossed his arms and his expression hardened.

Burke's shoulders bulked bigger. "More deaths are caused by amateurs than professionals. I have attitude about people who own and carry guns that shouldn't."

No way did she want to get into some stupid argument with these chauvinists. She tried to calm her reaction. Didn't need to be defensive, she could just be firm. "I've been shooting since I was a kid. Besides, look what happened today, will ya? Did we or did we not just come under fire? If you hadn't shown up, Burke, I would have at least been able to return fire and get us to safety."

Burke's focus on her intensified. "Interesting timing, isn't it? You just happen to be carrying a gun for '*protection*'," he said, and she could hear the air quotes in his voice, "and then you come under fire. Almost like you were expecting it."

She stared at him like he'd lost his mind. "What have you got in that canteen, Burke? Vodka? Expecting it? Oh, yeah, every time I take a walk, people shoot at me. Happens all the time. You are such an idiot. Mountain lions. That's why I brought it today. Why are you making this into a drama?"

Burke's mouth went even uglier. "Whatever. I'd prefer if you unloaded the weapon and allowed me carry it for the duration of the day."

Straightening her spine, she thrust out her chin. "No fuckin' way." She'd kill him if he tried to take it from her.

Burke scowled, but backed off. "Fine. Just don't shoot me."

She sneered. "If I did, it wouldn't be by accident."

Burke sent her a nasty smirk.

"I agree with Burke," Paul said. "Why don't you let him carry the weapon? He is protecting us. I'd feel safer."

Sam shot him the cold, powerful *do-I-need-to-kill-you* glare that normally made her men cower in fear.

Paul's eyes widened, then he frowned. Clearly surprised by her response.

She thought of and rejected twenty nasty retorts. Since all her replies seemed to include profanity, she chose to say nothing. But she didn't diminish her Death Stare, nor did she look away.

Paul's steel-blue eyes darkened, his thick brow flattened into straight line, and his mouth tightened. He stood taller and a flash of fire blazed in his expression. He looked like he wanted to slap her. A slight chill went through her. Dude had a menacing, authoritarian edge she hadn't seen before. But she wouldn't allow herself to flinch, nor shift her attention.

Paul finally threw up his hands and stepped back. But he wasn't happy and clearly didn't like her defiance.

Despite his hotness, the dude had better be careful about throwing his weight around or he might just throw himself right out of her life.

Both men kept their attention on her gun until she tucked it into her pack. Neanderthal morons. Why was she always attracted to cave men? High time she put out a fatwa on her sex drive.

Slipping on her pack, she followed Paul through the forest, Burke right behind her.

Sam mentally kicked herself with every step. She should have stayed in Seattle until she copied the information and returned the originals to Linda Anderson's apartment.

But how did the bad guys find her so fast? She'd worn a disguise to the apartment. Shit, this was crazy.

How was she supposed to trap or kill Larry while outsmarting a team of security professionals while avoiding a group of professional hit men? Absolutely insane.

She kicked a rectangular piece of shale and sent it sailing off the edge of the trail, down toward the creek far below. Would her life ever return to normal? Would she ever be safe again? Sam punted another rock off the single-track trail. A loud crash from below was followed by a *thoomp-splash* as the rock hit water.

"Sam? Could you please stop alerting the snipers to our location?" Burke bit out in a snide tone from behind her.

"Sorry," she grumbled without turning around.

Keep it together, Murdock. Maintaining her sanity and composure was paramount now. She needed a clear head to get to Seattle and cover up her theft. Once the Patriots had their evidence, she could disappear. Eventually, the bad guys would find out that the Patriots were in possession of the information again and would stop trying to find her. By then, she'd be mostly through her plan of attack on Larry. Chances that anyone would link her to the dickhead were slim to none.

Before he knew it, he'd be dead or in jail for life.

Looky here, Larry. Pretty photos of you and little girls frolicking naked together. But wait, there's more! A thumbdrive chockfull of evidence about your offshore criminal enterprises and bank accounts!

Sam grinned as she followed Paul up a steep incline. Couldn't wait to see the look on his face. *Yes, Larry, I'm still alive and see these objects in the jar I'm holding? These are your balls. They belong to me now.*

And if for some reason her new plan didn't work, she always had her original, assassinating the fucking deviant.

Burke followed Sam and her date on the trail, his attention torn between possible sniper vantage points and the tantalizing Miss Murdock. He loved the way her heart-shaped ass moved against her tight hiking shorts. Her long legs were perfect appetizers for the nirvana hidden between. And her gorgeous breasts should be in a museum. High, rounded, perfect handfuls. Not too big, not too small. Tight.

But it was the fire within her that made him hard as obsidian. Her hazel eyes, flashing with red-hot passion. That sock on the jaw she gave him. He should have been pissed. All it did was make him want to throw her to the ground and fuck her until she screamed.

Dangerous. He wanted her in a blinding, crazed sort of way. Every cell in his body wanted to possess her. Dominate her. Care for her. Keep her safe.

Insane talk. He couldn't lose his mind over another woman. It wasn't possible. Emma was the only one with that power. Or had been the only one. Last time he saw her, his lust and love had faded. Surprisingly fast.

But Sam was different. She wasn't afraid of him. In the least. He normally liked his women to be a bit fearful of him, kept them in line better. But Sam would constantly challenge his authority. Which for some reason, made him want her even more. She was a tornado disguised as a beautiful woman. Winning her would be pure poetry.

She glanced over her shoulder at him. He smiled.

Pursing her lips, she turned around with a haughty little toss of her head.

Blood surged into his cock. Sultry, wicked siren. He loved the way her wavy shoulder-length auburn hair fell loosely about her slim shoulders, the way her full burgundy mouth quirked when she was being sassy, and the way she sneered at him.

Smoldering. Defiant. And so very fuckable.

He smelled his hands. Sam's heavenly flowers-and-fresh-rain scent filled his nostrils. He got even harder and grinned. Just so happened she needed a bodyguard.

She turned again, did a double-take and frowned. "You'd better not be staring at my ass," she snarled.

"Wouldn't dream of it." He forced his face to go neutral. Had to watch himself. Didn't want to show his hand too early in the game.

"Yeah…" She sent him another glare, but as she turned away, she smiled.

He had to hold back his laughter. She wanted him, too. Badly and so soon.

This was going to be fun.

Well, the seducing-Sam part would be fun. Getting her to give up the package, not so much. Sam had a lot of fight in her, great for sex, not so great for coercion.

He was ninety-nine point nine percent sure she had the intelligence. When he'd questioned her, her pupils had dilated slightly and there'd been a flash of fear on her face before her obvious attempt to control her reaction. She must have gotten the box from the postman after she left the apartment building. The Patriots were in the process of verifying the delivery.

His gut burned and twisted, and his throat constricted. Holding a bleeding Joseph, the strained cough, the light fading from his eyes. "*Sent it…to…Linda Anderson.*" His stare had fixed and he'd stilled in Burke's arms.

Joseph better not have died for nothing.

Lying in a swamp with him. Sharing a cigarette. Joseph pushing him out of the way in that Iraqi back alley and taking a bullet for him. Only Rollin and he had been closer. Joseph had been a smart, loyal, strong man. To see what those fuckers did ripped him apart. Joseph hadn't deserved to die that way. Burke would make sure that the men who tortured him to death and the Cabal paid for that.

Ten minutes late. Ten minutes that cost Joseph his life. How would he ever forgive himself?

He only wished Joseph had stayed alive long enough to tell him *how* he'd sent the information to Linda Anderson. When he'd checked Joseph's pockets, he'd found no delivery confirmation slips, no paperwork of any kind. Nothing indicating Fed Ex, UPS, private courier or USPS.

But since no package had arrived at the apartment since and Sam had spent time with the mailman—plus her reaction—she must have it.

Strong turned around and checked on him.

Burke kept his expression passive. Strong was clearly behind the sniper attack. At first he believed the assailants were Cabal, but as the gunfire continued—by the pattern of hits: the trees next to Paul, the ground near him, but nothing close to him—and the fact that the bullets hadn't come within ten feet from Sam—it became obvious that the operation had been staged.

After Burke had sighted the two white men in camo, by their youth and because one kept taking phone pics of the other—who flashed some sort of gang sign—he'd pegged them as recently discharged Army grunts. Strong had said he worked for DAE, he probably had a military background and plenty of contacts.

To test his theory, Burke had ripped off a hit to the upper right arm of the more aggressive shooter followed by a quick shot through the top of the other kid's hat. The boys had erupted in screams and disappeared so fast, they almost left their weapons behind.

While relieved that the Cabal hadn't located Sam yet, why the hell would Strong stage an attack? More than likely trying to infiltrate the Patriots. Burke's news about her pursuers must have fed perfectly into Strong's plan. Allowed him to comfort her and appear protective. The asshole. Poor girl was just a puppet.

Maybe Strong was trying to recruit her. He could have been sent after that evidence, but he and Sam had hooked up before it had come into play. She had thrown herself into the middle of events just the day before.

Maybe Strong was behind Sam's theft of the evidence. Why else would she have grabbed the box?

But if Paul hadn't put her up to it, he must be out of his mind with joy now that he knew she had the evidence. Unless he'd been up in Seattle and had seen Sam take it. Or had gotten word from his network that Sam was Linda Anderson.

Or perhaps he worked for another organization.

Whichever, as soon as Burke had determined that Paul was a spy, he'd made every effort to hide his suspicions. Which was why he'd had been so "forthcoming" with information when he was questioning Sam. He had to keep the man feeling safe so he'd drop his guard.

Burke would have a full report on him by that night. And assign a detail not only "protect" Strong, but to keep an eye on him.

Sam sent him another glance. This one guarded.

Seemed like everyone on that trail had secrets. If he was right and Sam had the information, why would she want it if she weren't a spy? Hadn't she been able to tell by the contents how dangerous it was? None of her actions made sense.

She hadn't been surprised when she'd come under fire; she'd been surprised the attack pertained to Linda Anderson. And she'd nearly gone rabid when he'd suggested he carry her gun—she clearly didn't feel safe without it. But who would want to murder Sam? From what he understood, she'd been a cocktail waitress at high-end clubs until taking charge of Emma's new store.

But Sam? A spy? With that sassy mouth and flamboyance? Did not fit the profile.

So who was after her? An ex-boyfriend? Did she have a stalker?

Wasn't a stretch to think some man got obsessed. Hell, he was almost there himself.

Whatever she was hiding, he'd find out. As soon as they cleared the woods, he'd call Bobby and get a full background check on Miss Sam Murdock.

He chuckled. Then he'd know all her weak points. He'd have her —and the packet—in no time. Protect her from the hired killers and that snake Paul Strong, find out who she was afraid of and help her defeat them. He'd come into her life at exactly the right time. She needed him. He'd keep her safe.

And fuck her blind in the process.

Payback is available now

www.janetperiat.com

www.ingramcontent.com/pod-product-compliance
Lightning Source LLC
LaVergne TN
LVHW050920080826
845145LV00001B/142
* 9 7 8 1 9 3 7 8 1 3 0 3 1 *